"You were the cowgirl..."

Travis stopped laughing, and they just looked at each other for a minute. Should have been awkward, but it wasn't. It was good. "I recognize you," he whispered.

Maggie's heart pounded in her chest. All he'd said was that he recognized her. So what? But it felt as if he'd said *You're mine.*

Not that she ever could be. A guy like him...

She cleared her throat. "I never said thank you for helping me that day."

Travis moved closer. They were practically nose to nose. She kissed him sweetly on the cheek. "Thank you," she said.

"You're welcome," he whispered. Then he gave her a feather-soft kiss on the lips.

It was nothing. Just a peck. A whisper of a peck, really, but she felt it all the way to the tips of her toes. She felt the gravitational pull of his blue eyes and warm lips.

And she wanted more.

Big Bad
COWBOY

CARLY
BLOOM

FOREVER

NEW YORK BOSTON

Copyright © 2018 by Carol Pavliska

Excerpt from *Cowboy Come Home* copyright © 2018 by Carol Pavliska

Cover photography by Rob Lang, design by Elizabeth Turner Stokes. Cover copyright © 2018 by Hachette Book Group, Inc.

Forever

Hachette Book Group

1290 Avenue of the Americas, New York, NY 10104

forever-romance.com

twitter.com/foreverromance

First Edition: October 2018

Forever is an imprint of Grand Central Publishing. The Forever name and logo are trademarks of Hachette Book Group, Inc.

The publisher is not responsible for websites (or their content) that are not owned by the publisher.

The Hachette Speakers Bureau provides a wide range of authors for speaking events. To find out more, go to www.hachettespeakersbureau.com or call (866) 376-6591.

ISBNs: 978-1-5387-6343-8 (mass market), 978-1-5387-6342-1 (ebook)

Printed in the United States of America

OPM

10 9 8 7 6 5 4 3 2

To Jeff, my real-life cowboy. You and your boots, cargo shorts, and Red Hot Chili Peppers T-shirt just plain do it for me.

Acknowledgments

It takes a village just to get me out of the house before noon. It took a global network of enablers to help me write *Big Bad Cowboy*.

Extra special thanks to my B Team—Amy Bearce, Alison Bliss, and Samantha Bohrman. You long-suffering ladies read every version of this manuscript with a bottle of wine and a stress ball. I see right through your empty threats of *Never Again!* and I know you'll be there for the next This Has to Be Fixed Right Now crisis. How awesome is that (for me)?

Thank you to Jessica Snyder for coming all the way to Texas for a taco-eating brainstorming session and for introducing me to the hilarious Pippa Grant! You make writing fun. And to Erin Quinn—I'd be a nobody without you! Thank you for "discovering" me.

Warm hugs and kisses to my reading group, Carly's Bloomers, and to my fellow SARA's in San Antonio Romance Authors. You inspire me every day.

Thank you to my wonderful agent, Paige Wheeler, for working so hard on my behalf. I still remember our first phone call, and how Freddy Mercury crowed his wicked heart out the moment I said *hello*. I might have been your first client to apologize for her rooster.

Thank you to Michele Bidelspach for letting me know that Travis's secret dream was to be a real cowboy. He'd have no hat without you!

And thank you to my editor, Madeleine Colavita, for pretending I don't have an italics problem. Your invaluable wisdom and guidance brought Maggie and Travis to life. Please don't ever stop dropping smiley-face bombs on my manuscripts. And to everyone else at Grand Central Publishing, especially Joan Mathews, huntress of dangling modifiers, thank you for knowing what you're doing!

Extra special thanks to my family. You are my world, and without your faith and support, I'd never reach *The End*.

Finally, thank you to my readers. You complete me.

Big Bad
COWBOY

Chapter
One
❦

White caliche dust clung to Travis Blake's boots as he slammed the squeaky door on the mailbox. Or tried to anyway. It was smashed nearly flat, because not much had changed in Big Verde, Texas, during the twelve years he'd been gone. There were still a few idiots who thought it was fun to hang out of truck windows while blasting down dirt roads taking out mailboxes with baseball bats.

Travis stuck the mail under his arm—he'd face whatever holy hell it contained when he got back to the house—and squinted up and down the dirt road. Whoever had destroyed his mailbox was long gone. He added *Replace mailbox* to his endless mental list of things to do and headed for his truck idling on the road.

He dumped the stack of mail on the center console and put the truck in Drive, just as a small voice piped up from the backseat.

"Uncle Travis, you're not s'posed to leave me in the truck while it's runnin'."

Travis jerked and looked over the seat, blinking slowly until reality clicked into place like a steel vault door. It had been eight weeks since he'd gotten out of the Army with meticulous plans for the rest of his life, and six weeks since those plans had been annihilated by a phone call from a social worker.

Six weeks since he'd met his nephew, Henry, for the first time.

"You were fine. You couldn't get out of that contraption you're buckled into to save your soul. And even if you did, why would you be stupid enough to try to drive the truck?"

"Because I'm a kid!"

Travis didn't have much experience with children, but Henry struck him as being smarter than the average five-year-old, which was probably the very worst kind of five-year-old.

Henry kicked the back of Travis's seat because he knew Travis hated it, and Travis clenched his jaw and ignored it because he knew Henry hated *that*. He slowly drove up to the big iron gate adorned by the ranch's brand, an H with a rising T in the shape of a horseshoe.

When Travis was thirteen, his father, Ben Blake, moved him and his brother from a trailer park on the outskirts of Houston to the two-hundred-acre Texas Hill Country ranch known as Happy Trails. Rags to riches. And often back again. That was high-stakes professional poker in a nutshell.

Being a naive kid, Travis had thought all three of them would immediately become real cowboys. His dad had even bought him a black gelding named Moonshine, who he'd promptly lost in a bet. The only thing the man had ever managed to hold on to was the ranch. Which was good, because Travis intended to sell it.

"Mrs. Garza says you don't know what you're doing," Henry said, seeking another button to push.

"Well, thank God for Mrs. Garza," Travis said. And he meant it, too. If it wasn't for Mrs. Garza taking care of Henry after school and on weekends while Travis did light landscaping work, he didn't know what he'd do. His final pay from the Army was being held up in a tangle of bureaucratic red tape, and he couldn't start his new job in Austin until he'd tied up the loose ends at Happy Trails. He glanced at Henry in the rearview mirror. The child was more of a thrashing, uncontrollable projectile than a dangling loose end. It was hard not to feel sorry for him, though. Henry's daddy was currently a guest at the Texas State Penitentiary in Huntsville. And his mama had just died of ovarian cancer.

The social worker seemed to think Travis was Henry's only living kin not serving time behind bars.

Yep. Definitely hard not to feel sorry for the kid.

Travis pushed the remote on the visor and waited for the gate to open.

And waited.

"Goddammit."

"That's a bad word," Henry spouted.

The remote for the gate didn't work. Travis got out—turned off the fucking truck so Henry wouldn't chide him about it—and trudged over to open the gate manually. A white piece of paper flapped in the breeze.

You are in violation of Agricultural Code 246.4B again. It is not my responsibility to keep your cows off my property. It is yours. Fix your dang fences.

Travis yanked the note off the gate, crumpled it up, and dropped it.

"Litterbug!"

Henry was in prime form. He'd fallen asleep in the car seat, something he invariably did about three minutes before they got wherever it was they were going. Stopping the truck was like poking a nest of hornets, and that's why Travis had left it idling.

He leaned over and grabbed the wadded piece of paper, held it up for Henry to see, and then shoved it in his pocket. The gate groaned loudly as he pushed it to the post and hitched it on the wire. Then he got back in the truck, started it, drove through the gate, stopped the truck, turned the goddam thing off while giving Henry the evil eye, and climbed out to close the gate behind him.

By the time he finally got back in, an audience had lined up on either side of the lane; young bulls on one side and heifers on the other. At least those fence lines were holding. The same couldn't be said for the one separating his east pasture from Honey Mackey's apple orchard. The crazy old lady kept leaving him threatening notes. He'd patched the fence multiple times, but it didn't hold. It needed to be completely replaced. The only things required were time and money, both of which were in short supply.

The herd followed them along as they drove up the lane, even though the bed of the truck was loaded with a lawnmower and a weed whacker—tools of his temporary trade—and not hay. Henry waved at the cows until the truck turned left at the split and continued up to the house.

The windmill rose above the trees as they hit the top of the hill, and Travis automatically depressed the accelerator at the tug of its familiar silhouette. His dad, always full of cowboy dictums, had said windmills made a horse's hooves trot a little faster and a man's heart long for hearth and home. The effect it had on Travis was surprising, since neither hearth nor home had ever quite risen to the occasion.

Unlike the windmill, the sight of the house stirred no warm, fuzzy feels. The attic windows stared angrily, like a glowering monster. A new coat of paint would probably do wonders. Make the place more *Southern Living* and less *Amityville Horror*.

"Let me out!" Henry said. Then he convulsed and rocked in his seat until Travis reached back and sprung him.

"Stay out of the cookies. You've got to eat supper first."

Henry jumped down, leaving supper—a greasy paper bag from the drive-thru hamburger joint—on the seat next to his backpack. It was the best Travis could do after a long day at work, where he'd grubbed, dug, and planted at the Village Chateau, the fanciest hotel in Big Verde. And when he was done with all that, he'd helped get the place ready for Annabelle Vasquez's Halloween party. She'd kept a watchful eye on him as he'd installed a fake graveyard and set up a pumpkin patch. He'd politely turned down the invitation Anna had offered when he left. He didn't much care for parties, and this one seemed especially awful as it required a costume. He shivered at the thought as he followed Henry through the back door.

Anna had also invited him to bid on a landscaping project for her new house. He'd turned that down, too. For one thing, he didn't intend to remain in Big Verde long enough to complete a lavish Annabelle-style project that he was woefully unqualified to install. For another, it wasn't a good idea to work for someone you'd slept with.

* * *

Fishnet thigh-high stockings with silly bows on the back and a skirt so short it might be illegal—both in red. Maggie sighed. Why had she trusted Claire to rent a Halloween costume for her? She kicked off her sensible shoes and tossed her jacket on the bed while eyeing her best friend and co-worker, who had never owned a pair of sensible shoes in her life. With dark auburn hair and curves right out of a 1950s lingerie catalog, Claire was the opposite of Maggie, who looked more like your average little sister. Or—she ran her hands over the area where most women had hips—your average little brother.

"What do you think?" Claire asked. One corner of her mouth twitched. She knew exactly what Maggie thought and was clearly enjoying the hell out of it.

"Were they all out of stormtrooper costumes?"

Claire rolled her eyes and then held up a microscopic wisp of fabric with laces. "This is going to look fantastic on you. Way better than a stormtrooper costume."

"Is that a corset?"

Maggie had never seen a corset in real life, much less worn one. Maybe it would give her some curves if she yanked those laces real tight…

"Red will look great with your platinum blond hair."

"It's dirty blond, not platinum, and red washes me out. Also, stop trying so hard."

She took the corset from Claire and held it up against her yellow work polo with the green Petal Pushers logo. Pop, her blue-haired French bulldog, gave a bark of approval.

"I'm not trying. This *will* look great on you." Claire lifted a few strands of Maggie's hair out of her eyes. "And you call this pixie cut dirty blond?"

"Well, it's not platinum." Depending on how much Maggie was outdoors—which was a lot since she was a landscaper— her hair color ran the full gamut of sun-streaked caramel to light blond. People thought it was lighter than it was because of her ridiculously dark eyebrows and brown eyes. "And it's not a pixie cut," Maggie added, tossing her bangs out of her eyes. "A pixie cut is a hair-*do* and I don't *do* dos. Anyway, I can't wear this costume. It's demeaning."

"It's sexy. You can't clunk around a client's masked gala in a stormtrooper costume."

The client was Annabelle Vasquez, who was doing her best to spend a recent divorce settlement. "Would you stop referring to this silly Halloween party as a masked gala?"

"That's what the invitation said."

Annabelle was a pretentious snob. But Maggie really wanted to do the landscaping for the McMansion she'd plunked on top of the highest hill in Big Verde. It would be a challenge to make something out of that mound of limestone, but Maggie was looking forward to it. It wasn't often that she was able to work on a project in this small town that utilized her master of landscape architecture degree from Texas A&M.

"Travis Blake better not bid on that job," she said.

A couple of months ago it would have been a given for Petal Pushers, the garden center and landscape business Maggie owned, to win the contract. But now she had competition. *Travis Blake.* Just the thought of him made her shudder in revulsion.

"He's been aggressive about getting business since moving back to Big Verde," Claire said. "So, I'm actually not surprised."

"He's nothing but a glorified lawn boy," Maggie grumbled. "He's not remotely qualified, and besides, I bet his landscaping business isn't even a legit operation. You know he's an ex-con, right? He's probably a bookie, and the landscaping thing is just a front." She didn't know what a bookie did, but it was something shady and involved gambling, which was a known Blake family vice.

"I don't think it's a front," Claire said, picking up the micro-skirt Maggie was expected to squeeze into and holding it up to her own frame. "And besides, he's not an ex-con. You're thinking of his brother, Scott."

Nice boys, those Blake brothers. One of them—Maggie didn't even know which—had married Lisa Henley, knocked her up, and then, in the words of Maggie's dear dead grandmother, Honey Mackey, *That boy done run oft.*

Lisa had recently passed away, leaving behind a young child. Maybe that was why Travis was back. The kid must be his.

"Maybe you could take him a pie," Claire continued. "And sit down like neighbors to discuss his power grab."

Maggie laughed at the audacity of taking Travis Blake a pie. And only a girl like Claire, raised on a twelve-thousand-acre ranch, would consider Maggie and Travis neighbors. Maggie couldn't even see the Blake house from hers. And unbelievably, she hadn't seen Travis either. She wouldn't know him if he held a door for her while tipping his hat. Although she doubted he was that polite.

"You really shouldn't mess with him the way you do," Claire said. "You know, just in case he is every bit as horrible as you like to imagine."

"I don't *mess* with him. I leave informative notes on his gate. He needs to keep his scraggly cows on his side of the fence." She smirked and added, "I quoted agricultural codes."

"You know agricultural codes?"

"No, but I'm betting he doesn't either."

Claire crossed her arms over her ample bosom. "You weren't terribly bothered by the cows getting into Honey's apple orchard before Travis got here. I think you're just itching for a fight with a Blake boy."

Grandma Honey had engaged in an epic battle of wills with Ben Blake over the damn cows getting in her apple orchard. But when he'd passed away four years ago, and Lisa and her baby had moved into the ranch house, Honey had merely chased the cows back in with a broom and a few choice words, because *That girl's got enough problems.*

Now that both Honey and Lisa were gone, and Travis Blake was back—stealing landscaping accounts instead of mending fences—Maggie had gleefully revived the battle in true Hatfield and McCoy style. "I won't have Blake cows destroying Honey's apple orchard," she said. "It's mine now, and I intend to defend it against all enemies."

Maggie walked to the window and squinted in the direction of the Happy Trails' ranch house. A patch of cedar trees blocked her view, which was just as well. Honey had said the place was pretty run down. It was more than Lisa had been able to keep up with on her own, even before she'd gotten sick.

"I hear he's really cute now," Claire said, joining Maggie at the window.

"I'd forgotten he even existed," Maggie said. He'd been a couple of grades ahead of her, and it wasn't as if she'd had a social life. Not unless you considered cow tipping with the Future Farmers of America a social life. She'd been the only girl in Big Verde High's FFA program.

"Listen, there's something you should know," Claire said, chewing on her fingernail.

Nothing good ever followed *Listen, there's something you should know.* "Spit it out."

"Travis did the new landscaping at the Village Chateau."

The Village Chateau was the nicest hotel in town and the venue for the night's gala. More important, it was Maggie's landscaping account.

"Are you sure?"

Claire nodded while twisting an auburn strand of hair around her finger. "I'm sure. He started doing the upkeep a few weeks ago, and when they expanded the courtyard, they asked him—"

"But we have a maintenance contract with the Chateau. That's our job," Maggie insisted.

"We never had a contract."

They *should* have had the Chateau under contract. They'd been careless and overly confident.

"Why didn't you tell me earlier?"

"I wanted to! But I knew it would make you all splotchy..."

Maggie glanced in the mirror above the dresser. *Dammit.* "I can't attend a party at the Chateau—an account we just lost—dressed like a hooker."

Claire pulled a shiny red cape out of the Halloween store bag. "You're not a hooker. You're Little Red Riding Hood. And the fact that we just lost an account is the very reason you must go. We're going to make sure Petal Pushers wins Anna's project. Not Travis Blake."

Maggie crossed her arms over her chest and glared at the costume. She might as well be going as a sexy nurse or a French maid. "More like Little Red Riding Whore."

Claire snorted. "You're going to look sexy as hell while kicking ass. Maybe you'll even have fun. And JD will be there." She looked at Maggie as if she'd just said checkmate.

Maggie had chased after JD Mayes, with pigtails flying, since she was ten years old. Honey had always said, "You're like a dog chasing a pickup truck, Maggie. If you catch that boy, you won't have the slightest idea what to do with him."

At twenty-seven, Maggie knew exactly what to do with JD. *If* she ever caught him. Unfortunately, he was like all the other guys in Big Verde and saw her only as a friend. A good friend, which made it even worse. She held the corset up again, scrutinizing her image in the full-length mirror. She didn't look awful. Even with her grubby jeans on the bottom.

"You haven't seen the best part," Claire said.

What could possibly top the micro-miniskirt, corset, and snappy little cape and hood?

"Ta da!" Claire held up two shiny red boots. "You didn't think I was going to let you get by with garden clogs, did you?"

Well, no. But Maggie had thought maybe her red Converse high-tops would work in a sporty Red Riding Whore way. But these boots were better. "There's only one more fashion accessory I need," she declared.

"Earrings?"

"No." Maggie took the boots from Claire's hand. "A cowboy to wrap these around."

Chapter

Two

🌰

Travis put Henry's hamburger and fries on a plate and squirted ketchup onto a saucer, so it wouldn't touch the rest of his food. The kid was weird about that.

"Henry!" he shouted. "Come eat."

Henry was settled in front of the television, not budging, and prying him away from it would be a bigger battle than Travis had the energy for. He popped a TV tray up in front of Henry, set his food on it, and went back in the kitchen to get his own burger. Maybe he'd eat in front of the TV, too. He didn't even care what was on.

His phone rang as he grabbed a plate. It was the realtor, George Streleki. "Hey, George," Travis said. "What have you found out? When can we get this place on the market?"

"Well, that depends," Streleki stated simply.

"On what?"

"Your brother—"

"Scott and I inherited Happy Trails when our dad died.

And we both want to sell." Was Scott's latest incarceration the problem? The idiot had been caught with drugs at the Mexican border.

"I believe you," George said. "But I've got to get something from your brother stating his intent to sell."

Travis should be able to get that. It would be unpleasant—every interaction with Scott was—but not difficult. "No problem."

"And did you know there's a lien against the property?"

This was news. "A lien? Why? How?" Shouldn't he have known about something this important?

Maybe if you'd ever bothered to check on your brother's wife and son, you'd know what the fuck was going on.

After their dad died, Travis had told Scott that he and Lisa could live on the ranch for as long as they wanted. What did Travis care? He didn't want it. All he asked was that they take care of the cattle to hold on to the agricultural tax exemption and...*pay the fucking property taxes.* He swallowed. Hard. Scott had been busted shortly after that conversation.

"You've got some back taxes built up," the realtor said. "You'll get a hell of a lot more money for the place if you can pay those off. Otherwise, folks will just be looking to take advantage of you."

The knot Travis had swallowed rose back up.

"Shit," Travis said. "I'll get back to you, George." He slammed down the phone.

"What's wrong?" Henry asked. He was covered in ketchup.

"Nothing." *Everything.*

He was going to need real money to pay off the taxes. There was no point in hitting Scott up for it. And the change he was bringing in mowing lawns was putting food on the table, but that was about it.

He chewed his lip. Where the hell could he come up with

a big chunk of money? The check he was expecting from the Army most likely wouldn't cover it. He stared at the invitation to Anna's costume party resting on top of the mail, the one she'd handed him as he left the Village Chateau. The *Dia de los Muertos* skeletons and their taunting, garish grins stared back.

"Henry, I've got to go out tonight. Will you be okay if Mrs. Garza comes over?"

Henry's eyes lit up. He'd seen the party invitation in the truck. "You're going to the costume party? Can I go?"

"Believe it or not, it's just for grown-ups."

Henry shot past him and ran up the stairs. "I've got a mask for you!"

Travis wasn't going to wear a mask. He dumped his hamburger in the trash and went upstairs to the bathroom. He needed a shower if he was going to the party. He sniffed a pit. And even if he wasn't.

While Henry scrounged around for a mask Travis had no intention of wearing, Travis stripped and stepped into the shower. He turned the water on full throttle, nice and hot, so it could pummel his sore shoulders and back.

God, he dreaded this party. He'd intentionally kept to himself since moving back to Big Verde. He hadn't exactly made a ton of friends here as a kid. And of all people, it sucked that it was Anna holding this power over him. But there was a chance her landscaping project would pay enough to take care of the back taxes.

He snorted, remembering himself at seventeen. He'd been a clueless, puny bookworm, and Annabelle Vasquez had never paid him any mind until he started mowing her family's lawn. He could still see her standing at her bedroom window, curling a strand of shiny black hair around a finger and licking her lips while she watched him work.

She'd been his first crush, and it had been a thrill. But

after doing an awful lot of Anna's homework assignments, he'd realized he was being used. He'd tried to end things as politely as possible, but it was Anna's first taste of rejection, and she hadn't much cared for it. She accused him of stealing a bracelet out of her car. Her father had even filed a police report. Nothing had come of it. There had been no witnesses, and of course, Travis hadn't stolen the damn thing. But he was embarrassed by it.

He'd worked so hard to be the *Good Blake Boy*. But he and his family were outsiders in Big Verde. Folks had believed Anna, their hometown girl, and everyone suddenly claimed to have seen it coming:

Apple doesn't fall far from the tree. Poor kid didn't have a chance.

How else was he going to turn out?

He groaned as the shower head did what it was supposed to, and his muscles melted beneath the pounding stream. He'd work up a bid for Annabelle as soon as he got out of the shower. How hard could it be? It wasn't as if you needed a damn degree in landscaping to move dirt or plant shrubs. Although *some* people seemed to think so.

Mary Margaret Mackey had gone to A&M and earned a degree in landscape architecture. Travis knew this because he'd stalked her LinkedIn profile after damn near every business in town had told him Petal Pushers did their landscaping: a college degree, an internship at a big company in Fort Worth, followed by a questionable move back to Big Verde, where she obviously hoped to impress everyone with her vast knowledge of potted plants. *Petal Pushers*—what the hell kind of name was that? Did she flounce around in a pink sundress and fancy hat?

He turned off the shower and shook his head like a dog as Henry pounded on the door. "Uncle Travis!"

Travis ran a towel over his body and wrapped it around his waist. He didn't trust the old lock and didn't need another bathroom invasion resulting in an awkward conversation about the size of his penis.

"What is it, Henry?" It could be something as simple as wanting a cookie. But it could also be the beginning of a fit. Travis hadn't spent any time around Henry before Lisa died. He didn't know if the fits were typical shenanigans for a five-year-old kid, or if they were the result of loss. Either way, he dealt with them. He seriously doubted his idiot brother could do half as well. He'd had little more to do with Henry than Travis had.

"I found the mask!"

"That's awesome, buddy," Travis called back. "But I'm not gonna wear a costume."

Holding the towel in place, Travis opened the door. A disappointed face met him on the other side, but it didn't appear Henry was about to go ballistic.

"I've decided to go to the party as a ruggedly handsome man, so I don't need a mask." He gave Henry his best cheesy smile and puffed out his chest.

Henry didn't laugh. "I don't think people will know you're dressed up in a costume. You'll just look like yourself, and you're butt ugly."

Travis laughed and mussed Henry's hair, and Henry threw his skinny little arms around Travis's waist. Travis took a step back at the sudden display of affection, dragging Henry with him. Then he patted Henry's back, feeling the tiny shoulder blades poking against his Spider-Man T-shirt. The contact was getting a little less awkward each day.

"You always tell it like it is, Henry."

"That's because you're not supposed to lie."

Travis peeled Henry off and squatted so he was eye level.

"You going to be okay with Mrs. Garza tonight? I might be late."

"Yes," Henry said, lowering his voice to a whisper. "But you have to tell her about my bedtime problem."

"You mean how you're a very sound sleeper and sometimes don't wake up to go to the bathroom?" Changing sheets and pajamas in the middle of the night was a pain in the ass, but Travis refused to shame Henry about wetting the bed. His own dad had been an asshole about that sort of thing, and Travis wasn't going to follow suit.

Henry nodded.

"I'll tell her. But go to the bathroom before she puts you to bed, okay?"

"It don't help," Henry said.

"It doesn't help," Travis corrected.

"That's what I said."

Travis sighed. "I wish I didn't have to go to this stupid party."

"*Stupid* is a bad word."

"Did your mom tell you that?"

A watery expression floated across Henry's face. Travis hated bringing Lisa up, but the lady at school who provided Henry with grief counseling told him he shouldn't avoid it.

"Mom didn't like the word *stupid*."

"I'll try not to say it so much then."

Henry's little eyebrows turned down for a frown. "I wonder when my dad's gonna come get me."

Henry couldn't have many memories of Scott. He'd seen him only a handful of times, and Henry had been awfully young. "Remember what we talked about? Your dad can't come to Big Verde right now."

Henry's lower lip began to tremble. "He don't want me."

"He *doesn't* want—" Travis shut his mouth. "You know

what, big guy? I think you're right. I need a costume. Let's see that mask."

Just like that, Henry snapped out of it. "I've got three little piggies and *this*."

Two yellow eyes and a pair of wicked fangs.

Who's afraid of the Big Bad Wolf?

Chapter

Three

☙

Maggie watched through the windshield as Claire picked her way across the Village Chateau's parking lot on stiletto heels. The full October moon lit up the witchy silhouette, complete with broom and pointy hat.

Maggie flashed the Jeep's lights to get Claire's attention, and then got out and leaned against the door. She ran her hands over the corset, barely recognizing her own shape. It was as snug as she and Claire could get it, and came just below her breasts, which were probably supposed to be pushed up and out, but Maggie owned no contraption capable of achieving such a feat. Instead, she wore a stretchy bandeau bra beneath the white off-the-shoulder blouse because it was the only strapless bra she owned. The boots were above the knee, and the red fishnet thigh-high stockings stopped about four inches from the bottom of her skirt.

She felt both sexy and silly.

A truck pulled into the parking lot, shining its headlights

in Maggie's face. She squinted as it swung around before backing into the space in front of her. She rolled her eyes at the bright blue "bull balls" hanging from its hitch, swinging obscenely to the bass beat of a Rascal Flatts song. Why did guys hang scrotum sacks on their trucks?

The music stopped abruptly as Bubba Larson opened his truck door and climbed out. "Howdy, Mighty Mack."

When would guys stop referring to her as Mighty Mack? It had been cute in high school, when she'd earned the nickname by being the only kid in FFA who could get Mini-Might, a two-thousand-pound Brahman bull, into the chute. But now it was just childish and unwomanly and didn't go with her new corset.

The lighting was too dim for details, but it seemed Bubba had poured his portly self into something tight. In fact, it looked like he might be *wearing* tights.

A light breeze blew Maggie's cape open.

"Goddamn, girl," Bubba said. "I'm Superman, but what are you supposed to be?"

"She's Little Red Riding Hood," Claire said, arriving just in time to give Maggie backup. "Isn't she cute?"

Bubba raised his eyebrows. "I don't know that *cute* is the word I'd use."

Humiliation crept in, and warmth spread across Maggie's cheeks. They were probably the same color as her cape, which she quickly yanked closed. Why had she let Claire talk her into wearing this outfit? She felt like a little girl who'd been caught in her mother's lingerie. She must look laughable! Since feeling humiliated was not something she enjoyed, she became pissed off instead. "Listen here, Bubba. You're one to talk. I mean, if anybody looks more ridiculous than me—"

"Who said you look ridiculous?" Bubba asked. "You look

smokin' hot, Mighty Mack." He nodded at Claire and added, "You, too."

Claire curtsied with her broom, but Maggie shifted nervously from foot to foot. Bubba looked as serious as a large man with a muffin top over his tights could look, so she let go of the cape.

"Come on," Bubba said, offering an arm to each of them. "Let's light this place up."

"Isn't Trista coming?" Claire asked.

"She's already here," Bubba said. "Came early to help out."

"Is she a superhero, too?" Maggie asked, taking Bubba's arm.

"Nah. She's dressed as a nun."

Claire laughed. "She must be at least eight months along by now."

"Seven," Bubba said. "Baby is due around Christmas. She just looks like she's about to pop. Don't tell her I said that."

"Do you know whether it's a boy or girl?" Maggie asked.

"We'll find out when it gets here. I figure it's another girl."

Bubba and Trista had three daughters. As Bubba liked to say, his swimmers wore skirts. He worshipped those baby girls, though. He and Trista had been together since high school.

Maggie's heel hit a pebble and she wobbled. "Don't let go of me." She might look smokin' hot leaning against her Jeep, but walking turned her into a spindly-legged newborn calf.

"You'll get the hang of it," Claire said. "Just try to walk normally."

"Which one of you is going to cut a rug with me?" Bubba

asked. "Trista can't do it. Not unless we want this party to get a lot more exciting than it should."

Maggie loved to dance. But she'd break her neck doing it in these boots. "I'm just learning to walk in these," she said. "No way I could keep up with you on the dance floor."

Bubba was a lumbering alligator on dry land, but set him on some sawdust and he turned into a sleek and nimble creature. He could drop into the splits and pop right back up. A crowd always gathered once he got going, and Maggie didn't need an audience watching as she stumbled around in her red porn star boots.

"You've got to dance tonight," Claire said. "Those boots were made for it."

Short of snowshoes, Maggie couldn't think of anything made *less* for it.

They passed the final row of parked cars. "There's the white horse," Claire said, pointing to a gigantic white King Ranch Special Edition Ford F350 pickup. "JD is here."

Maggie tripped, almost impaling herself on the iron railing of the Gothic fence surrounding the Chateau. Her heart hammered in her chest. "I wonder who he's with."

"It doesn't matter. You're dressed better. If JD keeps you in the friend zone after seeing you like this, then he just doesn't like girls."

Bubba snorted, and so did Maggie. JD liked girls all right. And they liked him. He'd probably dated every single woman in Big Verde, *with one obvious exception.*

* * *

The lobby of the hotel was covered in cobwebs, flickering lights, and ghoulish displays. Maggie had to give Annabelle credit for throwing a different kind of Halloween party. Instead of renting the VFW Hall, she had transformed the Village Chateau into a proper haunted castle for a party nobody would soon forget.

Maggie rolled her shoulders. Time to focus. She was here for one reason and one reason only. Well, two, really. But the first order of business was to show off her cinched-in waist and nice round ass (optical illusion) to JD Mayes. "You go kiss up to Anna," she said to Claire. "I'm going to find a certain cowboy."

"Both of us need a drink before our missions," Claire said. "Let's get some witch's brew."

A waiter whisked past with a tray of smoking goblets, and they each snatched one. Witch's brew was basically trashcan punch, and it went down easy. Maggie wiped her mouth on the hem of her cape. Then she looked around for JD.

Something shiny caught her eye, and since every cell in her body gravitated toward it, she knew it was JD. His boisterous laugh rose above the din, and Maggie's feet automatically headed toward the source. The crowd parted, and there he stood, dressed as a knight in shining armor.

"Go get him," Claire said. "I'll go compliment Anna on the party, and her hair, and her costume..."

Maggie kept her eyes on the prize—gosh, he was cute—but her mind went to business. "Remind Anna that I'm the only landscape architect within a hundred miles and that Travis Blake is a guy with a lawn mower."

Claire sauntered off and Maggie inhaled deeply, squared her shoulders, and strutted toward JD like America's Next Top Model if America's Next Top Model were wearing heels for the first time and was slightly buzzed on trashcan punch. JD stood with Alice, the town's librarian, who wore the familiar yellow ball gown from *Beauty and the Beast*.

"Hi, Alice."

"Oh my!" Alice squealed. "Look at you." She turned to JD and poked him in the ribs with her finger. "JD, look at Maggie."

JD took a long, hard look that turned Maggie's legs to jelly. Then he flashed his two-million-dollar smile. "I don't know who you're supposed to be," he said, "but red agrees with you."

"I'm Little Red Riding Hood."

JD wore a breastplate over his starched white shirt, and metal plates were strapped over his Wranglers to his thighs and shins. There was even a gilded faceplate attached to the brim of his white Stetson. He gave a deep, squeaky bow. "M'lady."

"Isn't he just precious?" Alice asked. She winked at Maggie from behind an open book.

"Oh yeah. He's just precious." Alice had pulled off coquettish, but Maggie sounded like she was having an asthma attack.

JD pulled a fake sword out of a scabbard hanging from his belt. "Check this out."

Why wasn't he drooling over her newly corseted curves? Maybe some pleasant conversation about his outfit would lead to some more comments about hers. She nodded at his boots. "You're wearing the white tops."

JD could afford hand-tooled Tony Lamas, but he always wore Justin Boots because that's what George Strait wore. *What's good enough for King George is good enough for me.*

"Of course," he said with a wink. "The prettiest girl in Big Verde helped me pick them out."

She grinned and fluttered her eyelashes. "Maybe we can do that again sometime. I love hanging out with you, you know." They'd gone to San Antonio to shop for boots, eaten dinner downtown, and then watched the Spurs game at a sports bar. Unfortunately, the evening had ended with a friendly pat on the back.

JD shrugged. "I don't really need any boots right now."

Alice patted Maggie's arm sympathetically. "Is Claire here?" she asked. "I need to see if she's coming to book club this month."

Maybe the conversation could move beyond swords and boots if it was just the two of them. "She was headed to the ballroom."

Alice nodded and swooshed off, popping open a book and nearly taking out a waiter. Dimples appeared in JD's cheeks, and Maggie made sure her cape was open and pushed her chest out. *Look! Boobs!*

"You want to hit the bar for a drink?" JD asked, taking her empty goblet and ignoring her boobs entirely.

"Um, sure." Feeling deflated, she renewed her effort at puffing out her chest and damn near threw her back out.

"You okay?" JD asked.

"Yeah, just stretching."

JD cocked a brow and shook his head. "There's a portable bar set up in the corner. We don't have to go into the ballroom yet if you don't want to." He knew Maggie always needed a few moments to warm up before jumping into the fray. He was thoughtful and observant like that.

"Do you want another one of those misty things? Or your usual Dos Equis?"

A nice Mexican beer sounded delicious, but she didn't want to be predictable tonight. "Another misty thing, please."

While they waited for their drinks, JD folded his arms across his breastplate and gave her another good once-over. "So," he said. "What happened to the stormtrooper costume?"

"Claire picked this out for me instead. Do you like it?" Her heart pounded while she tried not to blurt out that she'd worn it just for him.

"Like I said before, red looks good on you. You should wear it more often."

The bartender set her drink down and JD doled out some money before picking up his beer. Was that all he was going to say? That she looked good in red?

"Bottoms up, Mighty Mack."

She grabbed her trashcan punch and guzzled it down. Maybe JD was just dense. Maybe he was so used to the two of them being buddies that he couldn't see what was right in front of him. A warm, tingly sensation spread throughout her body. *Time to show him.*

A graveyard had been set up in the courtyard. She'd seen it when they'd parked. "Let's get some air."

They started for the courtyard with JD squeaking at every step and Maggie hobbling along beside him. "You'd better pace yourself with the drinking or you're going to regret it in the morning."

He offered his arm, but on a whim, Maggie grabbed his hand instead. He hesitated a moment, but then resumed his squeaky gait. Was he surprised? Maggie stared straight ahead, not daring to glance at his face. He didn't let go and scream *girl cooties*, but he didn't give it a sexy little squeeze either.

The courtyard was unreal. Tombstones leaned this way and that, casting long, sideways shadows across the ground. Every now and then a dismembered hand clawed its way out of the dirt.

"Hey, look," JD said, pointing at a tombstone. "They have names of people we know on them." He let go of her hand and started wandering around. "Listen to this one. 'Here lies Dr. Martin—finally got something in the hole.'"

"I sincerely hope that's referring to his horrible golf game and not his dating life," Maggie said.

JD laughed. "Knowing him, it could go either way."

There were more amusing tombstones, but Maggie wasn't interested. "Isn't that the most gorgeous harvest moon you've ever seen?" she asked, sliding next to JD and slipping her arm through his. "It's very romantic."

JD looked at her. At least she thought he did. It was hard to tell because his Stetson cast the upper part of his face in shadow. But she could see the lower half, and his mouth was set in a stern, straight line. Either he was about to grab her and take her right here on the fake tombstones, romance novel–style, or he was not in the mood at all—*at least where she was concerned.*

She decided to press the issue by mashing her breast into his arm. Actually, it was probably the trashcan punch making that decision, but whatever. It seemed like a good one. JD's biceps flexed against her breast, and then she felt it—a small shiver. It passed through JD's body and into hers. *She was getting to him.*

"It's a little chilly out here, isn't it?" she asked, giving him an opportunity to deny it was the cool night air giving him the shivers.

JD cleared his throat and stared at his boots. Then he slowly lifted his gaze to hers. Maybe it was just the neon glow from the Pump 'n' Go sign across the street, but his hazel eyes gleamed like they'd been struck by moonbeams. Maggie held her breath. This was it. She reached up and softly traced the outline of his jaw with her finger. And he . . . *flinched.*

It was just a flash of a flinch. If she hadn't known him so well, she might have missed it or been able to talk herself out of having seen it. But there was no doubt in her mind about what had just happened. JD Mayes had flinched at her touch.

It felt like a slap piercing the alcohol buzz as easily as a cartoon cannon ball shot through a cloud. Her mouth dried up. Her skin broke out in a light sweat followed by a chill. She wrapped herself in her cape.

"Maggie—"

"No." She held her hand in front of JD's face like a shield. She needed to block the words before they ripped her apart like bullets from a machine gun.

I don't like you in that way.

Let's just be friends.

You're not my type.

She'd known it. So why had she made such a fool of herself?

It was the stupid corset, the ridiculous boots, and Claire's infuriating optimism. Claire had never known rejection. She hadn't been stood up by Scott Flores for the eighth grade Sadie Hawkins dance, nor had she sat home the night of the senior prom, pretending she hadn't wanted to go anyway. Women like Claire were never tucked away into friend zones, forced to watch the objects of their affection cry into their beers over other women. They never stood in front of JD Mayes while dressed like the world's least shapely porn star, watching him flinch and shiver at their touch.

JD moved her hand away from his face. The contact was electric. Not the sexy shock of fireworks, more like sticking your wet finger into an electrical outlet.

"I need to tell you something, Maggie."

Her eyes stung. She hadn't cried since Honey died. She couldn't blink. If she did, a tear might escape. *Hold it in, Mackey.*

"No. You really don't need to say anything," she said.

Blink.

Dammit. A tear slipped out. JD wiped it away with his finger. How dare he touch her tenderly on the face?

"You need to know—"

"I got the message, okay? Loud and clear."

JD dropped his hand to his side. "Let me talk, Maggie. You're my best friend—"

"Not anymore," she said. "It's too cruel."

She couldn't look at JD's face for one second longer. She turned and walked steadily—how, she didn't know—in the direction of the bar. She needed to find Claire and tell her she was leaving. Corsets, red porn star boots, and smoky eyes weren't meant for women like her. She could only imagine what people were thinking.

Look at little Mighty Mack trying to be sexy.

"Maggie, wait!"

She walked faster. A blur of unrecognizable faces rushed past as she stormed into the hotel, pushing her way through throngs of people, ignoring the few who called out greetings. She held the cape tightly closed.

Through her watery eyes she saw the tip of a pointy hat. *Claire!* She sped up, zigzagging through people toward the circular bar. But just as she got there, the hat disappeared. She headed for the one empty seat at the bar. She'd sit there and wait for Claire. Just like always.

She started to hoist herself onto the stool—they were tricky things for short people in tight miniskirts—and her heel missed the rung. She lurched forward and landed in a pair of strong arms.

"Are you okay?"

The voice was deep and held a hint of humor. She looked up to see vicious fangs, a tapered snout, and pointed ears. She gasped, even though it was a mask.

"I'm fine," she finally said. "But my, what big teeth you have."

Chapter

Four

❦

The entire night had been so surreal that Travis didn't know why he was surprised when a pretty woman in red—almost elfin with large eyes set in a small heart-shaped face—fell into his arms with a sarcastic comment about the size of his teeth. He couldn't help it; he ran his tongue over them. They felt perfectly normal.

"Thanks a lot," he mumbled, helping to get the little blonde upright again.

He assisted her onto the barstool, getting a good look at the red boots she wore. They were probably the reason she'd flopped into his arms, but damn, they looked good on her legs.

Her eyes crinkled in amusement. "Your mask," she said. "It has fangs. I wasn't referring to your actual teeth."

He smiled with a dumb sense of relief. The child's mask only covered the upper part of his fully adult-sized face, and his mouth was framed by long, sharp, and appropriately named plastic canine teeth. "I'm not used to having fangs."

"Admit it. You thought I had a tooth fetish."

Travis leaned over and whispered, "Do you?"

She grinned, but her eyes were shiny, as if maybe she'd been crying or trying not to cry. And her makeup was smudged. "Wouldn't you like to know? Maybe I have a mask fetish. I think that's an actual thing."

Her voice was smoky and sultry, like a jazz singer's, and surprisingly low for such a small woman. And yes, he would definitely like to know if she had a fetish of any kind whatsoever. "Wolf masks, in particular, seem to turn women on," he offered.

He wasn't even kidding. He'd initially left the mask in the truck, but even though he did his best to avoid socializing, he'd been forced into a couple of awkward conversations with people he didn't know but who seemed to know him. He'd retrieved the mask and quickly found Anna to give her the bid. She'd seemed pleased and insisted he stay long enough for one drink. Since then he'd been growled at, petted, and a woman who might have been his freshman English teacher had called him a good puppy.

His new blond friend seemed fascinated by the dance floor, staring at it intently. "My, what big eyes you have," he said.

He cringed as the eyes in question turned their gaze back to him. He couldn't seem to stop the stupid from pouring out of his mouth.

"That's my line," she replied.

He swallowed. Her voice was such a turn-on. She practically channeled Kathleen Turner with a little Emma Stone around the edges. It made it hard to follow a conversation. "Pardon?"

"You said, *My, what big eyes you have.* I'm Little Red Riding Hood. That's my line."

She didn't look anything like the Little Red Riding Hood in Henry's bedtime storybook. "I'm the—"

"Big Bad Wolf. Yeah, I get it," she said, waving a hand dismissively. "Fancy meeting you here."

She called the bartender over with just a nod of her head. "Dos Equis," she said. "With lime."

Travis pulled out his wallet. "Let me get that for you."

"No, thanks. I've got it."

Was that a rejection? And if so, a rejection of what? He wasn't exactly looking for a romantic relationship, and even a hookup seemed complicated now that he had a kid at home. It wasn't like he could stay out all night, or even real late, for that matter. And he certainly couldn't show up at the ranch with Little Red Riding Hood in tow. What would Mrs. Garza think?

Little Red Riding Hood dug around in her purse while the bartender looked on. In only a few seconds there was an impressive pile of crap on the counter, but she hadn't scrounged up any money. She sighed in resignation. "Just water, I guess."

"I've already opened the bottle," the bartender said.

She turned her big brown eyes on Travis. "Do you mind?"

Heck, no, he didn't mind. It was why he'd offered. He handed some cash to the bartender as the blonde took a big swig of beer. And then another.

"Argument with a boyfriend?" he asked.

Her big eyes grew even larger. He probably shouldn't have said anything. "You just look a bit...out of sorts."

"Great. I look out of sorts."

He couldn't say the right thing to save his soul. "I didn't mean anything by it. Just wondering why your makeup is smudged."

"My makeup is smudged?" She dug through the pile of crap still on the counter and pulled out a small mirror.

"You look fine."

"Fine? Aren't you a sweet talker. And oh wow"—she stared in the mirror—"in what universe do I look fine?" She licked her finger and rubbed it beneath her eye. "And there is no boyfriend," she added. "Zero, zilch, nada."

A flicker of hope popped up and settled inconveniently in Travis's crotch. He had no intention of fanning it into a flame, so he took a sip of beer and tried to ignore it.

"I guess I do technically have a boyfriend."

Good. The flicker of hope fizzled out.

Little Red Riding Hood rubbed a cocktail napkin across the condensation on her beer bottle and smeared it under her eyes in earnest. "Lots of them, actually. That's the problem."

She was a player. The flicker flared back up. "Oh, I see."

"Oh, stop. You don't see a thing. I mean there are lots of men and they're all friends. Friends, friends, friends..." She wadded up the napkin and took another sip of beer.

Her makeup was more smeared than ever, and it was kind of sexy, just like the rest of her. "Would you like to dance?" he blurted. His hands immediately became damp with perspiration. Why had he done that? He hated to dance. It must be the mask. He felt like a different man with it on. He hoped the motherfucking wolf knew how to dance.

Little Red Riding Hood stared at him as if he'd just told her where he'd last seen Elvis.

"You want to dance with *me?*"

Had he been too pushy? "Only if you feel like it." He tried to make it sound like he didn't care one way or another.

Little Red Riding Hood's adorable mouth curved up into a slight smile, and she fluffed her hair. She wasn't pissed. She was pleased. And the little flicker of a flame that had started in his crotch moved higher, warming his insides and making him grin like a jack-o'-lantern.

Something squeaked behind them, and Little Red Riding Hood stopped fluffing and frowned. Travis turned to see JD Mayes dressed like the Tin Man. JD had been one of the few people who'd been friendly to him in school, and they'd had a few pleasant run-ins since he'd moved back to Big Verde. But JD didn't look friendly now. His lips were drawn in a tight line, his fists were clenched, and his hat was pulled down low, hiding his eyes. What had JD's blood boiling?

"What do you think you're doing, Maggie?" he asked.

So, her name was Maggie. Travis hadn't even thought to ask.

"I'm about to dance with the Big Bad Wolf, not that it's any of your business."

He should probably lift his mask, so JD could see who he was and stop glowering. He reached for it, but then something rubbed against the inside of his calf. He looked down to see a red boot delicately working its way up and down his leg.

Tonight, with this pixie in her sexy boots and little red cape, he didn't want to be Travis Blake and all it entailed. He wanted to be the Big Bad Wolf.

Little Red Riding Hood had said there was no boyfriend in the picture. But with JD flaring his nostrils in and out like a bull ready to charge, it seemed a good idea to keep the mask on. The last thing Travis needed was to get on the bad side of the town's golden boy.

* * *

Maggie had half expected JD to follow them onto the dance floor. Not because of jealousy. They were good and clear on that. The idiot was protective, which was offensive, because she didn't need protecting. She wasn't his sister. Heck, she wasn't even his buddy anymore.

The wolf was huge. And he smelled good, like woods and sunshine. His hand spanned her back from below her bandeau bra to her waist. She shivered all over, and it was becoming increasingly difficult to continue simmering over JD.

Friends and acquaintances blew past them, a blur of mind-dizzying motion, two-stepping across the dance floor with hardly a glance. But the wolf steered her through the melee until they stood in the center of the dance floor, arms around each other, settling into stationary swaying and rocking. They danced in the eye of the storm. She reveled in the sexiness of the slow, warm pace, and her body melted into his as the long, hard feel of him swiftly led to the blissful Zen of *JD Who?*

The song ended, but the wolf pulled her closer, as if he didn't want to let go. She tightened her grip around his neck... *yes, let's dance some more.* She nestled in just below his chin as the next song began. It was a slow dance, and this was typically when her partner thanked her kindly and escorted her off the floor. She was good for a fun spin through the sawdust, but her usual buddies looked around for women like Claire when it came time to get their slow groove on.

For the first time, Maggie wondered just who the hell the Big Bad Wolf was. He couldn't be local, or he'd have gotten the memo that she was basically a guy. It felt wonderful to be perfectly anonymous. She was just a woman in a corset, stockings, and sexy boots dancing with a mysterious stranger.

The song ended, and the driving beat of electronic dance music started up. The wolf let go and stood there, stiff as a board, and gave a little shrug. "Not much of a dancer," he said.

"I beg to differ." He'd been doing just fine a minute ago. The man had rhythm in his hips. She grabbed his hands and started to move, hoping he'd become inspired. But dancing in red porn star boots was about a thousand times more difficult than swaying in them, and she felt like she'd just put on her first pair of roller skates. And from the grin on the wolf's face, she looked like it, too. "Fine. Let's head back to the bar."

The wolf practically wagged his tail in relief, and he grabbed her hand and steered her through all the sweaty, bobbing bodies, including Bubba and the crowd that had already formed around him. Their drinks still sat on the bar, but hers had gotten warm, so she pushed it aside. She didn't need any more alcohol anyway. The trashcan punch buzz had worn off as she'd danced, and that was a good thing.

"What are you thinking about?" the wolf asked. He held his head slightly tilted. He looked every bit the part of a curious puppy, and Maggie wanted to offer him a belly rub. She knew from slow dancing that the belly in question was lean and hard. She fanned her face with a napkin.

"I'm thinking that you are a very good distraction from my troubles," she said. Not to mention an excellent and timely ego boost.

"Troubles," he said. "We've all got 'em." He took a swig of his beer, no easy task since he had a snout.

She scanned the rest of him. Nice suit, excellent fit. Maybe he was a businessman. He clearly didn't know who she was, so he wasn't from around here. "Are you a friend of Anna's?" she asked.

"Not exactly."

It must be a business relationship then. Except Anna was engaged in no business to speak of... Oh! Maybe he was a divorce lawyer. She waited, but he didn't offer anything further. Maybe he enjoyed the feeling of being anonymous as much as she did.

Her gaze journeyed to his feet. Square-toe boots—dressy, but very worn—provided no clue. Almost every man in Big Verde wore boots, no matter their occupation.

The wolf set his beer down, and the corner of his mouth turned up in response to her scrutiny. "They're comfortable."

"I love a man in boots," she quickly assured him.

He gazed pointedly at her legs. "And I love a woman in boots."

Her cheeks grew warm at the compliment. Was it possible that this was leading to a *hookup*? She'd never had a one-night stand. She'd had a couple of boyfriends in college, and she enjoyed the occasional romp with a seed salesman who called on Petal Pushers. But she'd never hooked up with a stranger. The idea was exciting, and considering her extremely recent rejection, it was also one humdinger of a rebound. *Swoosh! Nothing but net.*

The Big Bad Wolf jerked as if poked by a cattle prod, and then began digging in his pockets. "Sorry," he said. "Got a text."

He'd better not claim that his poor, sick mother had suddenly taken a turn for the worse. Maggie watched the wolf fumble with his phone before breathing a visible sigh of relief. "Everything's fine," he said.

Maybe he'd just gotten the results of a biopsy or been approved for a loan. Whatever it was, she wasn't about to ask. She was determined to keep the Big Bad Wolf as her mysterious, sexy stranger.

Clearing her throat, she turned on her stool and brought her legs out from under the bar. The wolf picked up on the motion. Very slowly, Maggie uncrossed her legs, and then crossed them again. This was one of Claire's signature sexy moves. Maggie's skirt climbed up from the activity, and the wolf noticed. He set his phone on the bar. "Where were we?"

"Here," Maggie said, running her leg up his calf. Her skirt slid even higher, and she was rewarded by a very wolfish smile. This man oozed sex, and he was directing it all at her.

"I knew it!"

They both swiveled on their barstools to see Claire, standing with her hip thrust out, a broom in one hand and a drink in the other, pointed hat set properly askew. Speaking of oozing sex...

"Knew what?" Maggie asked. She hoped the Big Bad Wolf wasn't about to trade her in for a witchier model. But his warm knee pressing against the outside of her thigh indicated he liked his women in little red hoods.

"Y'all are the perfect pair. As soon as I saw this guy"— Claire poked at the wolf with her broom—"I knew you would end up together."

They hadn't *ended up together*. Not yet.

Claire stuck her broom beneath her arm and thrust out a hand. "I'm Claire Kowalski."

Oh no! Claire was going to blow their covers. If the wolf introduced himself, she'd be forced to introduce herself, and once she said the words *Maggie Mackey*, the magic would disappear.

"I'm..."

The wolf seemed to have forgotten his own name.

"I'm the Big Bad Wolf."

Whew! He was just as determined to remain undercover as she was. He pointed to an empty seat next to him. "Want to join us?"

"Absolutely," Claire said. Without falling, tripping, or otherwise planting herself onto the wolf's lap, she sat on the barstool. As if she'd blown an invisible dog whistle, the bartender trotted over, ignoring the throng of other guests holding out money and trying to get his attention.

Claire leaned over the bar, gave the guy an eyeful of cleavage, and ordered a whiskey sour. The wolf winked at Maggie. His eyes hadn't strayed. *Good boy.*

"Listen here," Claire said to him. "This is my best friend. No leg humping on the dance floor."

Awesome. Claire was talking about leg humping.

The wolf grinned. "I admit to being a leg man, but I'm not much of a humper. You're thinking of Labrador retrievers. Wolves have more self-control."

"Really?" Claire said. "I thought wolves were wild, untamed animals."

"Wild, yes. Drooling, excitable idiots, no."

The wolf clearly had experience with Labrador retrievers.

"I think we're done dancing anyway," Maggie said. The dance floor was not the wolf's natural habitat. Although she would love some more body-to-body contact.

"You are not," Claire said with a mischievous grin.

The DJ's voice came over the sound system. "I've had a request," he announced. "Better get your howl on, folks, it's 'Li'l Red Riding Hood,' by Sam the Sham and the Pharaohs."

Claire started laughing and scooted a mortified Big Bad Wolf off his stool. Maggie began to apologize—give him an out—but then the familiar opening howl of the song rang out. The Big Bad Wolf grinned and extended his hand. "They're playing our song."

Chapter

Five

❧

Travis was unbelievably turned on. It took everything he had to avoid the dreaded leg humping that Claire Kowalski had brought up.

He'd almost choked when Claire had introduced herself. Her father, Gerome Kowalski, owned the famous Rancho Canada Verde, which bordered Happy Trails. Although they'd been neighbors of sorts, he and Claire hadn't hung out in high school. She'd probably never given him a second thought, but he'd coveted everything she had: beautiful ranch, good family name, a dad whom everybody looked up to.

It was doubtful that Claire would be trying to hook him up with her friend if she knew who he was. And for that matter, what about Little Red Riding Hood? Travis had probably gone to school with her, too. But for the life of him, he couldn't place her.

He couldn't take the mask off. Not that she'd recognize him if he did. He was hardly the scrawny, thick-lensed-glasses-wearing runt he'd been at Big Verde High. But if his name came up, it might ring a bell, and then Little Red Riding Hood would politely excuse herself from the dance floor. Luckily, she hadn't shown any interest in exchanging information. Maybe she wanted to remain anonymous, too.

Maggie. JD had called her Maggie. It sounded vaguely familiar, but that was it. Unless they belonged to former tormenters or super popular kids—often one and the same—the names of his past were mostly forgotten. He let go of Little Red Riding Hood briefly to make sure his mask was secure, and then pulled her close again.

They were attracting a bit of attention, which he hated. They'd even garnered a few comments made in jest.

Make him keep his paws to himself, girl!

Watch out for that full moon!

He didn't feel comfortable dancing as intimately as they'd done earlier. People might not know who he was, but they sure as hell knew Little Red Riding Hood, and he didn't want to embarrass her.

Little Red Riding Hood didn't seem nearly as concerned about what people thought. She pushed her pert breasts into his chest, and his mind went blank as all the blood drained out of his head. He tried to put a couple of inches of space between them, but she was having none of it. She rubbed against him in a way that surely allowed her to feel every inch of his—more painful by the minute—*interest.*

The music wasn't helping. How could a song be so dirty without actually being dirty?

It's your mind that's dirty, bonehead.

It had been a while. There wasn't much room in his life for anything other than Henry. There was certainly no room for a relationship. But a little fun? Maybe. Especially if it was anonymous.

A soft hand ran up his back, briefly squeezed his neck, and then ran through his short hair.

"Are you staying at the Chateau?" she asked.

She must assume he was from out of town. Would it be intentionally misleading to let her think so?

"No."

There. That was the truth. And any lingering misgivings about honesty were promptly extinguished when he realized why she'd asked. She wanted to hook up just as much as he did, and was thinking about a place to do it.

Where could they go? Not to Little Red Riding Hood's house. That was too personal. She'd expect him to remove his mask.

There was an equipment shed on the grounds. It was on the other side of a patch of cedar trees, at the very edge of the property that backed up against a utility easement. It wasn't exactly a first-class solution, or even a second-class solution, but if the way Little Red Riding Hood was currently grinding on his thigh was any indication, he just needed a quick solution.

"There's a place we can go if you want to be alone," he whispered.

"Does it entail me following you through the woods?"

"Yes, actually. It does."

Little Red Riding Hood raised her eyebrows. For about five horrible seconds he thought she might say no thanks. But then she smiled and grabbed his hand.

"Into the woods."

* * *

Maggie followed the stranger—*stranger!*—through the trees and away from the party. He yanked on her hand, and it was all she could do to keep up.

She would never forget the look on JD's face as she walked out of the ballroom with the wolf. *Ha! Take that, JD. This could have been all yours*—She almost toppled to the ground as one of her heels snagged on a root. The wolf caught her, helped get her steady, and then gave a tug to get her going again.

"Hey, hold up," she said. "Where's the fire?"

The wolf stopped, and she bumped into him. After the giggling was over, he grabbed her by the waist and pulled her close. She rose up on her toes and wrapped her arms around his neck. It was hard to tell who kissed who first; their lips practically melted together. Maggie parted hers at the urging of his tongue, and he explored her mouth hungrily...impatiently...*deliciously*. Her head spun. She had never been so thoroughly kissed in all her life.

He straightened up to his full height and her feet left the ground. Pressed up against him as she was, she felt where the fire was. *In his pants.*

"You're so small," he whispered.

Like it was a good thing.

His mask was adorably crooked from the kissing. She straightened his snout.

"Have you caught your breath?" he asked.

Not even a little. But she nodded anyway.

The wolf set her down, and for the first time since she'd taken his hand and followed him into the woods—a generally bad idea for Little Red Riding Hood or anyone else—she wondered where they were going.

"The shed is just behind that clump of trees."

"The shed?"

"We're not headed to Grandma's house."

A shiver went up Maggie's spine. "We're going to do it in a shed?"

The wolf cocked his head. "God, I hope so. And it's actually a pretty nice shed."

"That's probably the worst pickup line ever."

The wolf laughed. Then he leaned over and planted a whisper-soft kiss along the side of her neck, setting off a domino effect of goose bumps up and down her arms. He followed it up with a little lick. "Mmm..." he said. "Tastes like chicken."

"What?"

"Chicken. Big time."

He flapped his elbows and made squawking sounds. Maggie laughed, and the wolf made one final cluck before holding out his hand with a grin. Maggie took it without hesitation.

The shed was clearly visible in the light of the full moon. It was an old stone structure with a tin roof—kind of romantic. The wolf pushed the door open with a loud creak.

This was it. She could turn back if she wanted. She knew this man wouldn't stop her. But she didn't want to. She wanted to be ravished by a tall, sexy man in a mask. And it wasn't entirely to make up for the fact that she'd been rejected by a tall, sexy man in a cowboy hat. She really liked this guy. She liked his looks—what she could see of them. She liked that he was an awful dancer. She liked his laughter and his chicken imitation. She officially liked him enough to justify jilted sex.

She stepped inside and shivered as the wolf shut the door.

"There's no lock on the inside," he said. "But I don't think anyone will walk in on us."

Moonlight streamed through the dirty window, casting shadows. Frogs and crickets performed a raucous symphony that competed with the music floating through the woods from the reception. But it all paled in comparison to the sound of her pounding heart.

The wolf's chest rose with each breath, but other than that, he didn't move. His mask was still on. Menacing sharp fangs, frightening eyes...Maggie backed up slowly until she bumped into an old weathered worktable.

"Are you still down with this?" the wolf asked.

So, so down with it.

"I'm not afraid of the Big Bad Wolf," she whispered.

He closed the distance between them with one step. Her breath caught as he tilted her chin up with his fingers. Then that bit of gentleness disappeared, and he pulled her to him by grasping the back of her head. His fingers tangled in her hair as his mouth covered hers. She felt the mask slip up as his tongue slipped in. She opened her eyes, but all she could see were shadows playing off the angles of his face and the waves of his dark hair.

Her eyes drifted shut again as his hand moved to her neck and trailed down to her collarbone. Breaking the kiss, he followed his fingers with his lips. The mask slipped up on his forehead even higher as he cupped her breast.

She couldn't see his face, but that was okay. He was her Big Bad Wolf. She gave in and let herself be swept away by the fantasy. She'd never role-played before. Was this what they were doing? If so, it was fun, thrilling, and turning her knees into jelly.

With one move, the wolf had the laces of her cheap costume corset free and her blouse lifted. She wanted to cross her arms over her unsubstantial bra, but she resisted. The wolf pulled it up with a single finger, exposing both breasts to the kiss of the cool night air. Her nipples hardened in response.

"My breasts are small," she said, hating herself as soon as the words spilled out.

The Big Bad Wolf's mask had slipped back down. All she could see was the lower half of his face. He smiled wolfishly and licked his lips. "They're perfect. They match the rest of you."

He brushed both nipples with the tips of his fingers, and Maggie squeezed her thighs together. Her nipples were a Candy Land shortcut to other areas.

"And besides," the wolf added, "it's responsiveness that turns me on."

Her nipples were almost painfully hard. Definitely responsive. The wolf ran his tongue along the side of her neck. He palmed her breasts and squeezed. Not too hard, but hard enough to get her attention, and she inhaled sharply.

"Do you like that?" he whispered.

Yes. She wasn't sure if she said it out loud or merely thought it. Forming words wasn't a priority.

"I'm a hungry wolf," he said with a raspy voice. "These look good."

He covered a nipple with his hot mouth. The rest of her breast, exposed to the night air, had gooseflesh. But her nipple was on fire. The wolf sucked and tugged, moaning in the back of his throat like Maggie was the best thing he'd ever tasted. When he'd had enough of one, he went to the other.

The wolf was a wonderful mixture of rough and gentle. He gripped her breast firmly—almost painfully—and stopped sucking to brush her nipple with his tongue like a whisper. Fingers trailed up the inside of her thigh, past the top of her stocking, leaving a path of molten heat. When he bit a nipple, her knees buckled.

Her knees had never buckled before.

The wolf clasped her firmly around the waist with his other arm, steadying her.

"Can I see what Little Red Riding Hood has in her basket?" he asked, skimming the edge of her panties with his fingers.

"Yes," she whispered.

He pulled her panties aside, but he didn't touch her. He kissed her mouth softly and lifted her skirt, exposing her fully to the autumn air's sensual caress.

But he didn't look. And he still hadn't touched. She was desperate for it.

He leaned over and kissed her again, this time parting her lips with his tongue while he teased the sensitive skin of her inner thighs with his warm hand. Then he gently inserted a single finger.

She moaned, barely recognizing the sound of her own voice.

"Is that good?" he asked.

"Yes," she hissed. "So good."

He moved his finger slowly in and out, and she rocked against his hand. He picked up on her neediness, and his finger moved faster, with less gentleness.

And she loved it.

She moved against him, wanting his finger deeper. He obliged, and added a second.

He stopped kissing her. His face was inches away, mask intact, as he watched her intently, soaking up her reactions.

"I want to make you come," he whispered. "Just like this."

Orgasms were elusive things and usually required a vibrator. But Maggie didn't want to burst the wolf's bubble. And besides, something was building from a place deep inside that had never been touched like this. Not with this force, this rhythm... she moved against his hand and wasn't even embarrassed. Her need was too great. She wanted to explore this new sensation, this deeper, rougher arousal she'd never experienced before. "Harder," she whispered.

She braced herself on the table and let her head fall back. The table creaked from the force of his thrusting fingers. Her entire body shook. She tingled. She buzzed. And still, it wasn't enough. It left her starving and desperate and wanting more.

"Come on, baby," the wolf growled.

Pressure built. Instead of stilling and pulling her energy in, Maggie pushed, and her orgasm exploded in deep, rhythmic contractions that radiated from her very core. *This* was a different kind of orgasm. It rocked her entire body until she melted into the wolf, collapsing against his chest. She couldn't even open her eyes. Her lids were too heavy.

"You've ruined me," she mumbled.

The wolf jerked. "Did I hurt you?"

Maggie snorted into his chest. "No, you didn't break me with your big, strong man hands. But you just raised the orgasm bar to a ridiculous level. All the orgasms I have from here on out will be disappointments."

"Oh," the wolf said. He stroked her hair, and she sensed a smile in his voice as he said, "I think we can raise it higher if you're not too..."

"Too what?"

"You talked in tongues near the end. Are you coherent enough to move on to the next part of the story?"

"What part is that?"

The wolf put his lips to her ear and whispered, "The part where the Big Bad Wolf eats Little Red Riding Hood."

Everything below Maggie's waist woke back up. She wasn't about to ruin the moment by informing him that the Big Bad Wolf actually eats Little Red Riding Hood's grandmother. No need to be a buzzkill.

Chapter
Six
❧

Was it the fucking mask? Travis didn't know and didn't care. He'd driven a woman wild with just his fingers. He'd never done that before. Maybe Little Red Riding Hood was especially orgasmic, or maybe he was just a badass.

He wanted to do it again, but without fingers. He pushed her back against the worktable and adjusted his mask to make sure it was still firmly in place. She leaned back on her elbows, smiling contentedly. She might have had her fill, but he sure hadn't. Her shirt was still pushed up and her perfect breasts were on display. They were an offering he couldn't refuse. He leaned over and kissed each nipple, which made her gasp. Then he pinched them, which made her gasp harder. The sound set him on fire.

Little Red Riding Hood spread her legs. *Nice.*

He still held her nipples, pinching them both a little harder. She closed her eyes and dropped her head back in response. *She liked it.*

He tugged gently, pulling her away from the table by her nipples, which was a huge fucking turn-on, and even though she winced, Little Red Riding Hood raised her head and her glassy gaze told him she was totally on board.

"Turn around," he ordered.

It was very unlike him to order a woman to do anything, and he almost followed it up with a *please*. But they were role-playing. That much was clear. And he was the Big Bad Fucking Wolf, and the wolf didn't say please.

Little Red Riding Hood turned around.

"Bend over the table."

"I should have known this would be your position of choice."

Damn, she was cute. And incredibly sexy as she complied with his request, sticking her perfect little ass out in the process. She grinned at him over her shoulder as he flipped her skirt up. He wanted to give each exposed cheek a hard slap and see what replaced that grin. *Where had that come from? He'd never felt compelled to spank anyone before. Wolf was a dirty dog.*

He didn't dare spank her. He caressed each cheek instead, then squeezed. It opened her up and she gasped. Her panties were still pulled over to the side, and with a single finger he pulled them over farther. He wanted to see. "Spread your legs."

He'd lost some of his commanding tone. In fact, he could now barely find his voice at all. But she'd heard him and did as she was told. He dropped to his knees and gazed. Her stockings rose to mid-thigh and had sexy red bows on the backs. Might as well start there.

He licked from a bow to a sweet ass cheek. Damn, he wanted to *bite* her. He could just imagine her warm skin between his teeth. He couldn't do such a thing, though. It might hurt her or frighten her. Hell, it kind of frightened *him*. Little Red Riding Hood arched her back and spread her legs wider.

"Good girl," he said. He had never said *good girl* to a woman before.

He threw off the stupid mask because wet-nosing a woman wasn't sexy. He squeezed her ass again, still wanting to smack those perfect round cheeks. She moaned with that sexy voice of hers. He wished they were in an actual bed with an actual locked door. He'd make her moan all fucking night.

The sight before him made him weak. He gave her a long, slow lick. Her thighs quivered, and he did it again. And again. Then he sought out the hard little nub with his tongue to give it the special attention it deserved. She responded by pressing against his face, forcing him to behave like a hungry wolf.

When he couldn't take it anymore, and he sensed she couldn't either, he gave her one last lick and stood up.

She reached for him. He placed a hand firmly on her back and she stilled.

"Patience," he said, although he had none at the moment himself. He unbuckled his belt and pulled his zipper down.

"Condom?" she asked.

He knew he had a condom in his wallet. It taunted him every time he pulled out money to buy more shit for Henry.

"I've got it covered," he said.

His voice sounded solid, but he was a mess, fumbling with the condom wrapper as his pants fell and pooled around his ankles.

His rested his penis on her lower back, noting the contrast in size between what he had and where he wanted to put it. He was by no means a freak of nature, but larger than average would be an apt description. And Little Red Riding Hood was so tiny. But man, she seemed ready as hell. He had to step out of his pants to reposition his stance and get low enough to reach her.

Little Red Riding Hood squirmed with impatience. "Please," she said.

He edged in slowly with a groan. She opened up like a flower and pressed against him. Everything fit just fine. "I want to hear you," he said. "Make some noise for me."

She breathed raggedly, but that was all.

He increased the intensity with a forceful thrust, eliciting a gasp. It still wasn't the reaction he wanted, so he pulled almost all the way out and slammed it home. She cried out and it fed a fire inside him. "Do you want me to do it again?" he asked.

"Yes," she gasped.

"Tell me how you want me to do it, baby." Holy shit—who the actual fuck was he? He didn't recognize himself at all.

Little Red Riding Hood wiggled her ass, but she didn't say a word. It was very naughty to disobey him. "How do you want it?" he asked again.

Another silent wiggle.

Somebody needed to be taught a lesson. He pulled all the way out. "I asked you a question."

"Hard," she whispered. "I want it hard."

He obliged, and she responded with the most delightful moans he'd ever heard. Her voice alone could make him come, and he was close. Too damn close.

He wanted this to last forever. Right now, the back taxes and a million other worrisome details could go fuck themselves. He didn't have a care in the world. There was just the rhythm of their bodies, the sound of the workbench banging against the wall, and their ragged breathing.

She stilled, and then he felt her contracting around him, squeezing the last bit of his willpower. He let everything go. The emotional relief that poured through him was as intense as the sexual one. For about ten blinding seconds, he just *was*.

His normal senses returned slowly. He was bent over Little Red Riding Hood, panting, skin damp, pulse pounding. The music from the party floated in and out of his consciousness.

The woman beneath him was warm, still, and silent. She'd had an intense orgasm; he'd felt it. Maybe she was as wrung out as he was. "You okay?" he asked.

"Mm-hmmm," she mumbled.

He stood, peeling his shirt off her damp body. He'd never unbuttoned it, hadn't even taken his jacket off. He quickly discarded the condom in the trash and pulled up his pants. Little Red Riding Hood flipped her skirt down and started to straighten up.

"Wait," he said. He grabbed his mask and slipped it on silently. "Okay."

She turned and pulled her shirt down. He almost groaned at the loss. He could stare at her breasts forever. He tucked his shirt in while she went about putting herself back together. He watched, mesmerized by every move. Her short hair was mussed, her makeup was still smeared, and she looked like a woman who'd been thoroughly fucked and had enjoyed the hell out of it.

"That was..." Every word he came up with—*hot*, *good*, *amazing*—seemed woefully inadequate.

"Soul shattering?"

That was it. He nodded.

They stared at each other. Now what? Little Red Riding Hood seemed almost too good to be true. She was sexy. That much had been established. The little conversation they'd shared had shown her quick wit. She was flirtatious but completely unaware of the effect it had, which charmed the pants off him. *Literally.*

Maybe they should exchange names and numbers like normal people. Maybe after what they'd just done, she wouldn't care that he was a Blake.

What the fuck. He'd go for it. The worst thing that could happen was she'd say she didn't date Blake trash. He felt for his phone, quickly patting down all his pockets, including the ones in his jacket.

"Lose something?"

"Yeah. Have you seen my phone?"

"You had it at the bar. Did you leave it there?"

Shit. Had she had him in such a state that he'd left his phone on the bar? "What time is it?"

Little Red pulled her phone out of her purse. "It's about eleven."

"Crap." He'd promised Henry a bedtime phone call over an hour ago. "I need to get my phone."

He held the shed door open for Little Red Riding Hood. Cool air rushed in—they'd really made some heat in the small shed. A light fog had settled along the slope of the riverbank, and the full moon created a phosphorescent dreamscape. Travis reached for Maggie's hand, so she wouldn't lose her footing in the ridiculous boots. He would have enjoyed the romance of the moment if he weren't panicked about his phone.

The music got louder as they approached the party, which was still in full swing.

"Don't worry," Little Red Riding Hood said. "I'm sure Zeke picked it up."

"Who's Zeke?"

Maggie laughed. "You'd know Zeke if you were from around here. He's the bartender."

Travis swallowed the unease of his deception. But the farther away from the shed they got, the less certain he became about everything.

Maggie stopped in her tracks when they came to the parking lot. "You know what? I'm just going to cut out here. It's getting late."

She was right. It was getting late, and he needed to get home. But was it rude to end the night so abruptly? "Are you sure?"

Maggie glanced in the direction of the courtyard that led to the ballroom. Maybe she was worried their reentrance would come off as a walk of shame. "Yeah, I'm sure."

They stood awkwardly in the grass. This was the time to ask for her number. To tell her who he was.

She suddenly stuck out her hand. "Safe travels."

Stupidly, he accepted, and they shook. Before he could find the words to steer events away from the awful direction they were headed, Little Red Riding Hood spun on her heels, nearly fell, and then took off at a rapid pace for the parking lot.

Fuck it. This was for the best anyway. He'd had some fun, so had she, and now everybody needed to resume their usual personas. Little Red Riding Hood glanced over her shoulder at him but didn't stop walking. He gave a feeble wave, before heading for the bar.

Zeke held up his phone as soon as he saw him. "Claire handed it in," he said.

Relief washed over him at the familiar weight of his phone in his hand. But it was short-lived. He had six text messages, all from Mrs. Garza. They started with Henry woke up with a stomach ache and ended with On our way to urgent care clinic.

Chapter

Seven

❦

Henry was nestled in the crook of Travis's arm, breathing deeply and radiating heat. He didn't have a fever. He was just a little furnace while he slept. Travis had been the same way as a kid.

The room didn't look much different than when Travis had slept in it. It still had a stain on the ceiling that looked like a vagina if you squinted. Travis hadn't been much older than Henry when Scott had decided to dispense a bit of brotherly wisdom and point it out. "That looks like a pussy," he'd said.

No matter how hard Travis had tried, he'd been unable to convince himself that the stain resembled a cat. He'd said as much, and Scott had laughed at him. Then he'd pulled a ratty magazine from beneath the mattress and showed Travis a series of pictures that had further complicated matters.

Staring at the stain made him think of Little Red Riding Hood. Not a cool association, but he couldn't help himself.

An image of that part of the female anatomy, even if you had to squint to see it, was just too tempting an invitation to begin ruminating on last night's activities. That soft skin, those perky breasts with their perfect pink nipples...

Henry shifted, flooding Travis with guilt and embarrassment. He placed his hand on Henry's chest to settle him back down—he could use a few more minutes of peace before the little scoundrel woke up—and wondered if he'd ever been that innocent. If he'd even had a chance to be. His mom had run off when he was little. And his dad, instead of shielding his sons from things most people would consider solidly within the *adults only* realm, had practically reveled in exposing them to his vices. Travis had little to no doubt that Scott, if he was man enough to raise his own kid, would do the same to Henry.

He pulled Henry in a little closer, swallowing the unease that plagued him almost constantly now. *What was he going to do about Henry?*

Scott was not father material. But neither was Travis. Henry deserved better than either of them. And didn't Travis deserve better, too? He hadn't asked for this. Was it his fault his brother was a loser and the kid's mom had died? He was fresh out of the Army with his whole life ahead of him. His buddy had a pipe outfitting business and was holding a job for him in Austin. It wasn't as glamorous as being a rancher, but it was a hell of a lot more realistic. He was stuck in limbo until he could sell the ranch and get Henry settled.

He needed to call the social worker again. Surely there was a long-lost aunt or cousin somewhere who would be a good fit for Henry. Foster care had been mentioned, but Travis hoped it wouldn't come to that. Scott would get out of prison eventually and then... Well, hell. Travis didn't exactly want it coming to that either.

Henry stirred and opened his eyes.

"How are you feeling?" Travis asked. "Still up for our trip?"

Travis had chiseled out a chunk of time he didn't have to take the kid camping. Henry had never been, and that was a fucking sin.

Henry's foggy, sleep-encrusted eyes turned bright and clear. "That's today?"

"If you feel good enough."

Henry tossed off the sheet and launched himself like a rocket, jumping on the small bed and narrowly missing Travis's crotch. It was hard to believe he'd been in an urgent care clinic just a few hours ago. Who knew severe constipation could mimic appendicitis? And who knew little kids got constipated?

The doctors at the clinic had been all over him. *When's the last time he had a bowel movement?* Travis had no idea. *How much fiber does he get per day?* Again, no idea as to how much fiber the kid even needed per day, much less how much he got from a cherry Pop-Tart. *How much water does he usually drink?* Does juice count? Or milk?

Henry needed more fruits and vegetables. Less junk food.

Henry stopped bouncing as Travis stood up. "I want some Cocoa Balls with chocolate milk."

Travis had already thrown the box in the trash. "How about oatmeal? I'll put some raisins in it."

Henry looked at him as if he'd just suggested tarantulas with piss sauce.

"All the bad food I've been feeding you is what made your tummy ache. We've got to eat better."

Henry scrunched up his face, and then opened his mouth to protest.

"The longer you whine, the longer it'll take us to hit the road."

Henry switched gears. "Will we see bears?"

"Nah," he said. "The only bear you're going to see is me after a week of not shaving." By most men's standards, Travis's five o'clock shadow was more of a starter beard. A week would leave him pretty wooly.

"You won't turn into a bear, Uncle Travis. That's just silly."

Travis winked at Henry. "You're right," he said. "I'm more of a wolf."

* * *

Maggie pulled into the parking lot of Petal Pushers. It had been hard getting out of bed this morning. She stretched, noting the familiar soreness in her shoulders. It came with the business. She'd had trouble getting the weed whacker started at the courthouse and had dang near put her shoulder out.

She opened the door of her Jeep and leaned back in her seat expectantly. Pop flew over her lap and onto the asphalt like he'd been ejected from a cockpit. Then he ran straight for the fence that enclosed the outdoor garden area, barking and shaking his stub of a tail. He looked over his shoulder at Maggie, snorting impatience through his little smashed-in bulldog nose.

"I know you've got trees to water. Settle down."

Stepping down from the Jeep brought a second ache into focus, somewhat unfamiliar but not at all unpleasant. And it wasn't located anywhere near her shoulders. She slammed the door, catching a glimpse of her face in the side mirror. There was that stupid grin again. She'd been walking around like a brainless idiot all morning.

"Snap out of it, Mackey," she said aloud.

But no matter how hard she tried to tone it down, she was bouncing around like one of those people with a spring in their step. Surely it would wear off by the end of the day. It wasn't like she had a freaking boyfriend. She'd had sex with a stranger. And they had made no plans for future interludes. But he'd found her sexy. And irresistible. And it was just so dang utterly delightful that now she was stuck with this irritating bounce when she walked.

"Snap out of it, Mackey," she said again. Because she didn't need any man to boost her step *or* her ego.

He couldn't keep his hands off me.

She resigned herself to the bounce. But she was limiting it to twenty-four hours.

She unlocked the gate and Pop shot through to begin his daily watering. He would only squirt a little on the first two or three trees. After that he'd shoot blanks until he exhausted himself.

She followed him in, scanning the rows of plants and shrubs, breathing in their magic elixir. She tiptoed among the balled and burlapped trees heeled-in at the back of the nursery, as if not to wake them, and stepped gingerly over the trickle irrigation lines, working her way to the small building that used to be a farm implement business owned by her grandfather. Upon his death, Honey had made it a nursery. Maggie had moved home to be a partner, and Petal Pushers had flourished under the management of the grandmother-granddaughter duo. Honey had kept up her end, which included floral arrangements for all the funerals and weddings in Big Verde, while Maggie developed a successful landscaping venture.

Claire had recently stepped into Honey's shoes as florist, and they seemed to fit pretty well. But nobody would ever fill the hole Honey had left in Maggie's heart. Or her life.

She strolled among the blooming plants, removing a leaf here and there, deciding what needed to be moved into the direct sunlight of the nursery's entrance and what needed to be loaded onto the truck for the River Mill subdivision.

The Texas Hill Country was a beautiful region, and although Big Verde might not attract a lot of industry, it did attract tourists and wealthy folks looking for pretty country homes. River Mill was a great addition to her portfolio, and she was ninety-nine percent certain she'd be adding Anna's project, as well. There was no way Anna would hire Travis Blake for something that important.

He was a nobody.

She let herself in through the nursery's back door and started flipping on lights. She checked on the shelves of gardening tools, gloves, and bulbs, noting which ones looked bare and needed restocking. She turned on the ceiling fans to make the wind chimes jingle pleasantly, and then went to the counter to boot up the cash register—a fancy new one she barely knew how to operate. Honey's gloves and shears sat by the business cards like a memorial.

While the cash register came online, Maggie pulled out her phone to check e-mail.

She had a text. According to the time stamp, it had been sent last night from an unknown number.

Who's afraid of the Big Bad Wolf?

Her heart leapt straight to her throat. The wolf had texted! But then a sense of unease crept in. She scowled. How did the wolf get her number? Did he *know* her? If so, why hadn't he said anything?

Her stomach lurched. She'd assumed he was a stranger. What if she'd been wrong?

The best night of her life had suddenly turned creepy.

Someone tapped at the front door and Maggie jumped. She had the jitters. With her heart pounding, she slowly approached the glass door while hugging the fertilizer aisle so whoever it was wouldn't see her. She sighed in relief. It was just Norbert. He was here to start loading the trailer for River Mill.

Maggie unlocked the door with trembling fingers.

"Sorry," Norbert said, breezing in. "Forgot my key to the back."

"No problem." She hoped she didn't look as freaked out as she felt. "I haven't made coffee yet."

Norbert hung up his cowboy hat and put on his Petal Pushers cap. He looked at Maggie with a glint in his eye. "I would have thought coffee would be your top priority this morning."

The blood in Maggie's veins turned to ice. She hadn't seen Norbert at the party last night, but maybe that's because he'd been *wearing a freaking wolf mask!* Even though her veins were now officially frozen, her face was on fire.

Surely, she hadn't banged Norbert in a shed.

Norbert whistled and headed for the coffeepot in the break room. Maggie followed, watching him as he rinsed out the carafe and dumped yesterday's grinds. She had to remind herself to breathe as she sized him up to be about the same height as the wolf.

"I'm going to add an extra scoop," he said. "That was some gala last night, wasn't it?"

He'd been there. Maggie swallowed and clenched her hands into fists.

Norbert turned around. "Maggie? Are you okay?"

She took in his build. He was fit, but stockier than the wolf. And his hair was darker and longer. His hands... definitely not the wolf's. She closed her eyes and imagined the wolf's hands. *The things they'd done to her...*

"Whoa," Norbert said, putting down the coffee scoop and heading her way. "I think you need to sit down."

"No, I'm fine." She waved him off. Norbert's text wouldn't have shown up as an unidentified number. She was being freakishly paranoid. "You're right. I probably had a little too much to drink last night."

Norbert looked doubtful, but he turned back around and flipped the switch on the coffeepot. It sparked and sizzled. Norbert said something in Spanish and jumped away from the counter. The smell of ozone filled the small room.

"No coffee this morning," Norbert said, unplugging the coffeemaker.

Maggie didn't care about coffee this morning, which was saying a lot, and her mind went straight back to wondering who the Big Bad Wolf was. She turned and felt paper stuck to the bottom of her boot. Something yellow poked out—a sticky note. She peeled it off, noting Claire's handwriting. COFFEEPOT IS TOAST. LET'S GET A KEURIG!

She crumpled the note and tossed it in the trash. She'd only recently convinced Claire to start washing and reusing a real mug, and now she wanted to blow through plastic K-Cups.

Whatever. Back to the endless loop of anxiety and panic.

"Who was that wolf you were dancing with?" Norbert asked, like a mind reader.

"Um, just a guy," she said. "He was from out of town."

Unless he was the mailman. Or the guy who kept the books for Petal Pushers. Or the man who drove the UPS truck…She felt faint again.

Once Norbert was adequately occupied and Maggie's heart rate had dropped back into the normal zone, she went into the small office and closed the door. She stared at the message again.

Who's afraid of the Big Bad Wolf?

Her thumb hovered over her phone. Maybe she should just ask the idiot who he was. Then again, maybe she didn't want to know.

After twenty minutes of fretting, she decided to ignore it for now. And by ignore it, she meant think about it constantly while pretending not to.

She still hadn't checked her e-mail. Maybe that would provide a decent distraction. She opened her in-box. First up was a Groupon for a spelunking tour. In an earnest effort to continue ignoring the text from the Big Bad Wolf, she bought two. Next were erectile dysfunction drugs from Canada, political appeals, and an Indonesian prince who wanted to give her lots of money. *Delete. Delete. Delete.* But then she hit pay dirt. An e-mail from Annabelle!

Dear Maggie and Travis,

Wait…what? Why was Travis Blake included in the greeting? Why were their names side by side? Why were they being addressed as a single entity?

I am happy to award the landscaping and architecture bid to Maggie (gorgeous design). The labor bid is going to Travis (great price). I'm sure the two of you will work well together.

Congratulations!

Annabelle Vasquez

Maggie set her phone on the desk like it was radioactive. That dirty rotten scoundrel had weaseled his way in on her job! Maybe if she'd spent less time banging the wolf and more time talking to Anna at the party, this wouldn't have happened.

Whatever Travis Blake's price was, she'd go lower. She supplied her own labor: herself and a small crew. She was not going to share this job.

This had turned into a shitty day. In less than an hour, her mysterious sexy stranger had turned into a stalker, and her unqualified competitor had become her brand-new work buddy.

She might not be able to do anything about Travis at the moment, but she could confront the Big Bad Wolf. Was he trying to scare her? Well, it wasn't working. Much.

She pulled out her phone.

Who's afraid of the Big Bad Wolf?

Ha. Screw him.

Not me.

She sent it and strummed her fingers on the desk. Would he answer?

Five minutes went by with no response while she cleaned out her in-box. She picked up her phone.

And if you text me again I'm calling the cops.

There. That would put an end to it.

Pop started whining at her feet. She mindlessly leaned over and rubbed him between the ears while contemplating all the ways she could make Travis Blake miserable enough to walk off the job and go back to doing lawns with his little push mower.

Pop barked as someone began pounding on the front door. Maggie stormed out of the office. What type of gardening emergency couldn't wait fifteen minutes for the store to open? She was full of bluster and ready to shout, "We're closed!" But then she remembered she had a stalker.

Pop had beaten her to the door, and she listened for his ominous, protective growl. Instead, she heard his whiny *rub my tummy* growl. And from the frantic toenail ticking, she deduced he was doing his happy feet circle dance, too. Just when she'd thought the day couldn't possibly get any worse, she rounded the fertilizer aisle and saw the white Stetson.

She crossed her arms over her chest. JD had stopped pounding and now tapped politely on the glass.

"We're closed!"

Pop wasn't buying it. He kept whining. JD kept tapping.

"Fine," Maggie muttered, unlocking the door and yanking it open. JD walked in quietly. His hat sat firmly above his ears. He adjusted it once, twice, and then once more.

Oh, for heaven's sake. JD didn't realize it, but that stupid hat was an interpretive device. JD having a good day meant it was high on his forehead. JD having a bad day meant it rode low. JD hiding from everyone because of some shit he'd pulled meant it was yanked *way* down low, and JD setting the damn thing squarely on the ears meant he was shooting for a confidence he didn't deserve.

Maggie wasn't going to make it easy on him, so she said nothing. They didn't have a thing in the world to talk about. Pop clearly hadn't gotten the memo and ran figure eights between JD's ankles, yapping to be picked up.

JD removed his hat. *Dear God, he was going to do the Grand Gesture.*

"Maggie—"

"Save it, JD."

"Too soon?"

"Massive understatement. I'll reevaluate when Hell freezes over."

"I think it's best to do it now."

"I'd prefer to let it fester. And believe it or not, I have bigger things—"

"We need to talk about your feelings for me," he said, taking a step toward her.

"How about we talk about your feelings for *me?* Shorter conversation."

JD cleared his throat. "Maggie, you mean the world to me, and there's something I need to tell you."

He'd practiced! She could hear it in his voice. He had a speech ready. Well, she wasn't going to let him deliver it. "I was drunk. That's pretty much it." She put her hand on his chest and tried backing him to the door. "Bye now."

"I've seen you drunk. You were maybe a little buzzed."

"Okay, fine. I was on my period."

"I've seen that, too. You weren't telling me to fuck off—"

"Fuck off."

"And your skin is perfectly clear. You don't have those puffy things you get beneath your eyes from fluid retention."

She got puffy things beneath her eyes from fluid retention? "File it under temporary insanity. I've been under a lot of stress lately. Or"—she snapped her fingers—"I was horny. How about that? Even girls like me get horny."

"Girls like you... What does that mean?"

"You know what it means."

"No, I don't."

Maggie turned and started for the counter. "Do, too," she said over her shoulder. It was habit to argue childishly with JD. They'd been doing it for fifteen years.

"Do not," said JD. "So do you want to go to Tony's tonight and catch a game?"

Maggie stopped in her tracks, overwhelmed by the repetitious, deadening familiarity of it all. She didn't want to fall back into the same old rut of being one of the guys. And she didn't appreciate her feelings being swept under the rug by JD, even if she had refused to talk about them.

She turned. "I need some space. I don't think we should hang out anymore."

JD's jaw dropped. Hurt shone in his hazel eyes— genuine hurt. But Maggie couldn't handle going back to the way things were. Not yet anyway.

"Fine. If you don't want to be friends anymore, then we just won't be friends." JD resettled his hat, giving it an extra yank. "It was going to happen anyway."

What was that supposed to mean? Before she could ask, JD yanked the door open, violently jingling the little bell on top. He looked over his shoulder. "Stay away from that goddamn wolf."

Chapter

Eight

❦

Claire breezed in with a cardboard tray of steaming coffee cups. "JD just blew past me in the parking lot. What was that about?"

"Nothing," Maggie said.

Claire walked to the counter, her heels tapping out a Morse code of sexiness across the concrete floor. She perched on her usual stool and set the coffee on the counter.

"Is he jealous of you and the wolf?"

"Hardly."

"Are we in a one-word-only mood today?" Claire asked. "Because I need more from you. Like who is he? How was it? Are you seeing him again?"

"Dunno. Great. No." *At least she hoped she wouldn't.*

Maggie just couldn't believe the wolf was someone she knew. Nor could she believe the way he'd made her feel. Even as she sat there in her Red Wing work boots and grubby clothes, the thought of his touch weakened her knees. She'd been so feminine and sexy in his hands. He'd teased out a side of her she hadn't even known existed.

"Why don't you want to see him again?"

She wanted to tell Claire about the text, but she was afraid Claire would immediately begin accosting every man in Big Verde. *Did you bang Maggie in a shed?*

"I told you not to wear those high heels to work." The only time Claire wasn't wearing heels was when she was rock climbing. Although now that Maggie thought about it... "Hey, you don't wear those when you climb rocks, do you?"

"Oh my God. Are you seriously not going to give me details? And of course I don't wear them when I climb. I wear them to work because they're the only shoes that keep my leather pants from dragging in the muck."

"I told you not to wear those either."

"Stop telling me what to do, or I'll take back your skinny pumpkin spice latte with an extra dash of cinnamon and no whip."

Maggie picked up the cup and looked at it. "Is that really what's in here?"

Claire laughed. "Of course not. Where would I get something like that in Big Verde? It's a bitter cup of black goo from the Pump 'n' Go."

Maggie took a sip and grimaced. "It's dangerous to walk around here in those heels."

"I promise not to sue you if I fall. Now start squawking."

What could she say? She'd never had sex like that before. And it wasn't just that she'd never had sex with a masked man while bent over a workbench in a toolshed. It was that she'd never done *anything* remotely kinky before. The Big Bad Wolf had seemed to know every secret desire she'd ever had and just how to meet it. She'd been putty in his hands. A pliable, quivering mess of need that only he could fulfill.

She shivered at the memory of the low rumble of his voice when he'd said, "Good girl." She'd have done almost anything at that moment to please him. She'd trusted him completely. And look where it had gotten her. The freedom of letting go might have been exhilarating, but it had also been stupid. Her stomach churned as she considered the consequences. What if he tried to blackmail her or something equally sinister?

Maggie pushed her coffee away and then quickly hid her hand beneath the counter, so Claire wouldn't see it shaking.

But Claire had seen it. "Oh, honey, what's wrong?" The concern in her eyes was intense. In fact, Claire appeared almost panicked. "Did he hurt you?"

Maggie twisted her hands. "I'm just a little shaken up. I'll give you the details, but you have to promise not to tell anyone until I decide what to do."

Claire set her cup down. "What do you mean, until you decide what to do?" She grabbed Maggie by the shoulders and shook her. "What happened?"

"I was stupid. That's what happened."

Claire pulled Maggie in for a bone-crushing hug. "It wasn't your fault. Whatever happened; it wasn't your fault. Shit, Maggie what have I done?"

What had *she* done? Maggie pushed Claire off because she really wasn't much of a hugger, and because she suspected Claire was off her rocker. "You didn't do anything but request a song for us to dance to, and we'd already danced anyway. None of this is your fault. It was my decision to follow him to the shed—"

"That dirty bastard assaulted you in a shed?"

Before she could answer, Maggie was again enveloped in an awkward and brutal hug.

"He didn't—"

"And I've given him your number," Claire whimpered. "Now he's going to stalk you."

"You *what?*"

Claire released her. "Don't be mad. It's just that I could tell things hadn't gone well with JD—I'd seen him sulking—and when I saw the wolf, I just thought maybe he could make you feel better..."

Boy, had he ever.

"And so, you gave him my number?" What a relief! The wolf wasn't a creepy stalker out to blackmail her. Claire had given him her number. And he'd texted her!

"Not exactly," Claire said. "He left his phone on the bar while y'all danced, which is careless if you ask me, and—"

Everything clicked into place. "You sent the text."

"Yes. In case you were too shy or too stupid to exchange numbers, you know?"

Maggie's mind raced to keep up. She pulled up the text to confirm. Who's afraid of the Big Bad Wolf? She pushed the phone toward Claire. "This was you?"

"Yes." Claire had the good sense to avoid eye contact.

What a freaking roller coaster. First, Maggie had thought she'd accidentally banged Norbert in the shed. Or possibly the UPS guy. And that he might be planning to blackmail her. Then she'd learned it hadn't been Norbert or the UPS guy, just her glorious and mysterious Big Bad Wolf, and that he'd texted her, probably because he wanted to see her again. *Elation!* But then it turned out to just be Claire. *Disappointment.*

"Oh, well," she mumbled. "At least we had one great night."

"You had a great night? You mean he didn't, you know..."

"Goodness, no! He didn't do anything I didn't want him

to do." Her face felt like it was on fire and she lowered her eyes. She'd wanted him to do all kinds of things. "We had sex."

"In a shed? Are you kidding me?" Claire bounced on her seat and clapped her hands. "That sounds incredibly kinky and possibly uncomfortable. Tell me everything."

"I just did."

"I doubt that. Are you going to text him back? He might not even know he's texted you since he didn't really."

"I already did."

Claire clapped her hands. "What did you say?"

"I threatened him with calling the cops." She took a sip of her coffee before adding, "And that would be your fault, not mine."

"Apologize. And then send something clever or witty."

All Maggie could drum up in her head was white noise. "I got nothin'."

"Sext him," Claire said, eyes shining with mischief.

"I couldn't!" Maggie said. "And besides, I'm not so sure about this. We know absolutely nothing about this guy. What if he's married?"

"He's not," Claire said.

"How do you know?"

Claire took a gulp of coffee, hiding behind the cup.

"You looked through his text messages, didn't you?" Maggie asked.

"I have morals, Maggie."

Maggie mentally counted to five before Claire coughed it up.

"He was texting with the babysitter."

Maggie swallowed loudly. "He has a kid? How do you know he doesn't also have a wife?"

"Because *he* was the one texting the babysitter. And there

was no wife at the gala. The situation just doesn't have a married vibe."

He *had* been at the party by himself. Dressed in a costume. It certainly didn't sound like he was married. But who was he? And should she try and see him again? She shivered as the memory of his hands on her bottom rudely crashed into her thoughts.

She took out her phone and started texting.

Chapter
Nine
ॐ

Travis stared at his phone while he pumped gas. He hadn't had any service in the state park, so he'd expected his phone to go berserk as soon as they got through the winding hills surrounding Big Verde. But he hadn't expected a series of nonsensical and mysterious texts from a person he assumed to be Little Red Riding Hood to come pinging in just as he pulled into the Pump 'n' Go.

It was odd because he'd never given the woman his phone number, and what was even more puzzling was that he'd supposedly texted her first.

Who's afraid of the Big Bad Wolf?

He had not sent that text. Something was fishy. And Little Red Riding Hood had responded.

Not me.

Followed by a threat.

And if you text me again I'm calling the cops.

Followed by several humdingers that made absolutely zero sense.

Never mind. I'm not calling the cops LOL.

Why would I do that?

Claire sent the first text and I didn't know it.

What did that even mean? How had Claire sent the first text?

Are you mad?

Do you want me to stop texting?

Those had all been sent within five minutes. Then there was a three-day pause, which he hated, because that meant she'd thought he was ignoring her.

Hey, it's me, Little Red Riding Hood. I understand if you don't want to text.

She'd waited almost fifteen minutes before sending the next set.

But if you want to text I'm fine with it.

Unless you're married. I don't want you texting me if you're married.

Not that you are.

Texting me.

Or married.

His pulse sped up. He'd like to see her again. She hadn't been far from his mind during the entire camping trip. Heck, he hadn't been able to be fully present with Henry, although God knows he'd tried. He'd been haunted by Maggie. More like obsessed. Unable to keep the hooded pixie out of his head for more than five minutes at a time. But he hadn't known how to get in touch with her, and now that he did, he wasn't sure he wanted to.

First off, she seemed a tad anxious. Second, she thought he was a mysterious stranger in a nice suit from out of town. The reality of who he was couldn't be farther from the truth.

But all he had to do was close his eyes and he could see her. Feel her. Taste her. *Oh shit. Don't go there again.*

He went there.

As the display on the pump continued its upward climb to twenty gallons, his mind replayed the well-worn reel of their night in the shed. The softness of her hips, the sound of their skin slapping together. He could practically hear her moaning and begging—he'd made her beg—as he'd fucked her senseless.

"Uncle Travis?"

He landed back on Earth with a deadening thud. The pump had stopped. The guy in line behind him scowled, waiting for him to finish up.

Travis hastily put his phone in his pocket, removed the gas nozzle, and closed the cap on his tank.

"Why were you standing there with your mouth hanging open?" Henry asked. "Were you daydreamin' or something?"

Travis climbed in the truck. "Or something. Put your seat belt back on."

Henry had learned how to unbuckle the harness on his car seat, a development that was making Travis's life a living hell. Travis thought the five-point contraption was overkill for a five-year-old and didn't blame Henry for not wanting to ride in the damn thing, but Lisa had left very specific orders. Henry was to ride in the car seat until he achieved the recommended weight and height for getting out of it.

"It's for babies!"

In retrospect, a week in the wilderness had probably been about four days too long. Henry was worn out and melting down.

Travis started the truck and slowly pulled away from the pump even though Henry wasn't buckled in yet. The little guy was just getting wound up—Travis could hear it in his voice—so it was best to find a safe spot to park and ride it out.

He pulled into a space in front of the store just as Henry delivered a punch to his kidneys through the seat.

Travis swallowed the urge to yell as he turned the engine off. "Stop it, Henry," he said, knowing it wasn't going to stop.

Henry screamed like a banshee and gave Travis's left kidney another good kick. Then he flung himself to the floor and curled up into a ball. This was extremely bad timing. Little Red Riding Hood hadn't been the only female frantically texting him while they'd been camping. Annabelle had also repeatedly texted, asking if he'd received her e-mail about the bid—he hadn't—and letting him know about a meeting at her new house thirty goddamn minutes from now.

Travis reached back and tapped Henry on the shoulder, which caused him to explode in a mass of arms, legs, and shrieks. It would be impossible to get the stinker back into his seat like this. It would be easier to get an octopus into a straitjacket, so Travis turned back around and pulled his cap down to wait it out.

Kick.

Henry had climbed back in his seat to kick the shit out of him again.

Kick.

It was bad timing because Henry wasn't the only one who was cranky and worn out.

Kick.

"Henry, stop it right now, or I'll never take you camping again. In fact, I'll never take you anywhere again. Got it?"

Kick.

It was hard to tell over all the sniffling and muttering, but he could swear Henry had just called him a rat bastard.

Travis rolled out of the truck with a grimace and limped

to Henry's door. He yanked it open just as a small foot shot out, pegging him in the nuts. Blinding white pain bent Travis over for about twenty seconds. On the twenty-first second, he grabbed Henry by one ankle and pulled him out of the truck. He quickly took hold of the other ankle, and before Henry knew what had him, he was dangling upside down.

"Now listen," Travis wheezed. "You don't have a choice about whether to ride in your car seat. No choice."

"I hate you!"

"I'm not real fond of you right now either. And you're going to hang here until you're calm enough to get back in the truck and act like a human."

Henry made a vicious grab at Travis's leg, but Travis dodged him. "You missed me," he chided, feeling about the same age as Henry.

"Butthead!" Henry shouted.

Travis swung wide so that Henry went back and forth like a pendulum. "Yeah? Well, you're a wiener head."

They'd long passed the point where one of them needed to be an adult, and besides, sometimes the word *wiener* made Henry laugh. But not today.

Henry spit at him and wiggled like an earthworm. Travis tightened his grip, so he wouldn't drop Henry on his head. Just when he thought he might have to sit on the kid to get him buckled in, Henry wound down and quit wiggling. Which was good, because a car had pulled up next to them— an older couple in a big silver Cadillac. The woman in the passenger seat, no more than three feet away, gawked openly. Travis smiled all friendly-like, hoping that would be the end of it.

"Help! Help!" Henry shouted.

Great. The passenger window of the Cadillac rolled slowly down.

"Can we be of any assistance?" the lady asked.

"No thank you, ma'am," Travis said. "We're just having a seat belt debate."

"Are you his father?"

"Stranger danger!" shouted Henry.

Travis pulled Henry up even higher, so he could see his beet red face. "Are you nuts?" He hoisted the kid to his shoulder to get him right side up again, and Henry proceeded to pout like a pro, but that was it. Maybe the battle was over. "I'm not his father. I'm his uncle," Travis said to the woman. He held out a hand and introduced himself. "Travis Blake."

"My dad is in prison," Henry added helpfully. Travis's face heated up with embarrassment, just as it had been doing his entire life.

The woman looked at his hand like it was a rattlesnake, but her husband reached across and shook it. "I'm Judge Samuel Monroe, retired. I knew your brother."

"No doubt," Travis said.

"And your daddy," he added, just in case Travis needed to be reminded of all the times he'd driven the truck—with no license—to haul his dad out of the drunk tank. After he died, they'd retired his barstool at Tony's with a brass nameplate.

The good judge's wife recoiled in her seat. Travis couldn't blame her. After a week in the wilderness with no shower and no shave, he probably looked like an escaped convict. He was on his way to being Grizzly Adams, or worse, a hipster from Austin. He couldn't wait for a shave and a haircut.

"Henry is just about to get in his car seat, aren't you, Henry?"

Henry was redder than boiled beets, a combination of rage and all the blood rushing to his head while he'd hung upside down. He stuck his tongue out at Travis.

"Y'all have a good afternoon," Travis said. He plunked Henry into the seat, buckled him in, and started the truck. With a final wave at the busybodies, he backed up. Henry's red, tear-streaked face was visible in the rearview mirror.

"Listen, Henry, I'm real sorry about the way I handled that."

"That man was a judge. Is he gonna take me away from you?"

Where had that come from? "Of course not. Why?"

"Before she went to heaven, Mom told me I'd better be good for you or a judge might put me in frosted care."

"You mean foster care?"

Henry sniffled. "That's what I said."

Something had changed on the camping trip. Keeping Henry alive had been exhausting, and Travis had started to worry a bit about letting just anyone do it. But that wasn't what had caused the shift. It was the other stuff. The story-telling. The endless question-answering. The warm sleeping bag hugs that kept away the things that went bump in the night. But mostly, it had been the moment he'd reentered the tent after a middle-of-the-night whiz to find Henry sitting up, eyes wide and lips trembling. He'd said, "I missed you, Uncle Travis."

But what he'd meant was, *I thought you'd left me.*

"Over my dead body," Travis said. "You're not going to foster care."

But where would he go? It wasn't like Henry could stay with *him.* Hopefully the social worker would turn up someone soon. Or maybe Scott would get out of prison, straighten out his life, and take being a dad seriously.

And maybe pigs would fly.

* * *

Maggie sat in her Jeep seething with rage. She'd just witnessed some jerk holding a poor child upside down at the Pump 'n' Go. She'd been about ready to jump out and do something when an older couple had pulled up and handled it.

She should have been more proactive—maybe gotten his license plate number—but she'd been struck dumb by the ridiculous scene. If she ever ran into that idiot, she'd give him a piece of her mind. But she hadn't recognized him, which meant he was probably just passing through Big Verde.

Still shaking, she pulled out of the Pump 'n' Go and headed north on Main Street. It was Friday, so every storefront bore bright green messages in shoe polish cheering on the Big Verde Giants in tonight's game against the Sweet Home Beavers.

FEE FI FO FUM!

KEEP THOSE BEAVERS ON THE RUN!

There were other cheers about the Sweet Home Beavers—it was just too easy—but most weren't appropriate for storefront windows. The Big Verde pep squad usually managed to sneak in an oldie but goodie, though, and she smiled to see Mr. Chavez seated in front of a checkerboard in the Rite Aid drugstore window with LICK THE BEAVERS! scrawled above his head. Every single person in Big Verde got the reference, but since they'd all been feigning innocence since their own pep rally days, nobody could admit it.

As Maggie passed her alma mater, Big Verde High, the Jeep vibrated with the powerful cadence of the school fight song. The pep rally was in full swing. When the song ended, the entire stadium would yell *Ho ho ho, Big Verde!* It was a take on the Jolly Green Giant jingle and was totally lost on the current generation, but they used it anyway because tradition was important.

Maggie drove on by. It wasn't that she minded reliving what were certainly not her glory days; she just had a meeting at Annabelle's. And she was determined to talk Anna out of splitting the contract between Petal Pushers and Travis Blake.

Her phone buzzed on the seat next to her. She was the only car on Main Street, so she risked a glance with her heart in her throat and her spine on fire, because the wolf hadn't texted back yet, and it had been a full week.

Ugh. It was her mother. And it was long. She'd read it later.

She imagined the wolf receiving her texts. He hadn't seemed like a jerk, so why hadn't he at least responded with a No, thank you? How could he just leave her hanging like this?

Maybe he'd figured out who she was. He wasn't from Big Verde, but he knew Annabelle, didn't he? What if Annabelle had teased him about dancing with her? She could just hear it... *Saw you dancing with poor little Maggie Mackey. Bless her heart, Big Verde High didn't know whether to name her FFA Queen or FFA King. So sweet of you to give her some attention.*

The road turned curvy as soon as she passed the Big Verde city limit, and her cares automatically lightened. Nature did that for her. It was one of the reasons she spent so much time working outdoors even though she had a landscape architect degree and could basically have a desk job.

She rolled her window down. Perfect autumn day for the Hill Country. Clear blue skies and eighty-five degrees for a high. Her ears popped as she gained a little altitude, and the landscape changed slowly from scrub brush and cactus to juniper and cedar. The highest hill was her destination, and she could see the road switchbacking up its side in the distance.

When she drove over the cattle guard, a cloud of dust met her, stirred up by the truck ahead. It went left at the fork, and so did she, continuing to eat its dust all the way up to the top of the hill, where the house was still under construction.

Three trucks were already parked beneath a giant live oak, and the one she'd been following pulled up under a big cottonwood, leaving absolutely no space for her in the shade. Leave it to a bunch of men to try and squeeze her out. She parked next to a pile of gorgeous white rock she assumed would go on the outside of the house and jumped down from the Jeep with Pop on her heels.

Two of the trucks bore L&M Construction emblems. One belonged to JD, the other to Bubba. They were partners. She spotted JD's white Stetson right away.

With her plans in hand, she strode with confidence toward the group of men. JD wore a starched white shirt and a pair of Wranglers with perfect creases pressed into each long leg—his Sunday attire. Trying to impress Annabelle? It seemed to be working. Anna had plastered herself to his arm.

Bubba smiled and waved. "Hey there, Mighty Mack."

JD tilted his hat and nodded, then pulled it all the way down to "hiding" mode. Annabelle projected her usual beauty queen smile, looking at Maggie as if she were a stray puppy she'd love to take in if only it didn't have fleas. Her right boob was displaced by JD's biceps, rising out of the hot pink scoop neck sweater. Not fair. Anna had enough cleavage without the help of JD's biceps.

Because he was a good doggie, Pop jumped up on Annabelle's legs. She squealed and gave a delicate kick that Pop artfully dodged. "Do you have to take that dreadful little dog with you everywhere?"

Maggie wanted to offer Pop a high-five, which was one

of his very best tricks. "Sorry." She pointed at Anna. "Pop, show some love!"

That was another one of Pop's tricks. *Show some love* meant *lick person on face* and Pop happily obliged, jumping up to give Anna some tongue when she bent over to brush the dirt off her jeans.

"Oh!" Annabelle said, scrunching up her face. "Get away from me!" She stood and delivered a sizzling glare to Maggie. *I'll get you and your little dog, too.*

Bubba scooped Pop up into a football hold while JD walked over to Maggie. "She's your client," he said in her ear.

He was right. Being in Annabelle's presence turned Maggie into a thirteen-year-old. "I'll have those jeans cleaned for you."

"Don't bother," Anna said. She'd already lost interest and was headed toward the dark truck Maggie had followed to the house. Its driver had finally gotten out, and Maggie gasped when he turned around. It was the jerk from the Pump 'n' Go! And even though she didn't think he'd seen her, his stunned, slack-jawed expression suggested he recognized her, too.

Chapter
Ten
☙

Travis couldn't believe it. The mask had not done as good a job of concealing his identity as he'd thought. Little Red Riding Hood had shown up at his job site—*why?*—and recognized him immediately. He'd been thinking of ways to respond to her texts the entire ride here, and now she was right in front of him, looking seriously pissed off.

He stood like a deer in the headlights, glued to the spot as Maggie stomped her way toward him with those adorable eyebrows drawn into a menacing scowl. She pushed the sleeves of her sweatshirt up like she was heading for the center of the ring, and his heart nearly burst through his chest. Not only was it responding to what it perceived as a pint-sized, but potent, threat, but something stupid located in the part of the brain housing primal instincts screamed, *That's my girl.*

"I recognize you," she said, stating the obvious.

That voice. He wanted to pick her up and spin her around,

maybe push her up against the side of his truck and kiss her senseless, but he remained where he was, entirely paralyzed, while Ms. Hood went around him to peer into his truck. He couldn't help but notice her perky breasts responding to the enthusiastic stomping. And he wasn't entirely paralyzed. One part of him had definitely moved.

"It's good to see you again," he said as she breezed by. Little Red Riding Hood had practically mowed down Annabelle on her way to his truck, but now Anna was also standing there staring at the two of them and looking every bit as confused as he felt.

Little Red Riding Hood seemed interested in Henry, and damn near poked her head through the window of his truck. Luckily, Henry was sound asleep. "Listen," Travis tried again. "I've been out of town. I was going to answer—"

"Is this child okay?"

"What?" He looked at Anna, but she just gestured with her finger near her ear in a circular motion while mouthing *loco*.

"Is he *okay*," Maggie repeated, very slowly, as if Travis had a comprehension problem.

"Of course he's okay. He's sleeping. The window's rolled down. What's your problem?"

His exhilaration over seeing her had journeyed from excitement to confusion and had settled at irritation. Maybe Anna was right. It figured that his one and only hookup in months had been with a crazy person.

"Are you sure?" She opened the door.

"Please don't wake him. You have no idea what you're doing."

He'd kept his voice nice and calm, as if he were talking to someone on a ledge. He didn't want to make any sudden moves that might cause her to screech or anything else that might rouse Henry. Travis felt bad enough about bringing a child to the meeting—it wasn't professional—and the last thing he needed was a huge fit that would make Anna reconsider her decision.

"Well, a few minutes ago he was hanging upside down over the asphalt."

She'd seen him at the Pump 'n' Go? Did she know he was the wolf?

"I hope he hasn't had a seizure or something," she added.

She said that last part without much conviction, as by now JD and Bubba were also standing around—with dumbass grins—and she seemed to notice she was the only one freaking out.

"He wouldn't get in his car seat," Travis said, even though it was none of anybody's business. "I had to calm him—"

"That is not how you calm a child down."

She had no idea who he was. She just thought he was some sort of—

"People who abuse children might think it's calming," she continued. "But nobody else does."

Child abuser. Great. Not a good time to suggest a date, then. Plus, he was kind of getting pissed at Ms. Hood.

"I'm sure Travis isn't a child abuser," JD said.

"Thanks, JD."

Maggie's mouth dropped open like she had a steel ball attached to her chin. "Travis?" she sputtered. "Travis Blake?"

Travis stuck his hand out, but he couldn't muster a pleasant expression. "Did you follow me from the Pump 'n' Go all the way out here just to harass me?"

Maggie jutted out her chin, frowned, and grabbed his hand with surprising force. "I'm Maggie," she said, giving his hand one vicious pump.

"Don't hurt yourself," he said.

She yanked her hand back and glowered at him. "I did not follow you. I'm here on business."

"I explained it in my e-mail," Annabelle said. "Petal Pushers is doing the design, you're just doing the labor."

"But Petal Pushers is Mary Margaret Mackey's business," Travis said. Alarms went off in his head. He gulped and looked at Little Red Riding Hood. "I take it you're Mary Margaret?"

She stared angrily with her arms crossed, tapping a toe in disgust. "Only if you're my mother."

Travis's head spun. This couldn't get any worse. Mary Margaret Mackey thought he was a child abuser and had no idea he was the Big Bad Wolf she'd recently had very filthy and satisfying sex with in a shed.

Beneath Maggie's heated and somewhat quizzical gaze, he muttered, "I guess we'll be working together."

She stared at him even harder. Holy shit, did she recognize him as the wolf? This probably wouldn't be a good time for that to happen. She was glaring at him intently. Putting two and two together? He'd been clean shaven the night of the gala. Now he was scruffy with a starter beard, and she'd never seen the upper half of his face. She averted her eyes.

Henry chose that moment to wake up and contribute to the conversation. He muttered a few unintelligible words before his dull eyes settled on Travis. "I just peed my pants."

He hadn't even been home to change clothes before being thrust into a meeting over a bid award he didn't fully understand, only to be accused of child abuse, and now he had a kid with wet pants. He opened the truck door. A dark stain was spreading across Henry's lap, probably soaking the car seat.

Henry was already unbuckling the harness. Travis lifted him out, holding him at arm's length.

"I imagine that seat liner comes out," Maggie said, looking at the car seat, which was soaked. "Just throw it in the washing machine. Do you have a towel for when it's time to buckle him back in?"

"I'm not getting back in that car seat," Henry said, crossing his arms. "You can't make me."

Maggie raised her eyebrows, then glanced at Travis and those big brown eyes—like mood rings—clearly said, *Okay, I get it.* She smiled and shrugged.

Henry moved on to the next item on his agenda. "I'm hungry."

Travis set him down.

"Goodness, you're dirty, too," Maggie said, taking in Henry's appearance.

"We've been camping for a week," Travis said.

"That must be why you smell like a campfire."

"I'm always dirty," Henry said. "And I'm always hungry."

Travis glared at Henry. He was laying it on pretty thick — probably hoping Maggie had a candy bar.

"You can have a banana," Travis said.

"I don't want a banana."

Of course he didn't. "Granola bar?"

"Nope."

Maggie reached into the bag hanging off her shoulder. "I have a bag of chips—"

"Thank you," Travis said. "But we're trying to eat better, right, Henry?"

"I want what she has."

So did Travis, but it was doubtful they were thinking about the same thing. Maggie waited, arm in the bag, for him to give her permission to hand over the chips. He nodded. "Fine," he said. "Thanks."

"You've got a naked kid," JD said.

"What?"

Henry had stripped to his underwear in record time. "I'm all wet."

"Wait a minute there, Henry—"

"Anyone have an extra shirt?" Maggie asked, just as the undies hit the ankles.

Nobody did.

Travis had a bag of camping clothes, but unfortunately it had rained last night. Everything in their tent had gotten wet.

Henry kicked the underwear off and stood there, butt naked. "I'm cold."

"Aw, hell." Self-consciously, Travis pulled his T-shirt over his head, eliciting a whistle from Bubba.

Travis ignored Bubba and slipped the shirt on Henry's skinny little frame. It dragged the ground, but it would keep Henry from getting chilled and cover his willy. This scene couldn't get any weirder. He was at a business meeting and both he and Henry were partially naked. Bubba and JD looked entirely too amused.

"Ooh, nice ink," Annabelle said. Her eyes took their time tracing the dragon tattoo that went from his shoulder to his biceps. His face heated up as she gazed at the falcon spanning the width of his chest, and he really became uncomfortable when she dropped her eyes to the rattlesnake coiled on his lower abdomen. He turned slightly, feeling stupidly modest.

Maggie tilted her head as if watching Henry inhale chips, but she was doing an obvious bit of peripheral peeking. He was damn glad he'd kept his shirt on in the shed.

"I have a tattoo," Bubba said.

"That hula girl quit dancing a long time ago," JD said. "Keep your shirt on."

Bubba faked a sad frown. "She's still got some sway, bruh."

"That's just jiggle," JD replied.

Anna had finished her site survey of Travis's body. "I'm done with Tweedledee and Tweedledum here," she said, waving a hand at JD and Bubba. "Now it's time to talk landscaping."

* * *

This was insane. Maggie had come ready to protect her turf with actual facts and figures—she absolutely *could* match Travis Blake's bid on the labor and do a better job with more equipment and a crew—but it was all she could do to yank single-syllable words out of the vocabulary soup threatening to explode through her ears.

Him bad. Me good.

"Do you think you can work that little bit out between the two of you?" Anna asked.

Little bit of what? What had Anna been saying? While Maggie had been trying to form a sentence in the presence of a half-naked male centerfold covered in tattoos that dipped down into his low-riding jeans, Anna had been blathering on about something involving her and the said half-naked male centerfold.

She remembered Claire's description of Travis Blake in high school and thought, *Quiet skinny bookworm in glasses, my ass.*

"We can work it out," Travis said. "No problem."

Work what out? Also, he looked like he worked out plenty.

She leaned on the newly installed granite bar and pretended to know what they were talking about. "Sure. No problem." *Maybe we can work it out naked.*

What was she doing? Ever since her night with the wolf,

she'd been—for lack of a better word—horny. She shook her head and focused on why she was here. "Anna, I'd like to discuss the contract in private if you don't mind."

"We don't need to discuss anything in private. You two are a team. You *do* know how to collaborate, don't you?"

"Yes, of course. And I'm pleased you like my plans. But splitting the contract seems unnecessary. I can match Mr. Blake's—"

"Call me Travis."

She risked a glance at the gigantic lumberjack sucking up all the air in the room with his chiseled pecs. Big mistake. "Okay—Travis. Whatever. Anyway..." What had she been saying?

"It's too late," Anna said. "It's been decided. You're going to work on this project together, and if one of you refuses, you'll be replaced."

Replaced? Oh, hell no. Good sense finally overcame the pheromones leaking out of the gigolo lawn boy. "There's one—*one*—landscape architect in town. And it's me."

"There's plenty in Austin," Anna said.

"They're more expensive, though."

Anna shrugged her shoulders and grabbed Travis's arm, leaning in and displacing her boob again. Someone should shield poor little Henry's eyes—she glanced around—wherever he was.

"He's not going anywhere," Anna said.

Travis was Annabelle's man candy. To his credit, he appeared somewhat mortified. What little skin she could see through his beard was flaming red, and his delicious full lips—*stop it, Mackey!*—were not smiling.

He pulled away from Anna and folded his arms across his bare chest. "I better go find Henry," he said.

Annabelle smiled at him sweetly. "Run along then."

Travis hesitated, as if he had something to say. But he apparently thought better of it. He nodded at Maggie before heading out in search of Henry.

"Oh, don't look at me like that," Annabelle said.

Maggie tried to adjust her snarl into a more pleasant expression. "Like what?"

"It's not what you're thinking," Anna continued. "I'm just trying to help him out. I mean, good Lord, he's a pathetic case. No education, living in that trashy house at Happy Trails, and now he's inherited a kid that belongs to his prison inmate brother."

Wow. When she put it that way . . .

She looked through the French doors to where Travis squatted next to Henry, who was poking at an ant mound with a stick. Henry squealed, dropped the stick, and slapped at his hand. Travis brought the little fingers to his bearded face and delivered a quick kiss to make it better.

More than just man candy, then.

* * *

Henry had just learned his lesson about poking at a fire ant mound. Travis had already kissed his knuckles—Henry had taught him all about magic kisses—and swatted another twenty or so ants off his little legs before the fuckers had a chance to bite again. Henry's eyes were brimming, but he wasn't wailing. Yet.

"Suck it up," Travis said. Then he winced. That's what his dad used to say to him. "Sorry," he muttered. "You can cry if you want to."

Henry sniffled but kept a lid on the waterworks.

Travis looked toward the house, where Anna stared at him through the window just like old times. It was clear that she'd awarded him the bid to relive her lawn boy fantasy from high school. That hadn't ended well. Maybe he didn't need this job that bad.

Except that he did need it that bad.

He swallowed his pride—it got stuck about halfway down but he powered through—and waved at Anna. She wanted a lawn boy? She had a lawn boy. He didn't have to be happy about it, though.

He stood, brushed off his pants, and picked Henry up. "You ready to go home?"

Henry yawned in response.

Maggie came out. "Did you get attacked by some fire ants?" she asked Henry.

Henry nodded.

"Hurts like the dickens, doesn't it?"

Maggie mussed Henry's hair but didn't look Travis in the eye. "Can you be here at nine on Monday? We'll start clearing out the rocks behind the patio."

"Make it seven," he said. His voice was brusque. "An earlier start is better for me."

So much for being the Big Bad Wolf. He was Anna's goddamn lawn boy.

He loaded Henry into the car seat and climbed behind the wheel, yanking his phone out of his back pocket. Little Red Riding Hood's texts stared up at him. A sly grin crept across his face. Maybe he couldn't get the upper hand with Maggie Mackey, but he knew who could.

Her last text had asked him if he was married. He'd start there.

Not married. I'm a Lone Wolf. Sure you're not afraid?

Chapter

Eleven

❧

Maggie jerked awake and slammed her hand on Darth Vader's head to silence the "Imperial March" alarm. She'd bought herself ten more minutes. Pop recognized the beginning of the snooze loop and settled in at her hip with a satisfied grunt.

Maggie sank back into the blissful abyss. She'd been dreaming about a snake.

A snake tattoo! Today was her first day on the job with Travis Blake. Forget the snooze. She threw the covers off. Pop cocked an ear, looking offended.

"We've got to get up. That jerk insisted on seven o'clock and I'll be damned if he's going to get there first." She swung her legs over the side of the bed. The floor was cold, and she headed for her robe and slippers. No point in cranking up the ancient gas wall heater she always half expected to explode. It was supposed to hit the upper eighties by early afternoon. Such was life in central Texas.

She shuffled into the kitchen and unlocked Pop's doggie door. You couldn't live in the country and leave a doggie door unlocked at night. Not unless you wanted a skunk in your house. Pop shot through and disappeared into the early morning fog.

She rinsed out the stovetop percolator and filled it with grinds. She should probably buy a coffeepot like a normal person, but the percolator had belonged to Honey. She hadn't done much to the cottage since Honey died, and she had a half-baked idea to turn it into a vacation rental. It was originally built in 1901 by German settlers, and Maggie had been approached by several people wanting to buy it. Since she wanted to keep the cottage in the family but didn't necessarily want to continue living in it herself, turning it into a weekend rental was the perfect solution.

She turned on the gas burner. The wolf had responded to her texts on Friday—finally! And it had been a fun exchange. She didn't know what she'd expected, maybe a little innocent back and forth, but they were dirty texting. She couldn't wait to tell Claire.

She looked at the texts again.

Not married. I'm a Lone Wolf. Sure you're not afraid?

I've already followed you through the woods. Seen you at your wildest.

What makes you think that was my wildest? Wear sexy panties to work tomorrow.

The wolf wanted to play games. Maggie wasn't sure she'd be very good at it, but last night she'd set out a pair of red lacy panties.

Pop bolted back through the doggie door and skidded to a stop in front of his empty bowl. Maggie dumped a little kibble in it.

She wasn't looking forward to working with Travis

Blake. He wasn't qualified. He didn't deserve his half of the contract. He was getting by on his looks, while Maggie had to work hard to get what she wanted. Her entire life had been a struggle to prove she was tough enough, big enough, and smart enough to compete with the boys.

She headed to the bathroom to get dressed. The red lacy panties were on top of her work clothes. The Big Bad Wolf probably thought she wore sexy lingerie all the time. As far as he knew, she worked in an office. She tried to imagine herself in a pencil skirt and heels and couldn't. But thanks to a gag gift she'd taken home from Lou Stewart's bachelor party (because of course she'd been invited to a bachelor party) she did have those panties.

She picked them up, biting her lip. She'd never worn them. Not exactly her style. But she yanked the tag off and slipped them on, feeling a bit like Little Red Riding Hood. She grabbed a stretchy sports bra, but it ruined the mood. As did the white utilitarian one from Walmart.

Forget it. She didn't need a bra.

Instead of her work clothes, she grabbed a cinnamon-colored long-sleeved T-shirt with a scoop neck and a black sweater. Black jeans and boots completed the ensemble, and three minutes later a toothbrush and toothpaste had completed her morning beauty routine. She ran her fingers through her short hair and was done.

The coffee was finally ready. She poured it into her PETAL PUSHERS—WE'RE DIGGIN' IT travel mug, grabbed her bag, and followed Pop to the Jeep. It was forty minutes after six when they headed down the bumpy dirt lane that led to Peacock Road.

Dang it. The cows were in her apple orchard. She slammed on the brakes and honked the horn. Two of the cows looked up, apples in their dumb mouths. Maggie rolled down the window. "Shoo! Go home! Get back on your stupid happy trail to Blake land!"

Pop, excited by the shouting, flung himself out the window. Before Maggie could get the door open, he was running circles around the cows, nipping at their hooves.

"Stop it, Pop!" The cows were getting jittery, and Pop was going to get kicked or stepped on.

Pop did not stop. Focused on the biggest cow, he darted in and out of her hooves, growling and yapping, until he managed to sink his sharp little teeth into a leg.

The cow did not appreciate it. She dropped the apple and ran. The rest followed suit, and Maggie jumped back in the Jeep to avoid being crushed in a stampede, which would be a stupid way to die. And the worst part was, the damn things were running in the wrong direction.

* * *

Travis pulled up to the construction site, noting the absence of a certain yellow Jeep with extreme satisfaction. He'd figured Miss Mary Margaret for an early bird. Maybe he'd been wrong.

He wondered if she knew her grandmother regularly left threatening notes on his gate. Yesterday's had been, YOU KNOW WHAT WOULD LOOK GOOD IN MY LIVING ROOM? TEN COWHIDE RUGS.

JD's truck was here. He'd been one of the few kids to be kind to Travis when he'd been an outsider in a town where most other kids absolutely knew they belonged. Their families' names were plastered all over the town. KOWALSKI FEED AND SEED, MACKEY DRUGS, MAYES CARPENTRY AND CONSTRUCTION. The same names over and over, linking aunts, uncles, grandparents, and cousins. There was only one Blake family, and they were known for gambling debts, theft, and, thanks to Scott, drug smuggling.

And not paying property taxes. Couldn't forget that one.

Travis hadn't known how to find his place in the community, and his family's antics hadn't helped. He'd been a loner by necessity.

But the Mayes family had been kind. JD's dad had never failed to shake Travis's hand and ask him how he was doing when most adults acted like he was invisible or eyed him warily. And his mom had been nice, too.

Travis opened the console in his truck and dug through yesterday's mail and Henry's stash of snacks to find his work gloves. *Yesterday's mail...* He pulled out two envelopes. One was alarming—unopened letter from the tax office—and the other was depressing—his bank statement. He sighed heavily and crammed them both back into the console. Then he climbed out of his truck, stuffed his gloves into his back pocket, and gathered the tools he'd need: wheel barrel, pickax, shovel, and hoe. There was nothing glamorous about digging up rocks.

He wheeled the tools around to the back of the house. Little Red Riding Hood hadn't marked anything off yet, so he wasn't sure where he should start. He looked through the French doors and saw JD on a ladder, hammering away on some molding.

He went inside. "You're here awful early."

JD missed a nail. "Dammit," he muttered.

"Sorry."

"No problem. And Annabelle wants to move in like yesterday, so I'm not early enough."

Travis nodded. "Nice house."

"Divorce settlement. You remember Jim Henderson? His dad had the Chevy dealership on the highway."

"Obnoxious kid who wrecked a Corvette on his sixteenth birthday?"

"That's the one. Three years ago, he wrecked his life by marrying Anna. I kind of thought they were perfect for each other."

Anna was on the rebound. Great.

JD went back to hammering. "What'd you do after high school?" he asked.

"Oilfields, mostly. Then the Army."

JD stopped hammering. "Were you deployed?"

"Afghanistan."

JD set the hammer down on the top of the ladder, and then made a motion to tip his hat, realizing too late that it wasn't on his head. He grinned in embarrassment—being without his Stetson probably felt like being completely naked—and said, "Thank you for your service, Travis. You should have had a hero's homecoming here in Big Verde."

Travis didn't know what to say. He was no hero. He'd met some real heroes, and he didn't like being elevated to a pedestal that he didn't deserve to approach, much less stand on. "I didn't see combat."

"Doesn't matter. You signed up. You went. Most people don't."

Travis waved him off and pretended to admire the molding.

"When did you get out?" JD asked, picking up the hammer and sticking a couple of nails in his mouth.

"Just before coming to Big Verde."

JD lined his hammer up with a small nail. "Well, welcome home," he mumbled, careful not to spit nails. "Glad you're back."

Travis swallowed. Welcome *home*. Big Verde had never felt like home. It had felt more like an unkept promise.

"It's so sad about Lisa," JD said. "Mrs. Garza says you're really good with Henry."

And there it was. That uncomfortable feeling when you realized everyone in town had been talking about you. Another aspect of small-town life he could never get used to. And he didn't think he was all that good with Henry. But he was better than Scott would be, and he was starting to get a little worried about it. He shrugged his shoulders—a gesture JD probably mistook for modesty.

"I hear the ranch is looking good," JD said.

Was JD out of his mind? "Where'd you hear that?"

"Gerome Kowalski says you've got the herd separated, fixed some fences..."

Gerome Kowalski had been talking about Happy Trails? More gossip. Travis felt sick at his stomach. The enormous Rancho Canada Verde bordered Happy Trails on its western fence line, and with its pristine, perfectly maintained fences, manicured pastures, and award-winning Black Angus herd, it was the gem of the Texas Hill Country, and it made Happy Trails seem all the more pathetic.

"I've patched the fences in several places, but they need replacing. And I've managed to get the heifers and young bulls separated, but that's about it. The herd needs to be thinned out."

"Nothing that can't be done with a little help," JD said.

"I just need to get it in good enough shape to sell. I've got a job waiting for me in Austin."

JD's mouth hung open and three nails slipped out, bouncing off his boots. "You're selling Happy Trails? What about Henry?"

"I'm not real sure. There's a social worker looking into the possibility of other relatives and whatnot," Travis said, stuttering just a bit.

JD furrowed his brow. Reached for his nonexistent hat. And then he changed the subject, for which Travis was grateful. "I'm going to Tony's with Bubba and a few of the guys to watch the first Spurs game of the season tonight. You want to come?"

"Sorry, but I've already got some plans."

JD looked down at him like he didn't believe him. "Maggie will probably be there."

Travis's head snapped up in a completely involuntary gesture. He tried to cover it up by swatting an imaginary gnat. "So?"

"I realize she can be intimidating."

Intimidating? That tiny little thing? "I don't find her intimidating at all."

And I know just how to make her behave herself.

"You're a rare man then," JD said with a grin. "Anyway, I saw the way you were looking at her."

"What way was that?"

"Like she was a piece of cake and you hadn't eaten in three years."

"I think you're mistaken."

"And she was looking at you the same way."

"I *know* you're mistaken."

Whatever it was that was going on between Little Red Riding Hood and JD, it wasn't of a romantic nature. Because it sure as hell felt like JD was trying to fix him up.

JD set his hammer down and picked up a thermos. "If your plans change, you know where to find us. We'll keep a stool warm for you."

Although Travis appreciated the invitation, Tony's was one place he hoped to avoid. His dad had spent too much time there. Besides, he really did have plans. "I promised Alice I'd build a gazebo in the children's reading garden. Alice is the librarian," he added. "She reads to Henry at story time every week, and I couldn't turn her down."

"I've known Alice all my life."

Of course JD knew Alice. Everyone knew everyone in Big Verde. He wouldn't be surprised if Alice was JD's cousin or if maybe her granddaddy had married JD's great-aunt on his mother's father's side. That's how all the introductions went in Big Verde. *You know Sally...she married that nephew of Bob's down at Bippo's Shop...his mama was a Polinski...* and so on, and so on.

"Alice's uncle married my Aunt Fran," JD started. Then he grinned and reached for his missing Stetson again, cheeks turning pink as he realized the pattern he'd fallen into. "Sorry. You don't need to know all that. Anyway, I wasn't aware Alice needed help at the library. Maybe Bubba and I will sacrifice our barstools tonight and come by to help out."

This was another small-town phenomenon. Folks dropping everything to help out.

"Really?" Travis asked. Alice had already recruited some local teens for the project, but it sure would go a shit-ton faster with JD and Bubba on-site.

"Sure," JD said. "It'll be fun. And maybe we'll get done in time to catch the second half of the game."

A car door slammed. It was followed by the excited yaps of a little dog.

"Look," JD said, pointing out the window. "There's that woman who doesn't intimidate you."

Travis looked, but as he watched Maggie head his way, no amount of bracing could prepare him for what his heart did next, which was damn near grind to a stop.

Chapter

Twelve

❧

Twenty minutes late! All because she'd had to chase a bunch of cows off her property. She marched across the area where the backyard was going in and blew through Anna's French doors to find JD and Travis shooting the shit like they had nothing better to do.

She was going to light into Travis about his fences. Set his ass on fire. Toss him into a volcano of burning lava—

He smiled. Blue eyes. White teeth. A dimple she hadn't noticed before, just above the beard, only on the left side. Her heart flopped over like a fainting pygmy goat on a YouTube video. Maybe it wasn't professional to chew him out in front of JD.

"Good morning," he said.

His voice was low and echoed in the big room—the *great room*, as Anna insisted on calling it—vibrating its way through her bones, snaking its way up and down her spine, and generally making her feel warm and tingly all over.

Which was mighty inconvenient and vaguely familiar. Every time the man spoke, she had an uneasy sense of déjà vu. Her head spun for a moment.

"Sorry. I'm late because I was . . . I was—"

"Trying to decide what to wear?" JD was grinning like an idiot. "Because you sure look nice today."

She glared at him. "I was reevaluating my initial plan to install agarita bushes. Thinking about going with Anocacho orchids instead. It'll do better here, and it won't attract as many deer as the agarita." This was technically true. She had recently made this decision.

"Why don't you want to attract deer?" JD asked.

"Probably because they'll destroy the landscaping," Travis suggested.

"That's partially it," Maggie said. "It's also because I suspect Anna hates anything furry and cute with doe-eyes. She wouldn't think twice about eating Bambi."

JD laughed. "I would only eat Bambi if the Martinez Meat Market turned him into sausage first."

"Chicken-fried venison steak is the best way to eat Bambi," Travis added, rubbing his extremely flat and presumably hard stomach.

"Mm," JD agreed. "Or Polish kielbasa." He took to rubbing his own *Mr. October* abs with delight.

Maggie fanned herself with her landscaping plans. It was getting very warm in this room.

"Sausage talk getting to you?" Travis asked.

JD laughed. "It's getting to me."

Maggie raised her eyebrows slightly. "Oh, really?"

JD stopped laughing, and then blushed furiously.

Maggie snorted. "Keep going. You're doing so well."

"Nothing like a good, thick ring of sausage," Travis said with a wink.

"Y'all are awful." Maggie refused to blush. She literally willed the rising red tide creeping up her chest to stop at her neck. "And I'm not the slightest bit embarrassed by this banter, so you can stop trying."

"I don't know what you think we're talking about, Maggie," Travis said with a grin that indicated the opposite. "We're merely discussing the merits of venison in its many delightful forms."

Maggie grabbed his sleeve. "JD is already being a bad influence on you. Let's get to work."

The cool autumn air felt good on Maggie's flushed skin. She closed her eyes, stretched, and inhaled the scent of cedar and sage. When she opened her eyes, Travis was standing there with his mouth hanging open. Did the man not know how to dig up rocks? "Just start at the house and work your way out."

Travis blinked, and seemingly snapped out of whatever trance he'd been in. Who knew what ridiculous nonsense was going through his mind? Probably chicken-fried venison.

"Sure. I'll do that." He gave her a sharp salute, and then yanked up a pickax.

Maggie got right to work marking off plots. Within a couple of minutes, they were comfortably laboring side by side. Maggie measured, hammered in stakes, and strung lines while Travis dug up rocks, loaded them into his wheelbarrow, and piled them up at the edge of the site.

"I'm going to use some of them for terracing," she called to Travis. "So separate the good ones."

"That'll look real nice," Travis said. "And it'll be a good way to deal with the steep slope."

Yep. That's why she'd planned terracing. She didn't need him mansplaining her own business to her. She started to say as much but managed to bite her tongue. If they were going to survive the duration of this project, she'd have to keep a lid on the snark; the gate notes were bad enough.

By eleven o'clock the cool autumn air was long gone, and it had taken Maggie's sunny disposition with it. Sweaty and uncomfortable in her dumb clothes, she was seriously regretting her life choices. She ditched the black sweater and rolled up the long sleeves of her T-shirt. She'd ditch the boots, too, if she could. Both of her sweaty feet had blisters. The damn things were made for two-stepping, not for squatting and measuring gradations. They also weren't very flexible, and when she swatted at a gnat, she lost her balance and ended up on her bottom with a grunt.

Travis looked up. Because if you're going to squat, swat, and fall, you should do it when a handsome man is around to see it.

"You okay?" he asked.

"Yes," she said. She gave him her best *why do you ask* look. "Taking a little break." *Right here. In the middle of this pile of dirt.*

"Do you need to sit in the shade for a few? It's getting warm, and it's humid as all get-out." To demonstrate his discomfort, Travis dropped his hoe and grabbed the hem of his shirt.

He was going to take it off.

With the leisurely air of a stripper—not that Maggie had ever seen one outside of the movies—he slowly pulled the DON'T MESS WITH TEXAS shirt over his head. *Oh, hello, snake, falcon, dragon...*

"What did you say?" she mumbled. Or maybe she thought it. It was hard to know, because her mouth no longer seemed to be connected to her brain, which was probably a good thing.

"I said it's getting hot, and you've been working hard. Do you want to take a seat in the shade for a minute?"

Maggie managed to work her eyes up to his. They were so incredibly blue against the Texas sky. Maybe she did need to sit in the shade for a bit. "Shade sounds good."

Also, your eyelashes are unreasonable.

"I've got some tea in a cooler."

Cooling down sounded good, too. "You're going to get sunburned without a shirt."

Travis looked down at his lean, tanned torso. "Nah. I work outside like this all the time. You, on the other hand, could use some sunscreen on that pink nose."

Maggie started to get up, but the damn inflexible boots threw her off and she sank back into the dirt. Travis plucked her up like a dandelion, and she suddenly found herself smashed against his bare chest, eye to eye with the falcon.

"Oops!" Her fingers involuntarily grazed his abs on their way to his chest, which she only touched in order to push her face away from his warm, salty skin. It was a hard, unyielding chest. Pretty decent, as far as chests went. Her fingers might have lingered a moment. She might have pretended she needed the contact to steady herself as her head spun.

"Sorry," Travis said, lowering his eyes to where her fingers still rested.

The sight of a blushing lumberjack did nothing to help matters. She removed her fingers without looking to see if they were on fire, and then followed Travis to where his cooler rested beneath an ancient live oak. He opened the lid and grabbed a thermos. Then he snapped the cooler shut, brushed it off even though it was spotless, and invited her to sit on it as he lowered himself to the ground with a groan. Gosh, why did he have to be so —

"Sweet?" he asked.

"Pardon?"

"I hope you like it sweet." He held the thermos up. "Sweet tea. It's all I brought."

"That's fine," she said, hoping her ears didn't appear as bright red as they felt.

"Your ears are getting pink, too," Travis said.

Dammit. She was an ear-blusher. An ear-blusher with super short hair so everyone who witnessed her falling on her ass and then damn near kissing a bare chest could also witness the aftereffects on her ears.

"You should probably put some sunscreen on them. And that cute, upturned nose."

Did he just call her nose cute?

The ears. They were literally on fire now. She was like the "extra" version of Rudolph.

Travis poured tea into the thermos lid and handed it to her. "Bottoms up," he said with a wink.

Why didn't her voice work? Not even a squeak. She tapped her cup to his thermos and took a sip. It was good. She hadn't realized how thirsty she'd been. Travis must have been thirsty, too, because he tilted his head back and greedily drained the entire thermos.

"Hits the spot, doesn't it?" he said, wiping his bearded chin on the back of his hand.

There was definitely a spot she'd like him to hit.

Silence. *Talk, Mackey! How hard can it be?*

"There's supposed to be another cold front blowing in tonight," Travis said. "We might even get a frost."

Maggie nodded, the sound of her silence screaming in her head. This was so weird. Maybe all the blood rushing to her ears had left her vocal chords paralyzed. The same way erections caused stupidity in males. *Erections. Why was she thinking about erections?* She forced herself to grunt,

"Uh-huh." Which was way better than *Me horny*, the phrase playing on repeat in her head.

"It's still mighty hot in the sun, though," Travis continued.

"Uh-huh."

"Not so bad in the shade."

Holy cow. He was a weather rambler. A hot, topless weather rambler.

"In the shade it's downright nippy."

Then why did he wipe a bead of sweat from his temple?

* * *

It was all over. He'd spent the last three hours trying not to notice Maggie's breasts, and in an attempt at conversation, he'd chosen a tried-and-true category—*I'll take weather for four hundred, Alex*—and said *nippy*.

But damn, she wasn't wearing a bra. His mouth watered. He knew what those delicious buds tasted like. Could she see it on his face? What if she was putting two and two together and figuring out he was the Big Bad Wolf? He yanked his cap out of his back pocket and put it on, pulling it down low. Combined with the itchy beard he longed to be rid of, it might be a passable disguise.

Or he could just tell her that he was the man she'd had sex with in the shed. *Hey, want to hear something funny?*

Only she was kind of being nice to him at the moment. Why fuck it up? He slipped his shirt back on, so she wouldn't see the goose bumps she was giving him.

"When will you be finished with the rocks?" Maggie asked.

She sounded a bit breathless and shaky. The woman really couldn't take the heat, and it wasn't even summer. "Another day or two will do it."

"Do you think you might need some help?"

"No. I got this." Tomorrow would be a bitch, though. His back was already killing him, but he couldn't afford any help. He'd bid on the project, and now he had to deliver.

"On Wednesday we can start filling in with soil. I'll see about having it delivered that morning. Can you have a front-end loader here?"

"I'm just going to shovel it in by hand."

"You can rent one," she said.

"Nah." It cost too much. He couldn't swing it.

Maggie unrolled several sheets of plans on top of the cooler. "If you're thinking about doing it manually, you'd better have some help," she said, tapping the paper. "Big job."

For the millionth time, doubt crept in. What had made him think he could go from mowing lawns and planting shrubs to doing a large residential installation with no equipment and no crew? Why had he bid on this job? *Because you need the money, you idiot.* And why had Anna hired him? *To toy with you, you idiot.*

"I can provide a crew," Maggie said.

She might be cute, and he might know what her inner thighs tasted like—and want to taste them again—but the woman wanted him off the job. She'd been clear about that, and here he was sharing his tea and worrying about her sunburned ears. Time to toughen up. "You're just in charge of the design," he said. "I'm the crew. How I get shit done is up to me, and I'm going to get it done with my bare hands."

The dark eyebrows disappeared into her blond bangs, and she crossed her arms over her still-very-nippy chest. "But you're not a crew. You're one man. I honestly don't know what Anna was thinking when she split this contract."

Okay. Now his blood was starting to boil. She wasn't the

boss of him, and she wasn't going to steal his half of the project.

"If you want to split the labor," Little Miss Hood continued, "I'm sure we can talk some sense into Anna." She looked him up and down. As if the idea of him tackling this project was the most nonsensical thing she'd ever heard. Which it probably was.

Travis clenched his jaw. It was easier to ignore her hard little nipples poking through her shirt now that she was pissing him off. "You stick to your part of the bid, and I'll stick to mine."

Maggie stood and re-crossed her arms below her breasts, stretching the T-shirt even tighter.

Not so easy to ignore, after all.

"Just consider it. You might be in over your head here."

Why didn't she just cut off his balls and hand them to him on a platter? He snatched her plans, rolled them up, and handed them to her. Then he picked up the cooler. "Break's over," he said, heading for his truck to put the cooler away.

"Just think about it," Maggie called after him.

He could feel her eyes boring into his back. Why was he so fucking embarrassed? He'd known he was in over his head with this project. But he needed the money and was going to make the best of it. What he *didn't* need was to care what Maggie Mackey thought of him.

He did, though.

He remembered the way she'd melted at the Big Bad Wolf's touch. The way she'd acquiesced at the sound of his voice. The way those big brown eyes had looked at him as if he were the most important man on Earth. He climbed in his truck and pulled out his phone. He had a sudden desire to send a text.

* * *

Maggie stared at Travis sitting in his truck. She'd upset him. But dang it, he was going to slow down the entire project. He was behaving like a man-baby, and she had zero tolerance for man-babies. His feelings weren't her problem. Getting this project completed was.

Ping!

It was her phone.

How is your day going, LRRH?

She stifled a squeal and hurried to her Jeep for some texting privacy. It would just look like she was checking e-mail. Pop hopped onto the seat, put his little paws on the window, and started panting. "Chill out. We're not going anywhere."

Maggie tried to adopt an air of professionalism as she composed her text—in case anyone was watching—but she probably looked just like Pop, all slobbery and impatient.

How to answer the question? She tried to come up with something cute or sexy, but she wasn't good at cute or sexy, and decided to go with honesty instead.

Meh. At work.

You don't like work?

He didn't ask what she did. That was good. Let him think she had a fancy job somewhere sitting behind a desk in heels while everyone fell all over themselves doing her bidding.

I do. But I have a difficult co-worker to deal with.

Oh really?

Yeah. Thinks he knows everything.

Maybe he's all bark and no bite.

How about you? Are you all bark and no bite?

You know very well that I bite.

He'd never actually bitten her. But the thought of her skin between his teeth while he held her down and forcefully—

holy cow, where did these thoughts come from? The wolf had a strange effect on her. And it was not one that would make anyone's mama proud.

You might need obedience training.

You just gave me some ideas. Are you wearing sexy underwear like a good girl?

She was curious. Where did the wolf work? She remembered the look of his suit. The feel of his closely shaven skin, short-cropped hair. The square-toe boots—dark slate, not the usual black. He probably worked in a high-rise somewhere. But he'd just posed the question she'd been waiting for.

Red lacy panties.

She glanced around. Travis was messing with something in his truck, JD had left, and Anna still hadn't shown up. Nobody was paying any attention to her.

Little Red Panties for Little Red Riding Hood?

So very little.

Is there a Little Red Bra to go with them?

Not wearing one.

That was the truth.

Are your nipples hard?

Her face exploded in crimson.

Yes.

She couldn't believe she was having this conversation. In her Jeep. At work. With some businessman dressed in a suit with his secretary out front. Or maybe a client in front of him.

Pinch them.

She gasped. No way! She bit her lip, trying to think of a single reason to comply with the wolf's request. She came up with two: it was delightfully dirty, and it gave her a thrill.

Pop had caught on to the fact that he wasn't going anywhere and started whining. Maggie opened the door and let him out. No need to expose him to the depths of depravity to which she was about to sink. And then, after another quick glance to make sure Travis wasn't looking, she slipped her hands inside her T-shirt and did as she'd been told. The thrill was more psychological than physical, but it was intense. She fumbled for her phone.

I did it.

I knew you would. Enjoy the rest of your day.

A door slammed. Travis stood next to his truck, stretching. He glanced in her direction, smiled, and peeled off his T-shirt again.

It was going to be a long afternoon.

Chapter

Thirteen

❦

Travis had barely had time for a shower, much less dinner. Luckily, Mrs. Garza had seen fit to provide tamales. And not just enough for him and Henry. She'd made enough for everyone who was going to help with the library.

"Mrs. Garza, you didn't have to do that." He sure was glad she had, though.

Mrs. Garza, wearing jeans with rhinestones on the back pockets and a shiny purple blouse, continued packing foil-wrapped packages of tamales into an old, beat-up ice chest. "It was no trouble. And Henry helped."

Travis was certain it had been a lot of trouble. And he also knew that Henry's help generally amounted to the job taking twice as long as it should. But looking at Henry's face, beaming with pride, Travis realized he needed to let the kid help with ranch chores more often. Even though it was a pain in the ass.

"I didn't even know I liked tamales!" Henry said. "But the ones I made are real good."

"You have the magic touch, *mijo*," Mrs. Garza said.

"I do?"

Mrs. Garza stopped what she was doing and put her hands on her hips. "I said so, didn't I?"

Henry had something that looked suspiciously like chocolate on his chin. Travis grabbed a paper towel and wiped it off.

"We made cupcakes, too."

"I see that."

"I gots the magic touch for all kinds of cookin'."

"You *have* the magic touch."

"That's what I said," Henry replied, with no attempt at hiding his irritation. "And it's a good thing, too, because you can't cook."

Travis couldn't argue with that. Mrs. Garza had no doubt noticed all the frozen food in the freezer and the fast-food bags in the garbage. When she babysat for Henry, she almost always made dinner.

Beneath the aromas of cumin, garlic, and chocolate was the faint lemon scent of furniture polish. Looking around the house, it was clear that the one with the magic touch was Mrs. Garza.

"I don't expect you to cook and clean while you're here taking care of Henry." He didn't pay her near enough for that. He didn't really pay her near enough for anything.

"Well, the child has to eat," Mrs. Garza said. "And he needs a clean, safe place to play."

Mrs. Garza had zero filters and spoke her mind. She and Henry were alike in that way. You were getting the truth whether you liked it or not.

He picked up the mail from the counter. The notice from the tax collector's office glared up at him. He should open it. Face the music. See exactly how much he owed. He took a deep breath and . . . set it back on the counter. Covered it with a flyer from the local tractor dealership. Front-end loaders were on sale.

"I talked to my cousin about painting this place," Mrs. Garza said, closing the lid on the ice chest. "He says he can do it."

Travis gulped. He hadn't asked her to do that. The house needed painting, but he couldn't afford it. "I'm sure he'd offer me a good deal, but—"

"He wants a quarter."

Travis couldn't have heard that right. "A quarter?"

"That's for the interior. If you want him to do the outside, too, then he's asking for a half. He'll tell you how he wants it."

"How he wants it?"

"Is there an echo in here?" Mrs. Garza asked. She shook her head. "Anyway, I told him to stick with skirt steak for *fajitas*, some ribs, and to get the rest ground."

Beef! The man wanted beef. Travis might not have time or money, but he had sixty-two head of cattle, which was too much for the property in its current state. He'd forgotten how folks in Big Verde purchased large amounts of beef directly from the rancher. Almost everybody had a chest freezer on the porch for that specific purpose. Families went in together to buy a quarter, half, or even whole cows. Why hadn't he considered using beef to barter?

"Martinez Meat Market will process it," Mrs. Garza said.

Travis's bump of optimism took a dive. He didn't even have the cash to pay for processing. His concern must have shown on his face, because Mrs. Garza patted his arm. "Beto Martinez is my brother. He'll work something out."

Mrs. Garza was related to at least half the people in Big Verde. "You don't happen to have a cousin or a brother down at the tax office, do you?"

"Sorry, but no." She smiled and continued patting his arm "Everything will be fine. You just keep doing what you're doing."

Ignoring things. Putting off unpleasant tasks. Sure, he'd just keep doing what he was doing.

A few minutes later, loaded with tamales, cupcakes, and an ornery five-year-old kicking the back of his seat, Travis headed down the lane. Movement caught his eye in the east pasture. About twelve cows—he'd nicknamed them the Dirty Dozen—were walking in single-file, toe to tail. And they were headed straight for the weakest spot in the fence and Honey Mackey's motherfucking apples. He'd already come home to one note with a thinly veiled threat of poison. No doubt there would be another one tonight.

* * *

Maggie pulled to a stop in the back lot of Petal Pushers. She was pooped from her day at Anna's, having sweated her ass off in her stupid clothes while Travis paraded around half naked. Between his hot, gleaming torso and the wolf's dirty texts, she could use a cold shower. Too bad she didn't have time for one. The first frost of the season was on its way, and she had a ton of plants to move.

She got out of her Jeep. Norbert and Claire were already loading up carts.

"Can you believe this weather?" Norbert asked. "Hot as hell all day and dipping into the freezing zone tonight."

"That's Texas for you," Claire said.

Maggie picked up the handle on a cart loaded down with pallets of perennials and gave it a yank. What they couldn't haul inside would have to be covered with tarps.

As tired as she was, Travis had to be way worse. He'd

chipped away at the limestone forest all afternoon, one rock at a time. He'd made a decent amount of progress, but there was still so much more to do. Stubborn man.

Maggie dragged the cart backward, being careful not to trip on any hoses.

"Let me help you with that," Norbert said.

"I've got it. You just make sure all the faucets are dripping." She could damn well drag a heavy cart as well as any man, and the last thing she needed was frozen pipes.

She gave a huge tug on the handle, lost traction in the mud, and fell flat on her ass, which was apparently today's theme.

Claire covered her mouth with her hands, eyes wide, and nostrils quivering as she tried not to laugh.

"Not funny," Maggie said.

Claire held out a hand. "A little funny. And if you were wearing heels, this wouldn't have happened. Mine are dug in like anchors." To demonstrate, she lifted a foot. Clumps of dirt and roots hung from the narrow heels of what were ruined and probably very expensive shoes.

"Those are more like tent stakes," Norbert said.

Claire yanked Maggie up. "Either way, I'm not going down."

Maggie wiped herself off, picked up the cart handle, and went right back to grunting.

"Why do you have to do the heaviest and hardest job when you're the tiniest person here?" Norbert asked.

"Because she's trying to prove she can do everything Travis Blake can do," Claire said.

"He's the one who thinks he can do everything himself," Maggie said, noting with satisfaction that once she got the wheels out of the ruts, she could drag the damn cart quite well, thank you very much. "There's just no reason for it," she said, wiping her brow and leaving a smear of mud on her face. "We have a crew. We have equipment. He just has him-

self. Anna just wants him around because he looks good."
Boy, does he.

Claire had finished covering the citrus trees and picked
up a handle on a cart of succulents. "He is easy on the eyes."

"But he's not qualified. You can't hire someone just because he's hot."

"Men do it all the time. They have their secretaries and
assistants in their short skirts running around. Why can't
women have a little fun, too?"

"Because it's wrong," Maggie said. "No matter who
does it."

She deserved the contract. The *full* contract. This project
was right up her alley, and she didn't appreciate having to
share just so Anna could have a boy toy. Although he did
work ridiculously hard. She'd give him that.

"Anna and Travis have a bit of history, you know," Claire
said.

"Really? What kind?"

"The high school kind."

How could Anna and Travis have high school history
when Maggie didn't even remember Travis from high
school?

"They dated?"

"I don't think you could call it dating. But he used to
mow her family's lawn after school. I heard they messed
around."

"He was literally Anna's lawn boy? And now he is again?"

"You could say that. And supposedly Travis stole jewelry
from her. God, Maggie, did you ever lift your head out of the
dirt and look around when we were in school?"

She'd noticed lots of things in school—like JD, for in-
stance. But oddly, she hadn't noticed Travis. "There's no
way he stole anything. He's not that kind of man."

"Know him well, do you?"

"Are you absolutely sure he went to school with us?"

Claire laughed. "He's a pretty amazing case of metamorphosis. He's a hunky butterfly." She parked her cart next to Maggie's. "I think that's it. We've got all our babies inside."

"Yuck," Maggie said, lifting a boot. "Look at our feet."

"At least it's just mud," Claire said, taking the rag offered by Norbert and wiping off her heels. "We've stepped in worse. And that reminds me, you did have a run-in with Travis in high school."

"I did?"

"Remember when Danny Moreno put cow patties in your locker and they fell out when you opened the door?"

Yes, she remembered. It had gone splat onto her shoes, then she'd screamed and dropped her books in it, and then the vice-principal had walked by and told her to clean it all up. Danny was a pharmacist now, but Maggie still didn't trust him.

"The kid who helped you clean up the mess was Travis."

Maggie dropped the cart handle. "Get out," she said. "That was *not* Travis. It was some new kid."

"Why do you think that?"

"Because I'd never noticed him before." Or after, for that matter. Had she even said thank you? She tried to remember the boy who'd stopped to help her. He'd been small. His backpack was bigger than he was. He'd had brown hair and wore glasses—she'd been startled by his magnified blue eyes and *oh my God it was Travis.*

"Bingo," Claire said. "I can see from your dumb expression that you remember."

"This does not compute."

"It computes all right. He had a growth spurt. Lost the glasses. Hubba hubba."

"Wow. I mean, *wow*."

"I know."

Norbert pulled the outside gates shut and locked them. "We knocked it out with just the three of us."

"Is there a big party or something going on tonight?" Maggie asked. "I texted Derek and Frank to see if they could help, but they were both busy."

Derek and Frank were high school seniors who sometimes helped out at Petal Pushers.

Norbert's naturally dark complexion darkened some more. "Yeah, there's a...thing," he mumbled.

"What?" Maggie said.

"They're working at the library," Claire said quietly.

Maggie snorted. Derek and Frank didn't strike her as being big readers. Stoners? Yes. Readers? No. "Good one. What's really going on?"

"No, really. The library is redoing the children's reading garden and—"

"Redoing it how?" The library was city property, and Petal Pushers had the contract for landscaping.

"A gazebo is going in. And some new play equipment."

"Oh. That sounds nice. I should swing by and have a look. I bet we can propose some new landscaping to make it even nicer."

"Yep," Claire said, and then mumbled something over her shoulder as she headed for the garden center doors.

"What did you say?"

"She said Travis Blake is in charge of the project," Norbert said.

Maggie was speechless for almost two seconds, which felt like an extremely long period of time. Travis was going to ruin her. "You're kidding me, right?"

Norbert shook his head.

"How did he land that? Is every single person in this town so easily swayed by a bare chest?"

Norbert furrowed his brow. "What are you talking about?"

Maggie didn't have time to explain her theory about the gigolo lawn boy. Instead she held her fist in the air and proclaimed, "I'll go to City Hall! I'll stage a protest—"

"Hold on there, Norma Rae," Claire said. "I don't think we've lost a contract just because Travis is building a gazebo and installing playground equipment. Neither of those things are services we provide."

"He'll weasel his way into that contract. He'll be very polite about it. He might blush stupidly and say *aw shucks* and then, he'll take off his shirt!"

"Okaay..." Norbert said.

"And when he does that," Maggie continued, "nobody can think straight and there goes our contract."

She stomped over to the utility sink to wash the mud off her hands. He had weaseled into her business. He couldn't keep his cows on his side of the goddamn fence. "Enough is enough," she spat.

"Are you about to make a big scene at the library?" Claire asked.

"Don't try to stop me."

"I wouldn't dream of it. Hold up while I put on some lipstick."

Chapter

Fourteen

❦

Maggie pulled into the library at the same time as Claire. She wasn't quite ready to go in like the Terminator, so she waved Claire over. They needed to strategize.

It was after hours, but the small lot was filled with cars and bikes. Mark Polinsky's monster truck had its tailgate down, and two girls sat on it, legs swinging. An ice chest with its lid propped open was behind them in the truck's bed.

"It looks like a tailgate party," Maggie said as Claire climbed out and closed the door. "Travis has no idea how to direct a crew of young people. He thinks he can just turn on some loud music and set them loose."

They weren't exactly running around loose. Several were unloading bags of concrete while another group stacked lumber. Travis came around the corner. He wore a black T-shirt. Its hem rose when he hoisted a bag of concrete onto his shoulder, exposing nice ripped abs. Claire made a barely muffled sound of approval in her throat.

Something settled in Maggie's belly. It quivered and shook and sat at attention. Apparently, irritation and annoyance had slinked off like a twitchy-tailed cat, and dumb, dark desire had bounded in like a dog in heat.

"It looks like he's doing pretty well to me," Claire said. "Very well, in fact." She raised an eyebrow in a manner that suggested she was thinking of all kinds of non-concrete-related things.

Travis dropped the bag next to a wheelbarrow. He had to be dying after all he'd already done today. Yet here he was. Her eyes narrowed.

They must be paying him big bucks.

Alice came out of the library with a bag of books. Her face lit up when she saw Maggie and Claire.

"Oh no, she's going to ask me about book club again," Claire said.

"Just tell her no. Do you even read?"

"You know how hard it is for me to say no."

Maggie was so upset about Travis and his business-stealing bullshit that she let that little gem slide.

"Would you come to book club with me? You can read the book and tell me about it like you did for Honors English."

Maggie sighed. It wasn't that she didn't like to read. But she didn't relish the idea of talking about a book with a bunch of women who, like Claire, probably hadn't even bothered to read it and were just there for the wine.

Alice tapped on the window. Maggie rolled it down. "Hello, Alice. Heading home, are you?"

"Goodness, no. Not with this party getting started. Are you here to help us get the gazebo put together before the front blows in? We're expecting some freezing rain and whatnot—Travis doesn't want the lumber getting warped."

Maggie crossed her arms over her chest. "Oh, he wants everybody to help, does he?"

Alice shifted her bag to her other shoulder. "Of course! And everybody seems happy to do it. Travis even brought tamales."

Travis, Travis, Travis.

"That sounds nice," Maggie said through gritted teeth. "Claire and I were just going to check out a book, and I see we're too late so—"

The Jeep shook as Claire's door slammed.

"Where are you going?"

Claire shrugged. "Travis brought tamales."

"What book did you need?" Alice asked, opening Maggie's door.

Maggie's mind drew a blank. "What are you reading for book club?"

Alice bounced on the balls of her feet. "Are you coming to book club? We're reading *Bound and Determined,* Reyn Taylor's latest. It's just delightful—"

"Isn't she a romance author?" Maggie asked. She didn't think she'd ever read a romance novel.

"Yes, she is." Alice glanced around to see if anyone was listening and then whispered, "A dirty one. The genre is erotica."

"Sign us up!" Claire said.

"Wait—no—"

"We have one left and I'll put it on hold," Alice said. "Can you two share?"

"That won't be necessary—"

"You bet we can," Claire said with a wink at Maggie. Then she whispered, "I'm just going to read the dirty parts."

"Oh, goodie," Alice squealed, clapping her hands. "We could use some fresh blood. Between you and me, Miss

Mills isn't going to last much longer. Of course, we've been saying that for twenty years."

"Miss Mills is reading erotica?"

"Yes. When she's not teaching Sunday school at First Baptist."

Maggie snorted.

"This evening she's helping Travis by handing him nails—and no doubt a bit of heavenly advice—while he hammers on the gazebo."

The waver in Alice's voice and the red splotches creeping up her neck said she very much approved of Travis Blake's hammering skills.

The three of them walked up the sidewalk to the reading garden behind the library. Sure enough, Miss Mills sat as stiff as a board in a folding chair next to the gazebo, holding a nail up to Travis.

Maggie cleared her throat. It was time to broach the subject of the visit. "Alice, I'm a little surprised that Travis is here. Petal Pushers has a landscaping contract with the city—"

Alice smiled and patted Maggie's arm. "And they still do. Travis offered to build the gazebo and install the play equipment for free."

Cue gag reflex.

"I got some teenagers to help him because he was planning to do it all himself. Can you believe that?"

That aggravating, bull-headed man.

"He has touched up the landscaping a bit, though. You know, just in the places where it needed it," Alice added.

Maggie bit her tongue. The landscaping did *not* need any touching up. She went by regularly. And as for the Saint Travis act—ha! He was trying to worm his way into getting the city's contract for the following year. Which would include the parks, the courthouse lawn, city hall, the public pool...

"Well, we'd love to help," Maggie said with a forced smile. Because she could work for free, too, damn it.

"We would?" Claire asked.

"Absolutely. I just need to find a hammer."

"You're not going to kill him, are you?"

"I'm not planning on it. Accidents do happen, though."

"Oh, look! Bubba and JD are here, too."

"Goodie," Maggie said.

Ping.

A text! Claire raised an eyebrow. "Is it him?"

"I don't know." Maggie clawed her way to her back pocket, spinning around like a dog chasing its tail.

"Who?" Alice asked.

"A guy Maggie is sexting."

Alice stopped in her tracks. "That kind of thing goes on in Big Verde?"

"It goes on everywhere," Maggie said. "But we're not sexting. That's ridiculous." She looked at her phone and al most dropped it.

You've been wearing those panties long enough. Take them off.

"Well?" Claire asked.

"We're sexting."

Alice tried to sneak a peek at the phone.

"Alice, can I get in the library for a minute? I need to use the restroom."

Because good girls removed their panties when the Big Bad Wolf told them to.

* * *

Ping.

Travis grinned. That was fast. "Hold on a minute," he said to Miss Mills, who held up a nail.

He'd told Little Red Riding Hood to take off her panties. The red ones she'd supposedly worn to the job site this morning. The ones he'd been thinking about all day.

He looked at his phone under Miss Mills's watchful gaze. *They're off.*

He laughed. Who knew if she'd really done it? She might not even own a pair of red panties. For all he knew, Maggie had worn boxer shorts under her jeans at work today. No matter. He didn't care what kind of underwear she wore. It was what was in them that turned him on.

Henry yanked on his shirt. "Guess who's here, Uncle Travis."

"Just a minute." He needed a few seconds to think of a response.

"You young people and your phones," Miss Mills said.

"Uncle Travis—"

"Hush, Henry."

"Is it a woman texting you, Travis?" Miss Mills asked. "I swear you're blushing beneath that beard."

Could a guy not sext without commentary from an old spinster lady and a five-year-old?

"If it's a woman, she's a hussy. Young ladies shouldn't make overtures."

"Don't be jealous, Miss Mills."

Miss Mills huffed and fanned her face with a copy of *Ladies' Daily Devotions.* Travis grinned and added, "You can't keep me all to yourself."

Miss Mills stopped fanning momentarily. "Why, I *never*—"

"Maybe you should."

"Travis Blake! You should be ashamed of yourself for talking to a Christian woman this way."

"It makes your day," Travis said. "Now if you'll just give me a moment to respond to this hussy, I'll get back to hammering your nails in a jiffy."

Miss Mills fluttered her *Ladies' Daily Devotions*, but her cheeks were pink, and one corner of her mouth curled up. She daintily poked a hairpin back in her bun while looking at Travis over her horn-rimmed glasses.

"Uncle Travis—"

"One sec, Henry."

The thought of Maggie without her panties, eagerly awaiting instructions, made it hard to think. But he needed to type something.

"Hi, Maggie," Henry shouted.

Travis nearly dropped his phone. There stood Maggie and Claire, chatting with Bubba and JD. He quickly stuffed his phone back in his pocket and took a nail from Miss Mills to look busy. He poised the hammer and pretended not to see Maggie approaching in his peripheral vision.

"Hi, Henry. Are you working hard?"

That voice. *Goddamn, it was sexy.*

"Yes, very," Henry said, even though he was stuffing a cupcake in his face.

"And what about Uncle Travis? Is he working hard?"

"Nah, he's just hammering."

"It looks hard from where I'm standing," Maggie said.

Travis missed the nail and smashed his thumb. "Jesus Christ," he said, sticking it in his mouth.

"Don't take the Lord's name in vain, Travis," Miss Mills said. "And pay attention to what you're doing."

Travis glanced at Maggie, who was grinning from ear to ear. He took in the rest of her appearance—tousled blond hair, big brown eyes—and his heart seized. Why did she have such an effect on him?

Because she's Little Red Riding Hood and you know the kind of effect you have on her.

Inexplicably, Henry threw his arms around Maggie's knees and hugged her.

"Let go, Henry," Travis said. "You're going to make Maggie fall."

Henry didn't let go. If anything, he hugged Maggie tighter.

"You're going to get chocolate on Maggie's pants."

"Oh, it's okay. These pants are already ruined," Maggie said.

She turned around, taking Henry with her, and gave Travis a truly spectacular view of her ass. It was covered in mud.

"Have you been rolling around in a pigpen, Miss Mackey?"

"Practically," she said. "Not that it's any of your business."

And that's when he saw it. A small triangle of red lacy fabric poking out of her pocket.

She'd taken her panties off. Her tiny red panties. The ones she'd worn just for him.

She saw him looking, and her face lit up like a fuse. She quickly poked the bit of fabric back in her pocket. "Allergies are awful this time of year. I carry a hankie."

If there was a person less likely to carry a red lacy hankie than Maggie Mackey, Travis couldn't think of one. Of course, he also wouldn't have bet on red lacy panties. He cleared his throat and tried to act clueless.

"Anyway," Maggie said. "I just came down here to—"

"Rip me a new one?"

Maggie's eyes grew round as she feigned innocence. "To

help with the gazebo, of course. Do you have an extra hammer?"

Those big brown eyes lined with thick, long lashes looked straight at him. His stomach did something—it felt like a flip but maybe it was a flop—as she crossed her arms and stuck out her hip.

"You're a good girl, Maggie Mackey."

The last time he'd said that, she'd been bent over a table.

"Petal Pushers takes care of the library, you know," Maggie said. "It's our account."

Ah. That's why she was here.

"Good for you."

"Not interested in sharing it."

"Not asking you to."

She sure was cute when she was defensive, territorial, and pissed as hell.

"Come on, Uncle Travis. What do you want to nail next?"

Travis grinned. He knew *exactly* what he wanted to nail next. And it must have shown on his face because Maggie's eyes widened, and her cheeks turned pink. She fluttered her eyelashes like a prissy pants. "Well, I never—"

"That makes you and Miss Mills," Travis said with a grin. *And yes, you have.*

Chapter
Fifteen

It had gotten dark over an hour ago. Maggie stretched, feeling every vertebra in her back pop, and watched Travis load his tools into his truck. "Need help with anything?"

"Nope. I got this."

I got this. If Travis had a motto, that would be it. And as much as Maggie wanted to believe he'd taken on the gazebo to steal her business, it just didn't feel that way. Travis might be a Blake, but in his case, the apple had fallen from the tree and rolled far, far away.

"I'm waiting on Claire anyway. Have you seen her?"

Travis scooped Henry up and put him on his shoulders. "I wouldn't wait around if I were you." He nodded to the parking lot between the library and the Green Giant Burger Spot, where a pickup and horse trailer was parked.

It was right beneath a streetlight, and Maggie could clearly see the silhouette of a man leaning against the trailer with one foot kicked back on a tire and one arm wrapped securely around Claire's waist.

"Who's that?" Travis asked.

"If I'm not mistaken, that's Ford Jarvis," Maggie said in amazement. Why hadn't Claire told her she was hanging out with Ford? "He's a bit of a legend around here. Reclusive cowboy born in the wrong era. He's a throwback to the days of trail rides and chuckwagons."

Hardly Claire's type.

"Did he go to school with us?" Travis asked.

This was the first time Travis had acknowledged they'd gone to school together. Did he remember her? She swallowed the lump of disappointment. She kind of liked the idea of him not remembering her as Mighty Mack from high school. If she was honest with herself, that was a big part of her attraction for the Big Bad Wolf. Well, that and a few other things...

"No. He's from..." Maggie thought for a while. She had no idea where Ford was from. "He just showed up. Ranchers hire him when they need work that can only be done on horseback."

Travis perked up. "He's one of the Rancho Canada Verde cowboys?"

The cowboys who worked for Gerome Kowalski, Claire's daddy, worked cattle on horseback, not with ATVs or helicopters like other big ranches.

"I don't think he's a full-time employee. Claire says he comes in to help with roundups, but he travels all over Texas doing contract cowboying."

"Wow," Travis said, wide-eyed like a little boy. Maggie couldn't help but grin when he added, "Cool."

"Have you ever been on a horse, Travis?"

Travis frowned. "Just because I wasn't born in Big Verde doesn't mean I've never been on a horse."

"Just so you know, I was born and raised here, and I've

never been on a horse," she said. "I didn't mean anything by it. How many horses do you have?"

"We don't got no horses," Henry said.

"We don't have any horses," Travis corrected.

Henry, still perched on Travis's shoulders, yanked on one of his ears. "That's what I said."

Travis winced, but didn't do what Maggie would have done, which was put the little toot down.

"I had a horse as a kid," Travis said. His eyes turned wistful. "For one glorious summer."

"What happened to him?"

"My dad lost him in a bet," Travis said with a shrug.

"Oh, Travis. I'm so sorry…"

He smiled. "It's okay. It was a long time ago. And thanks for your help tonight. I guess Henry and I need to get going."

He hoisted Henry off his shoulders and plopped him into his car seat. Henry started to struggle and whine immediately. "I don't want to be buckled in! It huuuurts. I can't breathe! I can't move!"

Travis grunted and struggled to keep Henry in the car seat. "You're moving just fine. Settle down."

"No!" Henry yelled. Then he kicked the headrest of the seat in front of him.

Travis let go and rubbed his temples while Henry appeared to melt and slide halfway out of the seat. "I'm all out of tricks, kid. With Maggie standing right here, it's not like I can hold you upside down by your ankles."

Henry responded by jerking his body into a rigid imitation of one of the two-by-fours in the bed of Travis's truck. From jelly to rigor mortis in under two seconds. It would be hard to get him strapped in like that, and Maggie was beginning to see the logic in hanging him upside down.

"I want to ride up front like a big boy."

"You can't," Travis snapped.

Maggie had an idea. "Henry, do you like basketball?" He was wearing a San Antonio Spurs jersey, so it was a pretty safe bet.

"Yeah. Do you?"

"Of course! And the Spurs are playing tonight. First game of the season. It's on television. I bet you can still catch it if you hurry and get in your car seat."

"That's right," Travis said, giving her a look of utter gratitude as Henry resumed a normal posture and allowed himself to be buckled in.

"Can we watch it with Maggie?"

Whoa. She hadn't seen that coming. Surely Travis wouldn't want to.

"It's fine with me," Travis said.

Maggie's stomach began fluttering. It was annoying.

"I'm sorry," Travis said. "Awkward."

"No! It's fine. Really." Was it? Her hands were sweaty.

"Okay. I'll bring the leftover tamales to snack on. What's your address?"

They were meeting at *her place?* And why did he need her address when they were neighbors? Who did he think had been leaving him the slightly salty notes on his gate— the ones she may, or may not, possibly be regretting right about now?

"Are you sure it's okay?" Travis asked, probably sensing her hesitation because she was doing some serious hesitating. "JD said something about meeting you and Bubba at Tony's. I don't want to keep you from that."

She tried to organize her facial features into some semblance of normal as she pondered possible strategies. *Yes, I already had plans. Sorry. Bye. Ignore the note on the gate where I threatened to summon the Chupavaca to drain your cattle of blood.*

"We kind of invited ourselves over," Travis continued. "We'll understand."

Maggie looked at Henry. If you had to stick a label on him, it would say, PERSON LEAST LIKELY TO UNDERSTAND. How could she rescind an invitation to a five-year-old? "I'd love to have you both. I live at Honey's place. On Peacock Road."

Oh Lord. Watching it dawn on Travis's face—*you're the crazy lady who's been threatening me*—was both painful and hilarious. Maggie didn't know whether to laugh or cry. She fluttered her eyelashes and waved her fingers. "Howdy, neighbor."

Travis looked at her like she'd just smashed an ax through a door and said, *Here's Johnny!*

He was about to back out. Maybe he'd fake a sudden on-set of stomach cramps. That's what she would do.

"Let's go!" Henry said. He'd clearly run out of patience. "Let's go to Maggie's *now*."

Travis rubbed his beard as if trying to decide which one of them was scarier: her or Henry. "You sure you want us to come over?"

"Yes. Don't make me beg. It's weird."

Travis raised a single eyebrow in a way that made her tummy flutter again. Like maybe he'd like to make her beg. She pretended to be interested in her feet, so he wouldn't see the blush creeping up her cheeks.

"I'm going to stop at my house and put Henry in his pajamas first," he said. "Then we'll be right over."

Nothing like mentioning a five-year-old in his pajamas to vanquish the sexual tension. If there had even been any.

"I'm not tired! And I'm not wearing pajamas."

"Really?" Maggie asked. "I'm going to wear mine."

Travis raised the other eyebrow, and Maggie's cheeks heated up again.

"They're Spurs pajamas," she said. Just in case he was imagining something else. Something sheer. Or lacy. Or... *He wasn't thinking that, Mackey. Stop it.*

Travis grinned. Dammit. That dimple on the left side just plain did it for her.

"I have Spurs pajamas, too!" Henry shouted. Like it was literally his job to keep her from having inappropriate thoughts.

"Good. You wear yours and I'll wear mine."

Henry clapped his hands.

"If you're not wearing Spurs pajamas when we get there, Henry is going to have a royal fit. And I'll be a bit disappointed myself."

"I'm a woman of my word," Maggie said, watching Travis climb behind the wheel of his truck.

"I don't doubt it," Travis said. Then he rolled down his window and stuck a GO SPURS GO flag on top of his truck.

Well, hell. She was in trouble.

* * *

The headlights illuminated the Happy Trails' gate and the note flapping in the breeze.

I live at Honey's place, she'd said. She had to know about the notes. There was no way Maggie's crazy grandmother was keeping all the cow rage to herself. Maybe Maggie thought it was funny. Travis felt like an idiot.

He got out of the truck and yanked the note off the gate.

FIX YOUR FENCE OR I'LL SUMMON THE CHUPAVACA.

He tried not to smile, which should have been easy, considering how he felt. But he had to give the old lady her due—this was funny. According to Mexican folklore, the Chupacabra was a mythical creature who sucked the blood out of *cabras*, or goats. Travis had never heard of such a thing until he'd moved in Big Verde, where at least once a year, the local newspaper featured stories about Chupacabra sightings, usually next to pictures of dead goats who'd most likely fallen victim to mountain lions. It caused a lot of chatter at the Corner Café, where farmers and ranchers laughed it off before going home and making sure their shotguns were loaded.

Honey had replaced *cabra* with *vaca*, the Spanish word for *cow*. Probably thought she was clever.

Having to face Honey Mackey on her own turf with her feisty granddaughter as backup on the very night she'd literally threatened to drain his cattle of blood didn't sound like fun. What if tonight wasn't about basketball, but an ambush?

"Are we at Maggie's?" Henry asked.

Travis sighed. "Not yet. We're home. Let's get you in your PJ's."

Maggie wouldn't ambush a five-year-old. He was being paranoid.

The thought of her in San Antonio Spurs basketball PJ's—possibly plotting an ambush—made him grin, though. It also gave him an idea, and before he knew it, he was sending a text.

* * *

The wind kicked up, stirring Maggie's wind chimes into hysteria. She pulled her shoes off on the back porch just as the screen door slammed with a wham. She banged them together, shaking off the dried mud, and hightailed it inside to get the wood-burning stove going. The house was still warm, but it would be chilly within the hour.

A smile tugged at her lips as she lit the kindling. She was

glad she'd helped with the gazebo. It felt good, and she'd enjoyed working with Travis.

She added some logs and sat cross-legged on the floor, watching them catch flame. No matter how handsome Travis was, or how noble or perfect or adorable, she couldn't be sucked in. It would cloud her judgment, and she needed to protect her business. Despite what her mother might think about her decision to move back to Big Verde—*you'll waste away at Honey's flower shop until you marry some small-town man with a small-town mind and start having his small-town babies*—Maggie was on the road to success. She'd used her degree to turn Honey's beloved flower shop into a real business. She was building an impressive portfolio. One of her projects had even been featured in *Better Homes and Gardens*. By Big Verde's standards, she was a freaking rock star and had thus far not been approached by a single small-town man about making babies. *So there.*

And that was fine with her. Mostly. Maybe she was just one of those women who only needed fulfilling work, good friends, and a sexting relationship with a guy in a wolf mask. There were probably lots of women like that, right?

The fire popped, bringing her back to the issue at hand, which was getting ready for company. What did "in a little while" mean? She was filthy and needed a shower. She stood up with a groan and headed for the bathroom, just as her phone pinged.

Wear sexy lingerie tonight. I'll be thinking of you.

She didn't own any sexy lingerie, but even if she did, she could hardly wear it tonight with company coming. And anyway, she'd promised Henry she'd wear her Spurs PJ's.

She decided to respond honestly.

No can do. Having company.

Are you seeing another wolf?

Ha! Hardly.

Believe it or not, it's a man who's trying to ruin my business.

She waited a few minutes, but the wolf didn't text back, so she hopped in the shower. What had she expected? That her anonymous sexting buddy would want to have a deep and meaningful conversation about her job insecurity? He didn't know she worked in a male-dominated industry. He could never understand the scrutiny she underwent every single time she bid on a large job, just because she was a woman. She could handle the ribbing and jabbing and jokes at her expense. It was the lack of confidence that men—and women!—expressed in her ability to do the job because of her gender that really got her hackles up. She had to work twice as hard, and often for less money, to prove herself.

It wasn't Travis's fault that Anna had hired him to do a job he wasn't qualified for. But he should have turned it down. Or at least accepted some help.

After a super quick rinse off, she felt blindly around for her towel, shivering the entire time. It took only about twelve seconds before she was zipped up into her warm San Antonio Spurs footsie pajamas. Then she swiped at the foggy mirror with her hand and towel-dried her hair.

Ready for company.

She checked her phone to see if the wolf had texted back—he hadn't—and padded down the chilly hallway to check on the wood-burning stove. It was going gangbusters.

Note to self: Wolf just wants to talk dirty. No more personal revelations.

Travis was bringing tamales; but shouldn't she at least offer some chips and dip or something? She opened the refrigerator and stared for the obligatory five seconds before moving on to the pantry. It was a bust. All she had to offer were stale crackers and an expired carton of yogurt. She was a horrible hostess.

Pop started yapping. Maggie peeked out the window above the sink to see headlights coming up the lane.

"Settle down, Pop. It's just company."

Other than Claire or JD, Pop wasn't much used to company. He tilted his head as if considering what she'd said. Then he began yapping and growling again. He really got going when the headlights hit the house.

"Hush up, Pop. Do I look scared? It's not a serial killer. It's just Travis Blake."

Yap!

"Coming to our house."

Yap!

"Because that's not weird at all."

Yap!

She stepped onto the screened-in porch with Pop running circles at her feet as the truck pulled to a stop. It took a few minutes for Travis to extricate Henry from his car seat, but then she was covered in five-year-old.

"Hi, Maggie!"

Pop stopped barking to actively sniff the hell out of Henry. That turned to enthusiastic licking, which broke Henry out in a rash of giggles.

"Look, Uncle Travis. She still gots her dog!"

"She still *has* her dog."

"I know. That's what I said."

Travis sighed and smiled at Maggie. He wore a big wooly green sweater. *And glasses.* She hadn't expected those. Combined with his longish black hair and scruffy dark beard, it made him look like Rustic Outdoorsy Guy Who Likes to Read. She approved.

"You look nice in glasses."

Travis paused at the compliment, and then smiled. "My contacts were bothering me." He lifted his glasses and rubbed his eyes. "Cold fronts get me every time."

"Does your dog have a name?" Henry asked.

"It's Pop."

Travis eyed her Spurs basketball pajamas, took a closer look at Pop, and proclaimed, "I see the resemblance."

"Did you just insinuate that I look like my dog?"

"No. I insinuated your dog looks like Greg Popovich."

Greg Popovich was the head coach of the Spurs. And Travis had successfully noted the resemblance between him and the little blue-haired bulldog. "Impressive," Maggie said.

"It's the stubby silver hair and the, no offense, face only a mother could love."

Maggie laughed and picked Pop up, petting him between the ears. "Don't call my dog ugly."

"So, are you a real fan or just one of those girls who wears NBA lingerie and names her dog after Greg Popovich to attract guys?"

"Aw...you nailed it. I'm just trying to attract guys. I know nothing about sportsball."

"I bet you know more about it than I do."

Henry looked nosily through the open door to where Maggie's television glowed. "Let's go inside. I want to watch the game."

Travis came up the steps and reached over her head to hold the door open. He smelled good, like woods and sunshine.

How had this even happened? She took the bag of tamales from him and went into the house, where Henry was already rolling around the floor with Pop. Their relationship status had gone from Mortal Enemies to Comfy Pajamas Complicated in one afternoon.

Chapter

Sixteen

❦

Travis looked around the old farmhouse. Although he didn't see Honey Mackey—hopefully she was infirm and bedridden—evidence of her was everywhere. Gingham curtains, those ugly lace things that went beneath lamps, and about a zillion salt and pepper shakers shaped like roosters.

Maggie caught him. "It's my grandmother's house."

"Oh, I know. I just didn't realize you lived here, too."

Maggie looked at him quizzically. "I live here alone. I moved in after Honey passed away."

He was confused. And then it dawned on him. Miss Mary Margaret aka Little Red Riding Hood aka the Chupavaca Summoner had been leaving him the nasty notes.

She looked up at him with an angelic smile.

He folded his arms. "Sorry to hear about Honey."

"I'm surprised you didn't know, small towns being what they are."

"I haven't been back very long. And everybody still refers to this property as Honey Mackey's place."

Maggie nodded. "And they will still be referring to it as Honey Mackey's place a hundred years from now. Just like that drugstore on the corner is still called Harmon's, even though the Harmon's sign is long gone, and it's owned by a chain. You could say we're a little resistant to change."

"No kidding." Travis bet Honey's underwear was still in a drawer somewhere in the house. A mug on the counter said, WORLD'S GREATEST GRANDMA. Travis picked it up. It had about an inch of cold, stale coffee in it. "Unless Honey died last week, I'd say you're resistant to change."

Maggie stared down at her hands quietly.

Dammit! He was no good at making jokes. Especially ones about somebody's *dead* grandmother.

Maggie sniffled. "Actually..."

Oh, no. No, no, no, no. Her grandmother had *not* died a week ago.

Maggie sniffed again.

Jesus Christ. Maybe she had.

Maggie's pink cheeks slowly deepened to scarlet red. Her lips trembled, her eyes brimmed with tears, and it took everything Travis had not to turn around and fling himself out the window. This was worse than when he'd asked a nonpregnant lady when her baby was due. When would he learn to engage his brain before his mouth? No wonder Maggie had been so ornery. She was grieving a fresh loss.

"I'm so sorry. I didn't know."

Maybe Henry would barf now—he sometimes did that for no reason whatsoever—and they could make a hasty retreat.

Maggie covered her face with her hands. Her shoulders began to shake.

Instead of fleeing, Travis gathered her in his arms. And

even though everything about the scenario was mortifying, a party had started in his pants. He kept the necessary three inches between it and Maggie, so she wouldn't get the invitation. "There, there," he said stiffly. "It'll be okay. I have a horrible sense of humor."

For some reason, the sound of his voice seemed to unleash the beast. Maggie's shoulders shook so hard she rocked them both. He held on tightly as the first sob came. It cut through his bones and went straight into his heart. "Shhh…"

"Why are you lovin' on Maggie?" Henry asked.

When had Henry come into the kitchen? "Her grannie just died, Henry."

"Then why is she laughing?"

"She's not laughing—"

Travis loosened his hold as Maggie's sobs turned into howls. Travis held her at arm's length and stared into her face, which was distorted from *laughing*. Tears streamed down her cheeks.

Henry started to laugh, too, even though he had no idea what was going on. Laughter was contagious. In fact, Travis felt a little something stirring up, but he did his best to squash it.

"What's so funny?" Henry asked between giggles.

"Your uncle," Maggie wheezed to Henry. "God. He's gullible."

"Okay, so I fell for it," Travis said. "Big deal."

"Uncle Travis, do you have your feelings hurt?"

Now he felt even sillier. "Nah, it was a good joke." He'd love to make a joke about how the Big Bad Wolf was currently in Little Red Riding Hood's grandmother's house. What would Maggie's reaction be? He tried to imagine it. She'd be shocked. Embarrassed. Mortified, most likely. And he'd have to explain why he hadn't said anything sooner.

It was just one more thing he'd put off, and now it seemed too late. It was like when someone called you by the wrong name and you didn't correct them, and before you knew it, it was past the point of awkward, so you just pretended to have a new name.

It would be fine. Once the ranch sold and Henry was settled, he and Big Verde—and Maggie—would part ways. In the meantime, he should probably stop sexting her.

"Good," Henry said decidedly. Then he looked at Maggie. "Because it's not nice to hurt people's feelings."

Maggie rolled her eyes. "His feelings aren't hurt. Want some hot cocoa, pookie?"

"Yes, ma'am!" Henry said.

"I was talking to Uncle Pookie, but you can have some, too."

Maggie kicked a small stool over to the kitchen counter, while Travis glanced awkwardly around. Was Honey Mackey really deceased? Maggie had said she was, but she'd also indicated the woman was freshly in her grave, which obviously wasn't the case. Was the joke that Honey hadn't died recently? Or that she hadn't died at all? And who joked about dead grannies? Travis cleared his throat. "We're not disturbing your grandmother, are we?"

"God, I hope not," Maggie said. "She's been dead for nearly a year."

Okay. So that answered his question. Maggie Mackey joked about dead grannies. While wearing Spurs pajamas in a house full of rooster knickknacks. A grin took over Travis's face, and he realized he kind of liked twisted girls. Or at least he liked this one.

Maggie winked, but pain creased her forehead and her smile trembled. Honey Mackey was definitely dead, and her granddaughter, whacked sense of humor notwithstanding, was heartbroken.

"Were you close?"

"She was my best friend."

"That's pretty close," Travis said. "I'm sorry you've lost her."

"Thanks." Maggie looked down at her hands, took a breath as if she had something else to say, "She was the only person who truly believed in me."

Who wouldn't believe in this sexy dynamo of a woman? While Travis searched for something to say, Maggie turned away and opened the cabinet above her head. "Honey would have loved the little joke I just pulled on you." She stood on her tiptoes and still couldn't quite reach whatever it was she was looking for. "We had identical senses of humor."

"That's horrifying," Travis said. He walked up behind Maggie. "What are you looking for? I can get it."

Maggie came down to her heels just as he reached over, gently bumping into her. He backed up quickly, but the response of his dick had been swift. He now stood behind a grown woman in footsie pajamas in a dead lady's kitchen—with a raging hard-on.

"Oops," Maggie said. "Watch what you do with that thing."

"Excuse me?"

"You're gripping a cast iron skillet. I'm pretty sure my grandmother used it to kill my grandfather."

"Really?" Henry asked.

"No," Maggie said. "Another joke." She looked at Travis and whispered, "Somebody's as gullible as his uncle."

Travis let go of the skillet. He hadn't even known he'd grabbed the damn thing.

"The saucepan behind it," Maggie said. "That's what I need to heat the milk in."

"Got it." He handed Maggie the pan.

"Do you have whipped cream that squirts out of a can?" Henry asked.

Maggie set the pan on the stove and went to the refrigerator. "I might. Let's see."

Travis let out a low whistle at the sight of two bottles of beer, some ketchup, and a half gallon of milk. "That's some stock you've got there. Sure you're not a guy?"

Maggie frowned. Had he said something wrong? *Again?*

"Not a guy," she said with a sigh. "But thanks for asking."

He kept his mouth shut for fear of what might fly out next, and because the sight of her bending over looking in the fridge stunned him speechless. His penis kept hopping to attention like Maggie was a five-star general. He knew what they'd done together...

And she didn't.

"Ah ha! Look what I found, boys." She held up a white can with a spout in triumph. "Whipped cream."

Travis tried—and failed—not to think about all the places he'd like to put that whipped cream.

Maggie slammed the door shut with her hip, squinting at the can. "And it only expired two months ago. This is practically straight from the cow."

"I don't think that's ever seen a cow," Travis said.

Henry licked his lips. "Squirt some in my mouth, Maggie!"

"No, Henry. That's not a good—"

"Party pooper," Maggie said, breezing past him with the nozzle aimed at Henry's mouth. The unmistakable sound of the depressed tip of a whipped cream can came next, followed by hysterical giggles. Travis tried not to grin. Somebody had to be the grown-up.

"Go see what the score is, Henry," Maggie said, nodding at the television. "I'll bring the plates in."

"We can eat on the couch?"

"Where else would we eat on game night? Travis, grab those TV trays, would you?"

TV trays. The woman ate on TV trays while watching basketball and doing weird shit with whipped cream. She was a dream come true.

* * *

Maggie couldn't believe that she was sitting on the sofa sipping hot cocoa with Travis while the Spurs creamed the Mavericks. Henry sat between them, his little head already nodding. She pulled him in for a snuggle, and he curled right up.

A commercial came on. "I think Henry's asleep," she said, muting the television.

It was already the fourth quarter. The game would be over in a few minutes. Travis probably wanted to get home and put Henry to bed.

"Did Honey raise you?"

"Not initially. But when I started high school, my mom took off for Los Angeles. She's an artist, or at least that's how she sees herself. Big Verde stifled her creativity. She wanted me to come along, but even at fourteen I knew I didn't want that life. I'm a small-town girl at heart, which my mother finds terribly disappointing. Small towns, small minds, she used to say."

"You went off to A&M, didn't you?"

She raised an eyebrow.

"LinkedIn," he said. "Every time I tried to solicit business in town, I was told Petal Pushers had the account. I got curious. Had to scope out my competition."

"Stalker. And yeah, I did an internship at a landscape architect firm after graduation—"

"Vector."

She paused. "Seriously. You're a stalker. Anyway, it was a lot of sitting around behind a desk. I hated it. I decided to make a go of it here. I prefer sunshine to desks."

"Sunshine looks good on you."

She wasn't super adept at picking up social signals, but was that a flirtatious statement? It sounded like it. But what if she was wrong, and her ears were glowing for no reason at all? Travis was unbelievably hot, and surely, he knew that. What would he be flirting with her for? It hadn't been half an hour since he said, *Sure you're not a guy?*

Lord knew Travis wasn't the kid he'd been in high school—that skinny, short boy who'd helped her clean up the cow patty mess...Although when she looked in those blue eyes behind the lenses of his glasses, it was obvious at least part of him was still that sweet boy.

"I recognized you as soon as I saw you tonight," she blurted.

Travis sat up and inhaled sharply, as if bracing himself for an onslaught of high school memories. "I was going to tell you," he stuttered. "I wasn't sure you'd recognized me with the beard, and I thought maybe it was best to just not say anything. It's kind of embarrassing, isn't it?"

"High school is *supposed* to be embarrassing," she said. "It was the glasses that gave you away."

"High school?"

"Ho Ho Ho Green Giants!" She winced. That had come out of nowhere with comedic timing.

Travis stared at her as if she were performance art. Maybe she was. "Do you recognize me?" she asked.

He frowned at her. "Is this a trick question?"

"Aw, you don't, do you? Does a cow patty cleanup outside a locker ring a bell?"

Travis looked beyond confused. His blue eyes searched hers, and she did her best to look like fourteen-year-old

Maggie, which wasn't nearly as difficult as it should have been. Then his eyes widened, and a huge grin broke out on his face. "I do remember you! I knew we'd gone to school together, but you were a couple of years behind me. And I really didn't have any friends..."

He blushed, and it broke her heart.

"Anyway, you were the Future Farmers of America girl that hung out with all the redneck boys."

"I think that's what it says beneath my unfortunate yearbook photo."

"You had a nickname. What was it?" He rubbed his beard.

"Mighty Mack," she said. "And I'm trying really hard to outgrow it."

His eyes left hers and traveled down her face to the rest of her, and even though she was wearing what amounted to a blanket with a zipper, his voice deepened, and he said, "Oh, I'd say you've outgrown it. There is nothing remotely childish about you, Maggie Mackey."

Maggie could swear her ears were bathing the room in a rosy glow.

Travis's eyes worked their way back up to her lips, where they settled, making Maggie's heart pound in her chest. "I recognize you," he whispered.

All he'd said was that he recognized her. But it felt as if he'd said, *You're mine.*

Maggie cleared her throat. "I never said thank you for helping me that day."

Travis moved closer. They were practically nose to nose. His lips smelled like cocoa. They'd probably taste like it, too, but Maggie didn't have the guts. Instead, she kissed him sweetly on the cheek. "Thank you."

"You're welcome," he whispered. Then he gave her a feathery soft kiss on the lips.

He did taste like cocoa. Maggie didn't want him to pull away, so she parted her lips in invitation, and Travis accepted. With a quiet groan that nearly caused Maggie to come undone, Travis slipped his tongue between her lips. There was nothing feathery soft about the kiss now. His hand came up her back and settled at the base of her skull. She hadn't been kissed this way since her night with the wolf, and it awakened every cell in her body. This man who'd taunted her with his tattooed chest, his dimpled grin, and his endless blue eyes was now kissing her as if she were the best-tasting thing since chocolate ice cream. As if he wanted to devour her—*just like the wolf had.* She'd give anything to feel Travis's lips on her neck, trailing down to her breasts and maybe even lower. The only thing between her and Nirvana was the zipper on her PJ's.

Travis's beard was rough and soft all at the same time. It scratched and tickled—a delightfully wicked combination. She'd never kissed a man with a beard before. It was foreign and exciting, but somehow comforting, too. She brushed the side of his face with her fingers before tangling them in his wavy hair. With her other hand she toyed with the tag of the zipper at her neck. Should she do it?

A sensation of warmth spread across her upper thigh and soaked the leg of her pajamas.

She broke the kiss instantly, gasping in horror. They'd forgotten all about poor little Henry!

"What's wrong?" Travis asked.

"I think Henry wet himself."

Travis looked like he might say, "Henry who?" but then his eyes widened. "Holy shit."

Henry yawned and stretched. "Did the Spurs win?"

Maggie had no idea who had won the game, and from the dazed look on Travis's face, neither did he.

Chapter

Seventeen

❧

Travis collapsed on the couch and looked around in defeat. The place was hardly a model home under the best of circumstances, but after a bout of Hurricane Henry, it was a disaster. Spilled cereal under the table. An upturned laundry basket of clothes. All the couch cushions, save the one Travis was sitting on, dumped on the floor.

And it was only eight o'clock in the morning.

When he'd finally dragged Henry to the breakfast table, he'd discovered they were out of the little tyrant's favorite cereal. The socks Henry liked were dirty. The toothpaste wasn't the right flavor. By the time Travis had shoved Henry onto the bus, he felt like he'd been through the ringer.

Ping!

He looked at his phone and grinned. Hey wolfie. Cat got your tongue?

Close call last night. He thought for sure she'd recognized him as the wolf. It was an odd moment. Part of him had been relieved. He was ready for the deception to end, for Maggie to know the truth, and *choose him anyway*. He should ignore the text. Why make it worse? Maybe because making things worse was his specialty...

Just can't stop thinking about my tongue, can you?

He didn't like being deceptive. But Jesus, she thought he was trying to ruin her business. Other than Anna splitting her project between the two of them, what business had he officially stolen? He just had a few piddly-assed small businesses as clients. Although come to think of it, piddly-assed small businesses made up the overwhelming majority of Big Verde's business community. Had he inadvertently stolen clients from Maggie?

He'd stolen clients from Maggie.

Shit. He hadn't meant to fuck with her life. He'd finally met someone he really liked, and she thought he was out to ruin her. He doubted she'd take kindly to him being a lying dog—literally—on top of it.

He'd kissed her.

Thinking about it gave him a rush. If it hadn't been for Henry, they might have made out like teenagers for hours. Maybe they'd have done more than make out. He knew what was hidden inside that shapeless mass of fuzzy fabric Maggie had worn, and he'd wanted nothing more than to pull down its zipper and run his hands all over her smooth, warm skin.

You've got a pretty nice tongue.

A dumb smile took over his entire face. What did Miss Mary Margaret think about last night? Maybe he could get her to fess up.

How was your evening? You entertained the enemy. Refused to wear sexy lingerie.

What would she say? That she'd made out like a fiend with the guy she thought was ruining her business?

It was okay. He's a nice guy.

A nice guy? There were probably worse things than being a nice guy. Like being a lying bastard business-stealer who'd had sex with an unsuspecting business-maiden in a garden shed.

Should I be jealous?

He wanted her to say yes, that she was completely hot for the guy she was with last night.

He's no alpha dog.

Travis laughed, even though it was a slap in the face. How could he be jealous of the wolf when he *was* the wolf? Being both the alpha dog who made Maggie do dirty things and the nice guy who brought his nephew over for hot cocoa was emotionally confusing, to say the least.

But nice guy or not—I need to shut him down.

Travis raised an eyebrow. She wanted to shut him down? Irritation crept up his spine, along with a healthy dose of respect.

The back door slammed. Mrs. Garza wasn't supposed to come today, but Travis's nose picked up garlic, onions, and cumin. Not only had Mrs. Garza come on a day she wasn't expected, she'd brought food. His stomach growled as he went into the kitchen.

He smiled. Even with her jet-black hair teased high on her head, Mrs. Garza couldn't be much more than five feet tall. Today's outfit was a zebra-striped pantsuit, complete with a rhinestone-encrusted cane hooked casually over one arm.

"I brought you *carne guisada* and homemade tortillas. And I brought in the mail. It looks like nobody's done that for a few days. The box was overflowing."

"Thank you. The food smells delicious. I didn't realize you were coming today." He glanced at the huge stack of mail on the counter with dread, and then sighed and started thumbing through it. Magazines and other things addressed to Lisa, flyers…nothing from the Army. And finally, on the very bottom, a pink envelope from the tax office. He'd open it later when he had some privacy.

"I need to clean up a bit before Albert gets here."

Travis scratched his head. "Albert?"

"My cousin." She opened the foil-wrapped tortillas and a cloud of steam escaped. "He was supposed to paint the Janskys' house today, but they're not quite ready for him. He's going to work here instead."

"Today?" Panic. The place was trashed. "He's going to paint the interior today?"

"He'll at least get started on it. And my brother, Beto, is happy to process the beef if he can keep half of the cow. Plus the head, of course."

"The head?"

"*Barbacoa*. His is the best."

"He can have whatever he wants."

Mrs. Garza pushed him aside with her cane as she reached for a plate. "You'll eat some of this now, *sí?* I can hear your stomach grumbling. But save some for tonight. Henry will need dinner."

"Yes, ma'am."

She walked into the living room. "What happened in here?"

"Henry didn't want to go to school today."

"I'll clean up this mess. You make your taco."

She bent over to pick up a couch cushion from the floor. Travis rushed to snatch it up, fearing she'd topple on top of it. He set the couch cushion in place and gestured for Mrs. Garza to have a seat, but she spotted the cereal under the coffee table and headed for the broom in the corner.

"No, ma'am," Travis said. "You have a seat and I'll take care of that."

Mrs. Garza stopped and raised one of her eyebrows, which was quite a feat since it was painted on and already arched just below her hairline. "Did you say no to me?"

Travis swallowed. "Sorry, ma'am." He got her the broom and she briskly swept the tiny pieces of cereal into a pile.

"Go eat," Mrs. Garza said, shuffling to the trashcan to empty the dustpan.

"Maybe after I'm showered. I'm running late for work."

"Go on, then," Mrs. Garza said. "You get in the shower and I'll fix your tacos and warm up a plate."

"Oh, no, really. You don't have to—"

"Are you saying no to me again?"

Travis knew when he'd been beat. He went upstairs to the bathroom, took off his clothes, and got in the shower. Turned out it was the right thing to do. The stress of the morning dissipated under the rhythmic pounding of the showerhead.

He needed to tell Maggie he wasn't planning to remain in Big Verde. She'd probably be relieved to know he had no plans to take over her evil landscaping empire.

He shouldn't keep texting her. But it was fun. And so damn hot. Even as his mind pondered the depressing reality of his current predicament, his hand wandered down to the pressing, aching need that had risen in response. He closed his eyes and teased up an image of Maggie's sweet ass bent over the workbench in the shed. The bows on the backs of her red stockings had driven him wild. He gripped his cock, thinking about what she'd tasted like when he'd licked the bare skin of her thighs all the way up to her hot little—

The bathroom door opened. *Dammit, Henry.*

But Henry was at school. Travis frantically poked his head out of the shower curtain. "Mrs. Garza? What the—"

"Don't mind me, *mijo*," she said, standing in the steam like a zebra-striped apparition. "I'm collecting dirty towels, so I can start a load of laundry."

He was naked. Mrs. Garza was two feet away from him. And he still had his dick in his hand. Flustered, he let go and made sure the shower curtain wasn't gaping. "You don't need to do that," he said. "I can get to it later."

Mrs. Garza opened the laundry hamper and bent over, a vision that chased away any lingering fantasies involving Little Red Riding Hood. "It looks like later never comes around here. I'm happy to help."

Mrs. Garza grunted as she stood up, arms overflowing with towels, socks, and underwear.

"Thank you," he said with a feeble smile, hoping she'd quickly be on her way.

"Don't worry about getting this load in the dryer," she said, turning toward the door. "I'll do it while you're gone."

Ten minutes later, Travis blew through the back door, but then immediately screeched his heels to a halt at the sight and sounds of three men hammering and sawing right behind his house.

"Mrs. Garza!" he hollered, continuing to watch as the men climbed in and out of the mass of wood and metal that made up the long-useless cattle pens.

Mrs. Garza opened the door and poked her head out. "What is it, *mijo?*"

"Who are those men, and what are they doing?"

"Those are my cousin's sons. They're fixing up your cattle pens."

"Why?"

"Because he wants his *fajitas*," Mrs. Garza said. "That means getting a cow to the processor. Which means getting one into a trailer. And first you've got to get it into a pen."

Travis hadn't given that a bit of thought. More evidence that he had no business being a rancher. *Wait, when had he thought about being a rancher?*

He walked over and watched the men work for a few minutes. They asked him some questions, he thought about the answers, and by the time he got in his truck, he had a good idea of how to get cows into the shoot and trailer, and some plans for improving the design.

* * *

Travis pulled up to Anna's to see an entire herd of pickups parked beneath the trees. He found a spot and got out, gathering his tools from the bed of his truck.

JD stood with a group of men next to a pile of rocks. He waved his hat, inviting Travis over.

"Here's the brawn," JD said. "Where's the beauty?"

"I imagine she'll be here any minute." Travis nodded at the other men, most of whom looked vaguely familiar. That was the recurring theme since coming home to Big Verde—vaguely familiar.

"Beauty?" one of the other guys said with a smirk. "I thought you were going to say brains."

"Maggie's got both," JD said.

"I agree. She's a beauty with brains," Travis added, with a nod to JD.

"I don't think either one of you should get your hopes up," one of the guys said.

"Travis, do you remember Bill?" JD asked. "He was probably a year behind you in school. He's doing the masonry on the house."

Travis didn't remember him, but he nodded as if he did, and Bill did the same.

"I heard Maggie's a lesbian," Bill said.

"She is not," Travis and JD said together. Then they awkwardly eyed each other until Bill piped up again.

"I bet she's a virgin then."

"Definitely not," Travis and JD chorused. Then they stared each other down with what were no doubt identical expressions of surprise before Travis looked away first.

JD finally cleared his throat. "Bill, not every woman who turns your ugly ass down is a lesbian or a nun."

Mark Langley, who Travis remembered because his dad had been the high school principal, laughed heartily. "That's true," he agreed. "Unless ninety percent of the women in Big Verde are lesbians or nuns."

"Aw, fuck off," Bill said. "And I've never even hit on Maggie. I just have a very sensitive gay-dar. I mean, have you seen the way she dresses? Lesbian all the way."

"She dresses like a landscaper," JD said. "Stop stereotyping."

"Well, I've never seen her with a man," Bill said, crossing his arms as if that decided it.

JD yanked the brim of his hat down. "You obviously weren't at Anna's gala."

Mark Langley glanced around and lowered his voice. "I was there. She sure wasn't dressed like a landscaper that night."

Travis didn't like this one bit. The whole scene put a bad taste in his mouth. And as for how Maggie dressed, these were the kind of guys who catcalled. How was she supposed to dress? Who could blame her for wanting to be taken seriously?

JD stirred, and his fists were clenched. "She was Little Red Riding Hood at the gala. And I'd better not ever run into that wolf."

Travis broke out in a light sweat and pretended to squish a bug with the toe of his boot, keeping his face lowered because he figured it was fucking on fire.

"Who was that guy?" Mark asked.

"I have no idea," JD said. "I asked around, but nobody knew."

"You got a thing for Maggie?" Mark asked JD. "You guys more than friends?"

Bill, who Travis liked less and less by the second, broke out in hysterical laughter. "Are you kidding? JD here could have any woman he wants. Why would he be with Maggie?"

"Don't make me punch you in the face, Bill," JD said through clenched teeth.

If JD didn't do it, Travis might.

"Don't lose your shit. I'm just kidding."

It was doubtful that JD, in his pressed blue jeans and starched white shirt, ever *lost his shit*. But he could probably pack a powerful punch. The air was heavy with tension as all the men stood around worried that a fight might break out—and kind of hoping it would. But the sound of tires crunching on gravel drew their attention elsewhere.

"Speak of the devil," JD said.

The men scattered, getting busy at whatever tasks they had to do, but Travis stayed put, watching as Maggie parked. Pop sprang out the door, peed on all four tires, and then sniffed the air like he could smell the previous conversation. And it stank.

Maggie slammed the door. Then she looked up and smiled.

It was a big, genuine, beautiful smile. Her cheeks were already pink from the brisk autumn air, her light blond hair whipped around her face, and Travis nearly melted into his steel-toed boots.

Would it be weird to give her a hug? Because he wanted her body pressed against his in a bad way. Pop ran up, wagging his stubby tail, so Travis bent over and gave him a good rub.

"Did you have a hard time getting Henry up this morning?"

"It was awful. You're too much of a party animal for us."

"Just wait until the play-offs start. Then we're really going to party."

"Maybe I'll enlist the help of Mrs. Garza on school nights," Travis said. "That way we can watch without Henry."

Maggie raised an eyebrow. Travis grinned, put his head down, and headed for the patio. He'd just leave that there and see what Maggie did with it.

Pop barked as another car pulled up. Travis looked over his shoulder. Two young men got out of a beat-up blue pickup. He recognized one of them from last night—his name was Norbert—and waved.

"Hey, Maggie," Norbert called. "Where do you need us to start with the rocks?"

Travis stopped in his tracks. "What are they here for?"

What was it Maggie had texted? *I need to shut him down.*

"I thought you could use some help. These guys weren't doing anything today so—"

"I told you I didn't need any help."

"I know, but you really *do* need the help. You've got to be so tired, and it's no big deal to just let these guys join in. Y'all can be done by this afternoon."

Only it was a big deal. He couldn't spare any money to pay them. And he couldn't afford to get kicked off this job if Anna thought Maggie was having to help him.

He looked at the two men, who stared back in confusion. It wasn't their fault. He started for the rock mine. "Come on."

His pulse pounded in his head.

Maggie scurried along behind him, her feet scattering gravel, her breath coming in short pants. He had at least a foot on her in height, and she was no match for his long legs, so he increased his stride.

"Travis, are you mad?"

"Nope."

"Wait up. I was just trying to help."

He doubted that. She was competitive. And she'd been pouty about sharing this job from the beginning. If he didn't do something to put a stop to this, she'd have a full crew out here by next week, and he'd be out of a job.

He'd chat Anna up today. Make sure she remembered why she hired him.

Chapter

Eighteen

❦

Stop the truck!" Henry hollered as soon as Travis pulled onto Peacock Road. They were almost home, but Travis hit the brakes.

"Why?" There was nothing blocking the road. What in the world was he yelling about?

"Horse! Horse! Look, a horse!"

For a kid raised on a ranch, Henry sure had a strange re-action to seeing livestock.

Gerome Kowalski rode his chestnut mare down Peacock Road like it was the most natural thing in the world. Travis slowed down so as not to spook the animal, and Gerome waved and stopped. Travis rolled down his window.

"Howdy," Gerome said with a tilt of his straw Stetson.

"Out for a ride? It's a gorgeous day for it."

"That it is."

Gerome was an imposing figure, eyes shaded by the brim of his hat. Henry, for once, was quiet in the backseat.

Should Travis introduce himself? Surely, Gerome didn't remember—

"I haven't seen you since your daddy's funeral," Gerome said. "Have I changed as much as you have?"

"Not a bit," Travis said, flattered to be recognized. And Gerome hadn't changed much at all. Maybe a little grayer at the temples, but that was about it.

"My condolences about your sister-in-law. She was a good neighbor," Gerome said, not missing a beat. "Lilly thought highly of her, and of course, she's fond of that little man in the backseat."

"Hi, Mr. K!" Henry called out.

"Howdy, Henry. Your cows are looking good today."

"Yours, too," Henry said nonchalantly. Like it was normal for a five-year-old to discuss cattle with the owner of Rancho Canada Verde.

Gerome gazed at the front pasture of Happy Trails, and Travis wilted beneath the scrutiny. "You need to make some hay, or the cattle won't survive the winter. Manual Lopez will cut and bale it if you go in halves with him. He used to do it for Lisa."

Jesus. As big of a pain as Happy Trails was, Lisa used to manage it all herself. And here he was, not having given a single thought to what the herd would do for food for the winter. He hadn't planned to be around that long. "I'll give him a call this evening."

"And you need to thin out this herd. Sell some yearlings if you're not going to turn them into steers."

This was humiliating. Travis wanted to mumble, *Yes sir, thank you sir*, but he manned up enough to say, "Thank you for the advice."

"It'll help with your cash flow if you can sell a few."

Just when Travis thought it couldn't get any worse,

Gerome had brought up his cash flow. "How much is beef bringing right now?"

Gerome scratched his chin. "At market, I'd say these yearlings would get about a dollar a pound on the hoof."

Travis wasn't entirely sure what that meant, and it must have shown on his face, because with a barely perceptible grin, Gerome added, "They look to weigh about five to six hundred pounds each."

That was easy math. And a lot of fucking money.

"But they'll bring quite a bit more at the Texas Farmer's Market in Austin."

"Really?"

"And it's a better way to sell beef. Meeting with folks who want to know where their food comes from, selling them a healthy product you've raised while being a good steward of the earth... Well, it just feels right."

Travis's mind whirred with possibilities. It was surprising that he could make more money selling beef that way, but he trusted Gerome to know what he was talking about. "I never even considered that. And I agree, it sounds like a better way to sell beef."

"I'm going to miss it. But Canada Verde can't keep up with demand now that our focus is retail and we're the sole supplier to three big grocery chains."

Gerome wasn't bragging. Just stating facts. He stopped staring at the pasture and looked down at Travis. "Would you like our stall at the Texas Farmer's Market? You grow good grass and good cattle. Hell, thanks to your wandering bull and piss-poor fences, they're the same bloodline as my own. I'd be happy to endorse you."

Travis couldn't believe his ears. This would be a way to earn some quick cash, and well, it sounded like fun. "Mr. Kowalski, I would love nothing more than to take over your stall. Let's shake on it."

"Done," Gerome said, grasping Travis's hand in a firm shake, "You'll need a permit, but that's easy. And I'll send Claire with you to help out and show you the ropes. She loves working the market."

Henry started kicking the back of Travis's seat.

"Somebody's getting restless," Gerome said. "I'll let you two get back to your business, and I'll finish my ride."

Travis watched Gerome through his rearview mirror, literally riding off into the motherfucking sunset like a god.

Was it possible to make enough money to pay off the taxes with a stand at the farmer's market? He drove through the gate and past the cedar patch, whistling the whole way.

"Hey! Our house is clean!" Henry said as they rounded the bend.

It was only white primer, but by God, the house was painted. And yes, it did make it look cleaner. The place looked downright respectable. "It's just the primer," Travis said. "The real coat of paint hasn't even been applied yet."

"It sure looks real to me."

"Let's go see what the inside looks like." Travis didn't know which one of them was more excited, and they burst through the back door together.

"What's that smell?" Henry asked.

"Paint."

"Where's all my stuff?"

"Beneath those drop cloths." Albert had covered everything up.

Henry walked right up to a wall and put his hand on it. "Don't touch!" Travis shouted.

Henry snatched his hand back and stared at his white palm. Then he touched the wall again.

"Goddammit, Henry." Travis grabbed his tiny wrist. "I said don't touch. What the hell is the matter with you?"

Henry's bottom lip jutted out and his eyes started filling up with tears.

Here it comes.

Travis's entire body vibrated with frustration. He bit his tongue to keep from saying hurtful words. But man, they would feel glorious spilling out of his mouth. He could almost taste them.

"I don't want the house painted," Henry said. "I want everything just like it was!"

Travis started to count to ten. It was supposed to be a good idea, but for the life of him, he didn't know why. It only postponed the inevitable. "Get in the tub," he said through gritted teeth. "I'll have your supper ready when you get out."

Mrs. Garza had left tacos in the refrigerator. At least he wouldn't have to cook or feel like shit for going through a drive-thru.

"No! I don't want a bath."

Travis glared at Henry. *One, two, three...*

"You can't make me."

A dull ache began to throb behind Travis's eyes, and he brought his fingers to his temples. He was so fucking tired he could hardly move. And now he had a house full of wet paint and a five-year-old hellbent on touching every surface. And he still had forms to fill out for Henry's school and sandwiches to make for tomorrow's lunchbox. And there was the social worker to touch base with and the letters from the tax office to open—but he didn't plan on doing that without a beer.

Four, five, six...

"I want a cookie," Henry said quietly.

That was it. He'd only made it to six. "Do you know what I want, Henry?" The first words slipped out, and there was no going back. "I want to come home from work and not have to deal with a difficult little shit who isn't even mine."

Henry took a step back, as if Travis had slapped him. A wave of remorse and disgust rose immediately like bile. He'd just glimpsed the depth of his dark side, and it was fucking fathoms deep. If only he could take back those words.

Travis reached for Henry—his heart sinking—but it was too late. Henry turned away. What if he'd done irreparable damage?

"I just want things the way they were," Henry repeated with a sniffle.

Jesus. The poor kid wasn't talking about the paint. He wanted his mom, not an uncle he hardly knew who yelled and called him names. Some days were so trying that Travis had a hard time remembering how much Henry's world had been turned upside down. Travis squatted so he could look Henry in the eye. The one thing he'd longed for when his dad got drunk and said mean things was an apology. He'd never gotten one. But he could damn well give one. "I know you wish things were the way they used to be. You miss your mom, and I don't blame you. I'm sorry you're stuck with me instead. And I didn't mean what I just said. You are not a little shit. I'm tired and cranky is all. But that's no excuse for talking ugly to you, and I am deeply sorry. Can you forgive me?"

"Yes," Henry said, and his ready forgiveness somehow made Travis feel worse. "But you meant the other part."

"What part?"

"I'm not yours. That's why you don't love me."

Now it was Travis's turn to be stunned. Slapped by words. "You *are* mine. We're family, remember? Same blood running through our veins. And of course I..." It wasn't easy. He wasn't raised hearing or saying those words.

He took Henry by the shoulders. "Look at me."

Henry looked up, and it damn near broke Travis's heart. The pain in those little eyes was almost too much.

"I love you, Henry. I know you can't see it right now, especially when I'm like this, but everything I'm doing is for you. Do you understand? When we sell this place, you'll be set—"

"What does that mean?" Henry asked.

Not a good time to answer that question. "Just that we have better times ahead of us. I'm trying to do that for us, okay?"

Henry shrugged. He didn't understand. How could he?

"You say lots of bad words," Henry said.

"Sorry. I'll work on that."

"Can I say one?"

Travis couldn't squat any longer. He sat on the floor, popping his back and pulling Henry onto his lap.

"Just one. Make it good."

Henry put a finger to his chin, leaving a spot of paint, and considered which filthy word to utter. Travis felt bad that he had so many to choose from.

Henry straightened up—he'd made his decision. "I love you, too, Uncle Travis."

That wasn't what Travis had expected. "I'm happy you said that instead of a bad—"

"But sometimes you're a shit."

Travis bit the inside of his cheek to keep from laughing. When he had it under control, he solemnly said, "Thank you, Henry. I'll try harder."

"Can I have a cookie now?"

The kid knew when to strike a deal. "I'll split one with you. Then a bath."

Henry struggled out of Travis's grasp and grinned. "You need a bath, too. You stink."

Ten minutes later Travis finally popped open a beer and filled out Henry's field trip permission form. Then he wrote an e-mail to the social worker, asking if she'd had any luck locating extended family for Henry. His fingers froze when he tried to hit Send.

He'd leave it as a draft. Maybe he'd send it tomorrow.

He took a sip of beer and fingered the envelope from the tax office. Why was he so fucking afraid to open it?

Because he was an avoider and a runner, plain and simple. When things got bad, he took off. When Anna had done her stupid teenage drama bit with the stolen bracelet, he'd left Big Verde rather than stay and defend himself. When his dad got sick, he joined the Army. What if the amount owed in taxes was too much to fathom? Just the thought of it made him want to pack his bags.

Henry squealed and splashed in the tub.

He couldn't run this time. Not until he'd taken care of business.

He tore at the corner of the envelope just as his phone buzzed.

Fuck. Collect call from a third-party provider. It was Scott. Prison calls usually meant money for cigarettes or some stupid shit like that, and Travis often ignored them. But he needed to make sure Scott had signed the paperwork about selling Happy Trails. He downed his beer before answering.

"Collect call from a resident at the Texas State Penitentiary at Huntsville. Will you accept the charges?"

As usual, Travis hesitated for about seven seconds before replying that he would. The hesitation was real, he dreaded talking to Scott, and it had the bonus of making Scott nervous.

"Took you long enough," Scott said.

"Did you sign the papers about selling the ranch?"

"Whoa. No small talk? Can't I just call to talk to my little brother?"

"Not on my dime."

Henry screeched and laughed in the tub, and something tightened around Travis's heart like a noose. Would this dumb shit even ask about his kid?

"I haven't seen the papers yet. It's not like I have a butler skipping in with my mail and slippers every evening."

"Did you know we owe back taxes on this place? You said you and Lisa would take care of property taxes in exchange for living on the ranch."

"I didn't really get to live on it all that long, now did I?"

"That's your own fault. Your wife and son lived on it and somebody should have paid the taxes."

Henry and Lisa had probably never been more than a blip on the radar of Scott's self-centered universe, so Travis wasn't surprised by Scott's dismissal. "I figured Lisa would do it."

"Well, she didn't."

"Just pay it. Didn't the Army give you some money?"

"I haven't gotten my final check yet. And it probably won't be enough."

"*Probably* won't be enough? How much do we owe? Do you even know?"

Travis put his phone on speaker mode and set it down. He peeled back the corner of the envelope while sweat prickled the back of his neck. Slowly, he grasped the pink paper. He only had to pull it out about an inch before the number came into view.

"Jesus Christ. It's thirty-six thousand dollars."

"What?" Scott yelled, his voice ringing like tin through the phone's speaker.

This was more than three or four years' worth of back taxes. Their dad hadn't paid up during the final years of his life. Why hadn't Travis known anything about this?

Because you ran, dumbass. And never looked back.

"Brother, you better get your money from the Army and pay—"

"It won't be enough," Travis hissed. "How much do you think an enlisted man makes?"

"Don't you have a job waiting in Austin? Call that buddy of yours and ask for an advance."

"An advance of more than an entire year's pay? Are you kidding me?"

"Well, you'd better do something. Otherwise we'll lose the whole place. You realize that, right? But we'll both be rich if you can sell Happy Trails. Make sure it happens."

"You're going to set aside a chunk for Henry, right? This could take care of college for sure, and probably set him up pretty well with some proper investing."

There was a long pause.

"Did that social worker lady ever find a family for him?"

"You and I are his family." Poor kid.

"I'm not really daddy material—"

"No shit."

"It might be better for Henry if I just terminate my rights."

Travis let that sink in for a moment. The bastard didn't want to share his piece of the pie with his own kid. That's all it amounted to. Without another word, Travis softly touched his phone and hung up.

Chapter

Nineteen

❦

Maggie lay in her darkened room, propped up on one elbow, replaying the day in her head. It was like a stupid broken record.

She couldn't shake the look on Travis's face when he realized she'd brought Norbert and Alex to help. She should have known he'd bristle. He was stubborn and hellbent on doing everything himself.

He'd practically ignored her for the rest of the day.

He hadn't ignored Anna, though. Maggie had felt small and invisible, the total opposite from last night when the world had shrunk to just her and Travis. When she'd looked into his eyes, and it hadn't felt like remembering someone from her past. It had felt like looking into a future she hadn't seen coming but had always known existed. Those blue eyes behind the lenses of his glasses... they'd felt like *home*.

And they'd avoided looking at her all day.

But that kiss, though. It had been so hot. So sweet. And it had sent familiar shockwaves coursing through her body, which had initially cried, *Wolf!* But she hadn't needed a sexy costume to get a rise out of Travis. Unlike the wolf, who wanted a fantasy in fishnets, Travis had desired *her*.

Until today.

She rolled over, getting twisted up in her nightie, before flopping onto her back, lifting her ass, and dragging the hem back down where it belonged. She'd bought the stupid thing—black and lacy—at Cathy's Closet in town. Cathy had been curious, and Maggie had told her it was a gift for a shower. She'd been too embarrassed to admit it was for herself. That she'd bought it because the Big Bad Wolf had asked her to wear sexy lingerie last night, and the truth was, she hadn't had any.

Now it was serving as a torture device. She'd never get to sleep tonight, not with her nightgown trying to kill her.

She eyed the nightstand drawer. Five minutes with her silver bullet vibe —endearingly nicknamed Mr. Tatum—would take care of at least some of her restlessness. She slid open the drawer and dug around. Aha! He was hiding beneath *Bound and Determined*, the paperback she'd checked out for book club. She'd barely started the silly thing, and book club was next week. She squinted at the cover—a woman's near-naked ass and bound wrists. She might as well read it since she would soon be forced into idle chitchat about it. Maybe it would take her mind off things.

Leaving Mr. Tatum behind for Plan B, she pulled out the book, leaned back, and opened it to page twenty-seven, which she'd dog-cared. There were probably library rules against dog-earing pages, so she tried to un-dog-ear it by bending the corner back the other way. This made the whole situation worse, possibly permanent, and she'd just flunked book club with what the other readers would consider a crime against humanity.

With one more fluff of the pillow, she began to read:

Celeste didn't have time to ponder her predicament or how she'd managed to land herself in Ethan's bedroom. She needed to talk her way out of this, and she needed to do it quickly. She wasn't some drunken sorority girl who couldn't look out for herself. She was Celeste Harrington, CEO of Harrington Inc.

"Ethan, I demand you take these handcuffs off this very minute."

"Or what?" Ethan said, easy smile on his lips, as if he didn't have a care in the world. As if he didn't have to return to work the next morning, hoping he still had a job as Celeste's assistant. "Are you going to fire me?"

"I'd love nothing more than to fire your ass," she spat.

Ethan moved closer, but Celeste didn't flinch. "And I'd love to set fire to yours—with this paddle."

"You are so out of a job."

"Time to show you who's boss, Ms. Harrington."

Why were her panties so wet?

Surprisingly, Maggie related to that question. The book was effective. Unless, of course, you were trying to go to sleep. She could turn to Mr. Tatum. But he wasn't much of a talker. And right now, she wanted somebody to talk to her the way Ethan talked to Celeste Harrington.

Forget Mr. Tatum. She pulled out her phone.

Full moon tonight, Wolfie. Are you in control of yourself?

She counted the seconds. When she got to ten, she picked up her book.

Ping!

She dropped the book like she'd been caught with porn. Because she basically had.

Total control. As usual.

A chill went down her spine. When it hit the end of the road, it raced back up as a thrill. She should respond with something awesome. She waited for a brilliant bit of witty banter to materialize out of thin air. It didn't, so she typed out a very clever Ha.

Her wolf responded immediately.

I'm sure you're texting me in the middle of the night because you want to discuss lunar cycles. Not because you're horny.

Her thumbs hovered, hesitating. But then she went for it.

Up late reading erotica.

The phone was silent. She'd stunned it. Shocked it. It was probably dead. Then finally, Is it a fairy tale? I like those.

A fairy tale would be convenient. But alas, Maggie was reading plain old smut.

BDSM tale.

Seconds ticked by before the wolf finally spoke up.

???

Could it be he didn't know what BDSM was? Come to think of it, Maggie didn't even know what all the letters stood for. And it wasn't as if most guys had read *Fifty Shades* or the latest issue of *Cosmopolitan*. Not that she had, either, but didn't everyone know about this currently popular kink? Time to school the wolf.

The heroine has been a very bad girl. She's bending over for a spanking.

There. That should do it. She'd spelled it out for him.

Children's book?

Or not. How was she supposed to sext with the wolf if he thought she was reading *Anne of Green Gables*?

No!

The wolf responded with a devil emoji. He'd been messing with her. Wolves do not sleep in clothes. How about LLRH?

Oh! She wouldn't even have to lie.

Black lace nightie. Very short. Very sheer.

She rubbed her legs together and waited.

I want to do some very big bad wolfish things to you.

Now they were getting somewhere.

Like what?

Discipline first. You're wearing a naughty nightie.

The wolf wasn't as naïve as he'd seemed.

It is so naughty. You can see everything.

Was she really doing this?

Like your hard nipples?

Maggie shivered. Her nipples were rock hard and rubbing against the lace.

Yes.

Bad girl. Are you wet too?

Maggie gasped. She should have seen that one coming.

Maybe.

She couldn't bring herself to tell him the truth, which was yes, of course she was. The tiny strip of satin that barely covered her bits felt cool and damp against her skin.

Take off your panties.

She could keep them on and say she'd taken them off. The wolf would never know.

NOW.

Maggie jumped at the sight of the all caps. The wolf using all caps was hot. Quickly, she slipped her panties down her thighs, past her knees and ankles, and then kicked them to the floor.

Okay! I did.

She couldn't believe she'd done it. She should feel incredibly silly, but she didn't. She was a bit embarrassed, though. But she could always fake it. She could pretend to do what he asked. He wouldn't know.

Don't even think about faking.

Geeze! He was good. She sent an awkward "thumbs up" and waited. He didn't respond. The thumb probably killed his boner. If he'd even had one. What if *he* was the one faking? What if he was sitting on the couch in a pair of dirty sweats watching television and drinking a beer and pretending to sext?

Spread your legs. Nice and slow.

Okay. He was good at pretending. She obeyed. And it felt so very dirty.

Wider. Pull your knees up.

It felt like the wolf was watching her. Heat spread across her cheeks as she pulled her knees up and did as ordered. Then she picked up her phone.

Somebody's an impatient puppy.

But you're the one in obedience training. Pull up your gown and expose your breasts.

The room was chilly, but Maggie was on fire. She slowly pulled the lace up her body, shivering as it brushed her nipples. The light sheen of perspiration on her chest turned into gooseflesh when the cool air kissed her skin. Her nipples puckered as if touched by the wolf's breath.

Lick your finger and brush it over your nipples.

Oh God. They couldn't possibly get any harder, but she did as he said. She was completely under his control now. The day spent ordering people around and making decisions melted into a hazy bliss as she became the wolf's pliable puppet to do with as he pleased. Her muscles relaxed beneath the surrender, yet at the same time every nerve in her body was hypersensitive. Her blood warmed the surface of her skin and flooded to parts that swelled with need. She felt like a flower that had just opened under the sun. Without waiting for the wolf's orders, she arched her back and pulled her knees up higher.

Ping!

It took all her concentration to see what he'd ordered her to do now.

If I were there I'd check to see how wet you are. Since I'm not you have to do it yourself.

She didn't need to check. But she knew what he wanted her to do, and she did it. As soon as she touched herself, she dang near had an orgasm.

Don't you dare come.

The man was psychic.

I'm very wet.

Hard nipples. Dripping wet. You need a spanking.

Just like Celeste Harrington!

Yes. I'm a bad girl.

As soon as she sent the message, she realized the silliness of it. The difference between her situation and Celeste's was that there was nobody in Maggie's bedroom to administer punishment.

Three slaps LRRH. I'm going easy on you.

She couldn't very well spank herself, now could she? Were they going to pretend?

Did you do it?

Do what? Maybe he really did expect her to do it herself.

I'm not in the right position. Also, you're killing the mood with junior high ass slapping dance moves.

Who said anything about your ass? And you're in the perfect position.

The perfect position...What? He wanted her to spank her-self *there?* Even poor Celeste hadn't been asked to do that.

Maybe this was the place where she'd lie—Sure, I did that. It was great. Bye now!

Ping!

Maggie jumped and shamefacedly looked at her phone.

A picture popped up. Lower abdomen with a thumb hooked inside the waistband of a pair of black Hanes briefs, pulled down low enough to show off one side of his "V" and a nice leftward leaning bulge. She was weak with need and impatient for that waistband to dip lower.

Need some encouragement? I go lower after you've done it.

It was all so very encouraging! Maybe she would con-sider it—*Ping!*

NOW. Three slaps because you're a bad girl.

She closed her eyes. Could she do this? More important, *why* would she do this? Because she was a bad girl, that's why. And because the wolf had told her to. She braced her-self for the possible sting and definite embarrassment and then: *Slap! Slap! Slap!*

Okay, so it wasn't very hard. But it still stung. Maggie let out the breath she'd been holding just as the sting was replaced by tingling warmth. *Ooh.* She didn't want to wait for further instructions. She *couldn't* wait for further instruc-tions. Her fingers brushed the spot where her nerves were lit up, where she was swollen with the need for release. With-out the wolf's permission, she reached lower, rocking her hips. Her own breath filled her ears as she sought the perfect balance of touch and imagination—and oh, how her imagi-nation went into overdrive. *Those abs. That bulge.*

It didn't take long. Mr. Tatum had just been put to shame.
Ping!
WHAT DID YOU JUST DO?

How did he know? Still panting and engulfed in flames,
she fumbled with her phone.

I only did what you asked.

Plus a bit more.

I think you did too much.

No! He couldn't possibly know.

Her pulse had just begun to slow down but now it raced
back up. Did she accidentally have FaceTime on? Had he
been watching? Listening? She frantically checked. Nope.
The wolf was just guessing.

Took way too long Little Red Riding Hood.

I'm a slow spanker. Do I still get another pic?

What you get is another punishment.

Ooh! That sounded like a decent idea.

Give me a minute to recover from this one.

A minute was probably all it would take.

Not tonight LRRH. This was fun but I've had a bad
day. Should probably call it a night.

This was jarring. She'd nearly forgotten the wolf was a
real person. A man she'd teased with, danced with, *had actual sex with*... and he'd had a bad day.

Want to talk about it?

Maggie stared at the phone for nearly five minutes before
the wolf texted back.

No. And you already made it better. Get some sleep
LRRH.

Her phone stayed quiet, and Maggie turned off the light.
The wolf had had a bad day. He hadn't told her about it, per
se. But he'd shared something personal. A weird thing was
cropping up between them. It felt like trust.

Maggie rolled over and snuggled into her pillow. She was fully sated and pleasantly sleepy. But then her eyes popped open.

How could she trust a man in a mask who hadn't even told her his name?

Chapter

Twenty

Travis sat bleary-eyed at his kitchen table. He'd just returned from driving Henry down the lane to catch the bus. He had about ten minutes to chug down some coffee and scarf a Pop-Tart. His eyes darted to the clock on the wall. *Make that five minutes.*

He'd snagged only a couple of hours of sleep last night, thanks to Little Red Riding Hood. He felt as if he'd been smacked by a train and then run over by a semi. Come to think of it, that's what he felt like most of the time lately—a wreck. But this morning's exhaustion didn't carry the usual tension associated with the single working parent gig. His muscles felt like putty and he almost had a buzz going on. He had that wrecked, exhausted, loopy feeling that followed a good massage. Or a night of amazing sex.

It hadn't been *real* sex. But close enough. Without it, he'd have been up all night clenching his jaw with worry over the back taxes. He appreciated the distraction.

He took a gulp of coffee and leaned back in his chair, grinning. Maggie had absolutely zero self-control. He was glad he hadn't sent the second promised photo. It required some artful maneuvering to keep his tattoo out of the frame, and dick pics were generally a bad idea anyway. Last night he'd been like a drunken teenager, thinking everything sounded like a good idea, including using his only phone to carry on an incognito sexting conversation with the woman who was basically his boss.

He hadn't expected things to go so far. A couple of jokes or a few sexy comments were all he had in mind. But Miss Mary Margaret had surprised him. Who would have guessed she was into erotica? More specifically, who knew she was into *BDSM* erotica? And since he'd still been a little heated over her bringing her own guys in to finish the rocks, the Big Bad Wolf had doled out some punishment. *And she'd liked it.*

He laughed, thinking about her sleepwear. Black lacy nightie, his ass. She'd probably been wearing her basketball pajamas. Although, on second thought, she was honest to a fault. He swallowed. *Damn. She'd been wearing sexy lingerie.*

There were so many sides to Maggie, and he wanted to get to know them all. His Pop-Tart popped up. He grabbed it and licked some cherry goo off his fingers, thinking about how Maggie's fingers had surely dipped between her legs. Had she really done everything he'd asked? Had she really spanked herself in that way?

Yep. She had.

It was as if they'd been physically together in the room. The energy connecting them had been tangible. *Real.* All his problems had disappeared, and he'd been right there with Maggie. Watching her. Touching her. *Wanting her.*

He crammed half the Pop-Tart into his mouth and shifted

in his seat. There was absolutely no way for a decent outcome. He could never fess up about being the Big Bad Wolf now. Not after what he'd made her do. How could he look her in the eyes?

There would be no next time. He meant it. If nothing else, he was going to fuck up and call her Maggie instead of Little Red Riding Hood. And there was the phone situation. It was sheer luck that they hadn't already exchanged numbers.

He mentally made a note to get a new phone—like *today*—then crammed the last bit of Pop-Tart into his mouth before standing up and grabbing his sack lunch off the counter. There was absolutely no part of his day he was looking forward to...except for one.

Maggie.

Ping!

Dropping his lunch back on the counter, he frantically dug his phone out of his pocket. Was Little Red Riding Hood ready for some early morning shenanigans?

Hey Big Guy. Hope you got some sleep last night.

Yep. The intelligent decision to never, ever sext Maggie again went straight out the window.

You know exactly how much sleep I got last night. I hope you learned your lesson.

He waited for her to text back, like a puppy panting for a treat.

My lesson about what?

She wanted to play dumb. Where was she right now? Sitting in her Jeep at the work site? Maybe she was in her office at Petal Pushers, with the door locked, the shades pulled, and a dirty little grin on her face as she egged him on.

Do you need another spanking? Who cared if he was late for work? Maggie was being a bad girl.

Who do you think you're talking to?

He knew exactly who he was talking to. A very bad girl who needs another spanking. This time on her bare ass.

His mind hummed as he considered his options. Maybe he'd make her remove her panties and go commando. Nah. They'd already done that. Maybe he'd make her masturbate at work. He started to text, but she beat him to it.

I am a bad girl. It's been a long time. I'm glad you remember.

His brow furrowed, and a sense of unease crawled up his spine. That didn't make much sense. He squinted at the screen.

Holy shit. He was sexting Annabelle! He damn near dropped the phone. He had to think. The truth seemed to be the only option. I am so sorry. I thought you were somebody else.

He broke out in a delayed sweat as a wave of nausea washed over him. This was no game. What was he doing?

Too bad. If you ever need another ass to spank— or need a spanking yourself—you obviously have my number.

What should he say? *No thanks. I'm full up on asses to spank.* Seconds ticked by before he finally tucked the phone back into his pocket. Best to pretend it never happened. Maybe Annabelle would do the same.

* * *

Maggie poured coffee into her travel mug and grabbed her bag. She was late again! But the Big Bad Wolf hadn't let her get any sleep.

She blasted through the door with Pop in pursuit. She needed to beat the dump truck. Otherwise, the driver would automatically dump the topsoil in the place farthest away from where it needed to go. Murphy's Law ruled construction sites with an iron fist.

She'd call Travis. He was probably already there, and he could make sure the dirt was dumped in a convenient spot. She started the Jeep and her phone synced up with a pleasant chime. Time to give a shout out to her drunk girlfriend, Siri.

"Siri, please phone Travis."

"Okay," Siri said.

Maggie breathed a sigh of relief. Siri was being uncharacteristically cooperative.

"Calling Mavis now."

Maggie slapped the steering wheel in frustration. "No. Not Mavis. *Travis.*" Mavis was her hairdresser. The last thing Maggie needed was a thirty-minute conversation during a fifteen-minute ride about why she wasn't married.

"Who would you like me to call?"

"Siri, call Travis."

"I am sorry. There is no one in your contacts by that name."

Maggie frowned. Surely, she'd called Travis before, although now that she thought about it, she couldn't remember ever having done so. "Are you sure?"

"I am one hundred percent certain there is no one by that name in your contacts."

Well then, she'd call JD. He was usually on site early. "Siri, please call JD."

"Jay-Z is an American rapper and music producer, and he is also not among your contacts."

"Jesus Christ," she murmured.

"Jesus Christ is not among your contacts either."

"Siri, let's start over. Please call JD Mayes."

"Calling Jazzy Maids now."

When Maggie finally pulled under the big oak tree and parked next to JD's truck, her nerves were rattled, she was covered in dog hair, and someone was coming by to clean her house at three. She looked around for Travis's truck and didn't see it.

"Well, that figures," she said to Pop. "Hard to find good help."

She reached for the handle, but the door opened of its own accord.

JD Mayes, always the gentleman, stood in a golden ray of sunshine. "Good morning, pretty girl," he said with a wink.

"Why do you do that?"

"Open the door for a lady? It's how I was raised."

"No. I mean the flirting."

"I don't flirt. I give genuine compliments."

"Whatever."

Pop flew over Maggie's shoulder in a cloud of hair and landed in JD's arms.

"There's my pooch," JD crooned.

"Oh, brother." Maggie sighed, hopping out of the Jeep. JD even flirted with dogs. That should tell her something.

"How long are you going to be mad at me?"

JD stood there, earnestly staring at her, while giving Pop a groan-and-drool-inducing ear massage. Both looked totally clueless.

"Now's not the time to get into it."

JD shrugged his shoulders. "Well, I've got a few phone calls to make. I'm going to go sit in my truck for a while."

"You do that."

JD turned and headed toward his truck, pulling his phone out of the back pocket of his Wranglers.

Maybe it *was* time to get into it. "JD, wait."

He stopped in his tracks and turned, removing his hat as if somebody had died, which Maggie knew was merely his *I'm just a little boy—please don't hurt me* gig. He gazed at her through his lashes, and there it was. The glint. The hint of a grin.

"Stop flirting with me."

The hint of a grin turned into a full smile. "Aw, Maggie—"

"No. I'm serious."

The flirty pretense slipped as JD held his hands out. "Why are you acting so weird? And why don't we ever hang out anymore?"

"Because you're not interested in me, and yet you flirt with me constantly. It's rude, JD. And quite frankly, it's mean."

JD's mouth hung open as if she'd smacked him over the head with the plans she held in her hand. After a few seconds he replaced his hat, his signal that things were getting serious. "I'm sorry if you've misinterpreted my friendliness for flirting."

"I haven't. You're a flirt. Everyone says so. You just flirted with Pop for crying out loud. And I don't know why I didn't see it all these years. I don't know why I didn't get it, that your flirtation with me was no more significant than your flirtation with Pop."

"You know I care about you."

"Do you want to make out? Or maybe even have sex? Because that's what flirting insinuates."

JD tilted the brim of his hat down—nervous gesture that had the added benefit of shielding his eyes. But it didn't hide his cheeks, and they were flaming red. "I'm sorry. It's a habit. I've been doing it my whole life." He pulled the brim of his hat even lower and stared at the ground.

Maggie didn't care if she was making JD uncomfortable. He'd done it to her for years. "Well, stop it."

JD removed his hat again and held it in front of his belt buckle with both hands. He didn't look up, though. She rolled her eyes. He was doing the *Let us pray*.

"Yes, ma'am," he said with the earnestness of a Boy Scout.

"But Travis flirts with you, too." His earnestness was replaced by a playful grin "I bet he wants to make out with you."

"He wouldn't even look at me yesterday. Spent his time chatting with Anna."

"You shouldn't have hired labor. That's his part of the job."

"I was trying to help."

"It wasn't your place. It was unprofessional."

That stung. "I won't do it again."

"Good. Because he needs this job. Maybe that's why he gave Anna a bit of attention. Had you thought about that?"

No. She hadn't. Time to turn the topic back to JD. "His flirting doesn't hold a candle to yours. And you should be ashamed. There are rumors going around about you."

JD looked up sharply. "Rumors?"

"Bubba says you're going to Austin an awful lot. You're seeing someone, right?"

JD's mouth opened and shut again, as if he were going to deny it but had then thought better of it. She'd struck a nerve.

"You should know you can't keep secrets in Big Verde," Maggie chided.

His pink cheeks faded, and he turned a little pale.

"That's what I thought. Whoever she is, I doubt she'd appreciate all the flirting you do. So, knock it off."

JD pulled his hat down as low as it would go. "Maggie, I need to tell you—"

Beep! Beep! Beep!

The topsoil was here, and sure enough, the truck was backing up to dump it in the worst possible spot. Maggie didn't have any more time for JD. "If you've got something to tell me, you can do it tomorrow. Claire's coming over for the game."

"I'm invited? Does this mean we're hanging out again?"

She acted like she didn't hear him and ran off to catch a dump truck.

Chapter
Twenty-One

♡

Travis pulled up to the job site just in time to see Maggie and Pop attacking a dump truck. Or at least that's what it looked like.

He grabbed a shovel out of the back of his truck. Today was going to be spent spreading dirt the old-fashioned way: with his two hands.

His nose picked up on something floral and spicy.

"Hey there, Big Bad *Dom*."

His heart seized over the words *big* and *bad* as he turned to face Anna. *Calm down. She doesn't know.* He'd talked to her at the gala, so she'd seen him in the dumb mask. That's probably all she was referring to. She didn't know he was sexting with Maggie.

"Uh, yeah, about that spanking thing," he sputtered. "I was just messing around. Texting a friend. I'd prefer we not talk about it."

Anna licked her lips. "I didn't figure you for a spanker,"

she said, boldly ignoring him. "Who's the lucky bad girl? Anyone I know?"

Yaps cut through the air, coming closer and closer. Pop was heading their way, and his bad girl owner was right behind him. "Look who decided to show up," Maggie said.

She was out of breath from chasing the dump truck, and it made her voice even sexier than usual. He didn't have time to think about her sexy voice, though. Not with warning bells going off in his head—along with red alerts and whatever that sound is that submarines make right before they dive. He needed to get rid of Anna before she continued blabbing about spankings in front of Maggie.

He downed the rest of his coffee and held out his mug to Anna. "I sure could use another cup." Anna took the bait immediately.

"I have a fresh pot in the house."

"Great," he said. But instead of taking his mug, Anna took his arm.

"Why don't you come inside with me? You can fix your coffee however you like—"

"I just take it black," he said, digging in his heels. "Thanks."

Anna gave his arm a jerk. "Come on, silly. You haven't even seen the new crown molding yet."

And he didn't want to. But Anna was about to rip his arm off. He'd follow her inside, get his coffee, and come back out. Hopefully without Anna. "Okay. Sure."

Maggie narrowed her eyes at him. "Don't stare at molding for too long. You've got a crap-ton of dirt to spread."

"Maggie sure is cracking the whip," Anna said, pulling him to the house. Then she let go of his arm and slapped his ass. *Hard.*

"Jesus, Anna. Stop it."

She laughed. "I don't like being left out of the fun."

The urge to turn around and see if Maggie was gawking—he could feel her eyes on his back—was overwhelming. But he kept walking to the patio and opened the French doors for Anna to pass through like a queen.

The great room smelled of sawdust and fresh paint. Their feet echoed across the tile as Anna led the way to the coffeepot, which was about the only thing on the pristine black counters. "Place looks great," he said.

"Do you think so? I don't like the countertops. I'm not sure this is the color I chose, and I've changed my mind about the texture on the walls. I already told JD about it."

She must be driving Bubba and JD fucking crazy. He held out his mug as she filled it, standing way closer than she needed to. He took a small step back and brought his mug to his mouth.

"It's going to be a warm day today," she said.

Weather. Safe subject. "Yep. Another front's coming in, though. Not as big as the last one, but they're back to back—"

"Umm," Anna said, licking her lips. "I like front to front better." She closed the space between them and took his mug away, setting it on the counter.

"Wait a minute. I'm not done with—"

"Oh, you're done."

Her breasts pressed against his chest. She could probably feel his heart rattling his rib cage. He felt seventeen again as his body battled his brain. *This* is what it had been like all those years ago. Anna's relentless pursuit. His resulting awkwardness. And to think women experienced this shit all the time—some on a daily basis. How did they stand it? He took another step backward. "Anna, I've got a lot of work to do—"

"Who's your bad girl, Travis? I'm dying to know."

"I told you. I was just messing around with a friend."

Anna took another step, and Travis backed up against the counter. She had him cornered. "We're friends, aren't we?"

Travis swallowed loudly. "Um—"

The door swung open, and Bubba strolled in. He looked around the room, took in the two of them, and kept a poker face.

"What do you want?" Anna asked.

"I heard rumors about you not liking the countertops," Bubba said. "They're what you ordered." He pulled a wrinkled piece of paper out of his back pocket. "Got the order right here, with your signature. And the receipt."

"Do we have to talk about that right now?" Anna asked, as if she didn't really care about the countertops at all. "Travis and I are having a private conversation."

This was his out. "I'd better start shoveling," he said, scooting around Anna. Bubba gave a subtle wink as Travis passed, so subtle that Travis nearly missed it. As soon as he got outside, he inhaled deeply to clear his mind. He felt almost like he needed a shower and he hadn't even started working yet.

He pulled his cap down and grabbed the shovel just as JD rounded the corner of the house. "I have some good news for you, partner."

"I could use some. Shoot."

"The truck that was coming out here to haul off my front-end loader can't make it until Tuesday. Maggie says you might need it—"

"Maggie needs to mind her own business."

JD laughed. "That might be true, but it's not going to happen. Trust me. I know. But Maggie or no Maggie, the front-end loader is just going to be sitting here, taunting you while you shovel, unless you swallow your pride and use it."

The shovel handle was already burning against the

blisters the pickaxe and wheelbarrow had given him yesterday. It sure would be easier with a front-end loader. And faster—which was even more important.

"Okay. Thanks," he said. "I appreciate it."

Maggie was watching them, and JD gave her a nod. She headed their way, and Travis grinned. Goddammit, he couldn't help it. The wind blew the hair out of her face, showing off the dark eyebrows that didn't quite go with her light blond hair but nevertheless looked perfect on her face.

"You got plans tomorrow?" JD asked. "Claire and I are watching the game at Maggie's. I'm sure she wouldn't mind if you joined us."

Travis stuffed his hands in his work gloves. "Your matchmaker is showing, JD. It's weird. Put it away."

* * *

Travis and JD had been talking about her. That could mean any number of things, but hopefully it meant Travis was going to use JD's front-end loader and get the dirt spread today.

"Do you mind if Travis comes over to watch the game tomorrow?" JD asked.

Instead of rolling out a welcome mat, she rolled her eyes. "Why, JD? Do you need a buffer?"

"No. Well, maybe. But I thought Travis and Henry might enjoy hanging out with us. It's the weekend, you know. People do that on the weekends."

Oh, sure. Drag poor little Henry into this. She looked at Travis, who stood there like a kid waiting to be picked for the softball team. Although maybe he'd rather spend the evening with Anna.

"You're welcome to bring Henry," she said. "I'll need someone intelligent to talk to."

"You might be all talked out by tomorrow evening," JD said, "What's that book you're discussing at book club again? *Down and Dirty*?" He looked at Travis and stage-whispered, "They're reading porn."

She wanted to slap that silly expression right off JD's face. "It's called *Bound and Determined* and it's not porn. It's erotica."

She gave JD a look that would thaw an iceberg.

"I'm not sure Henry and I will make it for the post-erotica book club festivities," Travis said. "But we'll try. It'll depend on when I get back from Austin. I'm going to the farmer's market. We'll be selling Happy Trails beef at the Rancho Canada Verde stand."

"Oh?" Maggie said. "That sounds awesome."

"Claire is coming to help. Do you want to come along?"

A slight flutter started in her tummy. Butterflies! Maybe they were over the rock thing. "That sounds like fun. But I've got book club in the afternoon."

"You could just come for the morning."

"Y'all are cute. You know that?" JD said.

"Go away, JD. I came *this close* to not even inviting you over for the game. Maybe I'll un-invite you."

JD and Travis looked at each other and shrugged, and then JD adjusted his hat and shook his head with a smirk. "You do what you've got to do, Mighty Mack. And I was just leaving for another site anyway."

Bubba stepped out. "What's up? Are we meeting at Maggie's for the game tomorrow?"

"Shush, Bubba," Maggie said as he closed the door behind him. "I don't want Anna to hear." The absolute *last* thing she wanted was Anna rubbing all over Travis on her own damn couch.

"She went upstairs to her bedroom to pout about something," Bubba said. "I'll bring some wings and beer tomorrow. Trista is going to her sister's place in Round Rock. That means I'll be both hot *and* single. Tell all your friends."

Travis shuffled from one foot to the other. "So, about Austin..."

"I promised I'd take brownies to book club. I'll definitely need to leave early, but it sounds like fun! I'll go."

"Fantastic," Travis said.

Maggie started to turn, but then remembered about the phone number. "I didn't realize it until this morning, but I don't have your phone number."

"I have it," Bubba said, pulling out his phone.

"No, wait!" Travis said. "New number. I got it this morning. I need to give it to everybody."

After they'd exchanged contact info, Bubba took off, leaving them alone.

"Will you be wearing lingerie tomorrow night?" he asked.

Her face erupted into flames. How did he know she'd bought new lingerie? "Pardon?"

"Spurs PJ's. Henry will want to know."

God. She felt stupid. "Sure. We'll make it another pajama party."

Travis did that magic trick—the one where a dimple appeared out of nowhere in his left cheek, nearly obscured by his beard. Then he took off his flannel shirt and tied it around his waist. "Maybe I'll wear some, too," he said casually. "Although I don't usually sleep in any."

And with that, the jerk sauntered off with a shovel perched over his shoulder. He looked back to see if she was watching, and dang it, she was.

Chapter

Twenty-Two

☙

The Texas Farmer's Market was a madhouse of activity. Travis didn't know what he'd expected—booths of zucchini and onions maybe. But it was so much more than that. In addition to every fruit and vegetable in season, there were eggs, meats of every variety, honey, cheeses, herbs, and even growler stations from local breweries.

Taking over the Rancho Canada Verde stand was easy. Martinez Meat Market had processed several cows, keeping a percentage for themselves. Everything had been packaged, labeled, and frozen solid before being loaded into coolers. Claire had even made a banner with the Happy Trails' brand as a logo.

It looked official.

Luckily, Claire worked the counter, interacting with customers who wanted to know why the sign said HAPPY TRAILS instead of RANCHO CANADA VERDE.

"That's right," Claire said to a customer. "Same Black

Angus beef. Raised on a small farm right next to Rancho Canada Verde. All natural and grass fed. Rancho Canada Verde is thrilled to endorse Happy Trails beef products."

"Travis, we need a chuck roast," Maggie said. Her eyes twinkled. "This is fun, right? Maybe I could sell some of Honey's apples here, you know, if my neighbor ever gets his cows under control."

Travis ignored the side-eye she gave him, weighed the roast, marked it, and handed it directly to the customer, a young woman in tie-dye. "Enjoy," he said. "It's grass and apple fed. You won't find that just anywhere."

"Cool."

Maggie snorted and poked Travis in the ribs. "Watch it. This is Austin. Apple-fed beef will become a trend."

"Beef bones," Claire said. "And move it. We've got a line."

Travis reached in and grabbed a package. The beef bones were a surprising hit. Maggie said folks made broth out of them, that it was good for fortifying the immune system and aided healing. He might give it a try. It seemed like Henry had the sniffles every other week.

"Here's a bag!" Henry shouted.

It was his job to bag the merchandise, or at least hold the bag open for Claire. And he was obviously having the time of his life.

"You planning on growing into that hat?" Maggie asked him.

Gerome had given Henry a gigantic cowboy hat. "I think I already did," he said, wiggling the hat down over his ears. "See?"

Maggie laughed, then her eyes landed on Travis. "And what about you, cowboy? It looks like you've grown into yours."

Gerome had told him he couldn't sell Black Angus beef

while wearing a knit cap like a hippie. And then he'd pulled out a very nice straw Stetson. He'd dropped it on the ground and stepped on the brim before handing it over...*so it doesn't look like you just bought it at a department store.*

As if reading his mind, Maggie reached up and gave his beard a slight tug, which sent a tingle up and down his spine. "I like it," she whispered. "I like it a lot."

Her brown eyes darkened, and the tips of her ears turned pink.

Okay. The woman liked a man in a cowboy hat. Good to know.

"Excuse me," a man asked. "Do you raise turkeys at Happy Trails?"

"Turkeys? Um, no. Sorry," Travis said.

"That's too bad. We used to get our Thanksgiving bird from a small farmer near Moulton. We're looking for someplace closer."

"I'm pretty sure you can get one at your local grocery store," Travis said.

The man raised his eyebrows. "Do you know the conditions those turkeys are raised in? We don't eat meat that's been tortured. We're looking for naturally fed, free-range turkeys. Pigs and chickens, too."

Claire cut in. "And you can be sure that Happy Trails cattle are completely grass fed on one hundred and fifty acres of beautiful Texas Hill Country property. They drink the sweet, crystal-clear water of the Pedernales River, and are not treated with hormones or antibiotics, nor are they finished on corn in feed lots."

Damn. The woman knew her spiel. And it was obvious she felt strongly about it. Just like her daddy.

"Humane husbandry? Like Rancho Canada Verde?" the man asked.

Travis could answer this one. The cattle had gotten used to eating hay in the pens in preparation for the roundup. All they had to do was close the gate behind them, and then Gerome had shown him how to single out the ones they wanted in the shoot. "They're rounded up calmly," he said. "No prods. No loud noises. Heck, we don't even make eye contact—"

"Completely humane," Claire finished. She gave him a look that said, *Don't bore them with the details—these people do not realize the animals get slaughtered before they eat them.*

He shut his mouth. She was probably right. People didn't want to know the truth about where their meat came from. But most folks ate meat, and there were lots of ways to raise it. Most of those ways were downright awful, and Gerome Kowalski had opened Travis's eyes. It was fascinating to learn about the humane husbandry Rancho Canada Verde was known for. Roundups could be extremely stressful for animals unless done a certain way. Gerome had taught him how to stand quietly where you *didn't* want the cow to go. You didn't look at it directly—just watched with your peripheral vision. No sudden moves while you slowly shuffled forward, while your buddies did the same, until the animal had no place left to go but the shoot. Then you closed the traps behind it, one by one, until it walked on into the trailer, happily chewing hay the whole time.

Gerome had told Travis he had a knack for it.

"And do you help?" the man's wife asked Henry.

"Yes ma'am," Henry said. His hat wobbled as he vigorously nodded his head. He hooked his thumbs in his belt and puffed out his little chest. "Happy Trails is my ranch."

* * *

This morning the social worker had called: "Henry has no family other than you and his biological father." Travis had felt like collapsing beneath the weight of those words, and it wasn't until he exhaled that he realized it was from relief. There was no way he would have sent Henry off to live with strangers. His heart had already decided that.

Being all Henry had in the world might be terrifying, but they were family, and one way or another, they'd make it work.

But where would they make it work?

Travis climbed in his truck as a guy on a bike rode past in lime green skinny jeans and an ugly argyle sweater. "Thanks for the beef, man!"

Travis waved. The dude's man-bun was coming loose, but he was doing his best to keep Austin weird. Before Travis knew it, he'd shouted, "See you next month!"

Next month. He wanted to come back next month.

What was it Henry had said earlier? *Happy Trails is my ranch.* What right did Travis have to take him away from it?

None. He had no right to take Henry away from the ranch. And he realized he didn't want to. Henry had been so cute peddling beef. In fact, Travis wasn't sure who'd drawn more customers: Claire in her tight rhinestone-studded jeans, or Henry in his ten-gallon hat.

The farmer's market had given Travis all sorts of crazy ideas about raising free-range turkeys and chickens, goats, bees...maybe even planting a lavender patch. A lady had asked him about school field trips and eco-tourism. His mind was humming with fantastical notions. He couldn't wait to talk to Maggie about it. She'd left early and taken Henry with her. She should have dropped him off with Mrs. Garza by now.

He and Maggie had made such a good team today. Heck, they made a pretty good team as landscapers, too, even though Maggie was a micromanager to the nth degree and couldn't keep her nose out of his business. He liked her nose. And the thought of her being Suzy Homemaker and baking brownies for book club put a grin on his face.

It also gave him an idea. He pulled out his old phone; the one he'd stashed in his glove compartment, so it wouldn't tempt him. *The wolf's phone.*

Just one last time …

What are you doing today? Being a good girl?

He started the truck.

Ping!

That was fast.

A very good girl. I'm about to bake brownies.

He couldn't answer her right away. She needed to wait for it, worrying that bottom lip of hers while wondering what he'd make her do. And what would he make her do? A sly grin spread slowly across his face.

Do you cook often?

The response was immediate. HA HA HA HA HA. (That means nope.)

Do you have an apron?

Since she still probably had Honey's dentures in a jar somewhere—he shuddered a little—she probably also had an apron. Although like Honey's dentures, she'd probably never worn it.

Yes.

Bingo.

Good. Wear it. And nothing else.

He was very pleased with himself.

Nothing?

Nothing.

He was grinning from ear to ear when he decided to use the wolf's phone for good, instead of evil, and search for a nearby place to eat. Since this was Austin, he started to narrow the search by specifying *non-vegan*. But then he stopped. After all he'd learned about raising beef, did he really want to eat meat if he didn't know where it came from? He tailored the search by adding the words *local*, *organic*, and *beef*.

Hot damn. A grass-fed burger joint was ten minutes away. He headed for South Lamar Street, satisfied that he was about to enjoy a good meal while Little Red Riding Hood baked brownies in her birthday suit. A stream of X-rated images flowed through his mind. He particularly liked the one where Maggie was bent over, retrieving brownies from the oven. He was able to entertain himself with that all the way to the restaurant.

The parking lot was packed. A big white pickup caught his eye. White pickups weren't a rarity, but this one had the L&M Construction logo on its door. What was JD doing in Austin? Travis headed inside, happy he wouldn't have to eat alone.

There were three or four folks in line in front of him, so he looked around. All the indoor tables were full and there was no sign of JD. He must be sitting outside. Travis went back to examining the menu, which had his mouth watering with its pictures of thick, juicy burgers.

It was almost his turn to order when his phone rang. It was Mrs. Garza. "Everything going okay?" Travis asked.

He expected her to give him a blow-by-blow of what Henry was doing because that's what she usually did. But all she said was, "We're fine, Mr. Blake. But when are you coming home?"

She'd never called him Mr. Blake before. And her voice was filled with tension.

"I'm grabbing a bite to eat, then I'll be on my way. You

sure everything's okay? I can skip lunch and come straight home."

Travis had a bad feeling. Maybe Henry was sick.

"Everything is fine now, but earlier—"

"What happened earlier?" Had there been a fire? Had Henry choked on a pretzel? Did he have a rock up his nose? The list of alarming things that had possibly gone wrong was endless.

"It's just that we had a visitor."

Who would be stopping by to visit?

"Your brother, Scott," Mrs. Garza continued. "I didn't know what to do. I told him he'd have to come back later. Was that okay?"

There it was. The clenching of dread in his belly, the tightening of the noose around his neck. Scott must have gotten out early.

"Did he see Henry?"

"No. He was upstairs, and I didn't invite your brother in."

"You did the right thing, Mrs. Garza."

"Should I let you know if he comes back?"

"Yes, ma'am. Please do. I'll be home as soon as I can."

Travis wasn't hungry anymore, but it was his turn at the counter, so he mechanically ordered. Then he took his number and wandered out to the patio. He felt so numb he could hardly tell which way his feet carried him. There was no way he could let Scott take Henry. But did he have any right to stop him?

A white Stetson stood out among the crowd, and the sight of it calmed his raw, nervous energy. He was in bad need of a friend. Travis waved, but JD didn't see him. He didn't want to shout across the restaurant, so he quietly wove in and out of the tables, carrying his number and making his way toward JD, who was nursing an ice-cold beer. There was a second bottle on the table, so maybe JD wasn't alone. Didn't Maggie say he was seeing a lady in Austin? Travis hesitated. He didn't want to bust up a lunch date.

While he stood indecisive, a man in a gray suit entered the patio from the parking lot. JD looked up and smiled at the guy, who had a sharp haircut to match his suit.

Not the type of guy JD usually hung out with. Maybe this was a business lunch.

He expected JD to push his chair back, remove his hat, and rise for a handshake like the gentleman cowboy he was. But JD remained in his seat, smiling, as the newcomer walked over. He removed the cap from the second bottle of beer and pushed it toward the man just as he leaned over and gave JD a kiss. *On the lips.*

Travis's mind clicked along, gears grinding, and arrived at the only logical conclusion. JD was obviously not *out*. At least not to folks in Big Verde. He wouldn't appreciate being spotted by Travis. Maybe there was a free table inside now. Or fuck it, maybe he should just cancel his order and leave.

JD looked up just as Travis was about to turn. Their eyes locked.

Nothing to do now but smile and act normal. He waved and walked to their table.

The other man looked to see who JD was gawking at.

"Hi, JD," Travis said as normally as he could muster. "What are you doing in Austin today?" He sure hoped his outside didn't match his inside. And that his voice only sounded unusually high in his own ears.

JD stood. Travis expected him to pull the brim of his hat down, but he didn't. Good for him. The other man stood, too, and held out his hand. "Hi, I'm Gabriel Castro."

Travis shook Gabriel's hand and waited for JD to finally find his voice.

"Gabriel, this is Travis Blake. He's from Big Verde."

A huge smile appeared on Gabriel's face. "Nice to meet you."

Awkwardness descended in the form of silence. Travis wished there was a way to act as if a big secret hadn't just been unwittingly revealed, but saying, *How 'bout them Spurs?* seemed like a bad idea. In fact, he should probably find another table.

"Well, it was nice to meet you, Gabriel. I'll see you later, JD."

JD still didn't have a speck of color in his face. Even his lips were white. Did he think Travis was going to run back to Big Verde and blab?

"I haven't met many of JD's friends," Gabriel said. "Why don't you join us?"

JD's mouth tightened into a straight line.

"I don't know..."

A man arrived with a tray holding a gigantic double hamburger and a side of onion rings. "Number eighty-nine?"

"That's me," Travis replied.

"Sit with us," Gabriel said. "There's plenty of room. No need to take up another table."

The server set his food down and hurried off. It would be more awkward to leave than to just graciously accept Gabriel's offer.

"Thanks," he said, taking a seat. JD and Gabriel followed his lead and sat down, as well. "I wasn't looking forward to eating by myself. I saw JD's truck in the parking lot and came in here looking for him. I've been at the farmer's market."

Gabriel began snatching fries out of JD's basket. "No problem." Then he elbowed JD. "Thanks for waiting, cowboy. Did you even order me a burger?"

"You can have mine. I'm not hungry anymore." Only the lower half of JD's face was visible. But he looked pissed.

"Aw, come on," Gabriel said with twinkling eyes and a smile that lit up the room. "Eat up, man. It's your coming-out party."

Travis somehow managed to hold back a grin.

JD lifted the brim of his hat and narrowed his eyes at Gabriel. "This isn't anything to joke about."

Gabriel sighed. "I know, cowboy. But aren't you at least a little relieved?"

"No," JD said, adjusting his hat on his head. *Once, twice, three times.* He jerked his chin at Travis. "I guess you're pretty surprised."

Travis wiped his greasy chin and fingers on a napkin—motherfucking excellent onion rings—and took a sip of iced tea because he hadn't had the foresight to order a beer. "Not really."

JD's mouth fell open and he raised the rim of his Stetson. His eyebrows rose in incredulity. "You aren't?"

"Nah. You can't keep a secret in Big V."

"It's the pressed Wranglers, right?" Gabriel said with a grin. "With the seam down the front?"

"There've been a few rumors going around," Travis said.

JD looked downright incensed. "About me?"

"Who else? People have been saying you're seeing someone in Austin. We just didn't know who."

JD grunted. "Well, just wait until they find out."

"I'm not going to tell them," Travis said. And he meant it. He wasn't even going to tell Maggie, although he sure wished JD would.

"Have you two known each other a long time?" Gabriel asked.

"I went to school with him and his brother, Scott."

"Is Scott still in Big Verde, too?"

"Scott's in prison," JD said.

It irked Travis just a little that JD blurted that out. But maybe he wanted to share somebody's secret, too.

"Oh, wow," Gabriel said. "That's rough."

"Actually, he's out," Travis said. "Mrs. Garza just called and said he came by the ranch."

JD leaned forward in his seat. All his embarrassment and misery seemed to fade away as he said, "Did he see Henry?"

JD cared about Henry. Shit, it seemed the whole motherfucking town cared about Henry. It was his home. Maybe the crazy ideas creeping into Travis's head about turning Happy Trails into a real ranch—one that earned money—weren't so crazy. Something inside him shifted. It didn't quite settle yet, but it had definitely shifted.

"Travis, did you hear me?" JD asked. "Did he see Henry?"

"No. But he'll be back. Jesus, I hope he doesn't want to stay at the house."

"Who's Henry?" Gabriel asked.

"My five-year-old nephew."

"Your brother is the boy's father?" Gabriel asked.

Travis nodded.

"And where's the mom? Out of the picture?"

"You could say that," Travis said. "She died earlier this year. Cancer."

"That's too bad," Gabriel said. "My condolences."

"Anyway, I'm Henry's only family, other than Scott. And I think I'd like to..." He swallowed, knowing the words he wanted to say but fearing the reality of giving them form. He cleared his throat. "I'd like to adopt Henry. That is, if Scott goes through with giving up his parental rights."

There. He'd said it. And the noose that had been tightening around his neck for the past few weeks was finally loosened.

"That's great news!" JD said. "Really great news, Travis. You and I both know Scott has no business—"

"Are you sure your brother will relinquish his rights?" Gabriel asked.

"Scott doesn't want Henry," JD said. "He's a selfish bastard. Everybody in Big Verde knows that."

Travis agreed. "And even if he didn't want to give Henry up, wouldn't the courts see that I'm the better choice?"

"That would depend on a lot of things. But the state of Texas generally tries to reunite families. Scott is the biological father, so as long as he makes a good faith effort to turn himself around and live by the rules—"

Travis snorted. "He can't."

"Still. If he wants his son, it won't be an easy termination," Gabriel said.

A throbbing pain began building behind Travis's eyeballs. He didn't like the thought of Henry caught up in anything messy. "I think I might need a lawyer."

"Well, today's your lucky day," Gabriel replied. He pulled out a card and set it on the table next to a ketchup-smeared napkin. "I practice family law."

Travis took the card with gratitude. "Thanks, man. I might take you up on it. I don't have a lot of money right now—"

"Let's not talk about that. You're a friend of JD's. I'll do whatever I can to help you and Henry."

Relief washed over him. A month ago, it had been him and Henry against the world. Now he had friends and people who felt like family.

Chapter
Twenty-Three

❧

Maggie sat awkwardly on Alice's sofa, watching as everyone took dainty bites out of the brownies. Something was wrong. You shouldn't look like you had a cockroach in your mouth when eating a brownie.

"Mm," said Alice. "Yummy."

If it was so yummy, why did Alice look like she was suffering from a leg cramp?

"I'll just save the rest for later," she said, setting her plate on the coffee table.

Claire raised her eyebrows at Maggie. *What the heck did you do to the brownies?*

Maggie shrugged. She'd followed the recipe. Maybe she'd been a bit distracted because she'd been wearing an old frilly apron of Honey's and nothing else.

She picked up a brownie. It looked perfectly fine. She sniffed it. It smelled fine, too. She took a small bite, and her taste buds seized. Her salivary glands gushed in an attempt to wash out the offending foreign object. Maggie shuddered, looking for a place to spit.

"Here," Claire said, holding out a napkin just as a string of chocolate drool escaped Maggie's mouth in a slow descent toward Alice's carpet. Maggie took the napkin and spit the brownie into it.

"Well, now I'm intrigued," Claire said. "And clearly a glutton for punishment." She picked up a brownie and took a tiny bite. She managed to keep it in her mouth, but her scrunched-up face said she definitely detected what was wrong.

"God, Maggie. How much salt did you put in these?"

"I think just a spoonful."

"What kind of a spoon?"

"I don't know. Just a spoon."

"A big spoon? Or a teaspoon?"

How was she supposed to know? There were soup spoons, serving spoons, dessert spoons, and teaspoons. Who could keep them all straight? "It was one of the medium-sized spoons, I think."

"Do you even own measuring spoons? Next time you can bring the wine."

Maggie was more of a beer girl. And she wasn't too sure about a next time. So far, book club was like pretzel sticks—salty with very little substance.

Alice brought out glasses of water for everyone, and they guzzled them down like parched shipwreck victims on a desert island.

"Maggie, we're just so glad you're here," Alice said. "All you ever need to worry about bringing is yourself. But if you want to practice your cooking or baking skills, the Big Verde Book Club is happy to be your guinea pigs."

"Here, here," Claire said, raising her empty water glass.

Maggie laughed. There was nothing but kindness in the smiles of everyone in the room, except for maybe Anna, but kindness wasn't her strong suit, and she was at least looking pleasant. There were worse ways to spend an afternoon.

"You know, I once used baking soda when it called for baking powder," Alice said, blushing. "I took the cookies to the library's Christmas party and they tasted like copper. At the end of the evening, paper plates were scattered about, and the only thing on any of them were my cookies, each with a single bite taken."

"I put chili powder instead of cinnamon on the toast at Sammie's tea party," Trista said, rubbing her pregnant belly and bouncing a toddler on her hip. "Bubba ate it, of course. But the little girls, not so much."

"Oh, goodness," Miss Mills said, fanning herself with her daily devotional. "I still remember the first time I baked a buttermilk pie. The custard didn't set, and when I cut into it at the church potluck, it was a runny mess. I managed to sneak it into the trash when nobody was looking."

"You make delicious pies now," Alice said.

"Practice makes perfect. I had a particular young man in mind when I baked that buttermilk pie."

Maggie wondered if she'd baked it while wearing only an apron and thinking about being pushed up against the counter and ravished by a man in a wolf mask.

Miss Mills let out a long, ragged sigh. "It broke my heart that he didn't eat my pie that night."

"Yeah, I bet," said Maggie, avoiding eye contact with Claire, because that would be disastrous.

"That's what bakeries are for," Anna quipped. "I've never baked a pie in my life. But I set the kitchen on fire once when I tried to fry an egg."

Soon all the women were telling stories about their

culinary catastrophes. It escalated into a weird competition between Alice's burned lemon bars, Claire's twenty-five-pound frozen turkey, Miss Mills's cornbread full of weevils, and Trista's chicken and dumplings dripping from the ceiling.

Alice finally stood and spoke above the din, "Would everyone like to begin a discussion of the book now?"

One by one the ladies regained their senses, took their seats, and picked up their copies of the latest in literary porn. Claire leaned over to Miss Mills. "If you sat this one out, everyone would understand."

Miss Mills set her devotional down on the coffee table and dug in her bag. "Goodness, no. I never fail to complete a reading assignment." She pulled out a ragged and well-read copy of *Bound and Determined*. Post-it flags popped out from between every other page.

Somebody had done some deep, reflective studying.

"I really found myself identifying with the heroine," she said. "Sometimes you just want to let everything go—all of the trials of life and infinite worry with decisions."

You could have heard a pin drop. Alice recovered her voice first. "I guess it's a *let go and let God* type of thing, isn't it?"

Well, hell. It was going to be extremely disappointing if this discussion strayed from smut to Bible study.

Miss Mills looked at Alice as if she'd grown a second head. "Oh, goodness, no! Let's not bring the dear sweet Lord into this. And I don't approve of the premarital sex in this book. Not at all. And there was just so much of it. Nine sex scenes total, eleven if you count oral only."

There was a pause while everyone let that sink in. Then Trista said, "But who's counting?"

A few giggles here and there turned into howling laughter pretty quickly, and Alice had to fight to regain control. "I think Miss Mills is probably referring to letting the story's hero, Ethan Manning, take control with that paddle he loves so much."

Miss Mills picked her devotional back up and commenced fanning. "Ethan reminds me of Mr. Barret Hymes. Do you girls remember him? He taught sixth grade when I worked as a secretary at the school."

A general murmur went through the group. Who could forget Mr. Hymes? He was the meanest teacher Big Verde Middle School had ever seen or would likely ever see again. And he'd dressed like an undertaker.

Anna shuddered. "I was terrified of him in school. What in the world could he possibly have in common with our hot, sexy Ethan?"

"He had that paddle hanging by the door, didn't he?" Miss Mills asked. "I used to think about it sometimes."

It took another few seconds for Alice to get everyone settled down. She was like a referee. "Miss Mills, you never cease to surprise us."

"Don't think I've joined the ranks of those for whom fornication is the sin of choice. And I didn't choose this book, remember?"

"I'm sure Jesus understands," Alice said.

"I admit to enjoying the occasional spanking," Trista said out of the blue. "Once the kids are in bed, of course."

"Really?" Alice asked, eyes round. "I think I might have a problem with it in real life. And I hate to see women submit to men."

"Who said I was the one getting the spanking?"

"Bubba lets you spank him?" Claire squealed. "You realize we're all imagining it now. And that we can't unsee it?"

"Sometimes he's a bad boy," Trista said with a shrug and a wink.

"Goodness," Alice said. "I just didn't know that sort of thing went on here in Big Verde. Spanking, sexting—"

Anna perked up. "Sexting? Who's sexting?"

What the actual heck? Was Alice about to spill the beans?

"Yes," Alice said with a grin. "You might want to ask Maggie about it."

Shock must have shown on Maggie's face, because Alice immediately began apologizing.

"Oops. I'm sorry. I got carried away with the conversation and wasn't think—"

"Who on earth are you sexting?" Trista asked. She was clearly surprised that *anybody* would be sexting Maggie. "I mean, it's a man, right?"

"Not everyone with short hair is a lesbian," Maggie said. "And no, Trista. It's a cat. I'm sexting a cat."

"I'm not sure that's legal," Miss Mills said.

Anna had a fork of pea salad halfway to her mouth, but she set it back down on her plate. "I'm sure Maggie is sexting with a big, handsome hunk of a man. Am I right, Maggie?" Anna wore a sly grin that made Maggie distinctly uncomfortable. But that was the only kind of grin Anna ever wore.

"If you all must know, yes."

"Oh! Maggie has a suitor," Miss Mills happily exclaimed.

"And it's not a cat," Claire added helpfully. "He's distinctly more canine."

Anna's eyes narrowed as if she were connecting dots. The chance that Anna knew the wolf—he'd been at her party—both excited and terrified Maggie. Sometimes she forgot to think of him as a real person. Like, the Big Bad Wolf had a name. And a car or truck. Friends. And Anna might know all those things about him. It felt weird.

"It's just a guy and I don't want to talk about it."

"What's his name?" Trista asked.

"She doesn't know," Claire said.

Maggie shot Claire the evil eye and then risked a nervous glance at Anna, who'd set her plate on the coffee table and was dabbing her mouth with a napkin. She was grinning like a Cheshire cat.

"You don't know his name? What if he's a serial killer?" Miss Mills asked.

"He's not a serial killer. But he wishes to remain anonymous. And so do I for that matter." Another glance at Anna.

Anna cleared her throat. "I recently received a very dirty text," she said.

"From who?" Claire asked.

"It was a wrong number," Anna said.

"How odd," Alice replied.

"It was hot, though. He sounded like a Big Bad..."

Maggie's breath caught in her throat.

"*Dom*," Anna finished. "A big, bad dom. Which reminds me, let's get back to this book."

Maggie pulled her library copy of *Bound and Determined* out of her bag. A vague hint of unease hovered about, but she swatted it away by taking two big gulps of sweet wine fresh from a box. She wiped her mouth on the back of her hand as Alice asked the group if they could all relate to the heroine's desire to relinquish control.

Maybe she just had something in her eye, but Maggie could swear Anna winked at her.

Chapter
Twenty-Four
❧

Travis slammed the truck door and stared at the windows of Maggie's little house. They glowed with a warm yellow hue. Pop blazed through his doggy door, yapping hysterically. But he stopped and wagged his stub tail when he saw Travis, who leaned over and patted the French bulldog. "Nobody's sneaking up on Miss Mary Margaret while you're on the job, huh, fella?"

Travis straightened, looked around, and realized his truck was the only vehicle here except for Maggie's Jeep. Where was everybody else? He wasn't especially early. Maybe they were just running late.

"Let me out," Henry whined.

Travis reached in and unbuckled him, and Henry hopped down and began rolling around in the grass with Pop. "Don't get dirty," Travis said absentmindedly. "You're already in your pajamas." So was he. He'd stopped by Walmart and picked up a pair of Spurs pajama bottoms, which he'd paired with a black T-shirt. Henry was over the moon about the pajama party scenario.

He grabbed the bag of organic chicken nuggets he'd picked up at the burger joint and started for the porch. Henry wouldn't eat wings, but he'd do nuggets.

"Can I give a nugget to Pop?" Henry asked.

"You'll have to ask Maggie. He's her mutt."

"Kind of like Maggie asks you before she'll give me anything sweet," Henry said.

"Yeah. Because you're my mutt."

Henry laughed and dropped to all fours, yapping like a puppy.

"Get up. You're getting dirty."

"I don't care." Henry began digging a hole with his hands, tossing the dirt between his legs.

Travis bent over and scooped him up, then carried him to Maggie's screened-in back porch. Maggie opened the door and Pop jumped up and licked Henry on the nose. Henry dissolved into a fit of laughter. Travis set him down and held out the paper bag. "I brought some chicken nuggets to go along with Bubba's wings."

She stood back and held the door open. "Bubba's not coming. Neither is Claire or JD."

"Why not?"

"Let's see. JD says he has a headache. Claire is washing her hair. And Bubba says he has to watch some paint dry."

"Oh."

"Yeah. *Oh.* I suspect they're at Tony's gossiping about us."

Henry began running around on all fours, yapping and growling. The kid really knew how to make an awkward situation even worse.

"We can leave," Travis said.

"Why would you do that? You've already missed the first quarter. Come on in."

Henry upped the yapping to full-blown barking.

"Sorry, Henry. I don't have room for another dog in this house, so you'd better turn back into a boy."

"I don't know how. I'm a dog forever now." To prove it, he started to howl. Pop tilted his head to the side as if witnessing a freak show.

"Cut it out. And wipe your boots off."

"I don't understand people talk," Henry said.

"What was that, Pop?" Maggie said.

"Pop didn't say anything," Henry said.

"Oh, yes he did. He said that if you spin around two times and then touch your nose, you can turn back into a boy."

"How does he know that? Did he used to be a boy?"

"I don't really know. But I guess if he ever was a boy, and he wanted to turn back into one, he could."

"I want to stay a dog, too," Henry said.

"That's too bad," Maggie said. "Did you know dogs can't have chocolate?"

"They can't?"

"Nope. It makes them very sick."

Henry seemed to think about that for a while. Then he turned around two times and touched his nose. "Do you have any chocolate, Maggie?"

"I have a bag of miniature candy bars I've been hoarding since Halloween."

Henry scrambled into the house while telling Pop he was dumb for staying a dog.

"Thank you," Travis said.

"For what?"

"You just turned Henry back into a boy."

Maggie walked past him, and he caught a whiff of something very un-Maggie-like. Something fruity or floral.

"If you hadn't stepped in with your dog magic," he continued, "I was going to listen to Henry bark for at least three more days."

Maggie dismissed it with a wave of her hand. It hadn't even taken any thought. She just knew what to do around kids, and he never did.

"Are you wearing perfume?"

She avoided his eyes and fidgeted with the hem of her shirt as he pushed the back door open. "It's just some lotion for my hands. I went shopping with Claire, and now I smell like a girl."

"You look like a girl, too."

Maggie blushed all the way to the tips of her ears. She was dressed appropriately for their pajama party, but not in the footsie pajamas she'd worn last time. What she wore *this* time left less to the imagination—tight black leggings that went mid-calf and a little white NBA T-shirt. No bra.

She walked over to the refrigerator and grabbed a beer, stuck it in a koozie, and handed it to him. "You're not mad at me anymore?"

He pushed his glasses up on his nose. The combination of the season's cool dry air and dusty landscaping work was making it hard to wear contacts. "About what?"

"The guys I hired to help you. JD's front-end loader. We didn't have time to talk about it at the farmer's market today."

"I was never mad at you."

Maggie crossed her arms. "You sure acted like it."

"I acted like a pouty baby who had his ego poked. Not the same thing." He stared deeply into her chocolate drop eyes, hoping she could see what he felt. *I could never be mad at you, Maggie.*

"It wasn't my place. I'm sorry I hired help without talking to you about it. And I'm sorry you paid them—I'd intended to do that."

"Water under the bridge. And thank you for wanting to help. I don't know that my back could have held out for two more days. And you should know that I'm not out to ruin Petal Pushers. I don't intend to—"

"I know."

"You do? Because just recently you threatened to shut me down to save your business."

Maggie's eyes grew huge and round. Travis's heart nearly stopped. That was information Little Red Riding Hood had shared with the Big Bad Wolf.

"My, my," she muttered. "This is a bit embarrassing."

No shit. Travis took a sip of beer and wiped his brow.

"JD Mayes needs to learn to keep his mouth shut," Maggie added.

Whew! Travis took another sip—more like a gulp—and willed himself to relax between near-misses. "Anyway," he said, "I'm not sticking with landscaping. The farmer's market today gave me some—"

"JD told me. You've got a job waiting in Austin." Maggie looked in the direction of the living room, where Henry played with Pop. "You're not planning to stay in Big Verde."

"You're right. JD needs to learn to keep his mouth shut. And anyway, I'm kind of recon—"

"It would have been nice to hear it from you," Maggie said. "Because I kind of thought we were getting to be friends."

She came closer, the top of her blond head not quite reaching his shoulder, and looked up with her big, brown eyes. Travis lost his train of thought. "We were," Travis said. "We *are* . . . I hope."

Her eyes tugged at his like a magnet, and he lowered his

head as she rose on her toes. "Austin's not that far away," Maggie said.

"You're wrong," he whispered, softly brushing Maggie's bangs off her forehead so he could fall deeper into her dark brown eyes. "It's too far away." Right now, anything farther away from him than Maggie was at this very instant was *too far*.

He set his beer down on the counter and cupped Maggie's face in his hands. She seemed so small and delicate, yet she was tough as nails, and he loved it. She pinched his bearded chin and gave it a small tug until their lips met.

Travis had kissed his share of women, but nothing compared to the way his mouth was a perfect fit for Maggie's. He'd heard the *two become one* line before. It was sappy and sentimental and exactly what happened when his lips touched hers.

His decision was made at the sound of her soft sigh. He was staying in Big Verde. Staying at Happy Trails. Staying with Maggie.

He wrapped his arms around her, lifting her up effortlessly. He deepened the kiss as Maggie's breasts pressed against his chest. He could turn and perch her on the counter—

Pop barked, and it was immediately followed by the unmistakable sound of someone gagging.

Travis nearly dropped Maggie. Jesus, what kind of a... *parent? uncle?*... was he? He looked at the doorway, expecting to see Henry barfing over his and Maggie's inappropriate display of affection. But it was empty.

Maggie quickly disentangled herself from him, straightened her shirt, and then shouted, "What happened?" as she hurried into the living room.

Travis stayed behind in the kitchen. He needed a minute

for a certain part of his anatomy to return to the state it had arrived in.

Maggie was back in under a minute. "It's okay," she told him. "Henry threw up a little. It's an old pillow and I'll just toss it."

Great. So much for a fun evening. "Is he sick?"

Maggie went to the sink and washed her hands. "No. Just a gag reflex."

"Shit. The sight of us kissing literally made him vomit?"

Maggie shut the water off and briskly dried her hands. "No. It wasn't that."

"Then what was it?"

Maggie tossed the towel on the counter and turned to face him, hands on hips. Her cheeks and ears were pink, but he doubted it was from the steamy kiss they'd just shared. What the fuck was she so heated about?

"He ate one of my brownies, okay?"

One of her brownies. The ones she'd baked while wearing nothing but an apron. Travis tried to reel in the smile taking over his face. "Jesus, Maggie. Are they that bad?"

A grin tugged at Maggie's lips. "Want to judge for yourself? There's about a thousand or so left."

Travis grabbed her hand and gave a light yank, pulling her close. "You should steer clear of the kitchen and stick to things you're good at."

"Like digging in the dirt?" Maggie asked.

"No," Travis said, putting a finger beneath her chin and tilting her face up. "Like kissing."

Chapter
Twenty-Five

☙

The game was over. Travis had talked about Happy Trails through most of it. It was weird how excited he was about the place, considering he was going to sell it. It figured. She'd had two men notice she was a woman. One hid behind a wolf mask and the other was moving to Austin. And both seemed perfectly happy to carry on with her—one via sexting and the other through hot, steamy *yet completely temporary* kisses. Maggie had hinted that Austin wasn't that far away—JD was in a relationship with a woman in Austin—and Travis had responded that it was too far!

Message received.

She'd kissed him anyway. It was just a kiss, so what did it matter? If he wanted to smooch and rub his rock-hard body against hers while he was still here in Big Verde, who was she to protest?

Then again, maybe she should. Maybe she should end it right now. Kick him out. Say, *Adios, muchacho, it's been super fun swapping spit now buh-bye.* Of course, that meant saying good-bye to Henry, too. And she and Pop weren't ready for that.

She glanced at him, all stretched out with his long legs in front of him and his hands resting behind his head like he hadn't a care in the world.

It was ten thirty. He'd probably want to grab Henry from where he was passed out in the guest room and head home.

Only he wasn't moving.

Maggie's pulse sped up, which was stupid. Just because a tired man with a full belly wasn't jumping right up off the couch to sprint out the door didn't mean he wanted to make out.

Which was *fine*. Really. She'd only recently decided she could even tolerate Travis. She should ask him to leave right now, this minute, so she could begin the process of not kissing him ever again.

She cleared her throat to tell him it was time to pack up his hot self and his adorable nephew and get the heck out of Dodge. But what came out was, "Would you like another beer? Tomorrow's Sunday, and I don't have to get up early."

A small grin caused that dimple to pop out. "Nah. It'd probably put me to sleep." He closed his eyes.

Maggie let her eyes wander. Maybe it was because she'd baked brownies while almost completely naked. Maybe it was because of the book club discussion of *Bound and Determined*. Most likely it was because of their earlier Last Kiss Ever. Whatever it was, she really wanted to jump Travis.

The black T-shirt stretched across his chest and firm stomach, riding up just a bit. She'd love to slide it up and get another look at his tattoos. The waistband of his underwear peeked out of the top of his PJ's, and she tried—really, she did—not to look at the bulge.

Failure. She'd love to climb on top and rub herself all over him.

"How was book club?"

He was gazing right at her. Had seen where she was looking.

Her ears burned. "You're asking me about book club? When we could be talking about the flagrant foul that happened under that blind ref's nose?"

"Yeah, you went, right? Took the poison brownies? Tell me about it."

He just wanted to hear about her day? That was . . . *nice*. It was also a bit disappointing, considering there were other, more interesting, activities floating around in her head. "It was at Alice's house, and I kind of had fun. I think I might go back next month."

"That's good. I'm glad you enjoyed it. Alice seems nice."

"She is. She's a blabbermouth, though." *Could have done without her telling everyone I'm sexting the wolf.*

"What was the name of the book again?"

"*Bound and Determined.*"

"Is it the one on top of the microwave? The one with the bare-naked ass on it?"

She'd left that out? She turned to look at the microwave. At least it was too high for Henry to have seen it. "That's the one. I should put it away."

Travis stood up with a groan, stretched, and then lazily strolled toward the microwave. "Don't put it away. I might want to read it."

"You definitely do not want to read it."

"You're right," he said, picking up the book and looking at the cover. He glanced up at her with a very judgmental expression. "I'm not going to read it. You're going to read it to me."

"You've got to be kidding."

Travis brought the book to the couch, where he adjusted his glasses and read the back cover. He somehow managed to keep a straight face while Maggie sat quietly, engulfed in flames and wanting to disappear.

When he was done, he said, "Okay. This seems like a fine piece of literature. Let's take a peek."

The book automatically fell open to the nastiest scene. She should really stop dog-earing pages.

Travis scanned the page, a smirk forming at the corner of his mouth. He looked at Maggie with a raised eyebrow. "Seems like a good place to start."

He tossed the book at her and it landed in her lap.

"I have no intention of reading any of this out loud. You can forget it."

She held her hands up in the air as if she were under arrest, making no move to touch the book. Travis sighed and shook his head.

"Do I have to do everything myself?"

He reached for the book, but Maggie grabbed it first. "You're not reading any of this out loud either."

Travis took hold of the book with a big hand and tugged. "Yes, I am."

Maggie held on tightly. "No, you're not."

"Let go," Travis said.

"No."

"I can easily wrench this out of your scrawny little hands, but I'd prefer you graciously let go so I don't have to."

Maggie snorted. "Like that's gonna happen."

One yank, and it happened. She hadn't even felt it leave her fingers. "I'm not going to listen to you read that out loud."

Travis nodded to let her know he'd heard and registered her comment before opening the book. Then he dramatically cleared his throat.

Maggie crossed her arms over her chest and concentrated on actively not listening.

"Ethan firmly pressed Celeste against the bed."

It wasn't working. She'd had zero success in tuning that line out. So, she put her fingers in her ears and began humming because *Hey, we're all adults here.*

But she could still hear the low rumble of his big deep man voice as he read. He didn't even glance at her, just pretended she didn't have her fingers in her ears.

"Now that her wrists were bound to her ankles—"

He stopped reading.

He was probably shocked that Maggie and the other book club ladies had read such smut. He furrowed his brow and then said, "I'm not sure how that works."

"How what works? What do you mean?"

"How are her wrists bound to her ankles?"

"With those leather wrist cuff things."

He grinned and raised an eyebrow. "Leather wrist cuff things? Some girl really knows her bondage gear lingo."

Okay, she was sitting with Travis Blake in her very own house on her very own sofa and he had just said *bondage gear.*

Travis looked at the book again, as if he were studying a math problem in a textbook. "So, she's lying down, but where are her ankles? Does she have her legs lifted up?"

"Oh my God," Maggie said in exasperation. "Can you really not visualize this?"

"I guess I'm a little slow about these things. You might have to explain it to me. You seem to be the expert here— tossing out technical terms like *leather wrist cuff things.*"

"I'm not explaining anything to you."

"Ah You don't get it either. That's what I thought."

She did, too, get it. It wasn't rocket science. She got onto the floor—knowing full well she was playing into his hands—and lay down. She slid her feet up toward her bottom, but kept them on the floor because she was sure as holy hell not raising them into the air.

Travis got off the couch and kneeled next to her. He radiated heat. Maybe she should turn the ceiling fan on. Was it hot in here? She felt a bit warm.

"Okay, now see if you can reach your ankles with your hands."

Her neck was getting splotchy. She could feel it. Because nothing said *aren't I sexy* like a splotchy neck. Her arms were at her sides and she straightened out her fingers to clasp her ankles. Only she couldn't do it. She'd pulled her feet up so far that they practically touched her ass, but—

"You're shy a few inches," Travis said.

Why didn't her wrists meet her ankles? Were her arms too short? How had she lived all these years not knowing how disproportionate her arms were to the rest of her?

"It's like I'm a T-rex," she said.

Travis laughed. "I've heard there's an erotica market for that, too."

"And you would know this *how?*"

"Made the mistake of asking a lady in the doctor's office what she was reading. And anyway, your arms are fine. I don't think you can visualize this either."

"Okay, well, this doesn't work but I'm done. Who cares anyway? It's just a book."

"Now wait a minute," Travis said. "Don't be so hasty. This woman took the time to write a book. The least we can do is figure out what the hell she's saying."

He put the book down and touched a finger to his bearded chin. "Hmm," he pondered. "How about this?"

He moved so that he knelt at her feet. He took an ankle in each hand and said, "May I?"

Of course not!

"Sure," Maggie said.

Travis pulled one foot, and then the other, out to the side of her hips. It was hard for a girl to keep her knees together like a lady when a man was yanking her feet apart. But she tried, achieving a knock-kneed spread that was probably a negative three on the sexy scale.

"See?" Travis said. "This would work." He grunted as he gave her feet an extra shove. "Relax a little."

With his left hand, he managed to ensnare her ankle and wrist. "There we go," he said, seemingly very pleased with his accomplishment. He looked at Maggie as if she were a Rubik's Cube he'd just solved. He quickly snagged the other ankle and wrist with his right hand, and Maggie was rendered completely helpless.

There was a brief surge of panic, but then something inside her stilled. Travis was smiling like a goof, but she trusted him completely. All the tension seeped out of her body and dissipated like mist. It felt almost like being with the Big Bad Wolf, which was stupid because Travis was not the Big Bad Wolf and they were *not* going to have sex.

He smiled with a mischievous glint in his eye. "So, this works."

She couldn't speak.

"The question is, works for what?" he said.

He let go, and she crumbled inside. Her wrists and ankles had been so secure in his grip, and now she felt unanchored.

"Let's keep reading," Travis said, snatching the book up.

Maggie hesitated to move. Should she hold her position?

No, now that he'd let go, that would look stupid. She stretched out her legs and clasped her hands over her stomach, feigning relaxation. Like she was just chillin'. While Travis read erotica out loud.

Travis cleared his throat again. *"He pushed her knees open, displaying her for his pleasure, and she shivered in excitement."*

Travis's voice had become distinctly lower. Raspier. She glanced at his cheeks—what she could see above his beard—and they were pink. Bright pink. She crossed her ankles and tried to look casual. She remembered this scene. Next Ethan would—

"He firmly grabbed the spreader bar—"

Travis lowered the book, and Maggie quickly averted her eyes to examine the ceiling in great detail. "Oh, look," she said. "There are cobwebs up there."

"Maggie, what's a spreader bar?"

She really didn't want to admit to knowing what a spreader bar was. "How would I know?"

"Haven't you read the book?"

"What? Oh, well yes, obviously. But I don't remember every single detail and I don't remember a mention of spreader bars."

Except that she totally did. She'd broken out in a light sweat, even though it was cool inside. And she could hear her pulse in her head. "There's a moth hanging up there," she said, pointing at the ceiling.

Travis looked up. "I don't see anything."

Oh. It seemed her dilated pupils improved her vision. She now had special horny powers.

Travis looked down at the book again.

"He firmly grabbed the spreader bar and pulled her wrists and ankles up. Celeste was startled by this move.

Slowly, Ethan pressed the bar over her head, lifting her ass up with his other hand, until the toes of her feet came to rest just above her head."

He set the book down and squinted at Maggie in concentration. "I think I know what a spreader bar is now. But this seems like an advanced move. Not real sure I have a firm grasp of how she's positioned."

Maggie knew but she wasn't saying.

"I guess we'll keep reading." Travis turned the page.

He was really playing this up. It was adorable, sexy, and infuriating.

"Ethan held the bar close to the ground—no chance for Celeste to break free. She was exposed, open, and Ethan's face was so close to her—"

Maggie faked a sneeze.

"Gesundheit."

"I think I'm catching a cold. You should go now so I can get some rest."

"We can't stop here, and you know it. Also, that was the worst fake sneeze I've ever heard."

"It was the best I could do on short notice."

Travis shook his head and looked back at the book but then stopped and chuckled. "Jesus Christ, Maggie. Y'all read this with Miss Mills?" He was grinning from ear to ear.

"She loved it. Said it made her think of Mr. Hymes. Remember him?"

Travis's mouth dropped open. "That teacher who looked like a mortician—the guy with the paddle?"

"That's the one."

Travis closed his eyes. "Oh God," he said. "It's in my head. It's seared into my brain and I'll never ever get it out."

"Just imagine Miss Mills bent over Mr. Hymes's lap—"

Travis moved his hands to cover his ears. "I'm warning you, Maggie. Stop it or I'll—"

"You'll what?" She lightly shoved his knee with her foot. "What are you going to do, tough guy? Give me a spanking?"

She regretted it as soon as she said it.

Travis dropped his hands from his ears, having obviously heard every syllable she'd just uttered. He gave her a crooked grin. "You sure as shit deserve one."

"Me?" she asked innocently. "I deserve no such thing."

Travis narrowed his eyes. "I don't know about that," he said, rubbing the palms of his hands together as if gleefully contemplating the sound they would make on her bare ass. Her heart sped up at the thought of it. So, she quit thinking about it.

Travis picked the book up again. "Where was I? Oh yeah. He has her in a complicated martial arts situation. I'm not sure I understand the scene at all. I mean, where the hell are her feet?"

"What's wrong with you? Do you have to have every little thing you read explained?"

"It's just that—unlike some people—I'm completely innocent when it comes to this stuff. How long is a spreader bar?"

"No idea," Maggie said. "A foot maybe?"

Travis pulled out his phone.

"You're Googling it?"

"Yes." A few seconds later he looked up. "There's a lot of stuff on here."

"I bet. How long is the spreader bar?"

"This one is twenty-five inches. And forty-nine dollars."

He did a couple of finger swipes on the phone and then put it down. "It was Prime."

"You did *not* just buy a spreader bar."

Travis waggled his eyebrows before picking the book back up. "Okay, so we've got her ankles by her ears and her ass in the air. Sounds like yoga."

Maggie laughed. "X-rated yoga, for sure."

"I bet you can't even do it," Travis said.

Was he serious? She could do it. She wasn't going to, though. She had nothing to prove to Travis Blake.

"You'd have to be pretty fit and flexible to do this pose."

Maggie sat up. "I'm fit and flexible. And when I lived in Fort Worth, I even took a yoga class. I was so flexible I had to quit because I made everyone else feel inferior and it messed up their zen."

"I don't believe you."

"You are not tricking me into putting my feet by my ears."

"Okay."

"Seriously. I'm not doing it. I *could*, though. And that's what matters."

"Whatever you say."

"You don't believe me?"

Travis didn't answer. Just gazed at her calmly.

"Fine," Maggie huffed. "Watch this."

She sat up, curved her spine, and then shoved off to give herself some momentum. Up and over she went—easy peasy. But she couldn't stay that way without supporting her lower back with her hands.

"Ha! I told you." She held her position like a pro.

"Not really," Travis said. "You're supposed to have your wrists connected to your ankles, remember? You're holding your butt up with your hands like that lady on the senior fitness channel."

"That's just to get me started," she said. "Hold on. I got this."

She tried four or five times to remove her hands and to place them up by her ankles, but her rear end started to come down each time, pulling her legs and feet with it.

"Here, let me help," Travis said.

Before Maggie could stop him, he'd shoved his knees into her lower back and grabbed her wrists. He pulled them over her head, bringing them to rest beside her foot on either side of her head. He leaned over to do so, up between her legs, pressing his weight against her.

She was trapped beneath him. In a very naughty position that was obviously meant for a very specific activity. They were nose to nose and other parts to other parts, and his pajamas had developed a distinct tent.

"Breathe, Maggie."

She'd been holding her breath. She let it out.

"I can see where the spreader bar would come in handy right now," he said. His blue eyes were so intense. They looked like they'd darkened at least two shades. "I could hold it with just one hand, which would free up the other one for … other things."

Maggie lost all muscle control. She went limp.

She'd surrendered.

"Uncle Travis?"

"Shit," Travis said, letting go of Maggie and sitting up in the frantic and time-honored *I wasn't doing anything* tradition.

"What are you doing?"

Henry's hair was tousled, his eyes were puffy, and the likeliest reason for his wakefulness was spread across the front of his pajamas in a dark stain.

"Aw, man, Henry. Did you wet the bed?"

Obviously, he had, and there was no reason to fuss at him about it. Maggie stood up. "Let's get you out of these wet PJ's. Did you bring any extras with you?"

"Nah. But what were you and Uncle Travis doing?"

"We were reading a book."

"It didn't look like you were reading a book. It looked like you were wrestling."

"It was a book about wrestling," Travis said, standing. "Maggie, can we borrow a T-shirt or something?"

"I'm not wearing a girl's shirt," Henry said.

"You have to wear something, and your pants are wet."

"I'm not wearing a girl's shirt," Henry repeated.

With a sigh of resignation, Travis did a glorious thing. He pulled his shirt over his head. And there it was. The tattooed chest and ripped abs. To think it had all been on top of her just moments before.

"Excuse me," Travis said, yanking her out of her daze. "I don't mean to interrupt whatever it was you were just thinking about, but do you have a plastic bag for Henry's wet clothes?"

"You didn't interrupt a darn thing," she said, reaching under the counter for a grocery bag.

"Uncle Travis, when we get home, I want you to read me that wrestling book."

"That ain't gonna happen."

Travis slipped his shirt over Henry's head. Then he scooped him up. "Maggie, this has been a very entertaining evening, and I'm sorry it had to end." He glared a little at Henry, who seemed oblivious.

"I guess I'll see you tomorrow?"

"I look forward to it," Travis said with a wink. "I'll, uh...let you know when that bar comes in."

The more she blushed, the bigger he grinned. He pushed his glasses up on his nose and carried Henry to the truck.

She watched as they drove away, then she went inside and stripped the bed in the guest room. Before she even made it to the washing machine, she'd sent a text. Because a woman had needs, dang it.

Hey, wolfie. Want to play?

Chapter
Twenty-Six

♡

Travis rushed into his bedroom, quietly closing the door behind him. Henry was sound asleep, hadn't woken up even with the jostling of being removed from the car seat. He'd gone smoothly into bed without a problem, which was a relief, because Little Red Riding Hood had texted.

He'd sworn not to play the Big Bad Wolf role again. But after reading that book and doing those things with Maggie, he was just so fucking lit up. And Maggie was, too.

He'd looked straight into her eyes as she'd lain beneath him at his mercy—*she'd wanted it. So bad.*

The wolf was going to give it to her.

He'd pulled to the side of Peacock Road just long enough to text Get naked. Now he was finally in his bedroom. Did you do it?

Yes. And freezing. You sure took your sweet time.

Because he'd had to drive home from her house first.

You better not have taken matters into your own hands.

Although the idea of that excited him.

It's just me and Mr. Tatum.

Who the hell was Mr. Tatum?

??

My vibrator has a last name and it's T-A-T-U-M.

She named her vibrator.

Whatever you say.

First name is Channing.

That sounded familiar. He Googled Channing Tatum. What he found brought up all his old insecurities. This is what turned her on? For a moment he felt like his old long-limbed, skinny, stuttering self. But then he remembered he wasn't that kid anymore. He stood and looked at himself in the mirror. He was still shirtless. And he could give Channing Tatum a run for his money.

He picked up his phone. She should put that damn vibrator away. Mr. Big Bad Wolf was on the scene now. On second thought...

Just what are you doing with Mr. Tatum?

Getting warmed up for my wolf.

She'd called him her wolf. He wanted to be hers. And for her to be his.

I thought you were cold.

Not all of me. One part of me is very warm. And inviting.

He swallowed. He knew damn well just how warm and inviting that particular part of Maggie was. *Maggie.* He couldn't think of her as Little Red Riding Hood anymore.

He'd give anything if he could have her right here in this room. But since he couldn't, he'd have to let Mr. Tatum do the work for him.

Set the timer on your phone for 30 seconds.

Why?

Because I said so.

He knew she'd do it.

Done.

Now let Mr. Tatum tickle your right nipple until the timer goes off.

From what he knew of her nipples and their sensitivity, thirty seconds was going to be a long time. He grinned. He was a very bad wolf.

He busied himself with extremely filthy thoughts for the next thirty seconds. Then his phone finally pinged.

You're a horrible wolf. Don't make me do that again.

Now the left one. Thirty seconds.

NO.

Make that thirty-five seconds.

Silence. It was going to be about thirty-five seconds before he heard from poor Little Red Riding Hood again. He stared at the ceiling, thinking about her rock-hard little nubs and how he could outmaneuver Mr. Tatum with his tongue if only he could get to them. He pulled the waistband of his pajamas down to let his aching hard-on get some air. He took it in hand and stroked firmly. He could taste Little Red Riding Hood—no, *Maggie*. Maggie with her legs spread wide and his tongue buried deep inside her wet—

Ping!

Breathing heavily, he let go of his cock and fumbled for the phone. There wasn't just one text. There were three. How had he not heard them?

Done.

Hey, I said I'm done.

WHAT ARE YOU DOING?

Shit. He'd been caught.

I was in the bathroom

That's not sexy, wolfie.

No kidding.

I was slappin the salami.

LOLOLOLOL

Beating the bologna

Stop

Buffin the banana

I'm dying

Choking the chicken

I get it! I get it! Did you choke the life out of it? Are we done?

Nowhere near done. But you're talking disrespectfully to your master and his choking chicken. Go get an ice cube.

M'kay.

She sure fell in line quickly. Good girl. He imagined her running naked through her cold house and struggling to get an ice cube out of the tray while Pop looked on quizzically. He laughed out loud.

Got it.

Now what did he want her to do with it? His face burned. He knew exactly what he wanted her to do with it.

Put it in your mouth until I tell you to stop.

A second or two passed.

Ok. I'm sucking furiously because I want this thing as small as possible before you make me put it somewhere else.

He swallowed at the words sucking furiously and then grinned over her realizing exactly what was going to come next.

Right nipple. 5 seconds.

You're mean!

10 seconds.

He counted to ten.

Left one.

I have a completely numb nipple. Is that what you were going for?

No, that was not really what he'd been going for. God, he'd love to warm it up with his mouth.

OK 5 seconds on the left one.

He counted to five.

Still have ice left?

Yes. Where is it going next?

You know where to put it next.

For how long?

Until it's gone. And put Mr. Tatum to work too.

How long would it take? What if she got frostbite? Nah. It would melt quickly inside her hot—

He couldn't stand it. His hand went back to work. He groaned as the images took over. It wasn't his own hand sliding over his painfully hard cock. It was Maggie's hand. Maggie's mouth. Maggie's hot sweet—

In his mind, she was on top of him, riding him hard. Then that vision morphed into her beneath him, legs wrapped around his waist, hands clawing at his back. Now he was behind her pounding it home and . . . *Shit*. His strangled groan of release was enough to wake the neighborhood. He lay there panting and listening—all was quiet. No rustling sounds of Henry rousing. All the stress seeped out of his body and he waited for relaxation to take over and turn his muscles into putty. But it didn't. He was in *anguish*. He needed Maggie. Not this pretend relationship.

Maggie. He'd forgotten about Maggie.

Maggie? You still there?

His mind snapped to attention before he hit Send. That was close. He deleted her name. You still there?

Kind of. Partially. Sorry but I couldn't wait. It was so

cold and Mr. Tatum was so warm and everything was all melty and oh my god that was good.

He wished they could melt into the warm afterglow together. He'd love nothing more than to hold her all night long, only to wake up in the morning and treat her like a queen. He'd bring her coffee and breakfast in bed, and then Henry would come in for some morning cuddles.

Jesus. He was thinking in terms that could only be described as family. His pulse pounded. It should be coming down now, right? Not increasing?

His phone pinged.

Where are you wolfie? Not finished yet? Because I know what you're doing you dirty dog.

He laughed.

I'm here. You drove me wild though. I'm crazy for you.

He stared at the phone, waiting for a response. None came, so he added, You're my moon. That was romantic, right? Poetic? Also, it was true.

He got up and put on fresh boxers and a T-shirt. Then he peeked at Henry—sound asleep—and brushed his teeth. He checked his phone again before getting in bed. Maggie hadn't texted back. And even though he was dead dog tired, he had a very hard time going to sleep.

Chapter

Twenty-Seven

❦

Maggie yawned and put the windshield wipers on to get rid of the mist droplets coating her Jeep. Thanks to Travis's X-rated story time, she hadn't gotten a bit of sleep last night. Playing with the wolf had only served to make her more restless. And even worse, she felt kind of *ick* about it.

Travis had made it clear that they weren't in a relationship of any kind, so why did she feel like she'd cheated on him with the Big Bad Wolf? And for that matter, why did she feel like she was leading the wolf on, seeing as how he'd shown no interest in ever actually seeing her again, much less, removing his mask? *Because he'd gone all sweet on her last night, that's why.*

He'd called her his moon. She sighed dreamily, and then jumped when Pop barked. They'd just come around the curve and the apple orchard was filled with mother-luvin' cows!

She slammed on the brakes and honked the horn. As

usual, the cows looked up briefly, then went back to what they were doing, which was destroying the orchard. It was a good thing her window was up, and Pop couldn't get out to start a stampede.

She texted Claire. Going to be late. Cows in the orchard. AGAIN.

As soon as she set the phone on the seat, it rang. It was Claire.

"Why don't you call your cowboy and have him fix his fence?"

"Ha! Who says he's my cowboy?"

"JD. And everyone else."

"Who is everyone else?"

"Me. Anyway, I'm going to call my dad. His boys can have that entire fence line replaced in a few hours."

"Travis won't allow it."

"Just quote another agricultural penal code, summon the Chupavaca, whatever you have to do. Tell Travis he has no choice."

It was tempting. Maggie was tired of dealing with his cows. "Okay. Call your dad."

* * *

Travis's belly was nicely stuffed with *huevos rancheros*, and he had a sack lunch in his hand, filled with homemade pimento cheese sandwiches, pickles, chips, and cookies. Mrs. Garza patted his cheek. It felt good to be mothered.

Happy Trails was a hub of activity this morning. Men climbed up and down the scaffolding, putting the final coat of paint on the outside of the house. The inside was finished, and Mrs. Garza was busy hanging pictures like she owned the place.

Henry swung in the big tire that hung from the giant live oak out back, content for the moment. It was a crying shame Travis had to go work at Anna's. It was a good day to get some stuff done at the ranch. All the activity around him made him want to join in.

"How do you like the white?" Mrs. Garza asked, looking out the front porch window. "My cousin thought the personality of the house called for classic white."

Travis agreed. "I like it."

"He's getting a bid for central air conditioning," Mrs. Garza continued. "He thinks you might be able to work something out with the Jenkins brothers. They help out with St. Anthony's church picnic every year, and they'll need meat for the BBQ plates."

Travis hoped he didn't run out of cows. "We might have to hold off on that for a while." He grabbed his keys and headed for the door. "Listen, we'll talk about this later. I've got some work to do at Anna's. If my brother comes by, don't let him in. Okay?"

"Okay. Will you see Maggie today?"

"Yes. Why?"

"You should invite her to Thanksgiving." Mrs. Garza stared silently at him for a few seconds before adding, "Henry says she's your girlfriend."

"That little turd..."

"Well, I sure don't believe she's your wrestling partner."

Travis tried not to grin. This had escalated quickly. His heart started a weird rhythm—a fucking flutter—at the idea of Maggie here, in his house.

"I'm baking a turkey," Mrs. Garza continued. "And all the sides. You just need to get Maggie here with an appetite."

Mrs. Garza was having Thanksgiving at Happy Trails? "Don't you have plans with your own family?"

"My sister's daughter had a baby. First grandchild for her. The whole gang is going to East Texas, but my hip aches. I don't want to ride in the car that long. We'll just have Thanksgiving here. You, Henry, me, and Maggie. Smaller than I'm used to, but we'll have fun. You just wait and see."

Before he could say anything else, the old lady shooed him out of his own house. His head was still spinning as he stood on the back porch. *Thanksgiving.* He didn't usually celebrate, but he should probably do something now that he had Henry.

Lost in thought, he climbed in the truck, headed down the lane, and almost didn't notice the activity at the east fence.

"Whoa," he said out loud. To his fucking truck. As if he were thirteen years old again, dreaming of being in the saddle. Which he wasn't.

There were half a dozen guys working on the fence. Cedar posts were piled up on a flatbed trailer, and a tractor with an automated post hole digger was going gangbusters. Shit, it looked like half the fence was done. *Who the hell...*

And there she was. One hand on her hip and the other waving around in the air as she flapped her gums at Gerome Kowalski, who was leaning against a fence post, staring at the ground, and nodding silently, as cowboys were prone to do when women talked.

Travis stopped the truck and got out. He took a deep breath and starting walking.

"Oh, hi, Travis," Maggie said as he approached. She had a smile plastered on her face, but insecurity clenched her brow and shone in her eyes.

"I hope you don't mind me replacing this fence," Gerome said. "I understand you've got your hands full."

Maggie had complained about his cows to Gerome? "Not at all," he lied, wondering how he was going to pay for this.

His current bartering tool of beef didn't make much sense "I feel bad about putting you out this way, though."

"It's nothing. We'll be done in no time, and then you won't have to suffer any more of Maggie's rage." With a wink at Maggie, he added, "And won't that be a relief."

Travis attempted a smile.

Silence settled in, except for the hum of the post hole digger and the clanking of hammers nailing wire to the fence posts.

"I'm not real sure when I can pay you for this fence," Travis finally blurted.

"See that bull out there?" Gerome pointed to a huge Black Angus in the pasture, swishing his tail at flies. Travis didn't know much about bulls, but he admired the straight back, large neck, and powerful shank of the animal.

"You need to trade him out. It's a shame, though; he's a producer. I should know. He used to be a real pain in my ass, visiting my herd regularly. I figure I owe you for all the calves he's sired. So, don't worry yourself over this fence."

"Are you sure?"

"If I said it, I'm certain of it."

Travis was overwhelmed. And grateful. Because it really would be a fucking relief not to have his cows traipsing into Honey's apple orchard. He looked at Maggie, who was gnawing her lower lip and twisting her hands.

"Does this mean the threats will stop?" He tried to stare sternly at her, because watching her simmer tickled the hell out of him. Possibly turned him on a little, too.

"I don't have the slightest idea what you're talking about," she said.

Gerome looked at Maggie, glanced at Travis, and went back to contemplating the Black Angus. "Your daddy sure had an eye for bulls. I loved to watch him at the cattle auctions. He was rarely buying, but he'd advise anyone and everyone about which bulls to bid on, and they almost always took his advice."

"Are you shitting me? Dad didn't know a damn thing about cattle."

"I beg to differ. He had good instincts."

"I didn't know that."

"I figured you didn't."

Travis swallowed a knot in his throat. Learning something new about his dad, seeing him through the eyes of someone else, caused a small chunk of resentment to thaw and break away.

"In my experience, it runs in families," Gerome added.

And if Gerome said it, he was certain of it.

Chapter
Twenty-Eight

&

Maggie unlocked the front door of Petal Pushers, and Pop sprinted in. It was eleven thirty, so she had about half an hour before customers began showing up. People liked to do Sunday projects, and fall was a good time to plant shrubs and perennials. She wished she could get out to Anna's today. All the dirt had been spread, and it was time for the shrubs and trees to go in. Norbert had delivered them yesterday.

She walked through the garden center to the counter, where she booted up the computer. Then she went into the back to retrieve some more wind chimes to display by the cash register.

As she pulled a fourth box out to add to the stack, the bell on the door jingled and Pop went off like a car alarm. Claire was supposed to have the day off, but Maggie smelled Chanel. She came out of the stock room, carrying boxes, just as Claire slipped behind the counter.

"What are you doing here? I thought you were rock climbing today."

"Canceled," Claire said. "Everybody but me had other

plans. I figured if I came in and worked in the shop, you could get back out to Anna's and hurry that project along."

"Sure you don't mind?"

"Not at all. And I've been meaning to talk Thanksgiving with you."

"No worries. I'll bring a vegetable tray again." She'd spent last Thanksgiving with Claire. And she assumed she'd spend this one the same way.

"I'm going to Abilene with Ford for Thanksgiving. But my folks say you're still welcome—"

"Did you just say you're going to Abilene with Ford for Thanksgiving?"

"Yes."

"Ford Jarvis the Cowboy? That Ford?"

"Good Lord, Maggie. Unless you know some other guy named Ford who happens to be a working cowboy, yes, *that* Ford."

"Does your daddy know?"

Mr. Kowalski's parenting advice to every new mother in Big Verde was basically *Mamas, don't let your babies grow up to date cowboys.*

Claire drew her mouth into a thin line. Finally, she sighed. "Nope. Grown woman. Going anyway."

"Good for you! Also, I knew it! I knew you had more than just the hots for him."

"Who says I have more than just the hots?"

"Thanksgiving, that's who. You don't do Thanksgiving with someone unless it's serious, Claire. And don't worry about me. I'll go to JD's. Or maybe Bubba and Trista's."

"Speaking of cowboys, I hear yours is getting a fantastic new fence."

"Once again, he's not my cowboy. He's not anyone's cowboy. He's selling the ranch and moving to Austin."

Claire laughed.

"What's so funny?"

"My dad says Travis is a cowboy. And you know he doesn't say that lightly. Travis isn't going anywhere."

Maggie was filled with hope. Gerome Kowalski was never wrong.

* * *

Travis stood and wiped his hands on a rag as the rumble of tires on the gravel road made its way in from the distance. He'd finished early at Anna's and decided to paint the Happy Trails gate. It seemed a shame, with the house painted and the new straight fence lines in, to have a rusty gate at the entrance.

He took a big swig of water and wiped his sweaty face on the sleeve of his shirt.

The tire noise grew louder. Maybe it was Maggie coming down Peacock Road to get to her place. The cloud of dust made it difficult to make out the vehicle, but he was disappointed to see it wasn't a yellow Jeep.

It was a blue pickup. And it was slowing down.

With dread, Travis watched it turn in. All the painters had left, and nobody was coming back until tomorrow. The setting sun reflected off the windshield, concealing the driver's identity. But it had to be Scott.

The door opened, and a pair of grubby boots hit the dust. Travis inhaled and steeled himself for a confrontation, but the man who emerged was not his brother. "Hey there, runt, remember me?"

Runt. That brought back memories. Travis hadn't seen lowlife John Sills since he was seventeen. Because he didn't know what else to do, he offered a hand. "Hi there, John. What are you doing out here?"

"Shit. Look at you. I heard you got big, but *damn*, boy, I don't think I'd pick a fight with you now."

Walking up to someone who wouldn't fight back, smacking them in the face, and breaking their glasses was not a fight. And those were the kind of fights John picked. "I wouldn't if I were you," Travis said. "I hit back now."

John laughed and pulled his hand away. He hollered over at the truck. "You were right! He's a badass."

An arm dangled out of the passenger-side window, flicking ashes off a cigarette. Travis recognized the tattoos. "Are you going to get out of the truck, Scott?"

The cigarette was flicked to the ground. "Howdy, little bro." Unlike John, his brother was not grubby or disheveled. Menacing—yes. Messy—no. He could emerge from the flames of wreckage with his shirt pressed and hair combed. Today was no exception. He opened the door of John's decrepit truck with the cracked windshield and busted-out headlight as if he were climbing out of a Mercedes-Benz.

Scott walked over and thumped Travis on the back. "I feel like we're drifting apart. You never call or come by anymore. And when I stopped by yesterday, your *sancha* wouldn't let me in the house. She's a little old for you, by the way."

John laughed again. Travis just stared Scott down. "What do you want?"

"Maybe I just want to see my kid."

Travis worked at keeping his face blank. "Do you really think that's a good idea?"

"I need a phone. Then maybe money for a place to crash, unless you want me at Shitty Trails."

Travis broke out in a sweat. In addition to paying the back taxes, he'd have to buy out Scott's half of the ranch if he ever wanted to be rid of him.

"My wallet's in my truck. I'll give you some cash for a

prepaid phone and a motel room. But then you're on your own."

Travis walked to his truck to get some money.

"Somebody's coming," John said.

Indeed, there was another dust trail headed their way, and a yellow Jeep was the cause.

"Who's that?" Scott asked.

"The woman who lives down the road," Travis said, pressing a wad of cash into Scott's hand. "This should take care of things. I have to get back to work." *Just leave.*

"That crazy old lady who fought with Dad all the time? What was her name... Sweetie? Darlin'? It was something stupid."

"Honey," Travis said through clenched teeth. "She died. Somebody else lives there now. You should get going."

Travis nearly groaned as the yellow Jeep slowed down. Maggie stuck her arm out and waved. Then she turned in.

"Is that the little somebody?" Scott asked as Maggie pulled up behind John's truck. "She's cute."

Pop shot out the window. He pissed on all four of John's tires before trotting over.

"There's a good dog," Travis said. Scott bent over to pet him, but Pop responded with a low growl.

"Pop, stop that," Maggie said.

She wore her usual work jeans and long-sleeve polo with a flannel over it. But the flannel was open, exposing a pair of perky breasts. No bra. Travis glanced at Scott. He'd noticed, too, but wasn't openly staring. John, however, was not as suave as Scott. He leered, and Travis's pulse pounded like a jackhammer in his head.

"Are you going to introduce us to your friend?" Scott asked pleasantly.

Maggie smiled at him. She had no clue who she was dealing with. Scott was good looking, smart, and practiced at playing a nice guy, but Maggie's brows furrowed. She was wary.

"This is Maggie Mackey. She's a landscape architect."

Scott raised his eyebrows. "Holy shit. Mighty Mack grew up."

Maggie frowned. "Scott?"

"He's just leaving," Travis said.

Scott shook his head and laughed. "Received loud and clear, bro. Let me know when you get this place sold. I'm assuming you came up with a plan to pay the back taxes?"

Travis hadn't really wanted to do this in front of Maggie, but he was planning on telling her everything anyway. "I'm working on the back taxes," he said. "But I've decided not to sell Happy Trails. I'm staying on the ranch."

There was a deep intake of breath, and Travis looked to see Maggie with her hand over her mouth, eyes wide in surprise. Then those same eyes crinkled a bit as a smile crept out from behind her fingers. That was the reaction he'd hoped for. He winked at her.

Scott's face was a mirror opposite. Lips drawn. Nostrils flared. Vein pulsing next to his right eye. Travis dared a glance at his brother's fists. Both were clinched, and Travis took a step back. He wouldn't be surprised if Scott threw a punch, so he stuck his chest out and clenched his own fists, ready for it.

Scott raised an eyebrow.

That's right, motherfucker. I can take you now.

Relaxing his demeanor and adopting an easy smile that would have been pleasant on anyone else, Scott reached out and squeezed Travis's shoulder. Still wearing the smile, he said, "Sell the ranch, or you'll regret it."

Travis snorted. "Is that a threat?"

Scott stopped smiling. "Tell my son that his daddy will be back to see him real soon. It's time he and I got to know each other."

Travis tried to remain passive. Blank. Stoic. But the confirmation of his failure was reflected in his brother's satisfied gaze.

He'd just given away his weak spot.

* * *

The sun was setting in a brilliant Texas Hill Country display of orange, pink, and blue. Travis had pulled Maggie into his truck to talk, and it could have been the moment he'd been waiting for—the one where he confessed his feelings and his secret—but he was too frantic.

"He doesn't want Henry," he spat. "And he couldn't possibly take care of him."

"Exactly. So you have nothing to worry about," Maggie said.

"You don't know Scott. He's going to try and force me to sell the ranch. He obviously needs the money for something. Who knows what's hanging over his head? Scott's dangerous when he's desperate."

"Do you think he'll try to take Henry? Like blackmail? Sell the ranch, or else?"

That took the wind out of his sails. That's exactly what he thought Scott would do, but he didn't like hearing somebody say it out loud.

"What kind of custody do you have?" Maggie asked.

"I have temporary custody. That's all."

"Well, what do we do?"

She'd used the word *we*. God, he could kiss her. He could kiss her because she clearly didn't want him to think he was in this fight alone, and because she loved Henry. She really did. It was right there in those big brown eyes.

"I've got a lawyer," he said.

Her eyes melted with relief. "Good. Where did you find him?"

"He's a friend of JD's."

"JD is friends with a lawyer?"

Travis tried to keep his eyes on hers, but he couldn't. He was a horrible liar. He performed all the telltale *liar liar pants on fire* signs when he did it. Like avoiding eye contact. "Yeah. Just a guy he knows in Austin."

He glanced back at Maggie. She scowled in thought, trying to figure out who JD knew that she didn't. "You want *just a guy* to be your lawyer?"

"JD knows him well," he said, watching a moth flutter around the cab of the truck. "I trust him." He ran his hands through his hair. "Man, I really thought I had more time to get all this settled. Scott got out early. Gabriel thinks—"

"Who's Gabriel?"

"JD's lawyer friend." Back to the moth tracking. "He says the courts try really hard to keep kids with their biological parents. And even though Scott's been in prison, if he can pull off looking like he's making a good faith attempt at turning his life around..."

"I just saw him. He's not pulling anything off."

"I know. But he's a goddamn sociopath. He can be charming when he wants."

"Really? I think you're the charming brother."

Maggie looked at him almost shyly, and his heart thumped away like a tail on a dog that had been praised by its master. He was a roller coaster of emotions. "I should have jumped on this sooner. But I was reeling from my new responsibilities." He looked her straight in the eye. "Maggie,

I didn't want to be all Henry had in the world, I held off because I secretly hoped something else would work out." His voice hushed to a whisper. "I didn't want him."

"But you do now, and that's all that matters," Maggie said, touching his hand. "It'll be fine. We'll make sure of it."

There was that *we* again, settling over him like a comforting blanket. He brushed her bangs out of her eyes, and then he just fucking went for it. Leaned over and kissed her softly on the lips. Her fingers floated up to caress his cheek, then entangled in his hair. She parted her lips and moaned softly as he deepened the kiss.

Travis's heart thudded, threatening to burst out of his rib cage. When Maggie's tongue brushed up against his, all of his worries disappeared into thin air. *Well, maybe they didn't disappear. But they retreated to a respectable distance.*

There was only room for one concern, and that was to kiss the hell out of Maggie Mackey.

Chapter
Twenty-Nine
❦

Maggie sat in the break room at Petal Pushers, staring at her phone. She and Travis had gone at it like teenagers in his pickup truck yesterday. And Travis wasn't selling Happy Trails! Even better, he'd told her she was one of the reasons. Henry was the other one, so she was in good company.

She needed to do something about the wolf, though. His last text stared up at her. You're my moon.

It was the most romantic and sweetest thing a man had ever said to her. Especially since the man was a wolf. But she had to let him go. Travis was real. The wolf was not. The choice was easy.

Hey, wolfie. You there?

The response was immediate.

Right here, Red.

Best to just come out with it.

I can't play with you anymore. There's someone else.

She stared at her phone and counted, one, two, three... She'd never broken up with anybody before.

Is it serious?

I'd really like it to be.

Four, five, six...

Here's to your happily ever after.

Relief washed over her. Also, a bit of sadness. She'd miss her wild wolf, no doubt about it. But mostly, she was looking forward to kissing Travis again. Which would hopefully be sooner rather than later, since he would be dropping Henry off any minute.

Claire breezed in, carrying a tray of paints and paintbrushes for the craft class she was leading this morning. "Did you do it?"

Maggie nodded. "Yep."

"Good. Because you can't be two-timing on your cowboy when he just pulled into the parking lot."

Maggie's pulse picked up. "He's here to drop Henry off."

"He's leaving a five-year-old in our store?"

"Just for a few hours. It'll be fine."

The bell on the door jingled and Pop bounded out of the break room. Soon he came trotting back with Henry in tow. "Hi, Maggie!" Henry said, climbing onto a stool.

"Hi yourself. Where's your uncle?"

"He's in the truck lookin' at himself in the mirror. I got tired of waiting on him."

Claire laughed. "Aw, Maggie. He wants to be pretty for you."

"Boys aren't pretty," Henry said.

Travis walked into the room, proving Henry wrong. His shirt was pressed and tucked into his Wranglers, and his smile lit up the room. Honey would have referred to him as a *long, tall drink of water*.

"Thanks for watching him while I go to Austin," Travis said. "I wasn't prepared for a teacher workday, and Mrs. Garza has plans until three."

"No problem. I'm happy to have him hang out at Petal Pushers." Maggie went to the mini-fridge and grabbed a carton of milk. "Want a cookie, Henry?"

"Did you make them?"

"No."

"Then yes."

Travis poked Henry. "Manners."

"Yes, *ma'am*."

Maggie laughed and set a store-bought bag of cookies on the counter. Henry was a truth-o-meter. He didn't get all the subtleties involved in sparing someone's feelings. Not that her feelings were hurt. Baking was clearly not her strong suit. Now if someone were to criticize her landscaping, that would be another story.

"We're going to have fun today, Henry. It's time to decorate for Christmas."

"It is?"

"Not really," Maggie said. "But in the retail world we don't let that stop us."

Henry stuffed a cookie in his mouth and nodded as if he understood.

"The trees were unloaded early this morning. And we have all the Christmas goodies to set out. I'm talking snowmen, reindeer, You Know Who with the sleigh—"

"Santa!"

It wasn't usually this easy to make someone happy. It felt good.

"When are we getting a tree, Uncle Travis?"

Travis frowned. "Trees are a fire hazard and they make an awful mess."

"You're not serious," Maggie said.

"We never had one for those very reasons."

"You probably never had a lot of things. That doesn't mean Henry doesn't deserve them."

Travis rolled his eyes. "It's all a bunch of clutter, if you ask me."

Maggie wasn't exactly a glitter cannon of Christmas herself. In fact, she found a lot of it nauseating. But she was not going to let Travis Blake deny this kid a tree just because he'd never had one and apparently harbored an inner five-year-old who thought he didn't deserve one.

"We have ormy-ments at the house. And lights, too." Henry toyed with a second cookie but didn't eat it. "From before," he added quietly.

Maggie pulled gently on Travis's beard, so he'd look at her. "This is Henry's first Christmas with you." She gave him her very best *no way in hell you're denying this kid a Christmas tree after his goddamn mother died* glare. "He needs a tree."

"Fine. A small one."

Maggie gave a little yank on the beard. Travis winced. "Or a medium-sized one."

"Yay!" Henry took an enormous bite out of the cookie and began humming "Jingle Bells."

Maggie rose up on her toes and planted a kiss on Travis's cheek. "Thank you."

"What about you?" Travis asked.

"What about me what?"

Travis lowered his voice. "When are you trimming your tree?"

That sounded filthy, and Maggie's ears lit up like she wanted to pull Travis's sleigh tonight. "They're fire hazards and they make a mess."

"Are you kidding me?"

She wasn't, and she grinned to let him know it. "No tree for me. I'm hardly ever home, and anyway, I'm surrounded by them here."

"Maggie can come to Happy Trails and trim our tree," Henry announced.

Travis raised an eyebrow at Maggie. "How about it?"

"Sounds like fun," she said, heart fluttering. She'd never been inside Travis's house.

"I get to put the star on top. Uncle Travis will have to hold me on his shoulders like in the movies."

Something about the expression on Travis's face told Maggie that Henry wasn't the only little boy who'd imagined having a made-for-TV Christmas. This year they were both going to get one.

"I'd better get out of here. Are you going to be okay with Henry?"

"Of course. And he even gets to do a craft class with Claire. Right, Claire?"

"You bet," Claire said. "He'll like that."

"I'm not painting pots with a bunch of old ladies," Henry said. "That's what Uncle Travis says Claire does in her classes."

"Uncle Travis spouts off a lot, doesn't he?" Claire said.

"It's part of my charm," Travis said with a wink.

"They're making ornaments today. I think Claire should at least wait until after Thanksgiving, but some folks just can't help themselves." Maggie gave Claire the side-eye.

"If I ran the world, it would be Christmas all year long. Maggie's a Scrooge." Claire held out a hand to Henry. "Come on, let's go set up."

"Okay," Henry said, grabbing two more cookies before hopping off his stool. "What's a Scrooge?"

The tapping of Claire's heels and Henry's questions receded as Travis cleared his throat. They were alone. And Travis looked like he had something on his mind. If it was the same thing she had on hers, they might need to lock the door.

"Do you have plans for Thanksgiving?"

This was unexpected. And somewhat delightful. "Are you inviting me?"

"Yes."

What was it she'd said to Claire? *You don't do Thanksgiving with someone unless it's serious.* She swallowed. "I'd love to come."

"Good," Travis said. His voice was tinged with relief. It was so sweet! "I should be back by suppertime. You behave yourself now."

Maggie looked around the room. "Are you talking to me?"

"Is that the best Pacino you got?"

"It's the only Pacino I got, and I always behave myself."

"I doubt that, Miss Mackey." He kissed her on the nose. "I'll see you later."

He headed for the door and then stopped. "I've been meaning to tell you that package came in."

"What package?"

Travis waggled his eyebrows. "The long, skinny one. I think we determined it's about twenty-five inches."

Maggie's ears lit up like beacons. "You did not really order that."

Travis picked up a wooden ruler—MEASURE UP WITH PETAL PUSHERS!—and smacked it against his hand. Maggie jumped and squealed.

"Scare you? Guilty conscience got you thinking about a spanking?"

This was getting more and more Big Bad Wolfish by the

minute. Was there an animal lurking behind Travis's twinkling blue eyes? As she watched, they darkened a shade or two.

"Don't you need to be somewhere?" she asked.

Travis blinked like someone had just turned on the lights. "Yeah. Wow. I'd better get out of here. Don't forget about Thursday."

Like she could forget about Thanksgiving. "Wait! What should I—"

"Anything but brownies," he called over his shoulder.

* * *

Travis hoped his jeans were clean. And his shoes. And his hands. He'd never been inside a room that was so *white*. White rug. White furniture. White walls.

Gabriel Castro did not have kids.

Gabriel came back into the room with two cups of coffee. "It's black. Do you need cream or sugar?"

Travis took one of the mugs with extreme care. If Henry were here, he'd choose now to jump on his back. "Black is fine. Thank you for meeting with me."

Gabriel sat down and set his mug on the coffee table. "I'm happy to help. Any friend of JD's is a friend of mine."

Time to get some unpleasantness out of the way. "Listen, before we start, I need to know how much this will cost."

"I told you not to worry about that."

"I have to worry about it."

"It's pro bono, brother."

"You don't need to—"

"Yes, he does."

JD strutted out of the bedroom. Shirtless and damp from a shower, he wore nothing but athletic shorts.

"Jesus Christ, JD. I've never seen your legs before. Where are a pair of sunglasses when you need them?"

Gabriel grinned. "When I decided to go for a white boy, I went for a *white boy*. Check out that sexy farmer tan on his arms."

"I'd have worn a shirt, but I didn't know you were coming." JD glared at Gabriel.

"I forgot to mention it."

JD disappeared—probably to grab a shirt—and Gabriel popped open his laptop. "Has Scott ever paid child support?"

"Are you kidding?"

Gabriel wasn't smiling.

"No child support. Ever."

"So, you support the child?"

The child had a fucking name. "His mom used to support Henry. Now I do. Lisa had some life insurance—not much—but it's in trust. Henry gets it when he's eighteen. And there's some social security."

"Scott has been incarcerated multiple times, correct?"

"Yes." This was sounding better and better. What judge in his right mind would grant custody to Scott?

"Has he been involved with Henry at all?"

"Not enough to be noteworthy."

"It's all noteworthy. And I've talked to his parole officer. Scott took a parenting class in prison, and as of this morning, he's signed up for a series of parenting workshops that start next month."

"Shit. That was fast."

"He's looking for work. Doing all the right things."

What had seemed black and white was now murky as fuck.

JD came back into the room wearing jeans, a T-shirt, and a red face. He glanced at where his hat hung.

"Not in the house, cowboy," Gabriel said, and JD sat down and crossed his arms, staring straight ahead. Hatless.

Gabriel typed on his laptop, JD scowled, and Travis became more nervous by the minute.

"Scott reports that he's attempted to see Henry twice since his release. The first time was the day he got out—it was supposedly the first thing he did. And then he tried again yesterday."

"He did not try—"

"Says he did."

"I have custody. I don't have to let anybody see Henry if I don't want them to." He was getting pissed.

"Actually, you have temporary guardianship. You do not have custody."

Travis tried to quell the rising panic. "Are you sure?"

"Yes. Guardianship was granted due to parental incarceration. And that has ended."

"Early," Travis said. "It ended early. And he said he wanted to relinquish his rights."

"Verbally?"

"Yeah. I bet that doesn't mean shit, does it?"

"That's right. Verbal doesn't mean shit."

Travis rubbed the bridge of his nose. "I should have jumped on it when I had the chance."

"His crimes were not violent," Gabriel continued.

"Oh, he's plenty violent."

"I can only go by his convictions. And according to those, he's not violent, and none of his crimes are against children."

Gabriel typed for a few minutes while Travis and JD fidgeted. Finally, he looked up. "I don't want to give you a false sense of hope. But my gut says Scott doesn't want Henry, especially if he verbally agreed to relinquish his rights. He's fucking with you. I'm going to petition for nonparental custody. That's our first step. And since he's looking for a job, I'll also begin the paperwork to garnish future wages for child support. He'll hate that."

"What if it doesn't work? What if he still goes after Henry to try and force me to sell the ranch?"

Gabriel raised an eyebrow. "He'll have to prove to a judge that he can care for Henry better than you can. But we'll cross that bridge when, and if, we come to it. If you think there's a chance Scott isn't going to relinquish his parental rights voluntarily, then we need to go on the offensive and file."

After a few minutes of idle chatter to wind things down, Travis asked about Thanksgiving plans. "Having Thanksgiving with your folks, JD?"

"No. Not this year."

Gabriel sighed. "I hate being the reason you're not with your family."

"I'd rather be with you." JD grabbed Gabriel's hand.

"What about you, Travis?" Gabriel asked. "You got big holiday plans?"

"Believe it or not, I'm having Thanksgiving at Happy Trails. Mrs. Garza and Maggie are coming over."

"Maggie?"

"Yeah," Travis answered. "We're kind of dating, I think." Although he hadn't taken her anywhere. He should probably do that.

The corner of JD's mouth curled up; the little smirk that drove women—and at least one man—wild. "You think?"

Travis didn't want to talk about Maggie. He wanted to talk *to* her. Badly. Time to head back. "I can't thank you enough, Gabriel," he said, standing. "I feel better knowing you're on my side."

"We both are," JD said.

Gabriel stood. "We'll walk you out. I need to get the mail."

When they got to the door, Travis had a thought. "Would you guys like to come for Thanksgiving?"

JD looked at Gabriel, whose eyes were hopeful.

"Mrs. Garza is cooking, if that's any incentive."

JD put an arm around Gabriel's shoulders. "As long as it's not Maggie."

Travis laughed, but then he turned serious. "Don't worry. It'll all be fine."

Chapter Thirty

༄

The house was warm from the oven and the wood-burning stove, and the best part was it smelled like apple pie. Satisfied and basically pleased as punch, Maggie removed her apron. She was fully clothed—no naked baking this morning.

She hoped two pies would be enough. Travis had said JD was coming with a date. It seemed everyone was getting serious with somebody.

A few minutes later she pulled through the freshly painted Happy Trails gate. Travis had done some gorgeous landscaping with cactus and sage. The fences, she noticed with satisfaction, were straight and strong. Round hay bales sat majestically in the west pasture, surrounded by apple-deprived cows.

When the house appeared, she literally gasped. She didn't know what she'd expected, but it wasn't a gleaming white two-story with a wraparound porch and hanging baskets of blooming Christmas cactus. It looked like a home. A real one.

Travis was really staying.

She grabbed the pies and climbed out of the Jeep, just as Travis opened the front door. He wore a black long-sleeved Henley and jeans. He'd tamed his wavy hair and trimmed his beard, and his blue eyes twinkled as he said proudly, "Welcome to Happy Trails."

Maggie stepped onto the porch and handed him the pies. They were still warm. "You baked these?"

"Yes. Technically, I baked the shit out of them."

"Technically?"

"I put them in the oven raw and took them out done."

"And before that, did you take them out of a box and let them thaw?"

"Look at you knowing where your food comes from."

The door opened and Mrs. Garza, decked out in a gold lamé dress covered by a well-worn apron that had never seen a store-bought *anything*, waved them inside. "Come in, come in. Henry's been waiting for you, Maggie."

"Maggie! Come watch the parade with me." Henry wrapped himself around her knees.

"Let me see if I can help Mrs. Garza first, okay?" She looked around. "Travis, I'm . . . Well, heck. I guess I'm speechless." The living room was warm and inviting. Picture windows, high-beamed ceilings, a view of the valley called Canada Verde. "No wonder you've decided to stay here."

Travis took her hand and grinned. "The reason I'm staying here has pink ears."

"SpongeBob!" Henry shouted. "Look, Maggie!"

Henry was mesmerized by a gigantic yellow balloon being led down a street lined with freezing New Yorkers. He let go of Maggie's legs and plopped himself back in front of the parade.

"Travis, I need you to get down the turkey platter," Mrs. Garza said. "Maggie, you can set the table."

"It's such a relief to have someone in charge," Maggie whispered to Travis.

"Don't cross her," Travis whispered back as they followed Mrs. Garza into the kitchen.

"Wow. This kitchen is bigger than my living room."

It was nothing fancy. Some might even say it was strictly utilitarian, since it was clearly built for making big meals for hungry cowboys. But it was charming. It had tons of cabinets, endless countertops, and a walk-in pantry. Maggie wasn't the type of woman who typically got excited over such things, but she was still pretty dang impressed. And was it weird to imagine her landscape plans all rolled out under the bright and cheerful lighting?

"The plates are up there," Mrs. Garza said, pointing at the cabinet to the left of the stove. "I put the silverware on the table already."

The cabinet doors were glass, which Maggie knew was kind of "in" since Anna had chosen them for her new house. A stack of mismatched plates nearly hid the pretty white ones in the back. Maggie pulled them down. Adorned with a cheerful bluebonnet pattern, they were absolutely perfect. Had they been Lisa's Sunday dishes? Would she be pleased about their use today? Maggie tenderly carried them to the table, which was a long, rustic polished pine beauty.

"Where did you get this table?"

Travis handed Mrs. Garza the turkey platter he'd retrieved from the top shelf. "My dad made it for my mother. It went with us everywhere we lived. Sometimes it literally took up half the house—or trailer. We never ate on it, though."

"Goodness, why not?"

"I don't know. My mom left when I was little. My dad

kind of lived in suspended animation after that. I think he was waiting for her to come home so we could be a family again. Until then, it was TV trays and frozen dinners."

Maggie had never asked Travis about his mom. She'd assumed the woman was dead since he and Scott were raised by their dad. "Do you know where she is?"

"The last I heard, she was a showgirl in Vegas." Travis smiled sadly. "But I doubt that's where I'd find her now."

Maggie couldn't imagine a woman abandoning her children. Sure, her mom had taken off, too. But Maggie had been a teenager, and her mom had begged her to come along. They still talked as often as Maggie could tolerate, which was about once a month.

"I'm glad we're going to be sitting at this table today," Travis said, snatching Henry's backpack off the back of a chair. "Oh, and I'd better put this out of the way, too," he added with a grin, holding up a skinny box.

Maggie nearly dropped the plates.

"I'm going to run upstairs and put it in the bedroom. Care to join me?"

"Travis, stop it," Maggie whispered. "It's Thanksgiving."

"I know. I need to talk to you for a minute." He grabbed her hand and pulled her to the stairs. She followed him up, and he opened a door and shoved her through. A king-size bed took up almost the entire room.

"We need to talk about JD," Travis said.

So much for being thrown on the bed and ravished. "What about him?"

"He's bringing someone."

He'd already told her that. She took a moment to compose her facial features into *Great!* before saying, "It's weird that he's bringing her here. Why isn't he doing Thanksgiving with his family?"

Travis shook his head slightly. "Listen, JD's a little nervous. Just be a good friend."

It finally dawned on her what this was about. "Oh my God. What else would I be? Does he think I'm going to launch into a jealous rage? What an ego!"

"It's not that."

Ha! The hell it wasn't. This was infuriating. Embarrassing. Humiliating. "Wow. I just went through the seven stages of grief in, like, three seconds flat. Easy peasy. I'm at acceptance."

"That's where you need to be," Travis said, rubbing his bearded chin.

"Travis, come here." She grabbed a few whiskers. "I don't have the hots for JD."

"Prove it."

She was happy to. His mouth was so soft. She felt his hand at the nape of her neck and things became unmistakably less gentle. Her heart pounded when he ran his fingers through her hair, pulling it a little and tilting her head back. It gave him better access, and she nearly collapsed when he parted her lips with his tongue.

The man meant business.

Maggie wanted to climb him like a tree and shout *Timber!* before pushing him onto the bed.

Travis closed his hand into a fist, pulling her hair a little harder and tilting her head back even more. Her pulse raced like someone had waved a flag and said *Go!* Thrills and chills ran up and down her spine at this unexpected show of...whatever the heck it was. She hesitated to think *dominance*. This wasn't *Bound and Determined*, and Travis wasn't the hero of an erotic novel. Nor was he the Big Bad Wolf.

Which made the whole thing way hotter.

Travis's lips left her mouth and worked down her jaw to her neck. She went limp as a noodle. At the same time, she felt like she might possibly be on fire. Every bit of skin his lips touched was set aflame.

"Oh, Travis," she whispered.

He responded with a groan. This was going someplace good!

Although now the groan sounded a little high-pitched and whiny—

"Gross, Uncle Travis."

Travis and Maggie let go with a start. "Jesus, Henry," Travis said, running his fingers over his mouth. His face looked like it might explode. "Can't you knock?"

"Why would I?"

Travis's hair was a mess. Maggie imagined hers was just as bad. She was still out of breath, her knees were knocking, and she wanted to send Henry packing. But instead, she said, "So you don't require therapy later."

Henry backed out of the room and shut the door. Then he banged on it.

"Come in," Travis said.

Henry opened the door. "JD is here in a fancy car."

"We'll be right there. Now close the door."

Henry slammed the door. "I'm gonna tell Mrs. Garza that y'all were wrestling again!" he shouted.

"Do you think we've traumatized him?" Maggie asked.

"Nah. We were just kissing. He's seen worse on television."

If that was *just kissing*, Maggie was the Queen of England. "You should probably do a better job of monitoring what he watches on TV."

"Probably. Brace yourself," Travis said, opening the door. "Be nice to JD."

When they got downstairs, Mrs. Garza was staring out the kitchen window. "Who is that handsome man?"

Maggie walked up and peeked over the older woman's shoulder. No white pickup. A sleek, black Audi coupe had parked next to her Jeep. She didn't recognize the car or the dark-haired man standing next to it, but she sure recognized the white hat that got out next. It was pulled down very low, shading the upper part of JD's face. *Hiding.*

Mrs. Garza fanned herself with her hand. "That's some Latino sexiness out there." She fluffed her hair as she ran to the door.

The guy with JD was handsome all right. And dressed up in a nice shirt and tie. He carried a platter of pastries, and JD held some flowers, although they hung limply at his side as if he'd forgotten about them. The two of them stood together, looking at the house but not moving.

Mrs. Garza opened the door. "Welcome! Come inside!"

They came up the steps, the stranger with a smile and JD with a frown. Was this guy holding JD hostage? Maggie didn't see a gun to his head, but that was the vibe.

Travis shook hands with both men, did some back-pounding and other ritualistic whatnot, and then everyone stood around awkwardly because men were absolutely horrible at introductions.

"Who's your friend, JD?" Maggie asked. Otherwise they'd never know.

JD cleared his throat and pulled his hat down even lower, if that were possible, as if he were trying to drag it down over his entire body.

"No hat in the house, cowboy," the other man said.

Holy cow! They were going to begin Thanksgiving with a fistfight. Nobody told JD Mayes to remove his hat. JD could wear his hat in a church if he wanted to, and nobody would dare say a thing about it.

JD removed his hat.

"This is Gabriel Castro."

His lawyer friend—the one Travis had gone to see. The one Travis had been reluctant to share details about. The one who'd just called JD "cowboy" and ordered him to remove his hat in the house.

Not just friends then.

Numbness spread throughout Maggie's body. This is what JD had been trying to tell her! She'd been so focused on her own feelings that she'd been an awful friend. JD's hands were trembling, so she took one and squeezed it.

She glanced at the others. Mrs. Garza smiled reassuringly. Travis looked normal. And Gabriel grinned brilliantly—gosh, he really was handsome—while JD looked like he might drop dead on the spot.

Travis smacked Gabriel on the back. "I'm glad y'all could make it. Gabriel, this is Mrs. Garza. She's responsible for all the delicious smells coming from the kitchen."

Mrs. Garza blushed as Gabriel took her hand and gave it a soft kiss. "The way to my heart is through my stomach," he said. Then he looked at Maggie. "And I've heard all about the infamous Maggie Mackey."

"You have?"

"You've been partners in crime with JD since you were little kids, correct?"

She nodded.

"And that's Henry," Travis said, pointing to where Henry sat in front of the television.

Henry looked up. "That's who I am all right. And I can't hear the TV with y'all standing in here talkin'."

"Henry," Travis said in his warning voice. "Manners."

"I can't hear the TV with y'all standing in here talkin', *please, thank you, sir, and ma'am.*"

Everyone laughed, and Henry rolled his eyes in annoyance.

Mrs. Garza took the platter from Gabriel. "Pumpkin empanadas!"

"I made them myself."

Mrs. Garza stroked his cheek as if he were the baby Jesus.

"I baked an apple pie," Maggie said. "Two of them, in fact."

Travis rubbed her back. "Yes, you did, sweetheart. You and Mrs. Smith."

Maggie smacked his arm. "And what's your contribution to the feast?"

"I'm offering up the elegant digs. *Mi casa es su casa.*" He opened his arms in a wide, welcoming gesture.

"*Gracias, hermano,*" Gabriel said.

While Gabriel was being talkative and outgoing, JD was being uncharacteristically quiet. He'd wandered over to stare at the television with Henry.

"Is he okay?" Maggie asked Gabriel.

"He will be."

"Television off," Mrs. Garza demanded. "It's time to eat."

Henry began whining, but when he saw all the food on the counters, bar, and table, he stopped. "Come on, JD. We gots to eat."

"We *have* to eat," JD said.

"That's what I said."

Gabriel grabbed JD's hand as they entered the dining room, but JD wrenched it away. Then Gabriel touched the small of his back, and JD stilled. Mrs. Garza's eyes flitted to where Gabriel's hand rested.

"You two sit here," she said, pulling out chairs. Then she nodded to Maggie and Travis to take their seats, as well.

"Where do I sit?" Henry asked.

Mrs. Garza pulled out a chair. "Next to me, *mijo.*"

"Can I sit on the big books?"

"You've grown a bit," Mrs. Garza said with a critical eye. "I'd say A through E ought to do it."

"He refuses a booster seat," Travis said in answer to their quizzical expressions. "It gives us something to do with the outdated encyclopedias."

After Henry had scaled a sixth of the alphabet, the rest of them took their seats. Henry immediately reached for the turkey. "Hey, slow down," Travis said. "I drove all the way to Moulton to get that bird."

"Why would you do that?" Gabriel asked.

"I wanted to try a fresh, free-range turkey. Thinking of maybe raising some."

"Nobody's touching it until we say grace," Mrs. Garza said. "Travis, would you do the honor?"

Travis was quiet for a moment. "Why don't we all say something we're thankful for?"

That was an excellent idea to Maggie.

"I'm thankful for unexpected blessings," Travis said. "The past few months have brought one surprise after another. I fought against every single one. And I'm glad I lost."

Maggie squeezed his hand. It was quiet for a moment, as nobody seemed to want to go next.

Mrs. Garza spoke up. "I'm thankful that we can choose to make our own families."

"I thought you had to be related to be family," Henry said.

"Not always, little one. I think of you as my grandson, did you know that?"

"You do? Can I call you grandma?"

"Of course. Or you can call me *abuela*. That's 'grandma' in Spanish. And Travis, I'm tired of you calling me Mrs. Garza. Lupe is fine. We're family."

Travis reached over and squeezed Lupe's hand. "I couldn't have made it without you."

"It's my turn," Henry said in his bossy tone. "I'm thankful for *abuelas*. I never thought I'd have one!"

Maggie glanced at Travis. This had turned into a Hallmark movie. The kind that usually made her want to stick a finger down her throat. But now she had something in her eye. Lots of somethings. She dabbed them with a napkin.

Gabriel shifted in his seat and reached for JD's hand. JD stiffened but didn't pull away. "I'm thankful for love," Gabrield said. "And for finding it where you least expect it."

Everyone looked at JD. Would he take a turn? He sat silently for a moment, but then in a blur of motion, he pushed his chair back and stood.

"I'm just not ready for this." He looked at everyone sitting around the table, then shook his head and headed for the door. "I need some air."

"Are you in love like Maggie and Uncle Travis?" Henry asked as he passed. "You and Gabriel?"

JD stopped cold. Maggie's heart stopped cold, too, because Henry had just suggested she and Travis might be *in love*. She kept her eyes on JD, trying to be a good friend for once and focus on someone other than herself. JD grabbed his hat off the hook by the door, crammed it on his head, and walked out.

"I'm sorry," Travis said to Gabriel.

"No, I'm the one who's sorry. I forced this on him. He talks about Big Verde and all of you so much, and I'm just ready to be a part of his life—his *real* life. I'm tired of being his dirty secret." He put his napkin on the table and started to rise.

"Sit," Maggie said. "You don't deserve to be anyone's dirty secret. JD is being a gigantic dick."

Henry laughed. "Maggie said *dick*."

Maggie stood. "Sometimes it's called for."

Without another word she stormed out the door, where she found JD standing on the porch.

"What the hell is the matter with you?"

"I'm gay. That's what."

Maggie made an X with her arms and imitated a loud buzzer sound. "Wrong. Try again."

"What do you want me to say?"

"I have never seen this side of you, JD Mayes, and I don't like it. I don't like it one bit. You are being an awful guest and a worse host to poor Gabriel."

JD turned, his mouth agape. "You're upset about my *manners?*"

"That, and the fact that you didn't trust me. That you hid something from me—something this *big*, for crying out loud. And I'm also regretful of the opportunity you just passed up with Henry."

JD shoved the brim of his hat up. "What opportunity with Henry?"

"Henry just asked you point blank, with all the innocence and honesty of a five-year-old, if you and Gabriel are in love. And you could have said yes. You could have shown him that love doesn't always look the same for everybody, but it's still love. You could have shown him that it's *normal*, JD. But instead, you chose to be a shamefaced weasel. And that will be what he remembers about this, probably for the rest of his life. You'd better hope that kid's not gay."

The red tint that had stubbornly stuck to JD's face throughout her entire tirade drained away, leaving him pale. "It's just that I—"

"Come inside, JD."

Maggie offered her hand. JD grabbed it and pulled her close. "I do love you, you know."

When they came back into the dining room, Henry was

attempting to cram an entire roll into his mouth. JD sat next to him, picked up his fork like nothing had happened, and said, "Yes, Henry. Gabriel and I are in love."

It took Henry about ten seconds to finish swallowing, but then he said, "I didn't know I could have an *abuela*, and I didn't know boys could love boys."

"Well, now you do," Mrs. Garza said. "It's a good day for learning."

"I don't want to see any kissing, though," Henry said. "I've seen enough of that today already."

Chapter
Thirty-One

༅

Travis brought Maggie a glass of wine. She leaned against his shoulder with a soft sigh, and he put his arm around her. The house was quiet, as Mrs. Garza had taken Henry to the bingo hall, a weird Big Verde Thanksgiving tradition for a certain older crowd.

Maggie pulled her knees up and settled into him. "You smell good," she said.

He'd put on cologne today. It wasn't something he did very often. Just for special occasions.

"It's familiar," she said, leaning in to sniff in earnest.

Travis's pulse sped up. He didn't know if it was because of her warm breath on his neck—which felt nice—or if it was because he'd worn cologne on the night of Anna's Halloween party.

"It's just the cheap stuff most guys wear." That wasn't entirely true. It was a department store sample.

"Well, I like it," Maggie said, nestling her head beneath

his chin. "And Thanksgiving was wonderful. I'm glad you invited me."

Travis sighed with relief. "I half expected Scott to show up. Made it hard to relax."

"He doesn't seem the type to drop in for family holiday celebrations. What are you going to do about him and Happy Trails?"

"Buy him out someday. Until then, I'm not selling, and there's not a damn thing he can do about it. My dad set it up so that both of us had to agree in order to sell. He knew what he was doing, since Scott and I have never agreed on anything."

"Can't Scott just insist on splitting it in half? You each get a hundred acres?"

"Dad thought of that, too. Property can't be split. It can be sold as two hundred acres, or not at all."

"Scott mentioned back taxes. Have you paid that yet?"

Travis winced. "I don't have all of it. As soon as Anna pays me the rest of my fee, I'll have about a third of what we owe. I'll have to see if the tax office will accept that for now."

Maggie brushed the hair out of his eyes. It really was getting too long. He wanted to cut it and shave off the beard. Would she recognize him if he did? Now that she'd broken things off with the wolf, it wasn't like he *had* to tell her about his hidden identity. Maybe he'd just keep the mop of hair and itchy beard forever...

No. Their relationship couldn't be built on deception.

"I can't believe JD didn't tell me he was gay."

"He was scared." Travis could fully relate to being afraid of sharing a secret with Maggie. "It's always a risk to let someone know who you really are. Most of us hide behind masks."

"But what was he afraid of?"

"Losing you," Travis whispered. He closed his eyes. He wasn't talking about JD any longer. "He was afraid of losing you if you knew."

"That's ridiculous. I would never abandon a friendship, and certainly not over something like a person's sexual orientation. What do I care? But the lying...I just feel kind of played, you know? He lied to me about who he is."

The words Travis wanted to say—*I'm the Big Bad Wolf*— were swallowed up by the room. He could practically see them escaping through the ceiling. What would Maggie do if she found out he'd been harboring his own secret? That he'd also lied about *who he is*...She thought JD had played her? Holy shit. She'd go through the roof over what the Big Bad Wolf had done.

He decided to change the subject. "So how about you come over this weekend and we'll trim the tree with Henry?"

"Are you nuts? Tomorrow is Black Friday. This weekend will be insane at Petal Pushers."

Travis snorted. "I can't quite picture a horde of frothing-at-the-mouth shoppers taking over Big Verde's thriving business district. I mean, we're talking the oil change place, Pump 'n' Go, and Petal Pushers."

"Make fun all you want," Maggie said. "You haven't seen Miss Mills when she's got her eye on the last inflatable baby Jesus. Can we tree trim on Monday?"

"You've got an inflatable Jesus?"

"And three wise men."

Travis shook his head in amazement and tried not to think about Miss Mills blowing into spouts to fully inflate three wise men. "I'm hauling some calves to market on Monday. Does Tuesday work?"

"Tuesday evening. Tell Henry we've got a date. And

speaking of Henry, I wonder how late he and Mrs. Garza will be out? How late do bingo halls stay open? I mean, I wonder if they'll be gone long enough for us to—"

"For us to what?" Damn, she was cute. She was panting like a puppy. "Play a game of Scrabble?"

"I'm not much for board games."

"Well, it so happens that Henry is going home with his *abuela* after bingo. We've got the whole night. What do you want to do to pass the time? Maybe read a book?" He grinned at her. "We never finished the last one. I recall that when we left off, our heroine was in the very indelicate position of having her legs up over her head, separated by a twenty-five-inch spreader bar."

"You must have thought a lot about it to remember it in such detail."

"Well, you did that nifty demonstration. It left an impression."

Maggie laughed. "I bet."

"It probably left one on Henry's mind, too."

"Oh God," Maggie said. "I don't think he knew what we were doing."

Travis scooted closer and raised an eyebrow. "What were we doing, Maggie?"

She started to speak, but nothing came out. He should give her mouth something to do.

He kissed her gently at first, but urgency soon took over. He wanted her on her back, legs in the air, inviting him to do whatever the fuck he wanted.

Go away, wolf.

Maggie broke the kiss first, but only to say, "This is so much better than Scrabble."

Travis agreed. "Let's go upstairs."

By the time they got to the bedroom, he was ready to give

orders. *Take off your clothes. Lie down. Spread your legs.*
But he didn't. That was the Big Bad Wolf's way. Not his.

He pulled Maggie's sweater over her head and dropped
it to the floor. She stood in front of him in a red lacy bra.
Again, orders bubbled up out of nowhere—*Take off your
bra. Push your breasts out. Twist your nipples*—but he kept
them to himself.

"I want to see you," Maggie said.

"I'm right here, darlin'."

She rolled her eyes. "Travis, take off your clothes."

"You want me naked?"

"Yes. I want you naked. Now."

"You're a bossy little thing."

If she wanted him to take off his clothes, he'd take off his
clothes. But he was going to do it nice and slow. Make her
suffer a little. "Okay. Sit on the bed."

Maggie sat, and he slowly lifted his shirt, flexing to define
his abs. He might have lost a little ground since settling
down with Henry, but he was still in good shape—better than
most men—and he knew it. Maggie stared intently at his exposed skin. Not that he let her see very much. Yet.

His jeans rode low, and he hooked a thumb in his waistband, pulling it down a little as Maggie licked her lips.
Turning her on was turning him on.

He was no dancer, but he knew how to move his hips,
and so he did…a little. He flexed his muscles the entire
time, keeping a close watch on Maggie's face, because if she
started to laugh, it was game over.

She was not laughing.

He raised the hem of his shirt to reveal the three rows
of muscles making up his six-pack. Maggie's eyes followed
the shirt's path, leaving a heated trail on his skin. He ran his
hand over the snake tattoo that coiled across his lower ab-

domen, and then raised the shirt higher. He stepped closer to Maggie. So close that her breath grazed his flesh. She kissed his belly, and he clenched his fists and fought for self-control.

Her fingers traced the fly of his jeans, and he backed away.

Too soon, princess.

He turned around to show off his back. Maggie exhaled a long, shuddering breath. He pulled his shirt off and dropped it to the floor. The belt came next, and he yanked it through the loops in one swift move.

"Gosh, Magic Mike much?"

Maybe he'd been a little too dramatic. He looked over his shoulder to see her grinning, but she wasn't making fun of him. She seemed to be enjoying the hell out of herself. He unzipped his fly and lowered his jeans to mid-thigh. With his feet hip-distance apart, he pulled his underwear down and flexed his glutes, one at a time. Maggie squealed, so he did it again.

He had a dumb smile on his face now. Maybe he had a little Magic Mike in him after all.

He pulled his pants up, which made Maggie boo and hiss, and then spun around. He ran a hand over his abs and up his chest, flexing his pecs as he walked toward her. Maggie covered her face with her hands, but she peeked between her fingers.

"Travis, you're prettier than me. There is no way I'm taking my clothes off now."

When he was mere inches from her face, he pulled her fingers away. "Oh, yes you will."

Maggie's eyes went to his fly. He hooked his thumbs in the waistband of his briefs and slowly dragged them over the head of his penis. Maggie licked her lips. Then she licked him.

He groaned and pulled his briefs the rest of the way down, letting his cock free. Maggie took it in her warm hands, and he watched as she slid them up and down his shaft.

"This is pretty impressive," she said.

He just smiled and tried not to come all over her. She took him in her mouth and he had to try even harder. His eyes met hers—big and round above her sweet mouth so full— and that damn near did it. He pulled back.

"Your turn. Lose the bra."

Maggie bit her lip and furrowed her brow. He was surprised by her shyness, until he remembered that, to Maggie, this was their first time. An uncomfortable wave of guilt crept up, threatening to ruin the mood.

* * *

Maggie couldn't believe the gorgeous man in front of her. He was like one of those guys on a calendar—all he needed was a firefighter hat and a cute puppy. What on earth was he doing here with her? And how the hell was she supposed to get up the nerve to take off her bra? It was possible Travis's pecs were bigger than her breasts. "I'm not much in the cup size department."

Travis knelt before her. "You're the perfect size. The perfect shape."

"Do you have your contacts in?"

Travis laughed. "I see just fine, sweetheart."

"It's really bright in here. Maybe we can turn off the overhead light and put a lamp on. Do you have a scarf to drape over it and set the mood?"

"I'm all out of scarves."

"Oh. Well, maybe we could—"

"You're killing me here. How about I count to three? On three, you lose the bra."

That might work. Maggie scrunched her eyes shut. "Okay. Count."

"You look like you're about to rip off a bandage."

That was kind of like what it felt like. "No. I'm fine. Start counting."

"One...two...three!"

Maggie tried. She really did. But nothing happened. Her fingers were frozen. What she needed was her red cape and porn star boots. Little Red Riding Hood would have no trouble losing the bra. If only she could feel that free and sexy again. But Travis was very unlikely to growl—or bark—orders at her. He was too polite. Too sweet. And she should be totally turned on by that, especially given the adorable striptease he'd performed.

"Try again," she said.

Travis sighed. "One...two...you're not going to do it."

"Sorry! It's just that you're all—you know—Channing Tatum-ish and whatnot. And I'm—"

"Sexy. Gorgeous. Making me so hard I could die."

"Really? Even in bright lighting?"

"Especially in bright lighting." He traced a finger along her collarbone, leaving a trail of gooseflesh, and dragged it around the curve of her breast. "Perfection," he whispered.

Maggie wanted to believe him. She saw his pulse pounding in his neck, watched as he licked his lips.

Slowly, she unclasped her bra and let it slide down her arms. She tried not to melt as she closed her eyes and let him look.

Warm breath brushed her skin. She shivered as his mouth covered her nipple. She was on fire. Places Travis wasn't even touching were lit up in anticipation, and Maggie arched her back when fingertips brushed her other nipple.

She didn't care about the bright lighting anymore.

Travis tugged at the button on the waistband of her jeans. "Let's lose these."

"You first."

Without an ounce of hesitation, Travis stood. And before Maggie could snap her fingers, he was butt naked, except for his socks. And he was clearly anxious to get on with things.

"Come on. Your turn." He pulled her off the bed with a glint in his eye. "Do I have to count to three?"

"Probably. But let me get my boots off first."

She yanked them off. Then she looked at Travis and waited.

"One."

She unbuttoned.

"Two."

She unzipped.

"Three."

Maggie pulled her jeans down, stepped out of them, and did a little dance in her red lacy panties. "Whoo-hoo! I did it!"

Travis offered her a quick high-five, then pulled her close as they collapsed onto the bed. Oh, but it felt good to have his naked body pressed against hers. She pushed on the top of his head, encouraging him to give attention to her breasts again. He seemed more than happy to oblige, and soon Maggie was floating on air, tingling with euphoria.

Travis kissed, sucked, flicked, and grazed. Maggie writhed beneath him, willing him to go lower down her body, but not wanting him to abandon any part of her. He moved against her, warm and hard, kissing down her abdomen, paying homage to her rib cage and belly button, making her giggle with his beard. "Sorry, I'm ticklish."

"I'm filing that info away for later," Travis said, blue eyes sparkling. "Now, let's see what else you've got for me to play with."

Maggie couldn't help it. Her eyes immediately darted to the long, skinny box on the nightstand.

"What are you looking at?"

Ugh! He'd caught her. And he was enjoying it.

"Nothing."

"Are you sure? Because it appears you're interested in that box over there."

Play dumb, Maggie. "What box?"

Travis dragged his finger lightly down her tummy, leaving a trail of goose bumps. He followed it with his lips, and even though his beard tickled, Maggie wasn't laughing. "You want to know what's in that box, baby?"

His voice had gone distinctly lower, gruffer, and there was something about the way he said *baby* that caused her to tremble. "Yes," she whispered.

Travis licked her just above the waistband of her panties, and Maggie could barely catch her breath.

"It's a—"

He licked her lightly again.

"Fully retractable—"

He kissed her through her panties.

"Self-assembly—"

He licked a little lower.

"Cardboard telescope for Henry."

What? Maggie smacked Travis lightly on the top of his head. "You big tease!"

"What did you think it was?"

"You know what I thought it was, and you're infuriating."

Travis pulled at the waistband of her panties. "I bet you won't stay mad long."

Holy cow. That beard. Those lips. *That tongue.* He was

right. Irritation no longer registered on her radar. She just wanted him to keep doing what he was doing, only lower.

As if he needed any more tricks, Travis proved to be a mind reader and hooked his thumbs in her panties, yanking them down in one swift move before tossing them over his shoulder. "Open your legs."

Ooh . . . there was that voice again. Low. Commanding. A hint of a growl. But it couldn't stamp out the stupid sense of modesty currently keeping her knees glued together. "It's really bright in here."

"I'm not turning off the light. We just got to the best part."

Maggie chewed on her lip and pulled her knees up.

"One," Travis said.

The menacing undertone nearly did it for her.

"Two."

She could do it.

"Three."

Nothing.

Travis put his hands on her knees. "Give me permission. It'll be over before you know it."

Maybe . . . "Okay—"

Bam. He slammed her knees open before she could add, *I guess.*

Travis held her knees firmly in place. She was trapped. At his mercy. *Displayed.*

"You're so beautiful," he whispered. "I have to taste you."

This is the part where the Big Bad Wolf eats Little Red Riding Hood.

Maggie stilled. Why had the wolf's voice butted in? There was no room for him in here. Was her mind playing tricks on her?

Travis's warm mouth erased that thought, and any that tried to form after it. *Rough beard. Soft tongue. The sensa-*

tion of being devoured. A low primal moan that she vaguely recognized as her own voice resonated in her head.

Her skin tingled. Her bones hummed. And when Travis's fingers traveled up her rib cage to pinch her nipples, she completely fell apart, trembling beneath waves of pleasure. And then she was floating...until Travis wrenched her knees apart with a gasp.

She'd been squeezing his head between her thighs.

"Sorry," she wheezed, still trying to catch her breath.

Travis grinned goofily. "It would have been a good way to die."

Slowly, he crawled up her body until they were nose to nose. She lost herself in his blue eyes, and even though she was thoroughly wrecked, she was madly looking forward to what came next.

"This has to be a dream. Pinch me."

Travis's eyes became a shade or two darker. "I just did. And you tried to strangle me with your thighs."

The flush crawled up Maggie's chest, spread to her cheeks, and lit up her ears. He'd noticed what had pushed her over the edge.

"If this is a dream," Travis continued, "I hope we never wake up."

She pulled his face back to hers, wanting his lips, wanting the full weight of him crushing her and holding her down. The bed shook as Travis fumbled around in the nightstand drawer without breaking the kiss. He was getting a condom. At least one of them still had the mental faculties to be responsible.

After he'd slipped it on, he kissed her sweetly and then gently—*oh so gently*—eased himself inside her. She wrapped her legs around him as he moved slowly and rhythmically. The man knew what he was doing. This was a delicious prelude, but Maggie longed for the pace to quicken, the intensity to deepen—

Travis moaned and bit his bottom lip as if trying to control himself. He was holding back, and she didn't want him to. She wanted him to give her everything, but how could she ask for what she needed? She dug her heels into his very fine butt cheeks and pulled on his shoulders.

"You okay?" he asked.

"Yes, I just want..." She couldn't finish.

"What do you want, baby?"

There it was again. The way he said *baby*. The sound of it made her tremble to her core.

"Maybe faster. Try it faster. Or harder. Or...something." She squeezed her eyes shut in embarrassment. "I think I like it hard."

Travis quit moving. He was frozen above her, inside her. She opened one eye for a quick peek at his face. Had she stunned him into silence?

Those eyes. Heavy lidded yet so intense she could feel their gaze. His mouth was drawn in a tight, straight line. Nostrils were flared. A tiny vein pulsed on his forehead.

Maggie dug her fingernails into his shoulders. He winced, and after a sudden, gasping breath, he grabbed both of her wrists easily with one hand. Before she could even squeak, he pinned them above her head.

Oh, yes. This was it. This was what she wanted. "Travis—"

His breath teased her ear, setting her on fire. "Open your legs and take this cock."

Her breath caught. She was so turned on she couldn't move.

"Now," he growled.

Her legs responded like good little soldiers, unwrapping

themselves from his back and falling open, knees raised. "Take me."

Luckily, he didn't need to be told twice.

* * *

Maggie lay next to Travis, listening to his soft snores compete with the ticking of the clock in the hall. While he'd done the man-thing and immediately fallen unconscious, she was wide awake. Her mind hummed along like a hamster on speed.

Best. Sex. Of. Her. Life. Not only was it steamy and, well, just the way she apparently liked it, it was sweet and funny. That striptease! Those ridiculous countdowns to get her clothes off! Followed by heat. So much heat. How had she gotten this lucky? Travis was literally everything she'd ever wanted.

So why was she unsettled? She felt as if she'd missed a doctor's appointment or failed to pick up the one thing she'd gone to the store for. Maybe it had something to do with work. It would come back to her if she could just freaking relax.

Travis had left the nightstand drawer open after rummaging for a condom. She'd somehow ended up on that side of the bed, and the open drawer stared up at her. She wasn't much of a snooper, but as she went to close it, the light from the hallway made it easy to spot condoms, sore muscle cream, and a book—*Bound and Determined*! How adorable and hilarious. She covered her mouth to keep from laughing.

She was about to close the drawer when a phone caught her eye. It wasn't the one Travis regularly used, but it was the same model. Why would he have a second phone in his drawer? She frowned. This shouldn't give her pause. She probably had four or five old phones tucked away in various places.

Her hamster mind spoke up. *Phones are used for texting. By wolves.*

Maggie sat up, pulling the sheet against her. This meant nothing. Absolutely nothing. And why was she thinking about the wolf anyway? She was just doing that worrying thing she sometimes did in the middle of the night.

She looked down. One of Travis's boots poked out from beneath the bed. A square toe. *Dressy, but very worn.* Just like the wolf's.

She sniffed the sheet. At one point tonight, Travis's cologne had sparked a flashback to the night in the shed. She'd brushed it off, feeling guilty for fantasizing about the wolf while she was with Travis.

Open your legs and take this cock.

Maggie gasped. She dropped the sheet and stood up, naked and shivering. She looked at Travis, sleeping peacefully. What was his jawline like beneath the beard? Her eyes darted around the room and spotted her jeans on the floor. She grabbed them and slipped them on, because she suddenly couldn't stand being naked. Too vulnerable. Her red sweater was also on the floor. Where was her bra? No matter. She pulled the sweater over her head. Stepped into one of her boots while looking around for the other one.

"Maggie, is everything okay?"

That voice!

A lamp flicked on, and she winced in its harsh light. Travis sat up sleepily, rubbing his eyes.

His eyes. She'd believed their familiarity was because of high school. But it was more than that. Way more than that.

She limped to the side of the bed, wearing only one boot. Maybe its partner had been kicked underneath when she'd tossed it off with wild abandon. This was all she needed to focus on…*getting dressed*. Nothing else. Not the way Travis's body had felt like the wolf's. Not the way his forceful thrusts and animalistic groans had driven her insane, or the way she'd gleefully submitted, feeling safe and secure—what a joke—and *just like Little Red Riding Hood*.

She looked under the bed.

"I figured you'd stay the night," Travis said.

Maggie had to stop searching for her boot to find her voice. "Henry will be home in the morning. It would confuse him."

"I don't think he'd be confused. He knows we're wrestling partners."

Don't be cute and funny right now. "Tomorrow's Black Friday, remember? I've got to work."

"Just get up early—"

"No, I've got stuff to take care of at home."

"Like what?"

"Pop needs to go out."

"Go get him. He can stay over, too."

He wasn't going to give up. "What part of *no* do you not understand?"

She'd snapped at him. His blue eyes widened in response. His mouth opened as if to speak, but then he faltered. *That's right, buddy. I've got your number. Or the wolf's number. Somebody's number.*

Travis got out of bed and slipped on his jeans.

"What are you doing?"

"Getting dressed. I'm not going to walk you out naked."

"Why would you need to walk me out? I'm perfectly capable of finding my Jeep."

"I don't know. Maybe because we just had soul-shattering sex?" He stuck his foot in a boot, not realizing he'd also just stuck it in his mouth.

Soul-shattering sex. That was how she'd described their night in the shed.

The two of them stood eyeing each other suspiciously, each wearing a single boot.

Maggie looked away first and picked up the bedspread they'd knocked to the floor. Where was her godforsaken boot? Maybe she'd kicked it through the open closet door.

"Listen, Maggie. We need to talk."

Maggie walked to the closet. There was a very nice suit hanging up. Same color as the wolf's. She touched the jacket sleeve. Same fabric. The feel of it against her finger triggered memories in high definition. She shivered, then she turned to look at Travis. "I think it might be a little late for that."

Travis paled. "I can explain."

She didn't want to hear it. *Couldn't* hear it. "What a fun little game you've been playing."

"It wasn't a game. I just didn't—"

"Is the mask in here, too? Do you keep them together?" She dug through the closet. Flannel shirts, T-shirts, jeans... no wolf mask. But it didn't change anything. She was certain. Everything clicked into place. She'd recognized his very first kiss, hadn't she? And tonight, she'd known who he was with every pant, groan, and forceful thrust. *Her wolf.*

And then there'd been Anna. Holy cow, just how many hints had she dropped? *Of course* she would know Travis had come to the gala as the Big Bad Wolf. And Maggie had been providing her with entertainment ever since.

What an idiot she was.

"I was going to tell you—"

She stomped her booted foot. "But you didn't! All this

time, and you didn't say a word. Did you think it was funny?"

She didn't stick around to hear his answer *or* to find her stupid boot. She grabbed her bag—it was right next to Henry's telescope and wasn't *that* another hilarious piece of the humiliation puzzle—and limped out the door.

Chapter
Thirty-Two

♡

Black Friday. In more ways than one.

Petal Pushers would rake in more money today than it had in the previous two months, and normally this obscene amount of consumerism filled Maggie's heart with cheer. But today, instead of doing the happy dance of a retail mogul smothered in jingle bells, she sat at the cash register with her head in her hands, mindlessly rubbing Pop's tummy with her foot.

She was ignoring Travis's texts. She should probably block him. And the stupid wolf, too. Although he hadn't texted since she'd broken up with him. Ugh! She had to stop thinking of Travis and the wolf as two different people.

They were one and the same.

All those texts. She'd sat in her Jeep taking orders from the wolf while Travis sat in his truck! She'd removed her panties at the library while Travis hammered nails in the gazebo! And she'd even talked to the wolf *about* Travis. And he'd never said a word. She'd been so thoroughly played.

She groaned and raised her head. Petal Pushers looked like Christmas had vomited all over it. Every surface was covered by wreaths, trees, bows, and ornaments. It had been cheerful earlier, but now it was disgusting. And if she heard Wham! sing "Last Christmas" one more time, she was going to explode in bloody chunks of green and red.

See? She could be festive.

Where was Claire when she needed her? Well, she knew where she was—somewhere between here and Abilene—but that wasn't the point. Maggie pulled out her phone to send another emergency text.

Claire, where are you???????

Claire.

Claire.

Claire.

Claire.

The door jingled, followed by the tapping of Claire's heels. It was music to Maggie's ears, and she jumped off her stool.

"What is wrong with you?" Claire asked. "My phone thinks it hit the jackpot."

"Travis is the Big Bad Wolf." There. She'd spilled the beans. Said it out loud for the very first time. Right in front of Ford Jarvis. "Hi, Ford."

She'd never heard Ford's voice; not that she could remember anyway. And today was no exception. He nodded and smiled.

"Ford, why don't you head out? I'll see you later," Claire said. Her voice sounded normal—even and tempered. But her eyes were huge and clearly said, *My friend has lost her mind.*

Ford seemed anxious to comply and, with a final nod at Maggie, quickly vacated the premises.

"Oh my God," Claire said. "Have you been eating chalk?"

"What?"

"Sometimes when people have nervous breakdowns, they eat chalk."

"Get some coffee and sit down. I've got a story to tell, and it begins with *Once upon a time there was a Big Bad Wolf.*"

Ten minutes later, Maggie's voice was hoarse, Claire's coffee was untouched, and George Michael was at it again, singing about how someone had thrown his heart away. "And I thought I loved him. The end," Maggie said.

"Okay. I admit this sounds incriminating. It really does. So, let's assume you're right."

"He lied to me!" Maggie wailed. "Like over and over again."

"Well, I imagine it got kind of awkward, you know?"

"I had no idea who he was, Claire. And he knew who I was. He had all the power—"

"Why do you think he knew who you were? Initially, I mean..."

Maggie thought back to the gala. She *had* intentionally avoided introducing herself to him. She'd assumed he was a stranger from out of town. Maybe he'd had similar misunderstandings about her.

"But as soon as he saw me at Anna's—that first day we worked together—he recognized me. He should have come clean."

Claire took a sip of her cold coffee and made a face. "True. Although he was probably pretty dang shocked. And there were other people around, right? What was he supposed to say? That y'all had already met via a shed bang?"

"He could have at least said that we'd met before. And then later, when we were alone, he could have told me—"

"You accused him of child abuse at that meeting, right? Maybe he wasn't anxious to add insult to injury."

The boiling rage in the pit of Maggie's stomach settled down to a simmer. Claire sounded reasonable. "It's just that he dragged it out for so long."

"It doesn't mean his feelings for you aren't real."

"How could they be real? How could *anything* he said or did be real?"

"Are your feelings for him real?"

"He lied to me," she said stubbornly.

Claire leaned closer to Maggie. "You were excited by it. So was he. This isn't necessarily a bad thing. You know what would wrap this up nicely?"

"What?"

"You, agreeing to be pre-surgery Meg Ryan in *You've Got Mail*. You meet Travis at the park. He's wearing a wolf mask. And you say, *I wanted it to be you so badly*. Then you kiss. And we all go, *Yay! And they lived happily ever after!*"

"Real life isn't a fairy tale, Claire."

"I was shooting for a romantic comedy."

The bell jingled on the door, and a blast of cold air hit Maggie in the face. She sighed. "We'll finish this conversation later." She turned to face the next round of customers.

It was JD. And Gabriel was with him. "Mighty Mack, we need a Christmas tree. What have you got?"

JD and Gabriel were buying a tree. Together. In Big Verde.

"I've got an eight-foot noble fir. That's what you usually get, right?" JD had a gorgeous home with high ceilings, lots of windows, and a huge, sloped lawn. He always went overboard at Christmas with lights, lasers, and his Uncle Jeb in a Santa suit sipping on a flask while handing out candy canes. Miss Mills was JD's only real competition, but whereas JD had Drunk Santa, Miss Mills believed Jesus was the reason for the season. Flying reindeer and magic elves were the work of the devil.

"The eight-footer is what we need," JD said.

We. Gabriel's smile outshone Maggie's. "You know what they say about men who feel the need to buy big trees," he said.

JD lifted the brim of his Stetson, so Gabriel could see his raised eyebrow. "But you know that's not true, don't you, Gabe?"

Gabriel's complexion darkened.

Claire cleared her throat, but neither JD nor Gabriel looked up. She did it again, less subtly, sounding like an eighty-year-old man choking on a chicken bone.

JD pounded her on the back.

Claire swatted his arm away. "Who's your friend?"

"This is Gabriel, and I imagine you heard all about him as soon as he and I left Travis's last night."

Claire shook Gabriel's hand. "Pleasure to meet you. I've been out of town, so I'm behind on the gossip. Did y'all rob a liquor store last night? Shoot holes in the Rite Aid sign? Pinch the wrong ass at the Purple Pony?"

"We're dating," JD said.

Claire looked behind them. "Dating who?"

"Each other."

It took about three seconds for it to sink in. Then Claire said to Gabriel, "Oh? You must be from Austin then. I knew JD was seeing someone in Austin. How nice. Are you enjoying Big Verde? Will you be staying long? Can I get you a piece of pie?"

"Claire," JD said. "You can stop babbling. It's okay to act surprised."

Claire slumped with relief. "Whew! Oh my God, JD, you're *gay?*"

"Yep."

"I wouldn't mind a piece of pie," Gabriel said with his two-million-dollar smile. "If it's not too much trouble."

Claire looked at him like he was nuts. "I don't have any pie."

"That's just something Southern girls say when they're nervous," JD whispered.

"Who all knows?" Maggie asked. "Did you tell your parents?"

"Yeah. Told the folks last night."

Maggie raised her eyebrows. "And?"

JD removed his hat. "Well, beneath the initial shock, they seemed to think that a lot of my childhood finally made sense."

"Like your fifth-grade obsession with Shania Twain?"

"Shut up. She's a queen and you know it. Anyway, next I told Bubba."

"How'd that go?"

"Once I convinced him he wasn't my type, he didn't much care."

Maggie led them to where the eight-foot tree stood on the lot. Even though it was the only one that size, JD and Gabriel went through the traditional decision-making angst— holding it this way and that, standing back and looking at it from various angles—before deciding they'd take it. Norbert helped them get it loaded onto JD's truck, with Gabriel snapping pictures and posting them to Instagram the entire time.

Maggie refused to let them pay for it.

"Why don't you and Travis come by for some eggnog after work tonight?" JD said.

"Thanks, but we're not really—"

A pickup turned into the lot and parked next to them. It was Bubba. Trista rolled her pregnant self out, looking ready to pop. Bubba got out next, and then they all watched, mesmerized, as the kids clambered out one by one, like clowns from a clown car.

"Merry Christmas, y'all," Bubba said. When he spotted Gabriel, he adopted a formal tone for introductions. "Trista, this is Gabriel, JD's gay boyfriend. I believe I might have mentioned him earlier."

"You mean when you shot through the door like a rocket on steroids this morning? Yes, I think you might have mentioned him." Trista smiled at Gabriel. "So nice to meet a gay boyfriend of JD's. The straight ones were all so boring."

* * *

Travis leaned on the shovel and wiped sweat out of his eyes. It had taken every ounce of willpower he had just to get out of bed and drag himself to work today. He'd been up all night.

Yesterday had started out perfectly. Wonderful Thanksgiving dinner at Happy Trails. His table surrounded by family and friends—neither of which he'd even *had* a few short weeks ago. And then he and Maggie had made love for the first time.

No, not for the first time, and that was the problem.

As soon as he'd realized what she wanted—*what she needed*—the wolf had come out to play. Maggie had complied so readily, and responded so thoroughly, that he thought he'd pulled it off. That she either hadn't put two and two together, or she had and didn't care.

He'd been wrong. She'd done the math *and* she cared.

The phone calls went straight to voice mail. The texts were ignored. And he felt fucking sick about it. He'd known she wouldn't take it well. How could she? He'd known all along that they'd had sex in the shed—kinky sex, by some standards. And Maggie thought it had been anonymous. He'd let her think that out of cowardice, and then he'd continued the charade out of weakness.

At first, he'd just wanted to avoid awkwardness at work. Later, he was downright fearful she'd blow a gasket, especially since he'd been unable to make himself stop with the sexting. And finally, after they'd grown close and shared their hopes and dreams, he'd been terrified of losing her.

He'd lost her anyway.

Would she stop by today? It was a busy time at Petal Pushers, so probably not. Either way, he had a lot of work to do. He stuck his sweat-drenched bandanna back into his pocket and drove the shovel into a pile of river rocks. Maggie wanted them spread throughout the walking paths of Anna's garden.

His phone rang. With a start, he yanked off his glove and grabbed it out of his pocket. It wasn't Maggie. With his usual lousy timing, Scott was calling. Maybe it was just a *hey, how was your Thanksgiving* call, but Travis doubted it.

"Hello."

"What is this thing I got about garnishing my wages?" Scott demanded.

Gabriel hadn't wasted any time.

"Happy Thanksgiving to you, too."

"I got a job, which is exactly what I was supposed to do—"

"Really? That's great news. Where?"

"Why does it matter? You're going to take all my money!"

"Actually, that money will go to help support your son. It's expensive to raise a kid. I just registered him for soccer. It was sixty-five dollars plus another thirty for the uniform. Want to buy some raffle tickets?"

Maybe Gabriel was right, and rattling Scott's money chain would cause him to drop the threat of taking Henry.

"If I get Henry, I won't have to give anyone any money. Maybe I should just go ahead and pursue that route. Unless, of course, you want to sell the ranch."

"I don't want to sell the ranch. And if you take Henry to punish me, you've got *all* the financial burden. Soccer starts next Thursday. Cleats are on sale at Walmart."

"Why can't you just pay the taxes and sell the ranch? We'll both be rich. And then you can pretend to be Henry's daddy all you want."

"I want to make Happy Trails into something. And I don't want to *pretend* to be Henry's daddy. I want you to give up your rights. If you don't, then the law says you must support your child."

Scott was quiet. Was it working?

"Fuck you. He's probably not my kid anyway."

Travis shook his head in disgust as he stared at the phone. *That's right, motherfucker. He's mine.*

There was no time to sit on this, so Travis texted Gabriel to get the ball rolling. No more procrastinating or avoiding unpleasant situations.

Feeling a little lighter, he put his phone back in his pocket and dug into the rocks with renewed vigor. It only took a few minutes for the endorphins to get pumping. He'd just slayed Goliath for Henry.

Next, he was going to get his woman back.

Chapter
Thirty-Three

♡

Travis watched the gathering storm clouds through the living room window.

It had been four days since Thanksgiving. No word from Maggie. He'd even texted her that he'd found her boot. He suspected she'd blocked him.

He wasn't the kind of guy to creepily stalk a woman, but Henry wouldn't stop asking about her. What was he supposed to do about that?

The Grinch was on TV. This was at least the fifth time Henry had watched the DVD today, all while giving Travis the stinky side-eye for his lack of merrymaking. The naked tree sat in the big front window. He'd bought it at Petal Pushers yesterday, hoping to see Maggie. She hadn't been there, but Claire had. She'd sold him the tree and said, *You're in Big Bad Trouble with a capital T.*

Like he didn't already know that.

"When is Maggie coming to decorate the tree?" Henry asked. Again.

It was Tuesday. Maggie was supposed to come after work, but somehow Travis doubted that was still the plan.

"She's at Petal Pushers," Lupe said, setting out a tray of fresh-baked Christmas cookies. "They close at six, so you've got another hour or so."

Travis gulped. "It's a busy day for Petal Pushers because of the holidays. So, don't be disappointed if she's too tired to come, okay?"

"That's silly, Uncle Travis. Maggie made a promise."

Travis pulled out his phone, looked at it, and tossed it on the couch. But then he had an idea. *Maybe she hadn't thought to block the Big Bad Wolf.*

He went upstairs and pulled the wolf's phone out of his nightstand drawer.

Once upon a time, there was a Big Dumb Wolf.

He sat on the bed and waited. It didn't take long.

And once upon a time there was a fair maiden who made the mistake of following him into the woods.

Travis wanted to remind her that she'd had a banging good time in the woods, but he didn't want to ruin it. He decided to go with what was in his heart.

I miss my moon. The world is dark without her.

Minutes ticked by. He should have known Maggie wouldn't react to romantic bullshit. He was going to have to fight dirty.

Henry wants to know if you're coming tonight.

I'll be there at 7.

When she didn't add anything more, he stood up. It was time to face the music. All of it. He'd been a conflict avoider his entire life. When you lived with a volatile, gambling alcoholic, you lay low, ducked into available open doorways, and waited for storms to pass.

But some storms didn't pass until you weathered them.

He was a little old to learn this lesson, but dammit, he'd recently come to realize there were three things that mattered to him—Happy Trails, Henry, and Maggie—and he wasn't going to lose any of them.

"You boys had better get ready for your company," Lupe said when Travis came down the stairs.

He ran his fingers through his mass of hair and rubbed his beard. Lupe was right. He needed to get ready. He went into the bathroom and pulled out a razor and shears. No more hiding.

Twenty minutes later, he emerged to hysterical laughter from Henry. "You look like a plucked chicken!"

Beard: gone. Mass of hair: clipped short.

Lupe walked up and rubbed his cheek. "Very handsome," she said with a wink. "And you, too, Henry."

Henry had put on what he called his fancy clothes: clean jeans with no holes and a long-sleeved blue shirt. He'd even stuffed his feet into the shoes he'd worn to Lisa's funeral. It didn't look like they fit anymore. That gave Travis a lump in his throat the size of Texas and, for some dumb reason, reminded him of the gravity of the situation. There were two possible outcomes: a new beginning, or an ending.

"You know you don't have to get dressed up for Maggie, right? She thinks you're awesome no matter what you wear."

Henry patted his hair and frowned. "I can't get the puffy part to stay down."

"I think Maggie likes the puffy part."

"You don't have to get dressed up either, Uncle Travis. Maggie likes you just the way you are. And that means she loves you."

Travis sighed. Maggie probably thought she didn't know him at all anymore. But she was wrong. She knew him better than anyone ever had.

"I warmed up some chili," Lupe said. "Your bowl is on the bar. You should eat before Maggie gets here."

Travis sat down and pulled the bowl over. He hadn't been able to eat much in the past few days, but now he thought maybe he had an appetite.

Lupe set a manila envelope next to him. "I found this on the gate a couple of days ago. I forgot to bring it in. You might want to open it."

Travis's heart pounded. Had Maggie resorted to leaving him notes on the gate again? And he hadn't even read it? He tried not to be irritated with Lupe—it wasn't her fault he was in this mess. Maggie had never put one of her gate notes in an envelope before. It must be personal. He tried to compose himself as he pulled it out.

AUCTION.

Shit! This wasn't from Maggie. It was from the tax office. He scanned the rest of the letter quickly, searching for a date.

November 29 Courthouse Annex Lawn

That was today!

"Travis, what's wrong?" Lupe asked. "You look like you've seen a ghost!"

Travis grabbed his keys and his checkbook. Maybe there was still time. Maybe nobody had bid on Happy Trails, and he could still do something.

"I've got to go."

"But where? Where are you going? Maggie will be here any minute."

It was raining, but he didn't have time to look for an umbrella. He had to get to the courthouse. "Tell Maggie I'll be back as soon as I can. Tell her it's important."

Fifteen minutes later, he pulled up to the courthouse annex. There was absolutely nobody on the lawn, and the place looked closed. He made a run for the courthouse door. It was locked, but he yanked on it anyway. He peered through the glass and saw a woman walking down the hall. He banged on the door.

"The offices are closed," she shouted. "You'll have to come back tomorrow."

"Was there an auction here today? For Happy Trails?"

The woman rolled her eyes and removed a set of keys from her pocket. She opened the door a crack. "Only one person showed up in this weather, but yes, there was an auction."

"Who showed up? Who was it?"

"Gerome Kowalski. He had the winning bid."

Travis took a step back. It was a punch to the gut. To the *heart*. Gerome's kindness had been an act. Travis had been an idiot to think a man like that would want to help a guy like him. Gerome had pretended to be, of all things, *fatherly*. And Travis had soaked it up. No wonder he hadn't wanted money for replacing the fences. He knew they'd be his. He probably had an ingenious plan to incorporate Happy Trails and keep it as a direct line to consumers, hence the farmer's market stall.

"Bye, now," the lady said, closing the door.

The lock clicked. "Wait, how does this work?"

She'd already walked away.

Travis trudged back to his truck, not feeling the rain or the cold or anything at all. Gerome Kowalski had just added two hundred acres to Rancho Canada Verde... *for chump change*.

Chump change that Travis couldn't come up with.

How would he face Henry? He'd fucked it all up.

He started the truck and headed for Tony's. The last barstool on the left already had his name on it.

Chapter
Thirty-Four

The Christmas music was going to be the death of Maggie. "Can we change the station, please?" she begged.

Claire, wearing what Maggie assumed to be a Mrs. Claus outfit if Mrs. Claus was a porn star, stuffed a wreath in a bag. "Yes, we can change it."

"Oh, thank God." Maggie sighed.

"On January first."

"But Claire—"

"Maggie, we're selling trees. We're selling wreaths. We're selling lights and inflatable elves. And we're going to listen to Christmas music, okay?" She smiled at Mrs. Parker as she handed her the bag. "Thank you and Merry Christmas!"

A large hand slapped a box of red and green ornaments on the counter. Maggie looked up to see Bubba peering over four more boxes. "Hey, Bubba. Why all the ornaments?"

"We got a cat," he said. "A cat that climbs Christmas trees. I told Trista that cats are useless animals."

Pop barked from beneath the counter.

"You don't need these then," Maggie said. She looked around for Kristen, the high school senior providing holiday help on weekends. She didn't see the perky blond ponytail anywhere. Which meant Kristen was probably hiding somewhere with her nose glued to her phone. "Come on. We have some that aren't breakable."

"I got the counter," Claire said.

Bubba followed Maggie to the ornaments. "I had to drive Travis home from Tony's last night. He was wasted."

Maggie stopped in her tracks. That asshole had stood her up to go to Tony's and get drunk? It wasn't quite the groveling she'd expected. And to think she'd been ready to forgive him.

I miss my moon. My world is dark without her.

Ha! She'd fallen for that. She really had. But then he hadn't even been at the house last night. She and Lupe had decorated the tree with Henry, looking at the door the whole time because they were freaking idiots. Honey's voice had played in her head on repeat. *That boy done run oft, Maggie.*

Maggie grabbed three boxes of unbreakable ornaments off the shelf and shoved them at Bubba. "You're a married man with kids and a pregnant wife. What were you doing at Tony's?" She really felt like railing on a man, and Bubba was the nearest one.

"Hey, settle down. Trista made eggnog, and I wanted mine with a kick. The liquor store was closed, so Tony slipped a little in a baby bottle for me." He lowered his voice to a whisper. "Don't tell anyone. I think it's illegal."

Maggie rolled her eyes. "I'll try to keep a lid on it."

"What happened with you and Travis? That boy was a mess last night."

Claire came around the corner. "That's just what I was coming back here to ask. Did y'all make up over the Big Bad Wolf thing? Did you pull a pre-surgery Meg Ryan?"

"The Big Bad Wolf? Meg Ryan? What the hell are y'all talking about?" Bubba asked.

"Did I hear something about the Big Bad Wolf?" JD stood at the end of the aisle, smoke coming out of both ears. Nobody had even seen him come in.

"Seriously, JD? Don't you have somewhere else to be? Don't *all of you* have somewhere else to be?"

Claire crossed her arms over her chest. "I work here."

"And I need more tree lights," JD said.

They all looked at Bubba. "I honestly can't remember why I'm here."

Maggie stomped her foot. "Listen, I know you're all curious, and you want to know what happened between me and Travis, but it's my business and for once the entire town of Big Verde doesn't need to know it."

"Know what?" Alice popped up at the opposite end of the aisle, arms full of tinsel.

"That Travis is the Big Bad Wolf who's been sexting Maggie," Claire said.

"Oh, my," Alice said with a grin. "Maggie, aren't you the lucky girl!"

"Wait a minute," JD said. "Are you saying that wolf who had his hands all over you at the gala was Travis? Why, I ought to—"

"Aw, cut out the jealous shit, JD. You're gay now, remember?" Bubba said.

JD yanked on the brim of his hat. "Yes, I remember, and I'm not gay *now*—"

"Well, that didn't last long, did it?" Bubba said.

Maggie wanted to scream. "All of you get out! None of

this is any of your business. Travis and I are done. Got it? We are *done*."

"This shit sucks," Bubba said. "After losing Happy Trails, I'm not sure Travis can handle losing you, too. He was even blubbering about Scott and Henry. The poor man thinks he's losing everything."

"One thing at a time," JD said. "He's not going to lose Henry. And no matter how pissed off she is, he's not losing Maggie either." Maggie started to protest, but JD glared her into silence. "What's this about Happy Trails though?"

Maggie's heart jumped to her throat. No matter how she felt about Travis being the wolf, he and Henry didn't deserve to lose the ranch.

"It was auctioned off yesterday," Bubba said. "Gerome bought it."

Claire gasped. "Daddy bought Happy Trails? That doesn't make any sense."

Bubba shrugged his shoulders. "That's what Travis said."

"That can't be true," Maggie said. Travis hadn't paid the back taxes yet, but would Gerome really take advantage of someone when he was down? Someone who'd been working so hard to dig out? Maggie wrung her hands. It didn't add up. Gerome wasn't that kind of man.

Although she'd recently learned she was a piss-poor judge of character.

"I'm going over there to find out what's really going on," she announced.

"Wait! I'm coming with you," Claire said. "Norbert and Kristen can mind the store."

"I'm coming, too," JD said.

Bubba put the ornaments he was holding back on the shelf. "Oh, hell. Me, too."

* * *

With effort, Travis peeled his lips apart. Next, he forced his eyes open. They felt full of sand, but unless it was a mirage, they were staring at a cup of water. And Tylenol. God bless Lupe.

With a groan, he sat up and popped the pills, downed the water. Yesterday played back like a nightmare. He'd lost the motherfucking ranch. How much time would they have to move out? And how was he going to tell Henry?

The bedroom door flew open. Travis closed his eyes and covered his ears.

"Uncle Travis, come see the tree!" Henry shouted.

"Talk softly, Henry. I have a headache."

Henry whispered, "Come see the tree."

"Okay," Travis whispered back. "Let me get dressed."

He didn't have the slightest interest in the tree. But he wanted Henry to be happy and carefree for as long as possible, so he'd pretend.

He managed to piss, brush the fur off his teeth, and get a pair of jeans on. Grabbing a T-shirt would involve bending over to open a drawer, so he'd go without.

The smell of strong coffee greeted him at the bottom of the stairs, and Lupe placed a mug in his hand. Holiday shit was everywhere—decorations, photos, an obnoxious musical Christmas village—and it dang near broke his heart. The place finally looked (and felt) like a home. A *real* home. The ones he used to see on TV.

They'd never had a tree at Christmastime. Christmas morning had dawned like every other, with Ben Blake hung over and Travis and Scott fighting over toaster waffles.

"Looks like Santa's elves were busy last night," he said, clearing his throat of whatever was making it difficult to speak.

"It wasn't elves. It was us!" Henry said. "You gots to help us put the angel on top."

"I *have* to help you put the angel on top."

"I know. That's what I said."

Lupe touched Travis's arm. "Come into the kitchen, *mijo*. Let's talk."

The kitchen was warm from the oven. Lupe had made cinnamon rolls, and even though his stomach wasn't in top form, the smell made Travis's mouth water. He reached for one, but Lupe slapped his hand.

"Are you loco? Not good for a hangover."

She grabbed a container out of the refrigerator and stuck it in the microwave. "I went to Rosie's Cocina this morning and picked this up for you. I'd have made it myself, but I didn't know you were going to need it."

Travis inhaled. Dear God. The woman was going to force-feed him *menudo*.

The microwave dinged, and he instinctively checked his phone for a text. Nothing from Maggie. It was over. Everything was over.

Lupe set a bowl and spoon in front of him. "Here you go."

He'd never tasted *menudo*. He didn't reckon himself for a tripe fan. But he knew not to mess with Lupe, especially where food was concerned, so he took a small sip. And it tasted pretty good. The second spoonful was even better. And surprisingly, his stomach was settling down, too.

"Good, right?"

He nodded. Maybe he'd get through this bowl before giving Lupe the bad news.

"I read the notice," Lupe said. "About the auction. Do you know who bought it?"

"It was Gerome."

He expected Lupe's face to reflect the same range of emotions that coursed through him, but she just nodded her head and made a little sound to indicate she wasn't surprised. Was Travis the only one who'd misjudged Gerome's character? The man was a sneaky, slimy bastard.

"Uncle Travis!" Henry shouted.

Travis winced.

"JD's truck is here, and a bunch of people are getting out. Oh! It's Maggie!"

"Shit." Travis jumped up from the table, heart pounding. He needed a shirt. He needed shoes. He needed—

"Hi, Maggie!"

Henry had already let them in. Talk about feeling exposed. Travis entered the crowded living room like he was on an episode of *Naked and Afraid*. What were they all doing here? His eyes settled on Maggie. She stared at him like she was seeing a ghost. Her cheeks turned pink, followed predictably by her ears. What was she thinking about? Thanksgiving night? The night in the shed? *His betrayal?*

"I told them about the ranch," Bubba admitted.

"How did you know about it?"

"Everybody at Tony's knows about it," Bubba said. "You're quite the showman. And they also know about your deep and meaningful feelings for Maggie and something about a spreader bar."

Maggie gasped, and the ears went to Code Red. Travis was pretty sure he was blushing, too, and he had no beard to cover it up. JD pulled his hat down low, shading the upper half of his face, but his grin was clearly visible.

"What's a spreader bar?" Henry asked.

Jesus. This was great. Travis glared at Bubba.

Bubba shrugged. "They're for lifting engines and other heavy stuff." Bubba gave Travis one of his poker face winks before adding, "The tractor supply place on the highway has some."

Henry had already quit listening, especially since Lupe was holding out a cinnamon roll. "Come into the kitchen, little one. I'll get you some cocoa to go with this." She paused at the door. "My cousin, Herman, works at the tractor place. He'll give you a good deal on the bar."

Wonderful. Travis was soon to be the proud owner of something used to lift tractor engines, right before he presumably moved into an efficiency apartment in Austin.

Maggie grinned at him, but then covered it up with her hand. Hope sparked in his heart. She was here, wasn't she? Her big, brown mood ring eyes couldn't seem to decide between concern, irritation, and something else he couldn't quite put his finger on. He went to rub his beard and realized it was gone. *Oh.* Maybe that was the thing he couldn't put his finger on. Recognition. Maggie was looking at the Big Bad Lying Wolf.

"Maybe you can buy this place back from Gerome," Bubba said, reminding Travis that there were other people in the room.

"With what? Do you know what this place is worth? I can't even afford the taxes on it."

"We'll figure something out," JD said. "Maybe a loan—"

"Someone else is here," Bubba said. "Man, you know how to host a fucking party, Travis."

Claire peeked through the curtains. "It's my dad."

Gerome Kowalski had come to take the ranch.

* * *

Every cell in Maggie's body cried *Wolf!* And judging from the stirring in her heart—*and nether regions*—they didn't feel a bit betrayed. Her mind, however, was another story.

Travis was pale, clearly hungover, and half naked. He

shouldn't face Gerome that way. "Go put on a shirt," she whispered.

His eyes searched hers, probably looking for clues as to whether she'd decided he was friend or foe. But she didn't have any to offer up. Not when she was in such turmoil. "Go," she repeated.

Travis bolted up the stairs just as Claire opened the door. "Daddy? Did you have to come so soon?"

Gerome enveloped Claire in a hug. "It's nearly noon. What are you doing here, sweetheart? Your mama's going to be upset that she didn't come along."

Yeah. Because if you're going to rip someone's home out of their hands, why not bring the whole family?

Claire closed the door, and Gerome, wearing a bewildered expression, glanced around the room. "Looks like I walked in on a party," he said. "A sad one."

Lupe came out of the kitchen and offered to take Gerome's coat, which he handed over, along with his hat and a tub of homemade pecan pralines from Claire's mom.

Who did that? Who offered candy in exchange for a family's ranch? This was some seriously weird business, and Maggie didn't dare open her mouth for fear of what might come out of it.

Gerome shook hands with Bubba and JD, both of whom were appropriately curt. Claire, who looked like she'd just discovered her dad had killed Santa, wrung her hands while blinking back tears.

Everyone parted like the Red Sea as Travis came down the stairs. Gerome held out his hand. "Howdy, son."

Travis was fully dressed in Wranglers, a long-sleeved shirt—pressed and starched—and the square-toe boots. Clean-shaven, clipped hair. He looked like a cowboy.

He looked like her wolf.

Travis smiled and shook Gerome's hand as if he were a welcome guest. "Can I get you some coffee?"

"Already had my two cups." Gerome glanced around with apprehension wrinkling his forehead. "Can we go into the kitchen to speak in private?"

Claire stepped forward. "Daddy, whatever you have to say to Travis, you can say in front of us."

JD and Bubba nodded, and JD topped it off with a vicious yank on the brim of his hat, a gesture that could possibly be interpreted as a direct threat.

Gerome shook his head as if trying to clear it of cobwebs and glanced longingly at the couch. "Why don't we all have a seat?"

Bubba took the recliner, leaning back and sighing as if maybe he'd take a nap after Travis was done losing his ranch. JD and Claire took the other two chairs, and Gerome sat on the couch.

Maggie stood next to Travis. She could feel the heat radiating off him. He looked calm and collected, but she knew better.

"I'm not sure how all this is supposed to work, Gerome," Travis said.

Gerome sat up straighter on the couch. "That's what I came to discuss."

Travis cleared his throat. "I'm hoping, on account of Henry, that we can remain in the house through the holidays. Then we'll be on our way."

"What kind of a man do you think I am?" Gerome asked. He stood, joints creaking. "Of course I want you to stay in the house through the holidays. And after."

"I don't understand," Travis said. "Didn't you buy Happy Trails?"

"No. I paid off the taxes and now I own the lien. According to the state of Texas, you've got two years to reclaim the property." He walked over to Travis and placed a hand on his shoulder. "What I did, son, was buy you some time."

Henry ran into the room and threw his arms around Gerome's legs. "Hi, Mr. K! I didn't know you was here."

"*Were* here," Maggie said.

Henry made bug eyes at her. "He's still here, ain't he?"

"Isn't he," Travis said.

"Is there an echo in here?" Henry shouted, sounding just like Lupe.

Travis picked Henry up. His Adam's apple bobbed as he swallowed and searched for words—probably trying to soak in what he'd just heard. Finally, he said, "Why would you do this, Gerome? Why would you spend so much of your own money just to buy me some more time?"

"Well, now, before you go making me a hero, you should know there's a bit of interest involved. But I did it because every boy deserves a chance to be a real cowboy." He pinched Henry's nose, and Henry erupted in giggles.

Travis nodded and ruffled Henry's hair. "Henry deserves a lot of things."

"That he does," Gerome said. "But I was talking about you."

* * *

Travis stood on the porch and watched Gerome drive away. The others, including Maggie, had left earlier, leaving Gerome and Travis alone to discuss the details.

Two years. He had two years to pay off the lien plus interest, and with what he'd already managed to save, it wouldn't take him nearly that long. But Gerome had suggested Travis wait the entire two years—plus one day. Happy Trails would then legally belong to Gerome, and he could sell it back to Travis without Scott's name being on the deed.

Travis wasn't entirely sure how he felt about that. He wanted to be free of Scott, but he didn't want to swindle him. Gerome had scoffed. Said he knew Scott's type and Travis wasn't doing him any favors by giving him money. But he'd agreed to help figure out a fair way to reimburse Scott for his half of the ranch, minus what Scott owed in rent, his share of back taxes, and of course, child support for the past five years.

It would still be a lot of money. But Travis had big dreams for Happy Trails, and he was going after them full throttle.

And those dreams included Henry and Maggie.

He went upstairs and retrieved the phone he kept in his nightstand drawer. Maggie had shown up today. She still had feelings for him. He just knew it. What they had was real, and even if it had started off with role playing and a fictitious *once upon a time*, Travis hoped it would end with a very real *happily ever after*.

The Big Bad Wolf was going to send Little Red Riding Hood one more text.

Chapter
Thirty-Five

❧

Travis leaned against the workbench and admired his handiwork. Bright twinkling lights hung from the shed's rafters. Softly glowing candles surrounded the champagne and glasses he'd set on a small folding table. He clenched a beautiful bouquet of yellow roses—Claire's creation—tightly in his hand. He'd even ordered dinner from the Corner Café. They didn't typically do deliveries, but Bubba's folks owned the place, and he'd offered to bring their steaks to the shed. Travis had no doubt as to Bubba's motives. Five minutes after he left, all of Big Verde would know how the date was going.

Travis shifted nervously from boot to boot and stared at the door. Would Little Red Riding Hood stiff him? It was just past seven o'clock. He dug for his phone and stared at the text he'd sent.

Can we start our 'Once Upon a Time' over? Follow the rose petals to the shed. I'll be there at 7.

She hadn't responded, but the text had been delivered. He stuffed his phone back in his pocket and resumed staring at the door.

Two hours ago, he'd stood up to Scott with Gabriel at his side. And Scott had consented to relinquish his parental rights. There were still details to work out; the court would have to approve the termination, but Gabriel said it should be no problem since Travis intended to adopt Henry.

Henry would be his son.

Only one element was still needed to turn this fairy tale into a reality, and that was Maggie.

Travis swallowed. Clenched his jaw. *She would come. She had to.*

The First National Bank of Big Verde was holding its annual employee Christmas party at the Chateau, and the music and frivolity floated on the breeze, just as it had the night of the Halloween gala. The night he'd passed up an opportunity to remove his mask and say *Hi. I'm Travis Blake. I know we just met, but I think I might love you.*

Because he'd felt it, even then.

Maggie was something special.

His tie was stifling, so he loosened it. Adjusted the dressy gray Stetson he'd bought special for the occasion. And then he just waited, while his heart threatened to burst through his rib cage.

* * *

Maggie parked next to Travis's truck and stared at the path that led through the cedar trees to the shed. It was covered in yellow petals, which was silly and seemed like a waste of good roses. She slammed her Jeep door and tried to ignore the smile tugging at her lips.

She headed down the path, slowing her pace when she realized she was hurrying. No need to go blasting through the door panting with enthusiasm and drooling forgiveness. Travis was going to have to work for it.

Hopefully he had more than rose petals up his sleeve.

The windows of the shed glowed with an inviting yellow hue. Candles? Had the man brought candles? Maggie swallowed and walked to the door. Her hand hesitated briefly on the knob, then she inhaled and slowly pushed it open.

Her breath caught at the sight of Travis stepping out of the shadows. The nice suit. The sharp, clean-shaven jaw. *The deep blue eyes.* How had she not known?

"Maggie—" His voice cracked, and he cleared his throat, held out his hand. "Please come inside."

She looked past him to the candles, twinkling lights, roses... Was that champagne?

"I promise I won't bite," he said.

He pulled her in gently, shutting the door behind her. His eyes roamed her body, clad in a red sweater dress—*of course she'd worn red*—and added, "Much as I might like to."

Maggie's pulse quickened. He was startlingly handsome. She longed to trace his jaw with her finger, remove the suit jacket, loosen his tie, unbutton his shirt...

Travis handed her the roses.

She was twenty-seven years old, owned a mother-luvin' flower shop, and nobody had ever given her roses before. "Oh, Travis. They're beautiful. Thank you." *Dang it, Mackey! Don't be this easy.*

"Claire made the arrangement. She fussed over the color. Said red is for romance, and yellow is for friendship. But yellow reminds me of you and your Jeep, and besides, you're the best friend I've ever had."

Had this conversation really headed so quickly into the

friend zone? Maybe she'd made some assumptions—*again*. "Listen, Travis—"

He touched her chin and tilted her face up, gazing intently. "Lupe says that friendship is the basis of true love. That you have to be a true friend to someone before you can ask for their heart. And Maggie, I haven't been a very good friend. I'd like to start over and do better, if you'll let me."

He wanted to ask for her heart? Would it be premature, at this point in the conversation, for her to yank it out of her chest and stick a bow on it?

Yes, it would. He'd *hurt* her. She needed an explanation. And an apology. Until then, there would be no swooning whatsoever. Her shaky knees were getting ahead of themselves. "Why did you carry on this charade for so long? I just don't get it. Were you trying to make a fool out of me?"

Travis closed his eyes as if steeling himself and then opened them with a sigh. "Nobody could ever make a fool out of you, Maggie. You're the strongest, smartest woman I've ever met. I never meant to hurt or—"

"Humiliate?"

"Especially not that," he said. "Never."

"I need to know why."

Travis pulled the brim of his hat down low and stared at his boots. "When I wore the mask, you thought I was a stranger. You were attracted to me—"

"Understatement, and you know it."

He looked up. "You *wanted* me. You didn't know I was Travis Blake, the guy who grew up on the rundown Happy Trails Ranch, accused bracelet thief, son of a man who couldn't afford to keep his fences intact but could afford to drink himself to death. The brother of a criminal. Fresh out of the Army with empty pockets and back taxes to pay and a newly acquired kid…"

But she loved that kid. And she hadn't known Travis had seen himself that way. It wasn't like *she* had seen him that way. She wasn't judgmental.

Previous words and thoughts slowly seeped into her consciousness.

Nice boys, those Blakes.

He's probably a bookie.

I hear he's an ex-con.

He's nothing but a glorified lawn boy.

Her face must have shown the realization, because Travis smiled sadly.

"Travis—"

He put a finger to her lips. "Let me finish. I liked being whoever you thought I was when I wore the mask. You made me feel like such a man, Maggie. In a way I'd never felt before. And I wanted to *be* that man. When I first saw you at Anna's, I thought you recognized me as the wolf, and that maybe you were a bit embarrassed. But then I realized you didn't, and when you learned who I was..."

Maggie blushed. She'd accused him of abusing Henry. She'd asked Anna to remove him from the project.

"You didn't like me," Travis said, "but you liked the Big Bad Wolf. I had a hard time letting him go for that reason."

"But after I got to know you—"

"You liked me?"

"More than liked you. I even quit messing around with the wolf because of you. You knew it, too. So why didn't you tell me then?"

"I wanted to. Desperately. But I was afraid you wouldn't understand. That you'd be humiliated, and angry, and that just when I'd finally earned your respect, I'd lose you entirely."

He was probably right. But it wasn't the *wrong* reaction.

It wasn't her fault she'd been lied to, deceived, and made a fool of. It was his. And so far, all she'd heard was excuses.

"Maggie, I am so sorry for hurting you. For lying to you."

Bingo! But was it enough? She'd never been the kind of girl to let go of a grudge very easily.

"If I could do it all over again..." Travis took her hands in his. "I'm Travis Blake. Not some mysterious stranger or intriguing masked lover. I'm just a man. And not always a very good one. But you bring something out in me. Something wild and fierce that wants to have you and protect you and all those things you probably don't like."

But a part of her liked it very much. "You clearly bring something out in me, too," she said, wondering how bright her ears appeared in the dim lighting. "And I'm not a sexy vixen in boots who hooks up with strangers. I'm a woman who'd rather watch basketball than go shopping. I don't need all of this." She looked around the room at the candles, champagne, roses...

"You like it, though."

Yes, she did. "Well, I'm also a control freak who doesn't like to share or be told what to do."

Travis's eyes darkened a shade. "Sometimes you enjoy being told what to do."

Maggie shivered. Travis didn't need the mask to flip her switch.

"I want to be with you, Maggie. I want to be with you when you're bossy and prissy—"

"I am not ever prissy."

Travis grinned. "And argumentative."

The best she could do was produce a disgruntled-sounding harrumph. And try not to smile.

"I want to be with you when you're sweet, kind, and nurturing. And when you're—"

"Ornery and cantankerous?"

"I was going to say sexy. Hot as hell. Naughty in ways I like to think are just for me."

"Oh."

He lowered his eyes. Licked his lips. And then he whispered, "I love you."

There it was. The three little words every girl longed to hear. She felt warm and tingly, as if she'd just guzzled a mixture of sunshine and honey. It made her eyes leak. "Oh, Travis, I—"

They both jumped at a knock on the door.

"Who on earth can that be?" Maggie asked. What if they were about to get in trouble for trespassing?

Travis looked at his phone. "It's seven thirty. I think it's our dinner. I hope you don't mind, I ordered some steaks from the Corner Café."

Maggie hadn't noticed that the table was set for two. Travis opened the door. And there stood Anna.

"Anna," Travis said. "What are you doing here?"

"Freezing my ass off," she answered, pushing him aside and strolling on in. "And delivering dinner."

Travis stood with the door—and his mouth—wide open. After a few awkward seconds, he finally managed to shut both. "Bubba was supposed to do it."

"Well, he can't. Trista popped that baby out right in the middle of St. Luke's *Las Posadas* procession down Main Street. I swear, it's just like her to try and upstage the Virgin Mary."

"Oh my!" Maggie said. "Are she and the baby okay?"

"Of course they are," Anna said. "Another girl. And between you and me, Trista is made for it. Wide hips. But anyway, it happened just as the procession stopped at the Corner Café. They shooed everybody out, and Bubba asked me to pick up your dinner elsewhere. So here I am."

This was a lot to take in.

"You're welcome," Anna added.

"Thank you," Travis said, taking the two large bags.

"I made it easy on myself and picked this up here at the Chateau," Anna said. "Why on earth you're in this shed I'll never know." She glanced around, taking in the lights and candles as if she were in the discount aisle of Walmart.

Maggie saw Travis pale as he pulled out his wallet. Dinner from the Village Chateau would be four times as much as one from the Corner Café.

Anna held up her hand. "No, don't do that. I've got it."

"Now, Anna, I can't let you do that," Travis said, opening his wallet. Maggie hoped there was enough money in it.

Anna crossed her arms over her chest. "Listen. I, um, kind of owe you for...things. I mean, well, there was the bracelet incident. And probably some other stuff."

What other stuff? And did this mean Anna had a heart? Holy cow, did she have a *soul?*

Travis looked at Anna for a minute, and then he put his wallet away. "Thank you," he said. "That's very generous of you, and I accept your apology."

Anna tossed her hair and raised an eyebrow. "It's not like I bought you lobster. It's just a couple of New York strips."

Whatever. A half-assed apology was still an apology, and Travis appeared to be satisfied.

"I'll just be on my way," Anna said. She glanced around the room again, and as Travis opened the door, her eyes met Maggie's. She smiled a little, and for a second, she seemed almost sweet. Then she flipped her hair and headed on out. "Later."

Travis shut the door. "Wow."

"Do you think it's poisoned?" Maggie asked, looking at the bags.

"Probably not," Travis said, taking Maggie in his arms. "Now. Where were we?"

"You just told me you love me, and I was about to say it back."

Travis kissed the tip of her nose. "You might want to get on with it then."

His breath was so warm against her skin. She turned her face up to his and whispered against his lips, "I love you, Travis. So very much."

Kiss me.

He took a small step back and removed his hat, holding it in front of him. "Can you forgive me?"

Maggie's heart melted and pooled at her feet, which was a sure sign she'd already forgiven him. "Of course I can. But no more deception, okay?"

"I swear I'll never hide anything from you again."

She believed him. And she couldn't hold back any longer. She wanted to touch him. Squeeze him. Kiss him. And that was just for starters. Without another thought, she flung herself at her big bad cowboy, wrapping her arms around his neck.

Something large pressed firmly against her tummy.

"My, Travis," she whispered against his lips. "What a big hat you have."

Travis placed it back on his head with a grin. "The better to woo you with, my dear."

Maggie's heart skipped a beat. She rose on her toes as Travis dipped his head, shadowing their faces with the (slightly bent) brim of his Stetson.

And they lived happily ever after.

The End.

Epilogue

❧

Maggie hit the remote and opened the Happy Trails gate with extreme satisfaction. It had been two years and one day, and Happy Trails now officially belonged to Travis and Mary Margaret Blake.

She couldn't help but roll her eyes as she drove past the gigantic wreath on the gate. She'd already spent the day drowning in Christmas at Petal Pushers, or as she liked to refer to it during the holidays, the Little Shop of Ho-Ho-Horrors. But Travis absolutely loved decorating the ranch for the holidays, and even though she cherished her role as Scrooge, she wouldn't deny him that. Or much else, for that matter.

A school bus was parked in front of the hay barn. Goodness, she'd forgotten today was field trip day. And Honey's Cottage was rented out to tourists for the weekend. They'd be arriving any minute, and she hadn't yet left fresh eggs in the fridge or flowers on the table.

She parked between the barn and the country chapel Travis had built for their wedding last April. It had been in constant use ever since. In fact, JD and Gabriel had it booked for Valentine's Day, and Big Verde was going nuts in anticipation of its "first gay wedding," as the newspaper called it.

Maggie and Travis just referred to it as what it was: a wedding.

The tractor rumbled over the hill and Travis waved. Maggie couldn't see his grin, but she felt it. The breeze brought giggles and shrieks from the passengers he towed, snuggled among hay bales and blankets on the trailer. They were coming back from the goat pens, which were currently home to eight baby goats and their mamas. Nothing was more fun and bouncy than baby goats, and Maggie expected their contagious enthusiasm to be reflected in the behavior of the second graders.

Good thing they'd decided against serving hot cocoa.

She went into the barn, where Lupe was ready to hand out educational packets.

"What are you doing out here?" Lupe asked. She insisted on wearing denim overalls for field trip days, which clashed adorably with her teased hair and bright red lips. "You've worked all day. You should be in the house with your feet up."

"I'm hardly lumbering around like one of the pigs. I'm barely pregnant! And this is Henry's class. I'm sure he's being a huge showoff, and I kind of want to see it."

"You should have heard him," Lupe said. "It was awful. Those are *my* cows. Those are *my* turkeys. That is *my* dad."

"How totally obnoxious of him," Maggie said with a huge grin. "Did JD and Gabriel come get their Christmas turkey?"

"They sure did. The rest are being shipped out tomorrow. And Maggie, you wouldn't believe it. One of those birds is going to Maine, and another to Hawaii!"

People came from as far away as Houston to tour the ranch, but Happy Trails did most of its business through a website. Thanks to Gerome and his Rancho Canada Verde stamp of approval, Happy Trails was cornering a market of its own.

The tractor pulled up noisily to the barn, belching smoke. Travis turned it off and the tailpipe backfired, causing an eruption of shrieks and laughter.

Henry was the first one off. Maggie grabbed him by a belt loop as he ran past. "Hey, aren't you going to say hello?"

"Oh, hi, Mag—" Henry turned pink. "I mean hi, Mama."

They'd decided *Mom* wasn't a good fit. It was what he'd called Lisa.

"Have your classmates had a good time?"

"You bet! They really liked the goats. I had to show them how to hold the babies."

Travis seemed to be having a hard time disentangling himself from a swarm of kids, so Maggie yelled, "Cookies!" to get their attention. She pointed to Lupe, and the swarm moved in unison.

"Did you get the cottage ready for guests yet?" Travis asked.

"Nope. I'm going to head over there now. I just need to grab some eggs. I've got the flowers in the Jeep."

"Forget the eggs," Travis said.

"But why? Guests of Honey's Cottage get fresh eggs. It says so on our website."

"Okay, fine. I'll grab the eggs and meet you there in a few minutes."

Holy cow, she was only a teensy weensy bit pregnant. It was doubtful she'd pop out a baby from picking up a carton of eggs.

As the kids lined up to board the bus, Maggie grabbed the

fresh flowers out of the Jeep and walked around to the pasture behind the house, where a familiar cow trail led through the apple orchard. It was the quickest way to the cottage.

A horse neighed behind her. It hadn't taken Travis long to catch up. He sat proudly atop his black gelding, Moonshine II, who he simply called Junior.

Her heart thudded in her chest. *That's my cowboy.*

She offered Junior an apple, which he happily whuffled.

"Did somebody get lost on the way to Grandmother's house?"

Maggie grinned. She was even wearing a red jacket. "Maybe."

"Can I offer you a ride?"

"I'm not sure it's a good idea to go with strangers into the woods," she said.

"It's worked out pretty well for you in the past."

That was true. Maggie put her foot in the stirrup and Travis had her in the saddle in one fell swoop. She settled in snuggly in front of him, grabbing the saddle horn. Travis would do the rest. One large hand pressed against her belly as the other held the reins, and Travis made that adorable little clicking sound with his tongue to get Junior started down the trail.

Maggie's hips rocked back and forth with the horse's stride, causing her rear end to rub against Travis. He shifted in the saddle, and she felt how much he was enjoying the ride.

He kissed her neck, nipped her ear, and ran his hand under her shirt to cup her breast.

"What do you think you're doing?"

"Getting ready to ride," he teased.

"Get that idea out of your head. We've got guests coming. They might be there already."

The cottage came into view. It was lit up with a string

of lights, and a tree glowed in the window. Like everything else on Happy Trails, it was awash in Christmas. The guests loved the extra bit of cheer.

Travis pulled the horse to a stop and helped Maggie down. There was no car parked in front, so they entered without knocking. Maggie rushed to put the eggs in the refrigerator, but Travis seemed in no hurry. In fact, he started putting kindling in the wood-burning stove.

"Travis! We can't leave the cottage with the stove going, and I'd prefer to sneak out before the guests arrive."

"They're already here."

"They are?" Maggie went to the window. She didn't see anybody. When she turned around, she noticed a suitcase in the hallway. "Is that my bag? It looks like my bag."

"Welcome to Honey's Cottage," Travis said. "We've got it all to ourselves for the entire weekend."

Maggie almost melted on the spot. That sounded dreamy. Divine, even. She rushed to Travis and jumped on him. He caught her with ease. "I've got all sorts of plans. And there's even a present for you under the tree."

"Really? For me?"

"Yes," he said, setting her on the couch. "Even though you've been naughty."

"I have not."

"Yes, Mrs. Blake, you have. On more than one occasion. And I got you an appropriately naughty gift."

Maggie peeked under the tree. A long, skinny package poked out from beneath its branches. It looked to be about twenty-five inches long. "Is that what I think it is?"

Travis knelt beside her and whispered, "It was Prime. And I promise it's not a telescope."

Keep reading for a peek at Claire
and Ford's story in

Cowboy Come Home!

Coming in Summer 2019

Chapter

One

❦

Claire Kowalski gazed across the table at Chad, her latest Sizzle match, and wished she'd swiped left instead of right. It wasn't his looks, because he was tall and trim with a full head of thick, brown hair and a sexy Prince Charming cleft in his chin. It was literally everything else.

"When you say rock climbing, you mean those walls in fitness centers, right?" He winked at her—gorgeous hazel eyes—and grinned. Why did he have a hard time believing she climbed? Maybe it was the Laurence Dacade heels or the shimmering silk shift she wore. It wasn't like she could wear climbing gear on a dinner date, and besides, if scaling granite was her first love, fashion was her second. She dabbed the corner of her mouth with a linen napkin. "I use walls for training, but I climb real rocks. Big ones. I'm the president of the Hill Country Rock Climbers Association."

Chad raised his eyebrows and his fork paused on its way to his mouth. He apparently thought better of whatever it was he was going to say and took a bite of steak instead. They'd suffered through enough stilted and boring conversation during the appetizers.

You sell respiratory equipment? How exciting!

She'd worked hard at keeping her eyes from glazing over. He was equally unimpressed by her job at Petal Pushers, a nursery and garden center, but her rock climbing revelation seemed to pique his interest.

"So, like, you climb up sheer rock walls and stuff? I thought you had to be pretty strong to do that."

Claire was aware she didn't look as tough as she was. Tall and curvy, with what her mother referred to as a "shock" of red hair, she was easy to spot while scaling a cliff. She was easy to spot period. She took a bite of dry salmon and downed it with a substantial sip of merlot.

"I'm no expert, but I've done some Class 5 climbs."

She waited for him to ask what qualified as a Class 5 climb. That's how this worked. *It's your turn.*

"I'm a runner," he said.

They were back to Chad's favorite subject: himself. That's pretty much all he'd talked about for the past twenty minutes, and the few times he'd shown interest in anything she had to say, it was slightly demeaning.

You didn't go to college? That's fine. Women don't really need to.

You've never been to Europe? Italy is the best. You should go.

You haven't tried sushi? How does that happen?

The arrival of their entrées had been a relief because it meant the date was closer to being over. She just needed to scarf down her salmon, politely decline dessert, coffee, and if she was reading this guy right, fellatio. Then she could get back to her comfy little house in Big Verde, put on her

PJ's, and find the dog-eared page of the Scottish Highlander paperback she was reading with her book club. In the meantime, she'd do her part for polite conversation. She might be a Southern girl who rock climbed, but she was still a Southern girl. "I see a lot of trail runners when I'm out and about. Do you run on trails?"

She placed her money on this guy being more of a city streets runner.

"I run at the gym," he said. "Where it's air conditioned. And I do cross fit, of course."

"Of course." She squinted over her wineglass, which had miraculously worked its way back to her lips, and concluded (a) he was everything she'd chalked him up to be; (b) his healthy glow came from a tanning bed; and (c) she might have to fake a text from her dying grandmother.

"I don't belong to a gym," she said, setting her wineglass down. "Big Verde is too small to have one, and I'd rather be outdoors anyway."

"I keep forgetting you're a small-town girl," he said. "You sure don't look like one."

What was one supposed to look like? Big Verde was only an hour from Austin and an hour and a half from San Antonio. It wasn't like she'd never seen a mall. Her dress had come from Nordstrom.

"This is Kobe beef, you know," Chad said, pointing to his plate. "You should have gotten the steak instead of salmon."

"That's not Kobe," Claire said. Kobe was extremely rare and most places who claimed to sell it were outright lying. The reason they got away with it was because there were an awful lot of people willing to be duped if it made them feel special.

"Well, I heard it was real Kobe. A guy from the gym told me they serve it here. And I'm pretty familiar with what constitutes a fine cut of beef." Chad picked up his knife and poked at his steak. "Look at this beautiful marbling."

It was barely marbled—Chad wouldn't know a good cut of meat if it bit him on the ass. "Marbling is just fat, and it's usually the result of corn feeding, which might be tasty, but it's not very good for the animal or the person consuming it. Have you ever been to a feed lot? Have you ever *smelled* one?"

"You act like you grew up on a ranch."

"That's because I did. My family owns Rancho Canada Verde."

Canada Verde meant *green canyon* in Spanish, and at twelve thousand acres, it was no small family farm. The Kowalskis had owned and operated it for three generations, but it had been Claire's dad who turned it into a household name among the growing organic, grass-fed market.

"Never heard of it," Chad said. "Do you have cows and stuff?"

Cows and stuff are what turned a chunk of land into a ranch. "Yes. And I typically don't eat anything with four legs unless I knew it by name."

"That's kind of...morbid, isn't it?" Chad shuddered a little.

"Yes. It's why I'm a pescetarian."

"Your profile says you're Baptist." Chad cocked an eyebrow. "I'm pretty sure they eat meat."

"True," Claire said, although she doubted they ate Kobe. She lifted her wineglass. "It's drinking they don't do. And anyway, pescetarian means I eat fish." She was surprised he didn't know that. It must not be a fad anymore. Maybe pescetarianism had been replaced by fake Japanese beef consumption.

"I bet you don't get out like this very often," Chad said,

looking around the restaurant. "I hope it's a treat, coming to the city and going to a nice place."

She wanted to point out that the restaurant was part of an overpriced chain, but why bother. Maybe she'd just have some fun instead. Then she was getting out of here. "Yes, thanks for giving me this opportunity to get dolled up and whatnot," she said. She picked up a fork and pretended to marvel at it.

"That's a dessert fork," Chad said.

Claire rolled her eyes and put the fork down. At what point did Southern manners become ridiculous? She wasn't going to go out with Chad again, and there was a Scottish Highlander waiting for her (in a kilt, no less) back in Big Verde. Did she really need to waste precious time with a cold fish? *Chad, not the salmon.*

Chad cleared his throat. Maybe he would be the one to end the date early. "I was thinking we could go back to my place after dessert."

Nope. Claire pushed her chair back and stood. "This has been fun," she said, because she couldn't shake those manners entirely. "But I really need to be getting back—"

"What for? What could possibly be happening in Big Little Town that you need to get back to?"

Somebody really wanted his blowjob.

"Listen, Chad. I can get a better steak for half the cost at the Corner Café in Big Verde. And speaking of Big Verde, people visit from all over to enjoy its scenic beauty and unique shops. Our mayor graduated from Harvard Divinity School, and I know that because she's my aunt. We're hardly a one-horse town, despite our single stoplight."

The only downside to Big Verde's size was its distinct lack of available men. Claire had dated every single one of them. Only Ford Jarvis had tickled her fancy.

In fact, he'd tickled it three times in one night.

But he had no plans to ever settle down. He'd been cruelly clear about that. And just when Claire thought she'd finally gotten over him, he'd come back to Big Verde. It was why she'd upped her activity level on Sizzle.

Chad stood abruptly, scraping his chair loudly across the floor. "You haven't even finished your dinner. And that was an expensive entrée."

Claire dug in her purse and pulled out two twenty-dollar bills. She dropped them on the table, along with the dessert fork, and then slammed back the last of her wine. "Dang," she said. "That's a decent merlot."

* * *

Thunder rumbled through the Texas Hill Country as Ford Jarvis leaned back in his kitchen chair, balancing on two legs. It had been raining on and off for three days. Nothing too hard, a light but steady shower, but the thunderstorm scheduled to hit this evening might be the straw breaking the camel's back. The ground was saturated, the creeks were full, and if the sky opened and dumped on Big Verde, they could see some flash flooding.

He pulled out his phone and checked the weather radar, letting out a low whistle that earned him a glare from Dwaine. "Things are about to get worse," he said.

Dwaine pulled his tiny ears tightly against his head. His beady eyes darted around the room, tail twitching while he looked for a place to hide. "Too bad you're a mean, mite-riddled cat instead of a friendly dog a guy could relax with," Ford said. Dwaine had shown up on a stormy night much like this one when Ford was living in a bunkhouse outside of Sonora. He hadn't wanted to take the nasty creature with him when he'd left for Odessa, but he'd been afraid the other ranch hands would let the poor thing starve. Same story for when he'd moved to El Paso, and from El Paso to Big Verde.

Four ranches in two years; five if you considered he'd hit Big Verde twice.

Who knew how long he'd stay? He'd been very firm with Gerome Kowalski, the owner of the infamous Rancho Canada Verde, about this stint as ranch foreman being temporary. Although if Ford was forced to admit it, he'd been downright flattered when Gerome had personally called him and asked him to come back to the ranch. Most cowboys would move heaven and earth for Gerome Kowalski, and Ford was no exception.

The radar showed a threatening cloud of red and hot pink just to the north, and it was headed straight for Big Verde. If they got a downpour, Wailing Woman Creek would swell, and the crossing would be under water. That meant he'd be cut off from the outside world until the water receded. He crossed his legs with a pleasant sigh. He and Dwaine had a thing or two in common.

Of course, the other folks living this side of Wailing Woman would also be cut off. He'd have to check on that old hermit, Ruben, and goddammit, he'd also have to check on Claire.

His right eye twitched. His thumb hovered over his phone. *Don't do it, dipshit.*

He did it. Clicked on the Sizzle dating app and logged in. Because yes, he had a fucking login for a fucking online dating site. Hell, he'd never used any form of social media. Had snubbed it, in fact. And here he was with a Sizzle profile. A password, username, the whole nine yards.

He wasn't even looking for a date. But Claire was. Buddy Moy had come across her profile last week, and he'd been all too happy to share the news.

Ford hadn't been able to see Claire's profile unless he set up his own. He'd hoped that the username *Ugly As Sin* and the lack of a profile picture would serve as a deterrent to all the single ladies, but no such luck. He had twelve new messages.

Ford ignored them and went straight to Claire's profile. His heart stuttered, and he dropped his chair back to all four legs at the sight of Claire's smiling face framed by that mass of red hair. A tiger's eyes, brown like honey with specks of fiery orange, stared back at him. No, *through* him. He shook off the sensation that she knew he was looking, that he was doing something wrong or invading her privacy. Hell, she had put it out there. Obviously, she wanted people to see it.

Username: Glass Slipper

Age: 29

On weekends you'll find me: Shopping for ALL the shoes. Rock climbing by day, two-stepping by night, and enjoying everything the beautiful Texas Hill Country has to offer.

Looking For: Prince Charming (NO PRESSURE LOL)

Ford had read these words probably ten or thirty times (who was counting?), but they still settled in his stomach like a block of concrete. He'd never be Claire Kowalski's ridiculous idea of Prince Charming. The boot didn't fit.

Claire's Sizzle profile identified her as an "active" member. What the hell did that mean? He sure hoped it didn't mean she was out on a night like this. Especially since she'd recently traded in her Range Rover for a bright red impractical chunk of low-clearance tin called a Mini Cooper. She'd said it was cute. *Cute!* Ford didn't care if it had dimples and a lollipop, mini *anythings* were not safe. This was Texas. People went big in Texas, and that included vehicles. If a truck, or even a goddam deer, smacked into a mini-whatever, it was going to do some serious damage. That bit of obviousness, combined with the fact that Claire drove her car even faster than she ran her mouth, worried the shit out of him.

He logged out of Sizzle and went back to the weather radar. The mass of thunder, wind, and rain would slam into Big Verde within the hour. He'd already checked on Coco, and the horse was settled snuggly in the stable. They'd weathered plenty a storm together, and Ford knew the Mustang would keep his wits about him. Nothing to do but ride it out. *And try not to think about Claire.*

About the Author

Carly Bloom began her writing career as a family humor columnist and blogger, a pursuit she abandoned when her children grew old enough to literally die from embarrassment. To save their delicate lives, Carly turned to penning steamy, contemporary romance. The kind with bare chests on the covers.

Carly and her husband raise their mortified brood of offspring on a cattle ranch in South Texas. Also? Carly is vegan. The cows love her.

Fall in Love with Forever Romance

USA TODAY BESTSELLING AUTHOR

DEBBIE MASON

The Corner of Holly and Ivy

"Heartfelt and delightful!"
—RAEANNE THAYNE

THE CORNER OF HOLLY AND IVY
By Debbie Mason

USA Today bestselling author Debbie Mason welcomes readers to Harmony Harbor! With her dreams of being a wedding dress designer suddenly over, Arianna Bell isn't expecting a holly jolly Christmas. She thinks a run for town mayor might cheer her spirits—until she learns her opponent is her gorgeous high school sweetheart. Connor Gallagher is not going to let the attraction sparking between them get in the way of his success. But with the help of some festive matchmakers, Connor and Arianna just may get the holiday reunion they deserve.

Fall in Love with Forever Romance

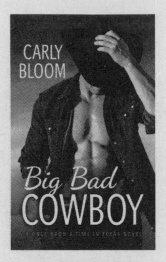

BIG BAD COWBOY
By Carly Bloom

Maggie Mackey is pretty sure she hates Travis Blake. He's irritating, he's destroying her business, and...and he's just so frickin' *attractive*. But when they're forced to work together, she discovers that the Most Annoying Man in the World is more than he seems. Maggie doesn't want to risk everything on a man who's so eager to leave town, but what if she can convince this wayward cowboy to stay? Carly Bloom's debut is perfect for fans of Lori Wilde and Maisey Yates!

Fall in Love with Forever Romance

CHRISTMAS WISHES AND MISTLETOE KISSES
By Jenny Hale

USA Today bestselling author Jenny Hale gives the magic of Christmas a whole new meaning in this feel good romance! Single mother Abbey Fuller doesn't regret putting her dreams of being an interior designer on hold to raise her son. Now that Max is older, she jumps at the chance to work on a small design job. But when she arrives at the Sinclair mansion, she feels out of her element—and her gorgeous but brooding boss Nicholas Sinclair is not exactly in the holiday spirit. Nick is all work and no play—even during the most wonderful time of the year. With the snow falling all around them, can Abbey make her dreams of being a designer come true? And can she help Nick finally enjoy the magic of Christmas?

Fall in Love with Forever Romance

THE BASTARD'S BARGAIN
By Katee Robert

New York Times bestselling author Katee Robert continues her smoking-hot O'Malleys series. Dmitri Romanov knows Keira O'Malley only married him to keep peace between their families. Nevertheless, the desire that smolders between them is a dangerous addiction neither can resist. But with his enemies circling closer, Keira could just be his secret weapon—if she doesn't bring him to his knees first.

TWISTED TRUTHS
By Rebecca Zanetti

New York Times bestselling author Rebecca Zanetti presents a sexy, action-packed story with twists and turns that will blow you away! Noni Yuka is desperate. Her infant niece has been kidnapped, and the only person who can save her is the private detective who once broke her heart.